OVER THE DISTANT MOUNTAIN RANGES AND BEYOND

DENNIS W.C. WONG

Contents

PART 1

Over The Distant Mountain Ranges

Chapter One

LIFE IS ONE OF THE MOST BEAUTIFUL THINGS

Life is one of the most beautiful things when spent with someone who truly loves you. The beauty of life is steeped in its challenges and uncertainties; otherwise, it would be drab, bland, and colorless. And when these challenges and uncertainties face those who one loves and those who love one, life becomes filled with eternal memories, memories that will never end.

She was her parents' favorite and their only child. They didn't have all the good and pleasant things of life. There was one thing they had that even money couldn't buy, and that was true love.

She got down from the foam mattress that she usually slept on and walked out of the house, going straight to the river to wash her face. Her family had that advantage because they lived close to the river. She had always wanted to ask why her parents chose somewhere close to the river, but whenever she tried to ask, she would swallow her question, hoping that one day they would tell her. She was named Lucinda, the daughter of a poor farmer.

"Lucinda, how many times have I warned you not to go close to the river? You can't swim yet; you might drown," Annalise said, shouting at Lucinda as she was already in the river.

"I don't know how to swim because you won't allow me. I'm already ten years old, and I want to learn how to swim. The water is so calm, and I feel I have this powerful connection with it," Lucinda replied as she emerged from the water.

"You're only ten and already talking about having a strong connection with the river. Will you get back home before I get mad at you!" Annalise shouted as she watched her daughter stroll back to their building, a stone's throw from the river bank.

Annalise then strolled into the river as she took out the clothes to wash. While doing the laundry, she turned and saw Lucinda standing at the bank, looking at her.

"I thought I asked you to go home? What did you come back to do?" Annalise yelled.

"Mom, you're always upset about everything, and besides, it was Dad who asked me to come and keep you company. So, can I step into the river?" Lucinda pleaded.

"No, you can't. Just stay there, and besides, I didn't tell your dad I needed help with the laundry. So please go back home," Annalise said while she turned to continue with her laundry.

"I'm not going back home," Lucinda shrugged and sat down at the riverbank, a little distance from her mom.

"Why is that so, young lady?" Annalise asked.

"It is so because you brought me up never to disobey my father. You always say I should help even without being asked to, but since you wouldn't want me to step into the river, I will wait here and help you carry the clothes home," Lucinda replied, rather adamantly.

Annalise smiled and continued with her laundry silently. Immediately she finished up, Lucinda helped her with the clothes as they walked home together. Annalise walked inside and left Lucinda to spread the clothes on the rope so they would dry. When Lucinda finished, she stepped inside and went straight to the kitchen to join her mom.

"Are you through with spreading the clothes?" Annalise asked as she saw Lucinda walked into the kitchen.

"I'm through, Mom," Lucinda replied.

Lucinda walked back into her room, and after what seemed like forever, her mom called her so she could come and eat. Promptly, she joined her parents at the table as they ate quietly.

One thing was sure: love lived here. Lucinda's parents had everything good, nothing valuable to boast of, not even their land. They couldn't afford to get a place to build in the village, and that was why they had chosen somewhere close to the river. Phil and Annalise didn't care about how the world felt about them; they only cared about themselves. Lucinda was their only child, and they treasured her.

When they had finished eating, Lucinda took the plates to the kitchen to wash while her mom and dad went outside to receive some cool breeze on the balcony. When she finished, she went into her room to stay. She had no one to play with, nor any toys or pets. It was her alone and her parents.

It was already late at night when Lucinda's parents walked into her room to kiss her goodnight; when they found out she was still awake.

"Lucinda, why are you still up? Is there any problem?" Phil asked.

"Can you tell me a story before I go to sleep?" Lucinda requested.

"Sure, that can never be a problem," Annalise said as she sat close to her daughter while Lucinda placed her head on her mother's lap.

"Here we go: Once upon a time, in a faraway kingdom, there lived a young boy who tended to the sheep. He had close to two hundred of them. However, the villagers feared the hyenas. They knew that this animal would always come for their livestock. So anytime the hyenas attacked the village, the villagers would come out in great numbers to chase them back into the forest. On a certain day, this young lad was sitting on the tree, feeling bored but thinking nothing in particular. Suddenly, he thought of a prank as he observed his sheep feeding happily on the field of grass before him. Suddenly, he shouted at the top of his voice and called the villagers to come to his rescue, that the hyenas were about to devour his sheep. The villagers heard his voice and came out in great numbers with several weapons but were disappointed to see that the young lad had raised a false alarm. Disappointed, they all went home angry as the young lad laughed so hard, feeling proud of the prank he just pulled. Well, he repeated it the next day, and the villagers rushed out again to see it was still mischief, but on the third day, the hyenas attacked his sheep, and when he called on the villagers to help, no one came out. They all thought it was a false alarm. The young lad lost about a hundred of his sheep that night. The ones left were brutally wounded as he walked home with them. He went home and cried himself to stupor. It was an expensive prank that cost him dearly. Here ends my story. So, tell me what you have learned," Annalise said, smiling at Lucinda.

"The first lesson is never to raise a false alarm to kill boredom, and then, one should always be sincere and honest in everything he or she is doing," Lucinda replied.

"That's true. So, my dear, raise no false alarm, and always be true to your words so that whenever you need help, people will come right away to help you. Is that understood?" Annalise asked.

"Yes, Mom," Lucinda said, smiling while Phil was sitting by the side, listening and watching his daughter.

Annalise and Phil eventually kissed her goodnight when they were sure she was fast asleep, and they both walked out of the room into their room, lying on the bed immediately to drift off to sleep. It was their usual daily routine.

On the next morning, Lucinda woke up as usual, and as she stood up from her foam, her back started aching again, which had been ongoing for several days now. Had her parents had the money, they would have gotten her a good bed, as this foam was already flat.

She walked out of the room and made it straight for the river, something that had become her morning ritual, something she hadn't missed for five years now. As early as five years old, Lucinda had gone to the river, and her parents would hurriedly come to bring her home for fear of drowning, but for those five years she was doing, they had never given up on that. She wanted to explore and know what it was like to be inside the water. After the first day she tried it, she hadn't stopped, although she has never dared to venture into the deeper part of the water.

She washed her face that morning with the river's flowing waters. Lucinda sat on the river bank, throwing pebbles into the river, enjoying the spluttering sounds of the pebble's impact on the surface of the river with the ripples they formed.

Annalise and Phil were at the back of the house planting seeds when they heard Lucinda's echoing from the river. They quickly dropped what they were holding as they ran towards the riverside. Lucinda was there, struggling to breathe as she kept shouting her parents' names. Phil jumped into the river and swam to save his daughter from drowning. Phil could grab hold of his daughter and swam back to the river bank. Annalise was in tears, praying that nothing would happen to her daughter. Phil laid Lucinda on the floor as he pressed her stomach, and water was gushing out from her mouth.

"She is alive!" Annalise shouted as Phil carried Lucinda and went back home. Annalise changed her daughter's wet clothes to dry ones. Phil came back and presented a cup of tea to Annalise as he raised Lucinda to drink the hot tea.

"What happened? Have I not warned you countless times never to go close to the river? What were you doing at the deeper part of the river?" Annalise asked, crying.

"You shouldn't be asking her that now. She needs to rest. Just wait until later on. Then you can start asking questions," Phil said.

Annalise managed to put Lucinda to sleep as she and her husband walked out of Lucinda's room and continued to their room. Annalise was still in tears. She couldn't imagine that she was about to lose her daughter. What would have happened if her husband wasn't around?

"Annalise, stop crying. Nothing is wrong with her. She just needs to rest, and she will be okay," Phil assured.

"What would have happened if you were not around or if we didn't get there on time? I would have been holding my daughter's corpse, of course. I have warned her countless times to stop going to the river, but she won't listen to me," Annalise whined.

"She is a little child and is bound to explore her curiosities. She has been going there ever since she was five, so telling her to stop now is a waste of time; rather, we can just caution her never to go to the deeper part of the river. Besides, she doesn't go that deep. Something must have happened," Phil reasoned.

"She is never stepping an inch close to that river," Annalise said with a tone of finality and evident fury.

"Don't be too harsh on her. Let's wait for her to wake up, and then she can explain to us what happened," Phil said as he wiped the tears dropping from Annalise's eyes.

"It's okay. Don't worry. Lucinda is safe. That's the most important thing for now," Phil said and hugged his wife.

Later in the evening, as Annalise was preparing dinner, she dished out a portion for her husband and daughter. She sat on the edge of the thinned foam as Lucinda opened her eyes and called out her name.

"Annalise!" Lucinda spoke with a faint smile.

Whenever she wanted her mom to smile, she called her by her name.

"Lucinda, how are you doing?" Annalise asked, smiling.

"I'm fine. Why are you crying, Mom?" Lucinda asked.

"I thought something bad might have happened to you. Why did you go deep into the water, knowing full well that you can't swim? What if we didn't get there on time? It could have been fatal. You know I can't survive the trauma of losing you, Lucinda," Annalise said.

"I was only trying to rescue this baby bird that fell into the water. Its wings were broken. I'm sorry I hurt myself while trying to save another life," Lucinda apologized.

"Don't worry, okay? I prepared something special for you. You will love it," Annalise said, smiling and patting Lucinda on the shoulder.

"Are you still upset with me?" Lucinda asked.

"Yes, I am upset with you, but I understand that you were trying to save a life. So, cheer up," Annalise said.

Annalise helped her daughter up as she ran a water bath for her, after which she helped Lucinda put on her nightwear and fed her quietly.

Nothing in this world mattered to Annalise except Lucinda and Phil, her two most priceless possessions.

◆ ❖ ◆

Chapter Two

LUCINDA SLOWLY OPENED HER EYES

Lucinda slowly opened her eyes to the dim sunray coming through the windows. She then stood up and walked towards the window, parting the curtains to let in the whole entrails of the sun. Having done that, she walked out of her room and went straight to her parents' bedroom, and on getting there, she quietly entered the room, seeing her mom was still fast asleep. Her dad had left very early in the morning. She walked to the window and opened the curtains to wake her mom.

"Good morning, Mom," Lucinda said, smiling.

Annalise slowly opened her eyes as she saw Lucinda sitting on the bed with her. Annalise got up slowly and took in her daughter, sitting down on the edge of the bed.

Lucinda would always wake up early, but she rarely came to her parents' room that early. She would instead go straight to the river to stay all alone.

"Lucinda," Annalise called.

"Yes, Mom. How are you, Annalise?" Lucinda asked, grinning.

"What are you doing in my room? You usually go to the river because that's where you go every morning, but you're still here," Annalise observed.

"You asked me not to swim, and you even warned me never to go near the river again so that I won't drown," Lucinda replied.

"What are you up to, young lady? How can I help you? In fact, what do you want?" Annalise asked, now wide awake.

"Thanks for asking. I want to pay a visit to Grandma and Grandpa up on the mountain. You've told me so much about them. I woke up this morning desiring to see them. Can you take me there?" Lucinda pleaded, pouting her lips.

"Lucinda!" Annalise called.

"Mom, please, I haven't asked for anything for God knows how long now, and today I'm making this request. Please don't tell me you won't grant me this request. I beg of you, Mom," Lucinda replied.

"Alright, I have heard you, young lady. I will take you there to spend some time with them. Maybe after two weeks, come back home," Annalise said.

"Just two weeks?" Lucinda asked, raising her eyebrows.

"Yes, young lady, two weeks. Is there any problem?" Annalise asked.

"But what will I be doing if I come back home? Nothing! So, I feel it is best if I stay there for at least a month," Lucinda replied.

"Leave my room now," Annalise said, pointing at the door, as Lucinda laughed and ran out.

Lucinda never took things seriously. She was always joking about everything, but she was fun to be with. Annalise didn't want her daughter to be far away from her. Although being the very playful and sometimes mischievous type, she always kept her company, although she had often made her talk too much. No doubt Annalise knew she would miss her daughter once she left for her parents' house.

As soon as Lucinda left, Annalise stood up and walked to the bathroom to have her bath. She didn't bother about preparing anything because nothing was at home, and that was the major reason her husband left very early in the morning to look for something they could eat for breakfast.

Annalise finished her bath and dressed up. Then she walked out of the room, meeting Lucinda sitting on the balcony.

"Lucinda, what are you doing outside?" Annalise asked.

"Nothing, just wanting to stay outside. Sit with me. Let's admire this beautiful natural scenery before us," Lucinda pleaded as Annalise came and sat down close to her.

"Mom, I'm hungry," Lucinda said after a few minutes of silence between the two filial friends.

"I know, just wait a little more. Your dad went to the farm, and he would branch out to the village market to get things before returning home. Once he is back, I will fix something for breakfast, okay?" Annalise said, patting her daughter on the back.

"Alright. So, while we wait for Dad to come back home, do you mind telling me a story?" Lucinda asked.

"What do you want me to tell you?" Annalise asked her daughter.

"I want to know more about your family, Mom. Why do my grandparents live on the mountain? Do they have neighbors?" Lucinda asked.

"Well, my parents lived on the mountain because of the calmness in that area, and nope, they don't have neighbors. I know the next question would be: how do they eat? Well, they travel to the village close to them to get foodstuffs every Friday. That's all," Annalise replied.

"Wow, that's nice," Lucinda said as she looked up, seeing her father coming back.

"That's Dad. He is coming home," Lucinda said as she ran towards her father and hugged him. She collected the hoe and cutlass her father was carrying and took them inside to keep behind the kitchen door. Lucinda then went back inside her parents' room and met her father sitting on the wooden chair. She went closer to him and sat on the floor.

"Dad, how are you doing?" Lucinda asked.

"I'm fine, and how about you?" Phil asked.

"I'm fine, Daddy, just hungry," Lucinda replied.

"Don't worry. Your mom is about to fix up something for breakfast. Wouldn't you like to join her?" Phil asked.

"I will, but Daddy, I need your help," Lucinda said.

"My help? Well, anything for my daughter. So, tell me, how can Daddy help you?" Phil asked.

"Can you convince Mom to take me to the mountain so I can visit Grandma and Grandpa? You know I've never been there, and I have this intense desire to see them. I promise after a month; I will be back," Lucinda replied.

"Is that all you want?" Phil asked.

"Yes, Daddy," Lucinda replied.

"Alright. I will do that, but I don't think Mommy will let you stay for a month. Don't worry. You will go," Phil said.

"Thanks, Dad," Lucinda replied, smiling and getting up, ready to leave the room for the kitchen.

"You're welcome," Phil replied.

"I'm off to the kitchen to help Mom," Lucinda said and walked out of the room into the kitchen.

When Annalise was through with the preparation, she dished out her husband's own and handed the dish over to Lucinda to set down on the table in the sitting room while telling her she was coming out shortly to meet them. Lucinda obeyed and walked out with the food. Annalise soon followed her with two plates inside a tray—one for herself and the other for Lucinda.

"Food is ready," Lucinda announced as her father smiled and shifted the chair close to the center table. Annalise and Lucinda sat down as they said a quick prayer before digging into their food.

"So, Mom, when are you taking your little angel to Grandpa and Grandma?" Lucinda asked.

"Lucinda, you don't talk while eating," Annalise chided.

"Daddy, won't you talk to Mom? She won't allow me to visit Grannies," Lucinda protested in between a munch of food in her mouth.

"Anna, don't you think this is a nice idea? Staying alone at home might tempt her into going close to the river. You remember what happened the last time she did so, and mind you: it's about time she visited them. I think it's nice you take her on a visit to the mountain ranges so that she can spend some quality time with them, even if it is for two weeks or a month," Phil said.

"Two weeks is too short. How do you want me to spend some quality time with them in just two weeks?" Lucinda asked.

"Lucinda, it's not that I don't want you to go. It's just that you are too stubborn. You're my daughter, and I'm your mother, and I tell you, you're very stubborn. You will visit my parents, and by the time you get there, you will start disturbing them and making outrageous demands," Annalise said.

"Aww! This isn't fair, Mom. How can you say your little angel is stubborn? I'm doubting whether I am still your little angel," Lucinda said, looking away.

"Hahaha! Remind me how old you are again?" Annalise asked her daughter.

"Ten, Mom," Lucinda replied, folding her hands.

"You're the mother," Phil chipped in.

"Oh yes, I know. It's just that she talks like she is an adult," Annalise replied.

"So, when are you taking her to your parents?" Phil asked.

"Yes, Mom. When are you taking me to your parents?" Lucinda asked, smiling.

"I haven't even accepted yet. You two are just the same, no difference," Annalise said, sighing.

"We're waiting for an answer, Mom; when?" Lucinda asked.

"Alright, I'll be taking you there by this weekend," Annalise replied.

"Aww! That's so sweet of you, Mom. One kiss for you," Lucinda said, blowing a kiss to her parents, one after the other.

"You both are the best," Lucinda said, smiling as she continued with her food. Phil and Annalise looked at their daughter and smiled back.

Lucinda was one hell of a child, very stubborn and intelligent as well. Aside from that, she was lovely, such that one could mistake her for a goddess. Her skin was as fair as snow, and her hair was so black, with her blue eyes and pink lips. Lucinda shared the exact resemblance with her mother, but one thing that confused Annalise most times about her daughter was how she acted and behaved like an adult, though she was just ten.

When they finished eating their food, Lucinda took the plates to the kitchen to wash. Then she retired to her bedroom to sleep. As Lucinda lay on the bed, she silently prayed that Friday would come quickly. And soon, it was Friday.

That morning, Lucinda was the first to wake up as she walked to her parents' room and knocked on the door. Her mom quickly rushed out, thinking something was wrong.

"Lucinda, what's the problem? It's only 6 a.m. Did you have a nightmare?" Annalise asked, looking surprised.

"Nightmare? That's the opposite of what I came here to say," Lucinda said, staring at her mom.

"So, what's the problem?" Annalise asked.

"I woke you up to let you know that today is Friday. Start preparing because I'm about to take my bath now," Lucinda said and walked out.

Annalise stood at the door looking at her daughter, wondering whether she was the one who gave birth to Lucinda. Quietly, she went inside as Phil grinned, having heard what Lucinda said.

"Your daughter is so unbelievable," Annalise said.

"How do you mean?" Phil asked.

"Can you imagine she woke me up so I can get ready to take her to the mountain ranges?" Annalise replied as Phil burst into quakes of laughter.

"What's funny?" Annalise asked, feeling surprised.

"She is your replica. So, anything she does now shouldn't surprise you at all. She is her mother's daughter," Phil said as Annalise frowned and walked out of the room.

Annalise walked straight into her daughter's room to help her sort out the clothes she would travel with.

"Mom, I thought you were going to get me some new clothes?" Lucinda asked.

"Lucinda, you know I don't have the money now. Don't worry; I would get you something better soon, okay?" Annalise assured.

Lucinda hugged her mother and whispered into her ears, "I was only joking with you. You don't have to feel bad about not getting me new clothes. We already have a roof over our heads, and we have something to eat. I'm grateful for that. So, smile, Mommy. Don't worry. In the future, I would get you all the finer things of life and would take you to the city."

Lucinda smiled and walked out of the room as Annalise wiped the tears that trickled down her cheeks. She looked up and said, "God, thank you for giving me a daughter like Lucinda." She then placed everything in the backpack and zipped it up.

Annalise prepared breakfast so they could all have something to eat. Phil bade them goodbye as he went to the farm. Annalise held Lucinda's bag, and together they went off.

"Who could that be?" Maya said as she stood up to check who was knocking at the door.

"Are you expecting anyone?" Greg asked.

"Of course not," Maya replied and opened the door to see her daughter and granddaughter grinning as she opened her arms to hug them both with so much excitement.

"Who do we have here?" Greg said, standing up as her daughter Annalise hugged him.

"I missed you so much, Mother," Annalise said, grinning.

"I missed you too, Anna beloved," Maya replied, pecking Annalise on the cheek.

"And who do you have with you?" Maya asked, looking at Annalise.

"My daughter, Lucinda, of course. Hahaha! Have you forgotten her? It's been a long time since you saw her. I think you saw her last when she was four. She wouldn't let me rest unless I brought her here. You know Lucinda and how stubborn she can be. I had to bring her here," Annalise replied.

"You did well. We missed her too, and we have been planning to visit again. Who would have known that my granddaughter was missing us as well? Aww!" Maya said.

"Don't worry, Granny. I will spend a lot of time here with you, okay?" Lucinda said as she smiled.

"Exactly, just as I wished, now that you're grown up. At least we are going to have good company," said Maya.

"Yeah, Grandma!" Lucinda almost shouted at the approval of her grandmother. They all sat down inside the parlor made up of mainly wooden furniture, with no modern gadgets. It was a small house with four rooms: one bedroom, one kitchen, one store, and a parlor. Inside the parlor where they all sat was an enormous couch, with very soft foam padding all around the wood.

A more miniature replica of it was situated opposite it, and the door to the parlor opened in between. Behind the colossal couch was a wooden table, chocolate. There were brownish curtains over the parlor's three windows, with a thick brown rug covering the entire wooden floor.

Here and there were sundry domestic Chinese utensils— contoured and chiseled flower vases, fresh flowers, and a fireplace for warmth.

Lucinda found the setting cozy. Her mother had thought the place would seem out of place for her. What held a unique attraction for Lucinda was the forest ambiance of the abode.

The house was located amid a forest upon a mountain, away from civilization. There was no threat of wild animals in sight.

As they all sat down talking, Maya walked into the kitchen and dished out food for her daughter and granddaughter, and while eating, they touched upon sundry subjects.

Later on, Lucinda became busy with her grandpa, teaching her a traditional Chinese game Lucinda saw for the first time. Later that evening, Annalise informed them she was about to leave.

After hugging her parents, she went straight to where Lucinda was sitting alone on the smaller couch and hugged her, whispering into her ears, "Please don't disturb my parents and better behave yourself." Lucinda stole a glance at her and smiled.

"Trust me, Annalise; I will be a good girl," Lucinda said, still smiling as Annalise laughed, her laughter triggered by the way Lucinda used to call her by her name.

"Take care of yourself," Annalise said as she opened the door and journeyed back home.

Chapter Three

BUT GRANNY, I DON'T
WANT TO GO HOME

"But Granny, I don't want to go home yet. Mom isn't even here to pick me up, so why do you want me to go home now?" Lucinda asked dejectedly.

Her grandmother had spoken to her about going back home, but it was apparent Lucinda wasn't taking that. The two weeks her mother gave had elapsed, and Maya needed to take her home.

"Your mom isn't here to pick you up because I will be the one taking you home," Maya said.

"Are you pushing me away from your house? I thought I was your granddaughter, or don't you enjoy my company?" Lucinda asked, folding her hands and looking at Maya disapprovingly.

"I enjoy your company, honey, but your mom's instruction should be obeyed," Maya replied.

"What's going on here?" Greg asked as he walked into the parlor from one of his many explorations of the woods—something that gave him holy joy.

"Thank God Grandpa is back. Grandpa, do you know Grandma wants to take me back home? I have asked her if I did anything wrong so I can apologize, but she said no. She wants to take me home, which means she doesn't love and enjoy my company anymore," Lucinda said, almost on the verge of crying.

"Oh, little one, don't mind your grandma. She loves you, sure. We both love you so much. Grandma is taking you home. Your mom and dad miss you a lot. She is taking you home so you can spend some time with them, and before you know it, you will be back here again," Greg said.

"Why is it that I don't believe you both?" Lucinda asked, placing her hands on her waist, standing akimbo.

"Has Grandpa ever lied to you before?" Greg asked, clearly flustered.

"Nope, you haven't, but I'm not having a good feeling about this. You both are trying to trick me into going back home, which is not fair. Going back home, I won't have the chance to do anything, like exploring the woods with you or going down to the river in the valley. Back home, Mom and Dad banned me from going close to the river. And when I'm there, I will be home alone most of the time with no one to talk to.

I wish I had a playmate or even a pet," Lucinda said and ran off into the lone room in the house with tears in her eyes.

"Indeed, Annalise gave birth to her replica. She acted like her when she was her age, yet she acts like an adult and reasons like one. Wow," Greg said as he sat on the oversized couch.

"You know we have to take her back home. Annalise can't stay a month without seeing her daughter. And even if we don't take her home, Annalise will surely be here in a few days to take her home, anyway," Maya whispered.

"Don't worry. I will convince her to go home with you; leave that to me," Greg whispered back, smiling.

"That sounds good. So, when will you talk to her?" Maya asked.

"This evening. Then tomorrow, you will take her home," Greg replied.

"That's nice," Maya said as she walked into the room.

That evening, Greg walked into the room and met Lucinda sitting down and staring out from the window into the woods.

"Are you still angry with your grandpa?" Greg asked as he sat close to Lucinda.

"I'm not angry with you as you did nothing wrong," Lucinda said with her eyes still staring out the window.

"I doubt it because you're not even looking at me, which shows you are still angry with me. Can you forgive me, my little angel?" Greg asked.

"Why do you want me to go home?" Lucinda asked. "Because…" Greg was talking when Lucinda interjected. "Don't lie to me, Grandpa. I'm not a baby," Lucinda said. "You're just ten years old," Greg replied, smiling. "Grandpa!" Lucinda exclaimed slowly.

"Alright, I'm sorry. The way you were missing us back then, even without ever meeting or knowing us then, is the same way your parents are missing you now. My dear, you see, that's the main reason you have to go home," Greg said.

"You will come back and pick me up, right?" Lucinda asked with eyes wide open in anticipation.

"I will, dear," Greg replied.

"Is that a promise?" Lucinda asked. "Of course, it is," Greg replied, smiling.

"It's not that I'm missing home, but if I go home, I won't be allowed to go close to the river. That's the only place I go to play, the only place I feel at peace, that even I cannot explain," Lucinda said.

"What could be the attraction in the river that you go there to play every day?" Greg asked.

"Well, I've not told anyone this, but sometimes in the morning, I get to find beautiful seashells washed ashore, and they are all beautiful. I can't bring them home, so I always hid them close to the riverbed," Lucinda said, smiling.

"That's nice, but don't worry; for once you meet with your mom, stay with her for some time, you will come back here, and promise you, we will go hunting," Greg said.

"You're not joking, right?" Lucinda asked, beaming with smiles. "I'm serious, Lucy," Greg replied as he hugged his granddaughter.

"So, are you the one taking me home, or will Grandma do that?" Lucinda asked.

"Grandma will do that," Greg replied.

"Alright, let's eat," Lucinda said as she stood up, and together they walked out with her grandpa. They had their dinner that night, and they all retired to bed, the two grannies on one bed, while Lucinda slept on a spare bed inside the same room. It was a large room.

The next day, Maya woke Lucinda up as she helped arrange Lucinda's clothes while Lucinda had her bath. Maya finished up and went out to have her bath. When she was through, she had to fix something for breakfast, although Lucinda claimed she wasn't hungry. Around 9 a.m., they both journeyed back home, with Lucinda asking her grandmother several questions.

In a few hours, they were home, and Lucinda was eager to rush inside to see her mom. She touched the door handle, and luckily it wasn't locked. She pushed it open, and they both walked inside. Lucinda screamed her mom's name and her dad's name as they both rushed out and hugged her tightly.

"Mom, please try not to kill me. I was only gone for two weeks," Lucinda said, smiling.

"I know. I missed you so much. I had already told your dad that if my mother didn't bring you home today, I would come there myself tomorrow and bring you back home," Annalise said, smiling.

"You both are only engrossed in your daughter that you did not even notice my presence," Maya said as Phil walked closer to her and hugged her.

"We're so sorry. It's just that we have missed her so much. Annalise won't stop talking about her since last night," Phil said, smiling.

"She is obsessed with her daughter, Lucinda. I'm so not surprised," Maya replied as she sat down, watching Annalise and her daughter.

Lucinda dropped her backpack while Annalise went inside to get something for her mother to drink.

"Why didn't Father come with you?" Phil asked as he sat next to Maya.

"He is busy, my dear, as always with the nature surrounding us. But don't worry; the next visit, we both are coming together," Maya replied.

"That sounds great," Phil said.

"So, Mom, here is your tea," Annalise said as she handed the teacup over to her mom.

"Thank you so much," Maya replied as she sipped the tea while grinning.

"Just like always, you're good with this," Maya commended.

"Mommy, I hope this drama queen didn't create a scene for you over there?" Annalise asked.

"You gave birth to her, and I'm happy you know she is a drama queen, but all the same, we enjoyed her company. Your father is coming to pick her up in two weeks. He made that promise to her," Maya replied.

"Oh! No problem then," Phil said as Annalise eyed him.

"Mommy, tell Dad to come over next month. I have missed him so much," Annalise pleaded.

"Maybe you should tell that to your father," Maya replied as she sipped her tea. They discussed other random stuff before Maya bade them goodbye and left for the mountains.

Lucinda had woken up that morning, but her parents weren't at home. And she wondered aloud, "Where could they be? They didn't even ask me to follow them." Quietly, she sat on her father's rocking chair. It was already getting close to three hours, and there was no sign of her parents, but she later ventured into the kitchen and found out her mother had left something for her to eat.

"Maybe they went to the farm, and probably they will go to the market to sell off some of the farm's produce," Lucinda soliloquized as she sat down on the chair and ate her food quietly. When she finished, she washed the plates and walked into her room. She didn't go close to the stream because of the incident that happened last time. She lay back on her bed and drifted off to sleep.

"Wake up, Lucy!" Annalise tapped her daughter as Lucinda slowly opened her eyes.

"Sorry, we didn't tell you we were leaving very early in the morning, and also, we are sorry for coming back late," Annalise apologized.

"No problem. I understand," Lucinda said, smiling.

"Let me fix up dinner; then I will let you know when it's ready," Annalise said. Lucinda smiled and watched her mother walk out of the room.

She stood up and walked into the bathroom and poured the little water remaining in the bucket on her body. Then she dried her body and quickly put on her nightwear.

After a few minutes, Lucinda went to the kitchen to meet her mom. Annalise was already done with the food as she dished out Lucinda's portion and gave it to her. Lucinda ate quietly and returned to bed. To Annalise, her returning Lucinda was unusually quiet, unlike the vivacious Lucinda that she knew she gave birth to.

Annalise suspected maybe it was because they weren't home all day. She, however, quietly ate with her husband, Phil, before they both retired to bed.

Chapter Four

ON A PARTICULAR MORNING

On a particular morning, some days after she returned from the mountain ranges, Lucinda woke up and quietly scampered into the kitchen to prepare breakfast for all of them. She didn't want to disturb her parents. She took the breakfast to her parents in their room. By the time she got there, they were already awake but discussing matters in low tones. There was an epidemic of flu spreading across the region, and so far, Lucinda was the only one out of the three members of this household who had not yet contracted it. Her parents were already down with the virus.

"Good morning, Mom. Good morning, Dad," Lucinda said as she dropped the tray of food on the table.

"Morning," Annalise replied.

"I prepared breakfast so we can eat," Lucinda announced.

"What a surprise! You're just ten, Lucinda," Phil said, more out of curiosity.

"I'm ten, but I normally stay with Mom in the kitchen. Although she hasn't allowed me to prepare anything, I've done it today; it's left for you to decide on the taste's goodness. Now that Mom is down, I'll have to step in," Lucinda replied.

"Lucinda, I want you to promise Mom and Dad something and just say yes when I tell you this," Annalise said weakly.

"I will always say yes, anything for you both to get healed and be back on your feet," Lucinda replied.

"Listen, Lucinda, this illness is spreading everywhere, and it's so contagious. I want you to go back to my parents' place, so you don't get infected. If we get healed somehow, then we will come back for you. Staying here with us and cleaning us up increases the chances of you getting infected," Annalise said.

"You want me to stay with Grandpa and Grandma? What will happen to you both? Who will take care of you, cook for you, and fetch water from the river for both of you? Who will keep it clean? No one. Mom, you still need me around to do all these," Lucinda said.

"We can cope on our own. Just go, Lucinda. I trust you. You're smart enough and know your way up there. Just leave, please," Phil said.

"I'm not going anywhere without you both. I don't care if I get infected or not. You both are my parents. I don't want to go anywhere without you both by my side. Please don't ask me to leave," Lucinda said as tears trickled down her eyes.

"We both want you to go now, Lucinda, for your safety because we love you and want you to stay alive. Please, dear," Annalise said.

"Can we talk about this later?" Lucinda said as she took out a spoon and started feeding her parents. She took the plates to the kitchen to wash. Soon after, she left the house and headed down to the river. Upon getting to the riverbank, she sat down quietly and later started soliloquizing.

"Mom and Dad want me to leave them. They want me to go up to the mountain and stay with my grandparents, but I'm going nowhere. How will they be able to cope without me? Have they thought of that? Who will do things for them? I'm not scared of getting infected. I just want us all to be together. If they die, I die with them. If they live, I live with them," Lucinda said to herself as she threw pebbles into the river. She stayed there meditating on sundry issues, gathering seashells, observing the river's flow, and watching fish darting here and there.

She didn't even know when the sun rose in the sky, and when it dawned on her, it was time to head back home.

When she got home, she saw her parents were asleep. As she walked to her room, she lay back on her foam mattress and slept off herself.

She later woke up in the evening and checked on her parents to see that they were still asleep.

"This is unusual. Mom and Dad have been sleeping since morning now. Well, let me leave them alone," Lucinda muttered to herself as she went to the kitchen to prepare something for dinner, after which she ate her portion and kept the remaining one for her parents.

She then walked back to her room and knelt to pray, saying, "Dear God, if you can hear me, heal my parents. I want nothing to happen to them. I know this illness is slowly wiping out everyone in the village, and no one is being spared.

Please, Lord, do this for me. I need my parents now more than ever. I can't do anything without them. They are my life, and I'm their life. I miss everything about Mom and how she scolds me, and the way she laughs. But today, she is struggling to even talk to me, same with my dear father. This illness has stolen the joy in our family. Please, Lord, return my prayer by healing my parents. Amen." After prayers, she stood up and lay back down on her bed to sleep.

In the morning, Lucinda yawned as she opened her eyes. She then stood up and opened the window curtains to see that the sun was already up. She walked out of the room and went straight to her parents' room as she tapped them to wake up, having been disgusted with their unusual sleep.

"Mom, Dad, please wake up," Lucinda said as she tapped her parents, but there was not even a whimper of movement from them as their bodies lay there like a log of wood and stone-cold as frozen beef. Frightened, Lucinda placed her ear close to her mom's heart, only to discover there was no sign of beating. She became more frightened as she did the same to her father. Her fright turned to hysteria.

"Mom, Dad, you promised you were not going anywhere. Please wake up!" Lucinda shouted with tears in her eyes.

"Please wake up. I prayed to God to heal you. I didn't tell him to take my parents away from me. Please wake up. I promise to do anything you want. Just wake up!" Lucinda yelled as she kept touching her parents, hoping that one of them would open their eyes, but nothing happened.

She ran out of the house and headed straight for the mountain, which took hours before she could get there.

"Who could bang at the door like that?" Maya asked as she stood up to check who it was. She was surprised when she saw Lucinda barefoot and looking fatigued.

"What's wrong with you?" Greg asked as he came out of the room.

Lucinda sat still and was crying.

"Who is after you? Talk to me, Lucinda. What's the problem? What about your mom and dad? Where are they?" Maya kept on with her barrage of questions.

"Mom and Dad, they left without me," Lucinda replied in between tears.

"How do you mean? I don't understand," Greg asked.

"They were sick. Everyone in the village is down with this illness, including Mom and Dad. Yesterday morning, they pleaded with me to come here and stay with you for a while, but I refused, telling them they needed me to be around them. And this morning, I woke up to feed them, but they wouldn't answer me. Their bodies were so cold. They had promised me they would not go anywhere without me," Lucinda said.

"Are you saying that Annalise and Phil are dead?" Greg asked with trembling lips.

Lucinda nodded with tears in her eyes.

"This can't be happening," Maya said as she held her granddaughter tightly, but Lucinda kept mentioning her parents' names until she fell asleep.

"They were sick, and they didn't let anyone know. Now her parents are gone. The last time I saw my daughter was when I went to take Lucinda back home. Death cheated me big time.

I didn't see my daughter one last time before she went on this journey. Annalise and Phil, you both should have waited a little longer. How will Lucinda cope without you two?" Maya asked as she wiped the tears from her cheeks.

"Although I felt something was wrong with me, I didn't know that my daughter and her husband were dying. If I knew, I would have brought them here and treated them with natural herbs.

I never got the chance to see Phil for some years now," Greg lamented bitterly.

"We can't leave the bodies there. We have to burn them and keep the ashes for Lucinda, their daughter," Maya said.

"Stay back, dear. I know how to do this! I'll be back before night falls," Greg said to Maya, who was still lamenting bitterly as she sat on the smaller couch.

"Take care of yourself, and when you see Annalise and Phil, tell them we miss them," Maya said as Greg was leaving the house.

Greg nodded as he stood up and walked outside. He took the horse and raced down to the village.

He got to the house where his daughter lived with her husband. As he came down and tied the horse to the tree, he walked inside slowly and met his daughter and Phil, just the way Lucinda had left them.

"You would have sent a message to me. Somehow, Annalise, I know you won't be dead because I would have tried everything humanly possible to heal you. Your child is in tears. She keeps saying that you both left without her. You made so many promises to her, and you didn't keep any. She yearns for both of you," Greg was saying in between sobs, slowly but surely grieving.

Gradually, he could pull the two bodies out of the house. He laid them on the wood and poured oil on them before setting them ablaze.

"Dust we are from, and to dust, we shall return," Greg said as he poured the ashes into the bottle that he had come with.

He climbed onto his horse and jogged back to the mountain top. He was in pain even though he refused to show it.

"Grandma, are my parents ever going to come back home?" Lucinda asked with tears in her eyes. She had woken up and kept bombarding Maya with questions concerning her parents.

"They will come home, but not soon," Maya replied. She felt terrible as she couldn't believe she had lied to her granddaughter.

"What of Grandpa? Where is he?" Lucinda asked.

"Oh, he went out to sort out some things. He will be back any moment from now," Maya replied.

"So, should I dish out your food now for you to eat?" Maya added.

"When Mom and Dad come back home, I will eat. You said they are coming back home, right? That's not a problem. I will wait for them," Lucinda said, with her hand holding her chin.

"I'm home," Greg said as he walked into the room.

"Grandpa. Grandma said my parents would be back home, so I'm waiting for them," Lucinda said, sitting up.

"Here, have this," Greg said as he gave a silver bottle to Lucinda.

"What's this?" Lucinda asked.

"It's a gift from your parents. They want you to keep it, and please don't misplace it," Greg said.

"A gift from my parents? Where are they?" Lucinda said, standing up as she ran outside. She came back a few minutes later and looked at her grandparents askance and said, "I checked everywhere, but I couldn't see them. Where are they?"

"Lucy, listen, your mom and dad gave me this to keep for you a long time ago. I want you to have it because you are of age," Greg lied.

"Why do I feel no one is telling me the truth here? Where are my mom and dad?" Lucinda asked with tears in her eyes.

"They want you to have this in memory of them. They might not come home soon," Greg replied.

"That's not fair. They promised they were going to go everywhere with me. They made that promise to me. Even if Mom would leave me behind, I trust my dad. I'm his little princess.

He makes sure I'm happy every day. He says yes to everything I want to do. You can't just tell me that my parents aren't coming home soon. I need them now. Get them for me. I want to go with them," Lucinda screamed as Maya hugged her tightly, patting her on the back.

"Granny, I want them home," Lucinda cried even more amidst tears.

"They aren't deaf to your cries, and please, trust me, Lucinda.

Your parents are coming back," Maya replied.

The atmosphere was awkward for Greg. He cast a furtive glance at them and walked out. He had cremated his daughter and son-in-law. If anyone had told him his daughter would be dead this day, he wouldn't have believed that person. He reasoned that death had played a fast one on them.

Chapter Five

GREG AND MAYA HAD TRIED ALL THEY COULD

Greg and Maya had tried all they could to make Lucinda leave the room, but all to no avail. She wouldn't budge and rarely touched the food. In the morning, Maya and Greg woke up and sat down on their bed, waiting for Lucinda to wake up too. They had agreed to talk sense to her.

Soon after, Lucinda stirred, opened her eyes, and had them focused on the wall. Maya wiped the tears that had gathered in her eyes that early morning. She was unable to sleep during the night.

The death of Annalise and her husband had been traumatic for her and Greg too. But like a man, Greg carried himself with the calmness the situation required. Maya was still wallowing in pain, sadness, and fear—the fear of losing Lucinda too.

They waited for Lucinda to become fully awake before they ventured into talking to her.

"Lucinda, how are you feeling now? I hope you slept well?" Maya said.

"Yes, thank you, Grandma," Lucinda replied without moving her eyes an inch off the wall.

"Lucinda, my dear, you're hurting yourself, and you're also hurting us. Had your mom been here, she wouldn't want to see you like this. You can't continue like this forever. Cheer up, my dear, and then we will go out and have some fun together," Greg said.

"If hurting myself would bring back my parents, then I'm willing to hurt myself until eternity. They didn't deserve this kind of cruelty. We lived far away from the village, yet somehow, they contracted the disease. Mom and Dad suffered so much.

Why didn't nature spare them? I need the love of my parents. I wanted them to be around me. I just want my mom and dad home," Lucinda replied as tears started rushing down her cheeks.

"We also want them home, but it had happened. Death is the only thing we humans have no power over. The least we can do is to respect their last wishes, and you are yet to tell us the last thing your parents told you before their death," Maya said.

"They said nothing! Nothing!" Lucinda replied and burst out crying.

"It's alright, child. Please stop. Please," Greg begged.

"You know Mom and Dad requested nothing; they only wanted me far away so I wouldn't contract the disease. Every day I prayed to the creator to heal my parents. I wanted a miracle. I cried and pleaded, but it's obvious it fell on deaf ears.

The day they died, I had woken up in the morning to cook for them as usual, only to meet their lifeless bodies. Mom, if you can hear me, know that you hurt me so much. Remember, you promised you would stay with me until the end of time, but you were quick to leave after spending a decade with me.

"Why couldn't you both defy death to be with me?" Lucinda yelled as Greg got up from the bed to hold her tightly, consoling her.

Maya left the room quickly with tears in her eyes as she walked into the parlor. She sat on the oversized couch crying. She took out an old wooden box, opened it up, and took out the seashell there as she ran her hands over it, with tears dripping on it.

Greg walked into the parlor after a few minutes to meet Maya holding the ancestral seashell.

"What of Lucinda?" Maya asked.

"I've been able to put her back to sleep. Why are you holding the seashell?" Greg asked.

"Well, this has been passed from generation to generation, and I know it must have cost a fortune. I don't mind selling it to give Lucinda the good life she deserves. I want to take her somewhere far away. It hurts to see her going through so much pain at such a tender age," Maya said.

"Taking her far away isn't what she needs right now. She only wants her parents back, and we know it is impossible, but I hope sooner she will let go of this terrible thing," Greg said.

"Annalise, why did you have to go? Can't you just come back somehow? I don't know how, but please, your daughter needs you," Maya said amidst tears, which dripped down her cheeks and dropped on the seashell.

Greg took the seashell from Maya and placed it back inside the box so he could be able to console her.

"You don't have to cry. I know you. Annalise and Lucinda share the same quality. Console yourself in Lucinda, please, my dear. You are so emotional right now, but please be strong for your grandchild. She needs you. She needs us," Greg said as he hugged his wife.

Lucinda later woke up before noon but refused to get up from her bed and refused every request to eat any food. In the evening, she got up from the bed, seeing an old picture of her parents hanging on the wall. She took it down and smiled, but the smiling quickly replaced with tears.

"I miss you, Annalise and Phil. I want you both to come home. I want to see that smile on your face whenever I call you by your first name, Mom.

I miss all the fun we had together. It's fun staying with Grandma and Grandpa, but I wouldn't trade you both for anything else in this world. Mom and Dad, why didn't you both stay for a long time? Why would you have to leave now?

I wish I could turn back the hands of the clock so we all could come here. If only you both listened to me, maybe you both wouldn't have contracted the disease, and you would be safe with me. I wish I tried harder in convincing you both to come here. I wish I tried harder," Lucinda said, wiping her tears with the back of her hand as she dropped the picture on the wooden floor.

Lucinda stood up and walked towards the window. She slowly opened the curtain, and after standing there for close to thirty minutes, she strolled back to her bed. When she heard her name, she turned around and looked but saw no one. She closed the window and shifted back the curtains as she walked out of the room.

"Grandma!" Lucinda called as she got to the sitting room. Maya rushed out of the kitchen as soon as she heard Lucinda's voice.

"Lucinda, you came out from the room?" Maya asked, feeling surprised and happy.

"Yeah, where is Grandpa?" Lucinda asked.

"He just stepped outside now. I think he will be back in a few minutes," Maya replied.

"Alright," Lucinda said as she turned to go back to her room. "Lucinda!" Maya called.

"Yes, Granny," Lucinda answered as she turned back.

"Why don't you sit here, please? Don't go back to bed now, please. You've been there since morning. You can sit in the parlor," Maya pleaded.

"But you're busy in the kitchen; who will be with me in the parlor?" Lucinda asked.

"I'm here with you. I'm not all that busy," Maya lied as she watched Lucinda sit down on the wooden chair beside the cooking stove. Maya heaved a sigh of relief as she sat down too. She was happy that finally, Lucinda had come to terms with the reality of losing her parents to death.

"So, what would you like us to do?" Maya asked.

"Of all the places in the world, why did you choose this mountain?" Lucinda asked with her hands on her chin.

"Because this place is quiet and heavenly. There is no disturbance. The tranquility of the environment gives us innermost peace," Maya replied, smiling.

"My mom, your daughter, did she ever like it here? She had no one to play with," Lucinda asked.

"Annalise, your mother, is a gift from God. She was unique. She was the main reason we chose here because she valued calmness more than anything else, and that was the main reason you and your parents lived close to the riverside. Annalise wasn't the type who had many friends.

She made friends with the animals. When she got married and moved away, I felt pain. My daughter is my most priceless possession. "She is gone, but I'm happy you are here," Maya said, trying hard not to cry.

"You know it's okay to let those tears out. That's what my mom taught me. That way, you will feel a lot better," Lucinda said as Maya stared at her. She was surprised this was coming from a ten-year-old girl.

"Lucinda, you—"

"I act like an adult, I know. Mom says that to me a lot. Anytime I cry, don't stop me. I'm only letting out my emotions. Having it stuck right there in me can lead to something worse for me. I miss my parents, and they are worth every single tear I shed for their demise. So, I understand when you cry because of your daughter, Annalise, and her husband, Phil. They deserve every bit of tears; they are worth it," Lucinda said.

"You know I miss her so much, and I'm scared. I want nothing bad to happen to you. Please, Lucinda, don't stay in your bed alone tomorrow. Try to come out like you did this evening. It hurts me so much that you're doing this to yourself," Maya said.

"I'm sorry if I was hurting myself, but I promise not to hurt myself again. Do you know why?" Lucinda asked.

"No, I don't, but why, if I may ask?" Maya said.

"Because my parents are back home. I heard their voice, and I can feel their presence," Lucinda said, smiling.

Maya was shocked when she heard that as she curiously looked at Lucinda.

"I'm not mad, Granny. I know what I'm saying; my parents are back," Lucinda said as she stood up and walked back into the room.

Maya placed her hand on her chin as she looked at the receding figure of her granddaughter.

"Please heal my granddaughter of this pain. She is too young and can't bear it anymore," she muttered to herself.

At that instant, Greg came inside and met Maya, lost in her thoughts.

"Maya!" Greg called, but there was no response from Maya. He went and touched her, and she jerked back to reality.

"Your body is here, but your mind is lost. What were you thinking about?" Greg asked as he sat down.

"Lucinda came out, and we talked," Maya replied.

"That's good news. Aside from that, why do you look lost?" Greg asked.

"Lucinda told me her parents are back, and she can feel their presence," Maya said.

"Wow! I wasn't expecting this," Greg said.

"I just hope she doesn't hurt herself. I'm scared of what she said. Talking about her dead parents being back is crazy," Maya said.

"Don't worry. I know Lucinda will overcome this. She is young, and anything happening now happened. She is young, and she will heal. Don't worry," Greg said as Maya smiled and walked back into the kitchen to fix dinner.

When Lucinda walked into the room, she laid down on the bed, and on looking up, she started talking: "I heard your voice today, Annalise. I heard when you called my name. That was your voice, Mom. I know you're back. I can remember what Granny said, that you and Dad would be back, and you know what? I believed every word she said to me that day because I know my parents can't just leave without coming home to know how their little angel is doing. This past night without you—just one night—has been hell for me. Grandpa and Grandma have tried to console me, but I want you both home so we can live together as one happy family again," Lucinda said as she closed her eyes.

"Lucinda!" the voice called again.

Lucinda smiled and said, "I can hear you; though I don't know where you are at the moment, trust me, I will find you."

Chapter Six

ON THIS FATEFUL MORNING

On this fateful morning, Maya had prepared breakfast, and after dishing out Lucinda's portion, she left for the next village with Greg for an emergency. Something cropped up. Lucinda was still asleep when they left, but Maya placed the food where she could see it before leaving the house and making sure that the front door was locked properly.

Later in the morning, Lucinda woke up to discover that her grandparents were not in the room. She went out to the parlor, but they were not there, and then to the kitchen. It was there she realized she was alone in the house, and on looking around, she saw her food neatly kept for her on a kitchen table.

She stood there looking at the food and wondering where her grandparents could have gone. She, of course, knew that they must have gone out on an essential assignment and that they didn't want to disturb her while she was still asleep.

"But where could they be? Where could they have gone?" Lucinda wondered aloud as she walked out of the kitchen back to the parlor. As she tried to open the front door, she discovered it was also locked from the outside. She then went out through the back door, opening it from inside.

When she stepped out, she went to the horse's stable by the house's side. Since her mourning period, she hadn't been there. On unlocking the stable door, she walked inside and saw the horses tied to the ground.

"Wow, they still look beautiful," Lucinda silently muttered as she ran her fingers over the bodies of the two horses.

"Do you have a name? What should I call you?" Lucinda asked. "I will think of a name for you two," she said, smiling.

"I think I have to come here more often," she added as she turned and walked out.

"Lucinda!" the voice called again.

"This is surely my mother's voice. Where can I find you, Mom?" Lucinda said, looking around to see who called her name, but with no form of fear.

"Lucinda! I'm here," the voice said. "Where are you?" Lucinda asked.

"What are you doing here?" Maya asked as she walked in.

"You and Grandpa weren't in, so I let myself out through the back door," Lucinda replied.

"And who were you talking to? I heard when you were asking, 'Where are you?' to the air?" Maya asked.

"My mom called my name, and she said she is in here," Lucinda replied.

Maya looked at her and then looked around before she said to Lucinda, "Your mother isn't here, Lucinda."

"If you came earlier, you would have heard when she called my name. I swear she is in here," Lucinda said.

Maya held Lucinda's hand and walked with her out of the stable. She locked it up correctly and walked inside with her.

"Lucinda dear, listen. No one called you. It's just that your imagination is playing tricks on you," Maya said. "That's not true. I know what I heard, Granny. My mom is back here. I can hear her voice. It's not my fault if you can't hear her," Lucinda said amidst tears as she rushed into the room.

"God, what is happening?" Maya asked as she sat down on the chair inside the parlor.

"Is everything alright?" Greg asked as he walked in to meet Maya with her head bowed.

"Everything isn't okay. I'm scared. I don't know what is happening to Lucinda," Maya replied.

"How do you mean? Is she okay?" Greg asked as he sat down.

"She is okay. I came back and figured out she wasn't in her room, but I could find her in the stable. Without her knowing I was behind her, I overheard her asking someone where she is.

I tried asking her who the person was, and she said it was her mom and that she is back. When I tried letting her know it was just a figment of her imagination playing tricks on her, she screamed and said, 'It's not my fault if I can't hear the voice.' Then she ran inside the room. I fear for her. I'm scared of how she is acting. What could be wrong?" Maya asked. "Maybe her imagination is indeed playing tricks on her," Greg said.

"But she wouldn't understand that, and she doesn't want to hear anything contrary to her thoughts," Maya replied, exasperated.

"Where is she?" Greg asked.

"Inside the room, of course. Where else?" Maya replied as Greg excused himself and walked into the room.

"Can I come in?" Greg asked as he stood at the door.

"Come in," Lucinda replied as Greg walked in and sat at the edge of the bed.

"You don't look okay. What's the problem, dear?" Greg asked.

"I heard the voice. It was loud and clear. I know my mom is somewhere around here, and I have to find her," Lucinda replied.

"What voice are you talking about?" Greg asked.

"My parents are back. I know I heard that voice. Grandma won't believe me. She thinks it's my imagination playing tricks on me," Lucinda replied. "How sure are you that your parents are back? And how come you're the only one who can hear this voice?" Greg asked calmly.

"I'm a hundred percent sure, but I don't know why you can't hear the voice. It's not my fault," Lucinda replied.

"Listen, my angel. Your parents are not back. Even if they are coming back, not soon. Perhaps because you have been thinking so much about them, that's why you have heard their voices," Greg replied.

"Have I ever lied to you before?" Lucinda asked, eyes blazing. "No, you haven't. Why do you ask?" Greg asked.

"So, why do you find it hard to believe me when I say that my parents are back? I heard the voice, and I know that's her voice. Nothing you would ever say or do can make me believe my parents aren't back. Don't worry, Grandpa, eventually, you will find out on your own that my parents are back here indeed," Lucinda replied.

"Lucinda, my dear, I do not doubt you, but my problem is that you're the only one that hears the voice," Greg said.

"I don't know, Grandpa. I can't know either," Lucinda replied.

"Alright, if you say so. I won't disturb you over this matter again," Greg said.

"Does that mean you now believe me?" Lucinda asked.

"Of course, I believe you," Greg said half grudgingly as he didn't want to stress the matter any further.

"Let me meet with your grandma. We have things to do," Greg said.

"Alright, take care," Lucinda replied, smiling.

Greg stood up and walked out of the room when Lucinda called him and said, "Thank you for believing me." Greg smiled and walked out of the room.

He entered the kitchen to meet Maya slicing onions. "Any luck?" Maya asked, still busy with her hands.

"No luck. Maybe her parents are back, and only she can hear the voices," Greg said, shrugging.

"Are you believing her?" Maya asked.

"Of course, I have no choice. This girl hasn't lied to both of us before. It isn't her imagination, or her mind is playing tricks on her. She knows what she heard, and according to her, it's her parents' voice. Even if we can't hear them, the only thing we can do is believe her. That's the only thing," Greg replied.

"But…"

"There are no buts in this case, Maya. Lucinda is already going through a lot. Her parents died right in her presence. At ten, she has gone through a lot, and you know Lucinda isn't someone who will wake up one morning to fabricate stories just to gain our attention. According to to her, she heard a voice, and that voice belongs to her parents. The least we can do is believe her, even if we can't hear the voice. But one thing is certain: Annalise and Phil are back, and their daughter only feels their presence," Greg replied. "But will Lucinda ever be okay?" Maya asked.

"Lucinda is more than okay. If she says anything, believe her. I beg of you. That's the only thing she wants from us," Greg replied.

"If you say so," Maya replied grudgingly.

"I will be in the stable. I need to check on the horses," Greg said and left immediately.

Maya finished cooking and dished out the food as she placed Lucinda's food on a tray and carried it to her.

"Thanks, Granny," Lucinda said, collecting the food from her. "You're welcome," Maya replied.

"Where are you going? Come and sit with me, please," Lucinda pleaded.

"Oh! Okay," Maya said as she sat down with her granddaughter.

"I went to see the horses today. They are beautiful and regal. They are such glorious creatures. I hope that I'm permitted to get close to them?" Lucinda asked.

"Yes, of course, my dear, you're permitted to go close to them. We bought them a week after I took you home. Grandpa needed something to ease his movement henceforth, and me too, whenever necessary," Maya replied. "I love the both of them," Lucinda replied, grinning.

"Oh, you do?" Maya asked.

"Yes, and I'm planning on naming both of them. I've been thinking of a suitable name, but by tomorrow, I should be able to come up with something," Lucinda replied.

"I'm fine with that," Maya replied.

"While I am here, Mom called again, and this time it felt like something was bothering her. She is sad about something," Lucinda replied.

"You mean Annalise, my daughter?" Maya asked, not entirely surprised anymore.

"Yes, my mom. I felt she was sad that I am taking time to find where she is," Lucinda replied.

"How do you know this voice is your mom's voice?" Maya asked.

"If you hear my mom's voice, can you recognize it?" Lucinda asked.

"Sure, I can. She is my daughter," Maya replied.

"Yes, it's true. She is your daughter, and you lived with Annalise for many years. So, you can recognize her voice when she speaks. That's the same way I can recognize her voice because she has been with me for a decade since she gave birth to me," Lucinda replied.

"So, if you find her, will you tell me where she is?" Maya asked.

"If she agrees to it, I will only tell Grandpa since you don't believe me," Lucinda replied.

"I believe you. You haven't lied to us before, so you can't start lying now or cooking up some stories. I believe you, dear," Maya replied.

"Wow! Thanks for believing me," Lucinda replied, smiling. "You're welcome," Maya said as she hugged Lucinda. "Now eat your food, my dear," Maya said, smiling.

Maya sat still as she watched Lucinda eat her food. She silently thought of the possibility of Greg being right after all and that Annalise is back. The fact is that only Lucinda can hear her mother's voice. She looked out the window as she continued speaking to herself: I made a wish that you come back.

I don't know how, but come back for your daughter. Guess you heard me. If truly you're back, Annalise, don't go; stay with your daughter, stay as long as you can even if we can't see you. Your presence has changed her a lot and is bringing back the old Lucinda who we know."

———◆❖◆———

Chapter Seven

LUCINDA STOOD UP FROM HER BED

Lucinda stood up from her bed and brought the lantern close to her. Slowly and noiselessly, she opened the door and walked out through the back door. Her grandparents were already sleeping, so Lucinda didn't want to wake them up. She silently tiptoed to the stable and quietly unlocked it, sneaking inside. She walked to where the horses were, figuring they were still awake as she dropped the lantern on the floor.

"It's me, Lucinda," Lucinda said as she ran her hands on the two horses. "Lucinda!" the voice called again as Lucinda looked around.

"I can hear you, Mom. Where are you?" Lucinda said, looking around.

The white horse shifted closer to where Lucinda was as she turned.

"Lucinda, it's me. My soul lives in this horse," the white horse said.

"Mom, you're in this horse? How come? How did you manage? What did you do?" Lucinda asked.

"Wow! My parents' souls live in these horses," Lucinda exclaimed happily.

"I have missed you. Your dad and I have missed you so much," the white horse said.

"I have missed you too and knew you both were going to come back somehow. I was certain when I heard your voice.

Even Grandma said my imagination was playing tricks on me, but I knew it wasn't my imagination. Thank you for coming back," Lucinda said as she hugged the white horse and went back to embrace the brown horse.

"Since your soul lives in this white horse, I will call you Anna, and since Dad lives in this brown horse, I will call him Phil," Lucinda said.

"Your grandparents will think you are losing it," Phil said.

"I will tell them. They will believe me," Lucinda said.

"I doubt it, Lucinda. They won't believe you," Anna said.

"What your mother said is true, Lucinda. They won't believe you, so don't bother trying to make them believe you. You're the only one who can hear us. They can't and can never hear us," Phil replied.

"Well, whether or not they believe, I don't care. You're my Anna, and you're my Phil," Lucinda said, touching the two horses.

"You should go back to bed now, Lucinda. It's late," Anna said.

"But I want to spend more time with you two," Lucinda replied, rather firmly.

"Your mother is right, Lucinda. Go back to bed. We will see you tomorrow morning. At least you now know that we are here. You can come anytime to see us," Phil chipped in.

"Yes, Lucinda, go back to bed as we also want to sleep now, too," Anna said.

"Alright, goodnight, Mom and Dad," Lucinda replied as she kissed the two horses and carried her lantern with her, walking out of the stable and locking it properly. On getting to the back door, she slowly opened it as she tiptoed inside and drove straight to her bed, lying down and covering herself up.

"Goodnight, Lucinda, we love you," the voices said.

"Goodnight, Mother; goodnight, Father. I can hear you all even though a distance separates us," Lucinda said as she smiled and closed her eyes and drifted off to sleep.

"Wake up, Granny," Lucinda said, tapping her grandma to wake up.

Maya opened her eyes slowly to see Lucinda sitting on the bed.

"Good morning," Lucinda said when she saw her granny was now wide awake.

"Good morning. You're up so early. Is there any problem? Did you have a nightmare?" Maya asked.

"Nightmare? No, rather I had the best night ever. About the horses. What are you feeding them with this morning?" Lucinda asked.

"Wait. Did you wake me up so early to ask me about what the horses will eat, or are you hungry?" Maya asked, sitting up.

"I'm not hungry. I'm talking about the horses. What will they eat?" Lucinda asked again.

"Hmmm. So, the horses are now your problem, Lucinda? Since when?" Maya asked.

"Oh yes, Granny. They had nothing to eat yesterday, so what will they eat today? They should have their morning food before ten a.m. at least," Lucinda said.

"Lucinda, is everything alright with you?" Maya asked.

"The horses need to eat. It seems you will not give me the food to give them. Let me talk to Grandpa instead," Lucinda said as she stood up to walk around the bed to get to her grandpa's corner of the big bed. Maya was watching her curiously.

She tapped Greg on the shoulder, waking him up. "Good morning, Grandpa," Lucinda said.

"Good morning, dear. Are you up already? You just woke me up. Hope everything is okay?" Greg asked.

"She also woke me up just to ask me for food for the horses," Maya turned toward her husband as Greg looked at Lucinda with questioning eyes.

"Well, Grandma wasn't saying anything, so I have to wake you up too. What will the horses be eating this morning? They are hungry. I'm sure they had nothing to eat yesterday," Lucinda replied as Greg looked at her with his mouth open.

"Are you joking, Lucinda?" Greg asked.

"I'm serious, Grandpa. What will the horses be eating this morning? They will be hungry any moment from now," Lucinda said.

"The horses are animals, Lucy. They are not humans like us," Maya chipped in.

"Speak for yourself, Granny. Who told you they are not humans? Well, I named the white horse Anna, after my mom, and the brown horse I called Phil," Lucinda replied.

"Please, hope I'm not dreaming," Greg said.

"You're not dreaming, Grandpa. You both are not saying anything. If there isn't any food available, tell me where I can get some food for them," Lucinda pleaded.

"Lucinda, is everything okay?" Greg asked.

"Yes, everything is okay, Grandpa," Lucinda replied. "So, why the sudden affinity to the horses?" Greg asked. "I wanted to ask that too," Maya replied.

"Let me say; they represent two people who matter most to me in this life, and that's my mom and dad. I'm super excited that they are back," Lucinda said, laughing.

"Lucy, is there anything you're not telling us?" Greg asked.

"Absolutely nothing. I just need food for the horses," Lucinda replied.

"You just want food, right?" Maya asked. "Yeah, just food, that's all," Lucinda replied.

"Alright, I will get the food for you," Greg replied.

"Okay, so you will bathe them, right?" Lucinda asked. "Yes, I will," Greg replied.

"Thank you, Grandpa. I need to bathe now," Lucinda said and walked out of the room.

"Something isn't right with my grandchild. Her parents' death is affecting her. Can't you see it? It's turning her into something else. I'm losing my grandchild," Maya replied.

"No, you haven't lost her. We just have to do whatever she wants. With time, she will understand the real thing that has happened to her parents. We have to play along with her until she is of age. If we try ruining this moment for her, she will go back to reclusion, and it's not what I want," Greg replied.

"For how long will this continue?" Maya asked.

"For as long as she takes to come to terms with the truth," Greg said while getting up from the bed.

"Let me get something for the horses to eat and also bathe them before Lucinda comes for my head," Greg said as he stood up and walked out of the room.

Maya followed suit as she walked straight to the kitchen to fix something for breakfast.

Greg himself went straight to the stable, opened it, and cleaned the inside, getting rid of the horse dung before taking the two horses outside to bathe them thoroughly.

He then went back to the stable, refilling the water and stocking up hay for them to feed. When he finished, he took the horses back inside the stable before walking back into the house to have his bath and eat breakfast. Lucinda, after taking her bath, had walked into the kitchen to meet her grandmother cooking.

"Granny, can I ask you a question?" Lucinda said. Maya's heart raced for a minute, but she held herself together so that Lucinda would not see the fright in her eyes.

"Sure, you can," Maya replied. "Can horses talk?" Lucinda asked.

"That's hilarious. Animals don't talk. No, horses can't talk," Maya replied.

"What if one comes out and claims she can hear the animals speak?" Lucinda asked.

"Maybe that will be if the person possesses some kind of magic," Maya replied.

"Does magic exist?" Lucinda asked.

"Magic sure exists, but I haven't seen one happen. So, I will say it's rare," Maya replied.

"Alright," Lucinda said as she went out before Maya stopped her.

"Why are you asking all these? Did anything happen?" Maya asked.

"I just wanted to know if animals can talk and if humans can hear them; that's all," Lucinda replied.

"Hey, Grandpa!" Lucinda said with smiles on her face as Greg walked into the kitchen.

"Have you…?"

"No need to ask, Lucinda. I have done everything," Greg replied.

"Oh, okay, that's very nice of you. Thank you, Grandpa," Lucinda replied.

"So, what are you doing in the kitchen?" Greg asked.

"I came to ask Grandma if animals can talk and if humans can hear them," Lucinda replied.

"Animals don't talk, and even if they do, humans won't understand them," Greg said.

"Maybe you shouldn't generalize. Just because you can't hear them doesn't mean they don't talk, and it doesn't mean some people can't understand them, either," Lucinda replied.

"Why did you say so?" Greg asked.

"Lucinda, are you now communicating with the animals?" Maya asked as she couldn't hold herself anymore.

"Oh, you don't call them animals. The horses have names, Anna and Phil, and address them with their names. Just because they are not humans like us shouldn't make us treat them like trash," Lucinda replied.

Greg and Maya looked at each other before Greg said, "Are you talking to Anna and Phil?"

"Oh yes, I spoke to them last night. We understand ourselves perfectly well," Lucinda replied.

"That's not possible," Maya said.

"Speak for yourself, Grandma. You don't always believe me, but I'm sure Grandpa believes me. When Mom was still alive, she always said that nothing is impossible in life. Just because they are impossible for others doesn't mean it will be impossible for you," Lucinda said as she stood up and walked out of the kitchen.

"My grandchild has lost it," Maya said, dropping the spoon she was holding onto the wooden floor.

"I'm so confused," Greg replied.

"You always believe her. Do you believe her this time?" Maya asked.

"It's impossible. Lucinda can't possibly be talking to animals.

Oh God, what's wrong with Lucinda?" Greg asked.

"First, she woke me up to feed the horses, and now she can talk to them. And this morning, she looks so radiant and lively; I'm scared that something bad might happen to her," Maya said.

"I don't know what to say, but I'm not worried," Greg replied.

Maya continued with her cooking as Greg left the kitchen to check on Lucinda.

Chapter Eight

LUCINDA, WHERE TO?

"Lucinda, where to?" Maya asked.

Maya had called Lucinda over to the kitchen to come and pick up her food. She rushed to the back door and was about to open it when Maya stopped her in her tracks, asking her where she was going with the food.

"I'm going to the stable; I want to eat there," Lucinda replied.

"Lucinda, you can eat here," Maya calmly said.

"But I want to eat there. I want to talk to the horses while eating," Lucinda replied.

"Talk to the horses? How can you talk to animals? You can't even understand their language, Lucinda. No one understands animals," Maya replied.

"Well, I understand them. That's why I want to eat there, so I will talk to them," Lucinda said and walked out with food in her hands.

Maya went to call Greg, who was sitting in the parlor, doodling.

"I don't know what's wrong with your grandchild. She said she wants to eat in the stable when I asked why she wants to talk to the horses. Lucinda has lost it. I'm sure of that. It's obvious her parents' death affected her, but has it got to the stage of talking to animals?" Maya raged.

"Where is she now?" Greg asked. "In the stable," Maya replied.

Greg got up and turned towards the front door exit, as Maya followed him in tow. Both of them went straight to the stable. They opened the door quietly, not to make any noise, and found Lucinda feeding the horses with hay cubes. When she finished, she then ate her food. Maya and Greg closed the door as they walked back to the house.

"Maybe we should sell the horses," Maya suggested.

"I see nothing wrong with her feeding the horses or staying in the stable to eat. The horses give her this joy that we can't give her. They serve as companions to her, and look, she is happy. If we sell the horses, she might hurt herself. We might lose her," Greg replied.

"But it's getting to be too much. Every night and day, she is in that stable with the horses, laughing and talking like she understands them," Maya said.

"If these horses were to be the only thing that can make her happy, then we should leave her. Taking those horses away will spell doom. I'm sure you don't want that old Lucinda who became a recluse because of her parents' death. Let her be, okay?" Greg asked and sat down heavily on the oversized couch, his favorite.

"But…"

"Let it be. She is still a child, and this makes her happy," Greg said.

"Alright, if you said so. Let me water the flowers," Maya said and walked out of the parlor.

"Mom, isn't there any way you and Dad can come out of these animals?" Lucinda asked.

"We barely have a few years left to stay here. Don't worry, Lucinda, we're okay here as far as we get the opportunity of being close to you," Anna replied.

"How do you mean?" Lucinda asked.

"Don't worry, Lucinda, you're still a baby. Don't worry, but with time, you will be able to understand," Phil replied.

"Okay, if you say so," Lucinda replied.

"Thank you so much, Lucinda, for everything. You made your grandparents show so much interest in us by bathing and feeding us every time, all thanks to you," Phil said.

"That's the least I can do, Dad. You and Mom live in the body of these horses, so I have to help. Grandma was even surprised when I told her I was coming to eat here. I can't explain anymore because they don't believe me. They think I'm going nuts," Lucinda replied.

"Lucinda, you don't expect them to believe you because they can't hear us. You're the only one who can hear us," Anna said.

"Okay. Should I get more hay cubes for you both?" Lucinda asked.

"Thank you, Lucinda. You're a daughter who is worth more than gold. Heaven blessed the day I gave birth to you. You have proven to be more than just our daughter, and luckily for us, you're blessed with exceptional wisdom. Thank you so much, Lucinda," Anna said.

"You're welcome," Lucinda replied, smiling.

"Can you take us outside? I need to feel the sun on my skin," Anna pleaded.

"Sure, that's not a problem," Lucinda said as she opened the small door and held onto the two ropes, walking out with the horses.

"Wow! It feels like ages," Anna said, sitting on the grass.

"I'm glad you like it. That reminds me, Dad, Grandpa gave me a silver bottle, and when I opened it, it contained ashes. When I asked, he said it's a gift from you both," Lucinda replied.

"Yeah, he is right. Keep that bottle safe with you. It's parts of us. It belongs to us," Phil replied.

"Your Grandpa is coming, and don't try convincing him because he won't believe you," Anna said.

Greg walked closer to where Lucinda was and said to her, "What if these horses run away?"

"They won't run away. Who leaves their house to go to a stranger's home?" Lucinda replied.

"I don't understand," Greg said.

"This is their home now, so they are fine here. They can't run away when a part of them lives here," Lucinda replied.

"How old are you again?" Greg asked with great surprise.

"I'm still ten but will turn eleven in a few months," Lucinda replied, smiling.

"Please take them inside," Greg pleaded.

"They wanted to feel the sun on their skin. When they are okay, they will inform me so I can take them inside," Lucinda replied.

"They will let you know?" Greg asked.

"Yes, they will let me know. Don't worry, Grandpa. I got this. Nothing is happening to them while I'm here, and trust me, they will not run away," Lucinda replied.

"But…"

"Do you trust me, Grandpa?" Lucinda asked. "I do, but…"

"No buts. Just know that nothing is happening to them," Lucinda replied as Greg looked around and walked away slowly.

Greg walked inside and called Maya, and together they went to the window to observe Lucinda.

"What's Lucinda doing with the horses?" Maya asked.

"According to her, she said the horses wanted to feel the sun on their skin, and that was why she brought the horses out," Greg replied.

"But what if they run away? She can't possibly handle two horses. She is just ten," Maya said.

"Same thing I asked her, but she reminded me that nothing of such will ever happen. But then it's awkward that the horses are so calm whenever they are with her," Greg observed.

"Wow! Indeed, nothing is impossible. I'm not talking to her about this attachment with the horses anymore," Maya said.

"Since she finds so much joy and peace in doing all these things, then we shouldn't interfere, but we should watch her closely," Greg said.

"Let me call her so she can have her lunch," Maya said.

"Alright. No problem," Greg said as he watched Maya walked out of the house.

Maya went out towards where Lucinda was with the horses and asked her to come and eat her lunch.

"I'm coming, Granny, just let me take them into the stable," Lucinda replied.

Maya stood still as she watched Lucinda lead the horses inside. She came out a few minutes later, and together she and Maya walked into the house. Lucinda walked straight to the kitchen as she washed her hands, took the plate containing her food, and walked into the parlor.

Lucinda sat on the smaller couch and ate her food silently. When she finished, she walked back into the kitchen and washed the plate before dropping it in its place.

"Where to again?" Maya asked as she saw Lucinda leaving the kitchen.

"Please don't tell me you're going back to the stable. Try to have some rest, Lucinda," Maya said.

"I'm not going to the stable. I'm going to the room to sleep," Lucinda replied.

"Alright, go and sleep, dear," Maya said as she watched Lucinda walk straight into the room.

Lucinda lay down as she closed her eyes. Before she knew it, she drifted off to sleep.

"I can't find them. Where could they be?" Lucinda asked, wailing.

"But we left them here," Greg said.

"They are not here. Who made away with the horses?" Lucinda yelled as she fell on the floor and cried herself into a stupor.

"Don't worry. I will get another horse," Maya replied.

"I don't want another horse. I want the two horses back. I need them back. Bring them back to me," Lucinda wailed the more.

Greg searched the entire area, but he couldn't find any of the horses. Lucinda was restless, sad, and melancholy. If only her grandparents knew why she wanted the two horses and that her parents' souls live in the horses.

"We can go out and search for them tomorrow beyond these mountain ranges," Greg said.

"No, let's go now; tomorrow might be too late," Lucinda said.

"But it's dark already. How are we going to find them? We have to wait until morning, and it looks like it's going to rain," Maya said.

"More reason we have to go today. The horses can't be out there in the rain," Lucinda replied.

"Please, Lucinda," Maya and Greg pleaded, hoping she would have a change of mind.

"I said no!" Lucinda shouted and woke up.

"Jeez, so this is all a dream?" Lucinda said, wiping her eyes with the back of her palm.

Maya and Greg had rushed inside Lucinda's room to know what was wrong with her.

"Lucinda, are you okay?" Maya asked.

Lucinda stood up and ran out of the room towards the stable. Maya and Greg followed behind as the trio ran to the stable. Lucinda unlocked it and rushed inside to see the horses still tethered to their places. She was relieved that her dream wasn't a reality. She then took turns hugging them.

"I thought I had lost you both," Lucinda said, smiling. "Lucinda, what's the problem?" Greg asked.

"I had a bad dream where someone had stolen the horses, and you and Grandma refused to follow me to search for the horses that night," Lucinda said.

Maya and Greg looked at each other and left Lucinda in the stable.

"I told you that should these horses be taken away from Lucinda, she might die. She dreamt that someone stole the horses, and she is acting like this. What will happen if it happens in reality?" Greg said.

"I hope no one takes them away from us. We have already lost so many animals in the past. The person who is behind the stealing should please pity my granddaughter and leave these horses because as it stands now, those horses are her joy and peace," Maya said as the duo walked inside to continue with what they were doing.

Chapter Nine

THIS WHOLE PLACE IS SO NOISY

"This whole place is so noisy that I can barely hear myself," Lucinda said.

"That's why it is called a market," Maya replied.

The three of them had gone to the nearby village market to get foodstuffs. This was the first time Lucinda had gone to the market. Even while her parents were alive, they preferred leaving her at home than taking her to the market.

They were almost home when Lucinda called out to Maya: "Granny," Lucinda said, tapping her grandmother.

"What's it?" Maya asked.

"The door. The door is open!" Lucinda said, almost shouting, pointing at the house.

"Oh no, please let it not be that they have stolen our things again," Greg said as they all hastened their steps. They got into the house and went to the rooms to check their belongings, but Lucinda went straight to the stable to check on the horses. When she got there, she saw the door was open. She hurried inside, and the horses weren't in sight.

"Mom, Dad, I'm here," Lucinda said, advancing closer, hoping the horses would come out of their hiding place. But there was no movement anywhere. And on looking at the ground, she saw that the horses' leash had been cut.

"No!" Lucinda said as she fell on the floor crying.

Greg and Maya heard her voice, and they ran to the stable to check what the problem was. They went there and found out that someone had stolen the horses.

Maya ran to where Lucinda was and held her tightly.

"Why are they doing this? Why didn't they choose to steal something else? Why would it be the horses?" Lucinda said as tears gushed freely from her eyes.

"Don't worry, we will get another one for you," Greg said, consoling her.

"That's the problem. I do not want another horse. I need Anna and Phil. I need them. They are not just horses; they are a part of me," Lucinda said, crying.

"But there is no way we can find them," Maya replied.

"I want them home. Please, Grandpa, help me," Lucinda replied, holding her grandpa's hands.

Greg was confused about what to do. He didn't know where to start to search for the horses. Maya tried consoling Lucinda, but all to no avail as she was confident of not accepting any other horse.

"Mom, Dad, please don't do this to me. Daddy, can you hear me? Please, you both shouldn't leave me alone here. You're my joy, happiness, and peace. I wouldn't have agreed to follow Grandpa and Grandma to the market.

I would have stayed to protect you both. Wherever you both are, please come back home, and even if you can't come home, tell me where you are, then I will come and take you home myself. I don't want to lose you both a second time.

Tell me where you are, Mom. Dad, talk to me, please. This place will be hell without you both by my side. Please come home," Lucinda said within herself as tears continued to gush freely from her eyes.

She was heartbroken. Her grandparents wouldn't understand why she needed the two horses back, and no matter how hard she explained, they wouldn't understand.

If only they knew that her parents' souls lived in those two horses, then they wouldn't bring up the suggestion of replacing them with new ones.

"Lucinda, help us, please," the Voice spoke.

Lucinda looked around and stood up with a start, to the amazement of her grandparents.

"Where are you? Tell me, please. Grandpa and I will come to bring you two back home," Lucinda muttered in an inaudible whisper. She made sure Greg and Maya didn't hear her, of course. She wouldn't want them thinking she was mad.

"That road that leads to the market. On the left-hand side lies a forest; search deep, and you shall find us. Please, be fast. If you waste any more time, you won't find us here," the Voice replied.

"Grandpa! I know where they are. Please follow me. Let's get the horses before they hurt them," Lucinda said, wiping her tears with the back of her hand.

"That's not possible," Maya replied.

"Please, Grandma, believe me this time, I beg you. I know where they are. If we waste any more time, they might hurt them. Please convince Grandpa," Lucinda said as she went to where her grandpa was standing and said, "Please, Grandpa, I'm begging you for this. If you follow me, I would be the happiest person. Please don't say no. You're not doing this for me. You're doing this for your daughter, Annalise, and Phil."

Maya and Greg looked at each other as Greg excused himself and went inside. He came out with his hunting gun.

"Let's go; let's bring them home," Greg replied.

"Thank you so much, Grandpa," Lucinda said as she hugged her grandpa.

Lucinda walked out as Greg followed suit. They had trekked a long distance until they got to the part that led to the market. When Lucinda tried entering the forest, Greg touched her and asked her to wait.

"What's the problem, Grandpa?" Lucinda asked.

"We're entering the forest, and I know you haven't even been here before," Greg replied.

"Trust me, Grandpa. She told me they are in there," Lucinda replied.

"Who is she?" Greg asked.

"Let's go, Grandpa, before they hurt them," Lucinda replied as she trekked into the forest while Greg followed from behind. They had gone so deep, yet there were no traces of the horses.

"Lucinda, let's go home. They are not here, and it's getting late," Greg pleaded.

"They are somewhere close. We can't come this far just to go home empty-handed. We have to go home with the horses," Lucinda replied.

"Please, Lucinda, we can't continue; let's go back," Greg replied.

"Where are you? Talk to me, please. We can't come this far for you to be silent on us. Grandpa wants us to go home, and he is right. Please, Mom, say something, I beg of you," Lucinda said within herself, hoping that her mom would reply immediately.

"Keep coming, Lucinda. Please don't go back," the Voice replied.

Lucinda smiled as she turned and held her grandfather's hand and continued leading him deeper into the forest.

"I think I saw them," Lucinda said as she ran closer to where the horses were and hugged them.

"Grandpa, help me untie them," Lucinda pleaded as Greg helped in untying the ropes.

"I'm so glad you both are safe," Lucinda said, touching the white horse.

"Thank you for coming for us," Phil said.

"I don't know what would have happened if you had gone back. Thank you, Lucinda," Anna said.

"You don't need to thank me. I'm simply glad you both are safe," Lucinda replied, smiling.

"Who is thanking you?" Greg asked, surprised.

"Oh, they are thanking me," Lucinda replied.

"When did you understand the language of the horses to know they are thanking you?" Greg asked.

"I can't explain, but trust me, Grandpa, you won't understand," Lucinda replied.

"Lucinda," Greg exclaimed.

"Grandpa, let's get going," Lucinda said.

Greg carried Lucinda and placed her on the white horse while he used the brown horse, and they headed home. Greg was amazed at how Lucinda was acting with the horses.

Maya walked into her room as she sat on the bed and said, "None of our animals lasts too long with us here. They always steal them from us, and just that, these are the sources of joy for our grandchild's happiness. They have also stolen them from us too. I hope they find the horses. I don't want that old Lucinda back. I don't want her staying in her room crying every day. God, please help us."

Maya bent down as she took out the old box and quietly unlocked it. She took out the seashell and held it and smiled. Maya was happy the thieves didn't make away with the seashell. She put it back, locked the box, and placed it back under her bed. Standing up and going into the kitchen, she prepared dinner.

Chapter Ten

GREG WAS STILL CONFUSED

Greg was still confused about how Lucinda knew where the horses were as they galloped back home. Suddenly, he felt Lucinda's hand tapping him as he turned to look at her.

"I have been calling you, but it seems your mind is far away from here," Lucinda said.

"Oh, sorry, my little angel. I was just thinking about something," Greg replied.

"Do you mind sharing with me? I can help," Lucinda said.

"How did you get to know the horses are here, and you were saying something about the horses thanking you?" Greg asked.

"When someone does something nice to you or helps in a time of need, what do you normally say to the person?" Lucinda asked.

"You say the word 'thank you,'" Greg replied.

"I helped them, and because of that, they said, 'thank you,'" Lucinda replied, smiling.

"That's impossible, Lucinda," Greg said.

"Since you can't hear them doesn't mean I can't hear them. We are two different individuals, Grandpa, and one thing that your daughter, Annalise, taught me is that nothing is impossible," Lucinda replied.

"I had taught Annalise, my daughter, that nothing is impossible in this life, and she had taught the same to you. But in this case, Lucinda, I don't think you can understand the language of animals," Greg said.

"I don't understand the language of animals. I understand these two. They are not animals, Grandpa. They have souls. I know you don't understand," Lucinda replied as she caressed the white horse.

"Tell your grandpa to hold on tight. We are leaving this forest soon before it gets dark," Phil said.

"Grandpa, can you hold on tight? We are about to experience a new ride," Lucinda said, smiling.

"Hold on tight, baby; hope you're ready?" Anna asked.

"Yes, I'm so ready," Lucinda replied as the horses started galloping swiftly through forest paths, and before they knew it, they were out of the forest. It didn't take up to an hour when they got back home and descended from the horses.

"I didn't know they were this fast," Greg said, panting.

"Oh yes, they are," Lucinda replied as she held the rope and took the horses inside.

"We are home now," Lucinda said as she walked into the stable with the horses.

"I thought we were going to die. Those hooligans were mean to us. They rough-handled us," Anna said.

"Thanks for coming," Phil said.

"Anything for my parents; I'm glad that you both are safe. What could be more than that?" Lucinda replied as she took the hay cubes and fed the horses.

"The dogs, rabbits, and the likes of other animals that they captured—we found out that they steal these animals from people, then take them into the forest and kill them for food," Anna said.

"That's so cruel. Why would they do that?" Lucinda asked.

"The question is who and who is telling them about these animals and where they are?" Phil chipped in.

"You're right, Dad, but who could that be?" Lucinda asked.

"Many questions need answers. You need to eat and rest, and then I will tell you everything you need to know," Anna said.

"Do you know who they are?" Lucinda asked.

"Of course, I do, and I know why they are doing what they are doing. Lucinda, go and rest. We will talk later, and thanks for the hay cubes," Anna said. As she brought her head closer, Lucinda touched her, placing a peck on her and doing the same to Phil.

"I'm making a promise to you both today. No harm will befall you again. Trust me. I will do everything within my power to make sure you both are safe. I know I just turned eleven a few days ago. I'm small but mighty. You didn't raise just any child. You both raised a fighter never to give up even when the battle gets tough. They will not take you back again; I promise," Lucinda said.

"That's a pretty big promise, Lucinda," Phil said.

"You both made promises to me in the past, and you all kept them. Now it's my turn to do the same for my parents," Lucinda replied.

"Your dad and I love you so much, and we are forever grateful to have given birth to you," Anna said.

"I love you both more," Lucinda said, smiling.

"Now run along, go eat and rest. We will see you tomorrow," Anna said.

"Goodnight," Lucinda said and walked out of the stable. She locked it up properly before going inside the house through the back door.

"I'm happy that you could get the horses. At least Lucinda can let us have some peace," Maya said.

"Yeah, but one thing still baffles me. It feels like she communicates with the horses in clear terms," Greg said.

"That's not possible," Maya said.

"The same thing I said to her. She told me nothing is impossible and that some things are better left unsaid," Greg replied.

"How did you know she was talking to the horses?" Maya asked.

"How was she able to know where the horses were kept? She said the horses were thanking her, and she knew where they were when the horses were about to speed off. She had to ask me to brace up for the ride and prompt me when the horses started galloping swiftly through the meandering paths in the forest, getting us home on time," Greg said.

"Hmmm. Really? You witnessed these?" Maya said, keeping quiet, obviously pensive. And after what seemed like an eternity, she added, "Ever since Annalise and Phil died, everything about Lucinda changed since she developed an unusual affinity for those horses, finding so much joy and peace in their company."

"I'm suspicious of her, too, whether she is a mere child, but I can't keep asking forever because I don't think I will ever understand," Maya replied.

"I'm simply watching in silence as things play out," Greg said.

"Don't worry. Lucinda is safe, and I know whatever is talking to her is a friendly spirit. So, let it be," Maya replied.

"What you said is true, but I need to be sure that I'm not losing my granddaughter," Greg said.

"And who said you're losing me?" Lucinda asked as she came into the room, leaning on the wall.

"How long have you been there?" Maya asked.

"Long enough to know when Grandpa said he feels I communicate with the horses," Lucinda replied.

"Were you eavesdropping on our conversation?" Maya asked.

"Yeah. I was coming in from the stable and was about to go into the room when I heard you both talking in here, and I had to eavesdrop," Lucinda said.

"Lucinda…," Maya called out.

"What you said isn't false, Grandpa. I communicate with you, but you both would never believe me. One thing you should understand is that those horses are part of me, and anything that hurts them hurts me. There is no need to be suspicious, Grandma. I have explained countless times, but it seems you both would never understand. Anna and Phil are part of this family. They are not just horses. I know with time, you both will understand," Lucinda replied.

"We…," Greg made to speak, but Lucinda mildly interrupted him.

"I know you're trying to take care of me; I understand, but no one is hurting me. Those horses can't hurt me because I'm part of them. I'm not going nuts, either. I swear I'm not losing it. I know sometimes I speak way past my age, but I guess that's how my destiny was mapped out. I only want to be happy, and those horses are the source of my happiness. I'm just sad that you both think something is wrong with me, but I'm okay. Your grandchild hasn't lost it," Lucinda said.

"She is sad. She just poured out her pains and bitterness to us. Even from the tone in which she spoke to us explains everything," Maya said.

"Maybe we should apologize, but I'm still confused," Greg said.

"Let it go, Greg. Maybe this is how fate has mapped out her life," Maya replied.

"I don't know what else to say. I will have a quick bath. You should be through with the food. Then we can go talk to Lucinda together," Greg said as he stood up and walked out of the kitchen while Maya continued peeling the potatoes When Maya finished with her cooking, she dished out Lucinda's portion, and on getting to where Greg sat on the oversized couch, she motioned to him so they could go and talk to Lucinda in the room.

Lucinda was standing close to the window looking outside when her grandparents walked in. She didn't bother to turn as her eyes were fixed on the stars.

"Lucinda, we brought your food, and we also want to apologize to you," Maya said.

"Look up there and see how beautiful the sky is," Lucinda said, still focused on the stars.

"They are beautiful," Greg replied.

"You know my parents always said to me, 'Lucinda, you're beautiful like the stars,' although I haven't heard them say that to me for a while now," Lucinda said.

"You don't need us to constantly remind you how beautiful you are, Lucinda, my dear. I'm so sorry," Greg said.

"It's not a problem, Grandpa, and thanks for the compliment. Maybe you both shouldn't be worried about me that much. I can take care of myself. Rest assured no harm will befall me," Lucinda said as she turned and sat on her bed.

"Eat up, my dear. The food is getting cold," Maya said as Lucinda picked up her spoon and started eating quietly and slowly.

Greg left even before Lucinda could finish her food, but Maya waited, and immediately Lucinda finished eating. She took the plate and stood up to leave. On getting to the door, she turned back to say, "If at all your parents are back, like you said, and you can hear them, tell them to watch over you because right now you matter a lot to us," Maya said.

"They heard that; don't worry," Lucinda replied as she watched Maya leave the room.

Lucinda stood up and looked at the sky one more time before closing her window. She drank the cup of water that was there as she lay on the bed and covered herself up to sleep.

"You know you're always beautiful, and you shine so brightly just like the stars, illuminating anywhere your feet touch because the light around you shines so bright and gives light to people." It was Anna's voice that spoke calmly, followed by a gentle breeze that seeped in through the windows.

"I heard that, Mom," Lucinda said within herself. "Good night, Lucinda," the voice said again.

"Goodnight, Dad and Mom. I hope to get to spend eternity with you both," Lucinda said as she closed her eyes and drifted off to sleep.

Chapter Eleven

LUCINDA WOKE UP THAT MORNING

Lucinda woke up that morning to have her bath as she hurried to the stable. She was eager to hear what her mom wanted to tell her. When she got there, she unlocked the door and walked inside. She dropped the hay she was carrying and watched the horses feed on it.

"How was your night?" Lucinda asked.

"Nice, at least we didn't sleep in that forest," Anna replied.

"Your mom said it all," Phil chipped in.

"So, don't you think it's time to tell me everything?" Lucinda asked.

"They only came for one thing: the ancestral seashell, which has been passed from generation to generation," Anna replied.

"Which seashell are you talking about?" Lucinda asked.

"This seashell is magical, and it has been passed from generation to generation. I was the next in line to have that seashell that I would pass to you, Lucinda, but things changed. Our spirits were already hovering, hoping to meet with the Creator when my mother Maya took out the seashell and made a wish. With her tears dropping on it, she asked that we return anyhow. She wanted us to come back because of you," Anna explained.

"But how come Grandpa and Grandma can't hear you, and I'm the only one who can hear you? I don't understand," Lucinda asked.

"Because she was specific in her wish. She said she wanted us to come back just because of you, Lucinda. The only living things that breathe here are these horses. That's why our souls came into them," Anna explained.

"So why did they take you both away? Who is behind it?" Lucinda asked.

"Stephen. He is behind all of this. She had lost count of the animals stolen here, which made her stop buying any more. Stephen had always quested after the magic seashell. He is Mom's cousin. He knows more about the seashell and what it can do. It broke his heart the day the seashell was handed over to Mom. He always comes to the house hoping to find it, and after each fruitless search, he makes away with the animals he can find here," Anna replied.

"So, you mean Grandma owns a magic seashell, but she doesn't know about its powers?" Lucinda asked.

"Yes, my dear. She only sees it as an ancestral seashell passed from generation to generation. The seashell has the power to grant all wishes except raising the dead," Anna said.

"Now I understand it better," Lucinda said.

"And when I said we barely have time here, I meant we have four years remaining," Phil said.

"You mean you both are leaving on my fifteenth birthday?" Lucinda asked.

"Yes, dear. Don't think we are going to stay with you forever. You need to know the truth," Phil replied.

Lucinda was quiet for some time before saying, "I guess I will see you both later. Let me have my breakfast first." Saying this, she walked out of the stable with her head bowed down. She went straight to her room and lay on the bed, crying.

Maya walked in and met Lucinda in tears. She dropped the food on the table as Lucinda sat on her bed.

"What's the problem, dear?" Maya asked.

"I'm just sad, Grandma," Lucinda replied.

"Sad? What's the problem? What makes you sad?" Maya asked.

"Don't worry about it. Can I ask you something?" Lucinda said, sitting up as she wiped her tears with the back of her hand.

"Sure. Go on," Maya said.

"Can you tell me more about the seashell?" Lucinda asked.

"Which seashell are you talking about?" Maya, shocked, asked to be sure of what she just heard because she had never discussed anything concerning the ancestral seashell with Lucinda.

"The ancestral seashell that has been passed from generation to generation," Lucinda replied.

"How did you get to know about that?" Maya asked, still in shock.

"Let me say, a wild guess," Lucinda said, smiling.

"Lucinda, answer my question," Maya asked, keeping a straight face.

"Alright, my mom told me about it. She told me about the seashell that it was to be passed to her, then to me, but since they are gone, I guess I will be the one to take it over," Lucinda said.

"Yeah, your mom is right. And since they are gone, you will have it," Maya replied.

"Seashell? What's so special about it?" Lucinda asked.

"Just like you said, it's an ancestral seashell but unique, and it costs a fortune because of the diamond on the body," Maya replied.

"Aside from that, is there anything about the seashell that I need to know?" Lucinda asked, hoping that her grandparents might know that the seashell was magical.

"Nothing else that I know," Maya replied.

"Who is Stephen?" Lucinda asked.

"He is my cousin whom I haven't seen for a long while. But who told you about Stephen? Because I don't remember telling your mom who Stephen was," Maya asked.

"Are you aware that he is the one behind all the stealing that has been going on here? Well, he is angry that the seashell was given to you instead of him. Anytime you both are away, he comes here and ransacks the whole place, hoping to find the seashell, and when he doesn't, he steals the animals so you both will get hurt. The last time he came, he didn't find the seashell; that was why he took Anna and Phil, asking the hunters to kill them and turn them into meat," Lucinda said.

"I know that my cousin was so angry and left the house after I was given the seashell, but how did you get to know all that, something that happened over three decades ago?" Maya asked.

Lucinda kept quiet and took her food to eat, but Maya wasn't taking that. She was anxious to know the answer to her question.

"Lucinda, I'm talking to you," Maya reminded Lucinda.

"If I told you, you wouldn't believe me, so there is no need to say anything to you. Trust me; you will not believe me. Aside from that, can you show me the seashell as I want to see it for the first time?" Lucinda asked.

"You want to see the seashell?" Maya asked.

"Yes, I want to see how it looks. That's all," Lucinda replied.

"Well, not until you tell me who told you about Stephen," Maya said.

"My mom told me about Stephen. She told me everything that happened, starting from when your grandpa gave you the seashell and how Stephen has been stealing your animals," Lucinda replied.

"That's not possible because I don't remember telling Annalise anything concerning it," Maya said.

"You see; you don't believe me. I told you so that you would believe me. So, I shouldn't answer that question, but I have answered you anyway," Lucinda said and continued with the food she was eating.

"Why were you crying?" Maya asked.

"The truth?" Lucinda asked.

"What else, Lucinda? I need the truth," Maya asked.

"I just realized I had gotten a few years to spend time with people who matter most to me in this world. I can't change it, but I will well use my time," Lucinda replied and continued with her food.

"Lu…" Maya made to say.

"Not another question, Granny. You will never understand," Lucinda said as Maya stood up and walked out of the room. Lucinda ate her food quietly.

"I don't know how she managed to get to know about Stephen," Maya said.

"I'm hundred percent certain you didn't tell Annalise about it, so how come she claims her mother told her about it?" Greg wondered.

"The same question I asked, and she told me no matter how hard she explains, I won't understand her or even believe her," Maya replied.

"It still baffles me how she got to know where the horses are, and today, I feel there is more to this," Greg said.

"Granny asked for an explanation, which I gave her, but she didn't believe me one bit. I will not lie to make her believe me. I wasn't joking when I said my mother told me about it. I'm serious," Lucinda said as she walked into the room and sat on the wooden chair.

"Lucinda!" Greg called, but Lucinda ignored him and came back after a while.

"You both think I'm lying to you or cooking things up. Don't worry. I know that in time you both will understand all these," Lucinda said as she sat down on the chair.

"So, tell me, why are you here?" Greg asked.

"So, Grandma will show me the ancestral seashell," Lucinda replied.

"Oh, about that, wait a minute," Maya said as she bent down and brought out the old box that was under the bed. One wouldn't even guess there was something under the bed or hidden in that old box. Maya unlocked it and opened it up as she brought out the seashell.

"Here," Maya said as she handed it over to Lucinda.

"Wow! This is beautiful," Lucinda said as she ran her hands over the body of the seashell.

"Is this a real diamond?" Lucinda asked.

"Yes. Sure," Greg replied.

"Maybe that's why Stephen is after it. He just wants to sell it and use the money for something else," Lucinda replied.

Greg and Maya looked at each other and kept quiet.

Lucinda felt something substantial as soon as she touched the seashell. The seashell indeed has its powers. She handed the seashell over to her grandma, who carefully placed it back in the box and locked it, pushing it under the bed.

"Aside from being beautiful, I felt an unusual inner peace holding it," Lucinda said.

"What do you mean?" Greg asked.

"I said aside from being beautiful, I felt unusual inner peace holding it," Lucinda repeated.

"I heard you the first time, Lucinda. I only asked what you mean by that?" Greg said.

"It's inexplicable to me too, Grandpa, but while holding it, it gave me this immense joy and peace," Lucinda said as she stood up and walked out of the parlor.

"If it weren't Annalise who gave birth to this girl, I would have said she is some sort of weird person. She doesn't speak or talk like her age," Greg said.

"You know Annalise acted like that when she was at this age. Remember?" Maya replied and smiled.

Lucinda went straight to the stable, unlocked it, and walked inside. She walked towards the horses and hugged each of them.

"It seems someone is happy," Phil observed. "I can sense it too," Anna added.

Lucinda smiled and sat on the wooden chair there. "I miss you both," Lucinda said.

"We missed you too," Anna replied.

"I spoke to Grandma, and she showed me the seashell. I can't explain the feeling I had when I held it in my hands, but it is so beautiful, so ethereal," Lucinda said.

"Did you tell them about the magical powers?" Phil asked.

"Even if I did, they would never believe me," Anna replied.

"I knew they would not believe me, but Mom and Dad, I'm making a promise to you both today: even if you both have few hours to spend with me, I promise to make every day count, and as for Stephen, be rest assured that he will never come back here again. I will see to that," Lucinda said.

"What do you intend to do?" Phil asked.

"You and Mom had always told me that nothing is impossible.

Let's watch and see," Lucinda said as she smiled.

She knew she would protect the horses at all costs as her parents' souls live in them. She just couldn't stand to watch anything happen to the horses anymore.

Chapter Twelve

You're Becoming Too Close to Them

"You're becoming too close to them. What's the problem, Lucinda? These horses are stealing much of your time," Maya complained.

"Granny, I already told you; they are not stealing my time," Lucinda replied.

"You eat with them. You play with them. God knows if it's also possible, you will sleep in that stable and eat their food. What's wrong with you, Lucinda?" Maya asked, very much disturbed.

"I will talk to you later, Granny," Lucinda said and was walking away when Maya called her back.

"Your grandpa and I are going to the village close by to get some food. Do you want to follow us?" Maya asked.

"No!" It was an emphatic response from Lucinda.

"Why? You can't stay here all alone," Maya replied.

"I can take care of myself, and I would like to stay back to protect the horses so they won't be stolen again," Lucinda replied.

"I'm set. Let's get going," Greg said.

"Lucinda isn't going with us," Maya said.

"Why?" Greg asked.

"She said she wants to stay here and protect the horses, just in case the thieves come again," Maya said.

"You're joking, right?" Greg asked.

"You know I'm not joking, of course, Grandpa. I'm serious. Take care of yourself, Granny," Lucinda said as she hugged Maya and Greg before leaving for the stable.

Greg and Maya looked at each other with unanswered questions written all over their faces. They, however, left the house without Lucinda. When Lucinda was sure they had gone, she walked into the house, locked the door, and went into the room. She bent down and took out the box, carefully unlocking it and taking out the seashell, running her fingers over it and smiling before she started talking.

"You've been said to possess magical powers that can grant wishes and make dreams come true. I only need one thing from you. Stephen will come back, and who knows, he might kill the horses immediately and dump their dead bodies here. I just want you to make him forget everything, everything about us, about this family, so he doesn't come back here again for any reason," Lucinda said as tears trickled down her cheeks, allowing the tears to drop on the seashell.

On noticing the appearance of the seashell glittering, Lucinda smiled and said, "Though I don't know what this means, I know somehow you have made my wish come true. Thank you so much." She quickly dropped the seashell in the box, locked it, put it back to where it was, and walked out of the room. She went to the stable, stepped inside, and pecked the horses.

"You seem excited," Anna said.

"Yeah, because I made sure that Stephen isn't coming back here again," Lucinda replied.

"What do you mean?" Phil asked. "Yes, what did you do?" Anna added.

"Well, I just made a wish," Lucinda replied. "Lucinda, what did you do?" Anna asked.

"The Ancestral Seashell; I made a wish with it, and I'm sure the wish has been granted because I saw it glitter. I wished Stephen doesn't come back ever again," Lucinda said.

"Thank you, my angel," Anna said as she raised her foreleg closer for Lucinda to touch, which she did with relish.

"Grandpa and Grandma already left the house. They went to the market in the village close by to get some things," Lucinda said.

"That's okay. Why don't you go and rest, Lucinda?" Anna asked.

"Then who is going to keep you both company?" Lucinda asked.

"Don't worry about us; just go in and rest. We are fine," Phil chipped in.

"Alright," Lucinda said as she pecked the horses before leaving the stable. She got back into the house, locked the door, and walked straight to her room, lying on the bed to see her eyes overpowered by sleep.

Maya and Greg had walked into the seer's house as they sat down on the wooden chairs and waited for her to come out. They had gone there because of Lucinda, just to make sure everything was okay with her.

The old woman walked out and sat on the wooden stool before them.

"You came here because of your grandchild, Lucinda. You both think she has been acting strangely," the old woman began saying.

"Yes, we are scared because she spends most of her time with the horses, and she acts like she understands the language of the animals. Aside from that, there is nothing else," Maya said.

"Your grandchild is special. She is a young child filled with wisdom who doesn't act her age. Yes, she understands the language of the horses. Lucinda, your grandchild, spends quality time with the horses because her parents' spirits live in the horses, and she is the only one who can hear them. Just let her be as she is bonding with her parents, and she barely has enough time because eventually, they will be gone forever," the old woman said.

"But how is that possible?" Greg asked.

"Nothing is impossible. Leave the young child alone. She only yearns for the love of her parents, who departed from this world at the wrong time. Just let her be," the old woman said.

"But how come we can't see or hear them?" Maya asked.

"Annalise and Phil only came back for their daughter, Lucinda. They want to spend more time with their daughter before they finally leave this earth's surface and its environs. Listen, any day you both try taking those horses away from your home, Lucinda might hurt herself. As it stands now, those horses, the brown and the white horse, give her immense joy and happiness. She goes out to meet them every morning, afternoon, and night. She has formed this bond with them that not even you two can break.

Don't separate her from those horses because you can't. She is not going nuts and hasn't lost it; she is still okay," the old woman said as she stood up and walked inside her closet.

Maya and Greg stood up and walked out of the building as they both trekked back home. "If Annalise and Phil's spirits live in the horses, why can't we see them?" Maya asked.

"Annalise and Phil only came back for their daughter and not for us. You heard what the woman said," Greg retorted, angry at his wife's stubbornness.

"We have one option, and that's to leave Lucinda alone with the horses since that's where her joy and happiness lie," Maya said.

"Yeah, it's for the best. Annalise will never hurt her child. She is protecting her," Greg replied.

"I worried because I only wanted the best for my grandchild," Maya said as they journeyed back home.

Chapter Thirteen

WHEN GREG AND MAYA
HAD GOTTEN HOME

When Greg and Maya had gotten home, they knocked on the door and waited for Lucinda to open it. It took little time before the door flung open.

"Welcome back," Lucinda said, opening the door wide as Maya and Greg walked in.

Maya handed a bag to Lucinda, who walked to the kitchen to set it down. She came out quickly and sat on the smaller couch with her hands on her cheeks, staring at her grandparents.

"Is there any problem?" Greg asked.

"No problem. I just missed you both, and thanks for coming back early," Lucinda said.

"Do you want to tell us anything?" Greg asked.

"Not now. I just need to have some rest. If I have questions, that would be later," Lucinda said as she stood up, walked out of the parlor, walked straight to the stable, opened the door, and walked in.

"Grandpa and Grandma are back. Do you think I should ask them about it?" Lucinda asked.

"Sure. I want to go home and see how the place looks. We will be back before they know it," Anna replied. Anna just wanted to see the house and have a drink from the river before their time on earth was up.

74

"Alright, let's do it," Lucinda said as she untied the white horse's leash, and together they walked out. Lucinda walked to the balcony and tied the horse's leash to the pillar while she stepped inside and met with her grandparents' discussion.

"Grandpa and Grandma, can I ask you both something? Please don't get mad, and promise me you're going to say yes to my request, no matter how weird it may sound to you," Lucinda asked.

"What's that?" Maya asked.

"Are you saying yes to it?" Lucinda asked.

Maya and Greg looked at each other and nodded, and then Greg looked at Lucinda and said, "Yes."

"I'm taking the white horse to our house," Lucinda said. "Which house are you talking about?" Maya asked.

"Our house, the one my parents and I lived in, the one close to the river. Anna wishes to have a last look at the house and have a drink from the river. Then, before you know it, we will be back home," Lucinda said.

"You can't…"

"Grandpa, please don't say no. The only thing Anna wants is to see the family house one more time," Lucinda said.

"Lucinda! Please!" Maya pleaded.

"You already said yes," Lucinda said as she ran out of the house, untied the leash, and immediately mounted the horse to race off together. Maya and Greg ran out of the house, but Lucinda and Anna were long gone.

"Please go after them," Maya pleaded.

"Just let them be, okay? I know they will be back soon," Greg said as he held Maya, and they both walked inside together.

Anna and Lucinda reached the family house as Lucinda stepped down and held the leash. They both strolled down to the river together. Lucinda dropped the leash as she watched Anna go deep into the river and dip her head into it. After a few minutes, she came out, and Lucinda grabbed the leash and climbed on top of the horse.

"I have missed everything, and that's why I wanted you to bring me here. I wanted to look at where I lived for decades and brought forth this beautiful angel named Lucinda. I wanted to have a taste of this river that wanted to steal my child from me. I wanted to see and feel it one last time. Thank you, Lucinda, for making my wish come true," Anna said.

"You don't have to thank me, Mother. I will always do anything you want because you brought me forth into this world, and I missed you and the river too. I have always wanted to come here. I'm glad I got to see this place together with you," Lucinda replied, smiling.

"Promise me you will come back here someday. I want you always to remember that this place is your home too," Anna said.

"I will always remember this place, Mom. I haven't forgotten," Lucinda replied.

"Let's go home then," Anna said.

"It's getting late already. Don't you think you should go after her?" Maya said, pacing around the sitting room.

"She will be back; I know that," Greg replied.

Just as Greg was still speaking, there was a shuffling of hooves outside, heralding Lucinda and Anna coming home. Maya heard the noise outside as she ran out to see Lucinda leading the white horse to the stable. She came out a few minutes later and walked straight to the balcony where Maya and Greg were and hugged them.

"Thank you for coming back," Maya said, smiling.

"Don't worry about me. Mom wouldn't let any harm befall me. She only wanted to look at our home one last time. I'm glad I could fulfill her wish," Lucinda said as she smiled and walked inside.

"Don't say a word, Maya. You heard what she said. Lucinda is fine," Greg said as they both walked inside together, locking the door behind them.

Chapter Fourteen

LUCINDA LAY ON THE BED, IMMERSED

Lucinda lay on the bed, immersed in deep thoughts, as she kept tossing around. Her mind wasn't at peace. She knew something was not right, but she couldn't place her hands on what the problem was. It was three months before her fifteenth birthday. Suddenly, she stood up and ventured towards the window.

"Your heart is troubled because you feel something unpleasant will happen soon," The Voice said.

"How do you know? I mean, how did you find out I'm sad?" Lucinda asked.

"I'm your mother. I can sense it, but you don't have to worry. Do you know why? Simple: Worry won't prevent what is about to happen. It has already been decreed, my dear," The Voice said.

"What's about to happen, Mom? I knew something was wrong. I can sense it. I can feel it, and I know whatever is about to happen won't bring happiness to me; rather, it will bring pinches of sadness. I'm not strong, nor am I ready to go through any more pain again. I don't want to lose you and Dad again," Lucinda replied as tears gushed down her cheeks.

"I gave birth to a sturdy daughter, and she is smart as well. She knows how to handle things, even in the face of tribulations. You have made life easy for us for these past few years, but the fact remains we can't be with you forever," The Voice said.

"I know you and Dad won't be with me forever, but I don't want you to go soon. Why do you keep saying you can't be with me forever? What's happening? What's going on? Explain things to me," Lucinda pleaded.

"Lucinda, you worry so much. I know that whatever happens, you're strong enough to handle it. I love you, Lucinda. Now go to bed," The Voice said.

"Please don't go. I need to talk to you," Lucinda said amidst tears. She closed the window and walked straight to her bed to lie down.

"You think I'm strong, Mother? The truth is, I'm not. I have been able to pull everything off because you and Dad were standing right next to me. I can start no journey without you two, and I don't intend to go on any journey without you two by my side.

I know you and Dad can hear me loud and clear. Whatever it is— whatever you're hiding from me—I know eventually you will tell me because I deserve to know every bit of the truth," Lucinda said, wiping off the tears on her cheek.

She turned to the other side of the bed as she closed her eyes and drifted off to sleep.

"Do you think we should tell her?" Anna asked.

"Yes, we have to. We can't keep hiding it from her. Yes, she knows we barely have enough time to spend here, but she doesn't know we have only three months left to be in this world with her," Phil replied.

"Do you think she will cope when we are away from her?" Anna asked.

"You worry so much about Lucinda. She is of age now. We should be grateful we were granted these five years to spend with her. We have watched her grow, and I know our daughter is a strong girl. She is growing to be a strong woman. I know she will cope without us when the time comes, but we have to tell her the truth before then. You wouldn't want her to wake up in the morning only to come here for us and find out we're leaving today. Would you? Think of it, Anna. She deserves to know now. We have ninety days left," Phil replied.

"Alright, I will tell her tomorrow. I just hope she will accept it," Anna said.

"She has to accept it," Phil replied. "I will do that," Anna said.

Maya woke up that morning and turned towards Lucinda, surprised that she was still in her bed by that time, but with her back against them. It was already 9 a.m. It was unusual for Lucinda to be in her bed by that time. Maya got up and walked to Lucinda's bed to see her moping in a fixated direction as if in a trance.

"Lucinda, is there any problem?" Maya asked.

"The truth: I think something bad is about to happen, but I don't know what it is. I can't seem to wrap my head around what the problem is," Lucinda replied.

"Maybe you have been overthinking, and just maybe there isn't any problem. So why are you worrying yourself?" Maya said.

"You don't understand, Granny. I can feel it, and I can sense it," Lucinda replied.

"If you say so, maybe with time, you will figure out what the problem is. Of course, I know you can fix it, but even if you can't, you should allow it to be," Maya said and walked out of the room towards the kitchen.

"Why is life so unfair?" Lucinda said amidst tears as she got up from the bed and put on her slippers. Then she walked out of the room to the stable. She opened it, walked inside, and went straight to where the horses were and patted them.

"You still look worried," Anna observed.

"Your face isn't bright. What could bother you?" Phil asked, feigning ignorance.

"My soul yearns for answers. I feel like something is about to go wrong. Please, Mom and Dad, you both should at least talk to me. What's about to happen?" Lucinda asked.

"My little angel, sit down and listen," Phil said.

Lucinda took the wooden stool, sat on it, and looked at her father, expecting answers.

"I wanted us all to spend time together for a very long time, but that won't be possible because we barely have enough time here," Anna began.

"What do you mean, Mom? I can remember you said that to me a few years back. Why are you repeating the same thing now?" Lucinda asked.

"You're turning fifteen in three months, Lucinda. We are leaving on your 15th birthday," Anna replied.

"Although I remember you telling me this about five years ago, I still don't understand. Are you leaving to go where? Where are you both going? Explain to me, please," Lucinda pleaded.

"Lucinda, we were only given five years' grace to stay with you here on earth, and the time elapses on your 15th birthday. When we said we barely have enough time to stay with you, that was what we meant. We wish to stay longer; we wish to spend eternity with you if that's possible, but right now, we can't because we are leaving for our eternal home," Phil explained.

"That's not true, Dad. You and Mom can't just leave me. It's not nice. Please stay with me," Lucinda pleaded as the tears started gathering.

"There is nothing we can do about it. The decision is beyond us. We wanted you to know so you can get ready," Phil said.

"Nothing? You both can't go. I beg of you," Lucinda pleaded all the more.

"This is the reality, Lucinda. Accept it. Be strong for us," Anna said.

"There is something I can do. I think I have an idea," Lucinda said, wiping away her tears, getting up, and was about to leave the stable when Anna called her back.

"Forget about the Seashell. It can't grant that wish you are about to make," Anna replied.

"If it can't grant this specific wish, then why did it grant the first one Grandma made?" Lucinda yelled.

"Stop, Lucinda; you're going to hurt yourself," Anna pleaded.

"This wasn't the plan, Mom, Dad. You promised to stay with me every day. Why are you both leaving now that life is getting more interesting? I'm not that strong, you know. I have been able to make it through all these years because I had you both. You both are my pillars. How do you expect the building to stand straight when the pillars are about to be destroyed? Tell me, how is that possible? It's not," Lucinda yelled again and walked out of the stable.

"Don't worry; she will be fine," Phil said to Anna.

"I hope she doesn't end up hurting herself," Anna said. "She won't. Your parents are there," Phil replied.

Lucinda walked into the room and locked the door. She brought out the Seashell, holding it in both hands, the one Maya had given her when she turned 13.

"There is something you can do. Yes, I know it. You granted the first one, and I believe you can still do something again. Please don't allow my parents to be taken away from me, I beg of you. Life will be meaningless without them. Please, I beg of you, grant my wishes, please, just this once," Lucinda said, crying, looking at the Seashell, but no light came out from it. She knew that her wish had not been granted. But Lucinda wouldn't give up.

"Keep my parents for me. I don't want them ever to leave, but even if they are going to leave on my 15th birthday, let them come back someday, please," Lucinda said, crying. She then dropped the Seashell on her bed and walked near the window, looking out into the woods.

"Let the universe hear me. If anyone is out there listening to me, please, I don't want my parents to go forever. Life will be ugly and meaningless without them. I want them to stay every day with me," Lucinda said as tears continued to flow down her cheeks.

The revelation from her parents had shattered her world. She was restless, sad, and worried. Why would they leave so soon? Where would they be going again without her? she wondered. And suddenly she started speaking again, this time solemnly, intensely, and gravely.

"If I had ever wanted one thing in life, it would be that my parents could stay with me until the end of time. I have dreams, and every dream of mine includes my parents in the picture. So, how do you think I was going to continue this journey without them? You brought them back somehow, and I know anything is possible. I'm just a young girl whose desire is that of her parents' love.

I want nothing more. You on earth. O ye wind, the sun, and fire; tell me, how do I continue this journey without my parents? I have interceded on their behalf. Please help me. They can't leave on the day of my happy day; I beg of you. You all have to hear me out and grant my wishes," Lucinda said as she walked back to her bed and lay down, suddenly enveloped in absolute solitude.

———•◆•———

Chapter Fifteen

It Was Just Two Days Before Lucinda's Birthday

It was just two days before Lucinda's birthday. She lay on the bed with tears gushing freely from her eyes. Maya and Greg walked in from the parlor and were surprised to see her in tears.

"What's the problem this time, Lucinda?" Greg asked.

"Please talk to us. Why are you crying, little angel?" Maya asked as she wiped the tears off Lucinda's face.

"My world is about to end. My whole world is crashing," Lucinda replied.

"What do you mean by your world is about to end? Is there any problem?" Greg asked.

"Yes, tell us, please. We may help you," Maya promised.

"No, you can't. You remember when you walked in here a few months ago and said if I can't solve the problem, I should let it be? The problem is that I can't just let it be. How do I continue this journey without them?" Lucinda replied.

"Journey? What do you mean, Lucinda?" Greg asked.

"My soul is bitter. My heart bleeds, and I yearn only for one thing: if only the universe can hear me and reverse this process, then I will be forever indebted to her," Lucinda replied.

"You speak in parables. How do we help if you won't let us know what you're going through?" Greg said.

"Your grandpa is right, Lucinda. You're our only eyes, and anything that bothers you bothers us. Please, I beg of you. Talk to us. We will help you," Maya pleaded.

Lucinda wiped her tears as she hugged her grandparents. She stood up and was about to leave but turned and looked at her grandparents and said, "The truth is you can't help even if I explained everything to you. I love you both, and I know that if it were something you both could do, you would do it for me. If only I had the power to go back in time, I would do it. Don't worry about me. This is my cross to carry," Lucinda said as she walked out of the room.

Greg bowed his head, exasperated, but wouldn't give up. He knew, however, that whatever was wrong with Lucinda was deep, and he was going to find out.

Lucinda made it to the stable, unlocked it, walked inside, and sat on the wooden stool.

"I wish I could change all this," Lucinda said in tears.

"Stop trying to fight it, Lucinda. Be grateful for having a grace period of five years with us," Anna said.

"I'm not ungrateful, Mom. I'm only fighting for what I love, which are you two. You can't understand. Do you think these past few months have been okay for me? Do you think those smiles were deep down from my heart? While being here with you, I was only trying to hide my pain and anger, but when I walk into the room, I face the reality that you both are leaving soon. How do you expect me to feel? Happy? Oh no! I can't! I just don't want you both to go.

"I swear I'm going to fight it, and I will win; even if you both leave in two days, I will find a way to summon your souls back to earth. That's a promise," Lucinda said as she wiped the tears from her eyes.

"You can't keep that promise. Do you know why? It's impossible," Phil said.

"I have always lived with the orientation from you both that nothing is impossible in life. Since I accepted it as a way of life when I became conscious of your existence, it may be impossible, but to me, it is not. I do not know whether those are mere words from you both, but they mean a lot to me. I have grown with it, and I believe whatever I want is possible to achieve. And when I say I am going to summon your souls back to earth, I will do it. Mark my words, Dad," Lucinda said and left.

"Where are you going?" Anna asked.

"I will search for answers. I'm coming back, and I'm sleeping here tonight," Lucinda said and walked away.

"She will never accept this. Hmmm, this girl," Anna muttered.

"Same here. I don't think this girl is going to give up. She is hell-bent on doing what's in her mind," Phil replied.

"I don't want her to get hurt. I wish there were a way we could stop this from happening. I'm in the body of a horse, and I'm fine with it. At least I got to see my daughter grow and see her smiling face again. I seriously don't want to leave. I want to stay and watch my daughter grow up to be a woman," Anna whined.

"We both desire the same thing, but it's time to bow to the call of nature," Phil said.

Anna turned her head as she lay on the floor. She would miss her daughter, and her daughter was already missing them, although they were still here.

That evening, Lucinda had her bath and changed into better nightwear to make herself comfortable throughout the night in the stable.

As she took her lantern to leave the room, Greg walked inside and shut the door.

"Going somewhere?" Greg asked as he sat down.

"Yes, to the stable," Lucinda replied.

"It's late, Lucinda," Greg replied.

"I'm sleeping there. Let me go," Lucinda replied.

"Not yet. Sit down first. I want to talk to you," Greg said as Lucinda sat down quietly on the bed.

"What's troubling your infantile mind, little angel? I know this is something deep. Your grandma is asleep on the couch in the parlor, so don't worry. You can confide in me. Please, I hate to see you in pain," Greg pleaded.

"But you won't understand," Lucinda said.

"I will when you explain. Give me a chance to experience your pain with you. I won't stand it if anything happens to you, child. Please, I'm begging you in the name of your late mother, Annalise," Greg said.

"She isn't late yet. Her body might not be here, but her soul lives," Lucinda replied.

"Please explain to me," Greg replied.

"I will explain to you. I will give you that chance to be part of this. Since she was your daughter, you deserve to know," Lucinda said, trying so hard to fight the tears.

Lucinda took time to explain everything to Greg, starting from when Maya made the wish and how Anna and Phil were about to leave in two days on her 15th birthday.

Greg hugged Lucinda tightly as she cried on her grandpa's shoulder.

"I know how you feel. I wish you had explained this to me all these years, as I wanted to be part of this bond. It's so sad I only realized it just a few days before their departure, but weep no more, Lucinda. I know they will come back someday. Nothing is impossible," Greg said.

"You believe me?" Lucinda asked, her eyes sparkling.

"I believe every word you said now. Trust me, Lucinda. Your parents will come back someday. Since they somehow cheated death to be with you, then they will come back," Greg reassured.

"Thank you, Grandpa," Lucinda said, smiling.

Greg wiped the tears falling from Lucinda's eyes as he stood up and held the door wide open for her.

"Go and be with them, dear. They need you," Greg said as Lucinda stood up and walked out into the night toward the stable.

"You came back," Phil observed. "Yes, I'm back," Lucinda replied.

"It's late; you need to sleep," Anna said.

"I know," Lucinda said as she spread out the nylon mat that she had come with on the floor to lie on it.

"What are you doing?" Anna asked.

"When I said I was going to sleep here, I meant every word I said. Goodnight, Mom. Goodnight, Dad," Lucinda said and closed her eyes.

In the morning, Lucinda woke up and left the stable. She went inside to have her bath, after which she returned immediately.

"It's not even been twenty minutes since you left here," Anna said.

"I know," Lucinda replied as she untied the leashes to lead the horses outside.

"Sunshine, finally," Anna said, looking up.

"Thank you, Lucinda," Phil said.

"Let me do it today, even though you both won't be with me tomorrow," Lucinda replied.

Greg walked up to them as he fondly touched the white horse and the brown one.

"I will miss you both. I wish Lucinda had explained things to me all these years. I wasn't part of this journey, but here I am, trying to say goodbye," Greg mournfully said.

"He knows, Mom and Dad. I told him everything, and he believes me," Lucinda said.

"Tell him we are saying thank you for taking good care of you, and we want him to continue when we are gone by tomorrow," Annalise said.

"What did she say?" Greg asked, seeing Anna's mouth opening and closing.

"She was only trying to say thank you for being the best to me," Lucinda said amidst tears.

"Annalise and Phil, I know you both can hear me. I love you both, and I hope you can stay longer. Well, I'm certain about one thing: I know fate will bring you both back somehow," Greg said.

"Thank you, Grandpa," Lucinda said as she watched her grandpa walk inside.

After spending some time outside with the horses, Lucinda took them back inside as she provided hay for them to eat while she went inside to have her breakfast. The day went fast as Lucinda kept wishing the hands of the clock would turn back.

That night, Lucinda slept in the stable despite Maya's pleas, but Greg had to convince Maya to allow her to be.

"I will miss you both. Goodnight," Lucinda said as she closed her eyes and drifted off to sleep.

"Wake up! Wake up! Lucinda!" Anna said as she brought her head closer to Lucinda's body. Lucinda slowly opened her eyes as she looked at the horses.

"We are still here. At least we got the chance to wish you a happy birthday," Phil said.

"May your days be filled with love, joy, and happiness, and most of all, peace," Anna said.

"You both are not leaving me, right?" Lucinda asked as she stood up.

"Yes, we are. Goodbye, Lucinda. Take care of yourself, and know that we will always love you. We will watch over you," Anna said.

"Farewell, my daughter," Phil replied.

"No! Please don't go, not now!" Lucinda shouted as she opened her eyes and watched the souls leaving the bodies of the horses.

"Please, this isn't fair! Grandpa!" Lucinda yelled, crying.

Maya and Greg heard the shouting coming from the stable as they ran to see the problem.

Maya and Greg walked inside to see Lucinda on the floor crying. Greg knelt close to Lucinda and held her.

"She is gone, Grandpa. She and Dad. They left after all my pleas," Lucinda said, crying.

"Don't worry, they will be back," Greg said.

"I want them back now. I need them back home. Why would they have to leave on my birthday? Why couldn't they stay longer? Why is life unfair? I'm only fifteen, but I have had my fair share of pain. Why is this happening to me?" Lucinda shouted as she left the stable, ran into the house, and locked the door.

Maya and Greg followed suit. "Please open up, Lucinda. We're here for you," Maya pleaded.

"Just leave me alone. I want to be alone. Go!" Lucinda responded.

They tried all they could, pleading, but Lucinda wouldn't budge.

"Why didn't you grant me that one wish I requested? Tell me why. Are you okay seeing me in so much pain and misery?" Lucinda said in tears as she threw the seashell on the bed.

It had already been months, yet Lucinda couldn't accept that her parents were gone for good. She would go to the stable, hoping the horses would talk to her, and after waiting a while, she would leave. Lucinda was hoping for a miracle. Every morning she would go to the stable and stay for a time before leaving.

Two years had gone by since the whole incident happened. Lucinda had woken up that morning, and after taking her bath and putting on her clothes, she went straight to the stable. She took out the white horse, climbed on it, and together they raced down to the village. She wanted to spend her 17th birthday in the house where she was born and raised.

She got there, tied the leash to a pillar, and walked into the house to see that everything was neat, which was unexpected. She held her breath, wondering what could be amiss, then walked cautiously into the other rooms.

Later on, she took a stroll down the river. When she got there, she removed her clothes, dove into the river, and felt peace. This same river would have taken her life so many years ago, if not for her parents' quick intervention. After spending a few minutes in the river, she swam to the shore, changed her clothes, and went back into the house. On getting there, she untied the leash and climbed on the horse.

She just wanted to go back home and cry since the house had too many memories. But she dried the tears from her eyes and forced a smile.

"Keep that smiling face, little angel," the Voice sounded. Lucinda was sure of the Voice; it was her mother's voice. "You're back!" Lucinda shouted.

"Yes, your father and I came back together. Happy birthday, my love. Even if you can't feel our presence, you can still hear us," the Voice replied.

"I can hear you, and I'm coming back," Lucinda said, smiling, as she turned the horse back towards her parents' house in the direction the Voice came from.

THE END.

PART 2

Beyond the Ranges

Introduction

Mysteries, mysticism, the supernatural—all became a mosaic of Lucinda's world. She never thought she was going to hear from them again.

Lucinda had gone back to her father's house hoping to see her parent's spirit, but only to realize once more that she wouldn't be able to see them. Instead, she could only hear them.

Chapter One

IT HURTS THAT I CAN ONLY HEAR YOU

"It hurts that I can only hear you, but I can't see you. I can't even see Dad. Where are you?" Lucinda screamed, with tears dripping down her eyes.

"I understand how you feel, Lucinda. But unfortunately, you can never see us again. We were given the privilege of communicating with you. So, let's be content with our voices only, okay, baby girl?" the voice assured.

"Dad, is that you?" Lucinda said as tears continued to stream down her cheeks.

"Yes, that's me. Let's be grateful, Lucinda, very grateful that you can still hear us," the voice replied.

"I am, Dad, I am," Lucinda said as she wiped the tears from her eyes.

"Time to go home," Lucinda said as she patted the horse, which slowly started moving and edged towards the mountaintop. Once home, she took the horse to the stable and went straight inside the house. Maya and Greg were sitting on the wooden chairs, chatting and laughing.

"You're back," Maya remarked.

"Happy birthday, beloved grandchild," Greg said, smiling.

"Happy birthday, my granddaughter. Where have you been?" Maya asked.

"I went to celebrate my 17th birthday at my parents' house and to see if I could see them again. It could have been the biggest gift in my entire life, but the situation remains the same. It's frustrating," Lucinda replied and walked inside, wanting to be alone at the moment.

"What is she saying? Did you promise her anything?" Maya asked.

"No. I do not know what Lucinda was saying. I will talk to her later," Greg replied.

After several minutes, Greg left Maya in the sitting room and walked into Lucinda's room.

"Can I come in?" Greg said, holding the door open.

"Grandpa, you are already in. Please come in," Lucinda replied.

"What's the problem, baby girl? You're not happy, and today is your birthday. You left early in the morning, and you came back with a frown on your face. To make matters worse, you said something that neither your grandmother nor I understood," Greg replied.

"How will you feel when you get a piece of cake only to discover that half has already been gone? How will you react to that?" Lucinda asked.

"I will feel bad, but I will be grateful for even getting hold of any cake at all," Greg replied.

"Why are you also talking about being grateful? I'm grateful. I am, but my parents should have just made the whole thing complete," Lucinda replied.

"Excuse me, young lady. Anna and Phil died seven years ago. So, what exactly are you talking about that your parents are making? What complete?" Greg replied.

"You don't understand, do you?" Lucinda asked.

"Of course, I don't understand. That's why I'm asking to know what you mean," Greg replied.

"Grandpa, my parents spoke to me actually."

"Lucinda, don't tell me you have finally lost it?" Greg asked.

"Grandpa!" Lucinda shouted.

"Lucinda, what's your problem?" Greg asked.

"I'm not crazy. You just asked me a question, which I was about to reply to, but you just cut me off. You know what? You can never understand, so don't worry about me. I'm fine. Never mind," Lucinda replied.

"Okay, since you said so. I have something to tell you," Greg said and waited for a split second before continuing, "We are moving."

"Moving? Moving to where? This place is nice. So, why do we have to leave here?" Lucinda asked, sitting up properly.

"The world is changing, and we have to move alongside it. We have to move to the city. I wanted to tell you that yesterday, but I had to wait to tell you today because today is your birthday. I thought you would be happy about it," Greg said matter-of-factly.

"Happy about what? I'm not happy. Why do we have to move? I want to remain here," Lucinda replied.

"Growth is constant just as change is. You don't have to remain stagnant," Greg replied, patting her on the back.

"Growth, change. All these you mentioned can still be experienced here. I like it here so much. There are so many memories to hold on to. You can't expect me to wake up and tell me we're moving. No, that will not happen. Listen to me, Grandpa."

"No, you listen, young lady; we're moving, and that's final," Greg said.

"Perfect, and my parents and secondly you completely ruin my birthday. So, you and Grandma can go. I can stay here, all alone. I want to be here; this is my roots. This place is my identity, and for me to leave here, I don't think it will happen," Lucinda replied.

Greg became intrigued the more. "How did your late parents ruin your birthday, Lucinda? What are you not telling me? You know you need to talk, young lady," Greg said, looking at Lucinda, expecting answers.

"You can't understand, so what's the need for explaining? You just asked me a few minutes ago if I had lost it. I'm not crazy, Grandpa," Lucinda shouted as she stood up and ran out of her room.

Greg stood up and walked out, only to meet Maya close to the door.

"What happened? Why did she run off like that?" Maya asked.

"It's going to be hard convincing Lucinda to move with us to the city. She doesn't want to go. She wants to stay here and keeps talking about her late parents. Maybe if we move to the city, Lucinda might accept the reality that her parents are gone for good, that they are not coming back. My grandchild is going crazy. She is losing it, and the least I can do now is to take her far away from here," Greg replied as he left Maya and walked to the backyard.

Maya sighed as she went to the balcony where Lucinda sat down, holding her chin in contemplation, but with visible traces of tears on her cheeks. Maya sat close to her as she wiped the tears off her face.

"Why will a princess be crying even on her birthday?" Maya asked, throwing her right arm around Lucinda's shoulders.

"Grandpa wants us to leave for the city. Are you aware of this?" Lucinda asked.

"Yes, I am. Although there are many memories here," Maya replied, "it isn't harmful to start afresh."

"I don't want to; I want to be here," Lucinda replied.

"Listen, baby girl. We need to leave. We are going with the horses if that's what you're scared of, but we need to leave. We need to see what the outside world looks like. Don't worry; if you don't like it, we will come back here, okay? It's a promise I'm making to you right now," Maya replied.

"Are you sure?" Lucinda asked.

"I swear on my very existence," Maya said.

Lucinda hugged her as they both smiled at each other.

"So, let's get back inside and have dinner. Today is your birthday, and I prepared your favorite for dinner. I bet you're going to like it," Maya said.

"Thank you so much, Granny," Lucinda said as both of them stood up and walked inside.

When they finished their dinner, Lucinda took the plates to the kitchen to wash. Then she retired to her bedroom and walked toward the window, opening it and looking outside and up to the sky to behold the sky covered with beautiful twinkling stars.

"Who would ever think that I would leave here so soon? This move to the city hurts so much," Lucinda muttered under her breath.

"Maybe you should just listen to them and leave with them. You can still come back here when things change in the city." It was the voice of her mom.

"Can you hear me, Mom?" Lucinda asked.

"Everything, Lucinda. I'm just like the wind, but I'm always around you. I only speak when it's necessary. Listen to your grandparents, and when it's time, you must return to the mountaintop so you don't put the lives of the innocent at stake," the voice replied.

"Lives of the innocent at stake? What do you mean by that? Does it seem you know so much about the future? Please tell me," Lucinda replied.

"Never mind. When you get to the city, and when it's time for you to leave, just leave with your grandparents. That's the only thing we know for now," the voice replied.

"My roots are here; my identity, everything. It hurts that even you and Dad are asking me to go. I can't do it," Lucinda replied, cleaning off the tears in her eyes.

"Even if you don't want to go, we need you to go so you can protect your grandparents. But Lucinda, my dear, this life is way deeper than you think. I already said this before: when the time comes for you to leave, leave with your grandparents. Because what we see, you might not be able to handle," the voice replied.

"If we get to the city, will I ever hear from you both again?" Lucinda asked.

"Of course you will. We will be with you every minute of the day. That shouldn't get you worried," the voice replied.

"Alright then. Mom and Dad, goodnight. I need to sleep. Talk to you both tomorrow," Lucinda said as she shut her windows and went straight to her bed. Her mom's words kept ringing in her mind: "When it's time for you to leave, leave so you don't put the lives of the innocent at stake." What does that mean? What is going to happen to us if we get to the city?

If something terrible is going to happen, why don't they ask me to stay back? Why do they want me to go? Why?" Lucinda kept thinking about so many things before she closed her eyes and drifted off to sleep.

The following morning, Lucinda woke up in high spirits and did her chores. She took time to bathe the horses, and when she finished, she went inside to have her bath.

Shortly after, Maya called her to come out for her breakfast, but she insisted on eating in her room. When she was through, she told her grandparents she was going to her parents' house to say goodbye before they leave for the city tomorrow.

"Won't you take the horses with you?" Maya asked.

"No, I'm okay. It can be a long journey, but I can do it. I did it when I was ten, remember?" Lucinda said.

"Lucinda!" Greg called.

"Yes, Grandpa!" Lucinda answered.

"I'm sorry about yesterday. Please be careful and make sure you come back before night falls. Don't worry; Maya will help you and arrange your clothes while you are away, okay?" Greg said.

"Thanks, Grandpa," Lucinda said and smiled as she walked out of the house.

It was already noon when Lucinda finally got to her parents' house. She stood momentarily at the entrance with mixed feelings and then sighed loudly before opening the door and walking inside. As soon as Lucinda entered, she looked around and let out a sigh again.

Finally, after staying for a few minutes without uttering a word, she walked out and went to her parents' bedroom.

"I'm leaving. I just came to bid the house my last farewell because I don't know when I'm coming back, but I will surely come back someday," Lucinda said as she walked out and went straight to the parlor, where her parents' portrait lay on the center table. She picked it up as she left the house.

She then went straight to the river. She sat down on the riverbank when she got there and brought out the picture as she stared at it.

"I know you can see me, Mom. I wish you were here to hold me and see how much I have grown and how much I look like you and Dad." Lucinda started sobbing silently. "This is the only thing I have in remembrance of you as I go to the city. I will never forget your face as long as I have this picture," Lucinda said as she stood up and started her journey back to the mountaintop.

Chapter Two

Lucinda and Her Grandparents Got to the City

Lucinda and her grandparents got to the city with a delay, but they could get to the house. No sooner had they settled in than Lucinda threw a question at them.

"You seemed to know much about the city. Where are we?" Lucinda asked.

"I've been here twice. After your fifteenth birthday, I had no choice but to decide to move to the city with you so you could forget what happened. I could buy this with the little savings we have, and here we are now," Greg replied.

"Grandma, did you know about this?" Lucinda asked.

"Sure, I did, but I felt it wasn't the right time to tell you," Maya replied.

"Interesting. Where is my room? I need to sleep," Lucinda said as Maya took her to her bedroom.

"This is your room, and it's bigger than the room you had on the mountaintop. I made sure I put everything you like," Maya said.

"Thank you," Lucinda replied as she sat down and pulled off her sandals. She then lay on the bed, and in no time, she was off to sleep.

In the morning, when Lucinda woke, she saw an owl perched on her window. When she stood up to go close to the window, the owl flew off.

"An owl on my window this early morning? What could that mean? Is this ominous?" Lucinda thought as she opened her windows.

"The environment looks beautiful and serene, as you will soon find out. We even have a garden in the backyard where we can plant whatever we want," Greg said as he walked into the room.

"Good morning, Grandpa. Yes, I just looked around through my window. It sure looks enticing. You know I'm in love with nature, just like you and Grandma," Lucinda said, smiling.

"Good morning, my little angel. Your Grandma asked me to give you this. You had nothing to eat throughout yesterday, so she woke you very early to prepare this for you," Greg said, dropping a plate of food on Lucinda's bed.

"Wow! Thanks. It was so thoughtful of her as always," Lucinda said, grinning.

"So, did you want to look around through the window, or did something else happen?" Greg was about to ask when Lucinda interrupted him.

"I woke up to see something off about here. I know you will say it's because I don't like the city, but I can feel it. It feels like I'm sensing something already," Lucinda replied.

"Don't worry. Once you get used to this place, I promise you will like it here," Greg replied as he walked out of the room.

Lucinda cast a glance at the food on her bed before walking outside. She made straight for the garden at the back of the house.

On getting there, she found a concrete bench and sat down to have a look around and savor the morning's freshness.

"The beauty of nature is right here in my presence," Lucinda muttered as she sat down, closing her eyes to inhale the sweet smell oozing from the many flowers in the garden.

Immediately, she opened her eyes and heard a noise, but she wasn't sure from where, which made her get up directly and race to her room.

On closing her door, she sat on the edge of the bed.

"I'm 100 percent sure I heard a rumbling of voice or voices. It felt like someone crying out for help, asking me to go and never come back. Who was that? What could this mean? Something is odd about this place; either the city or this very house," Lucinda had fleeting thoughts as she kept looking about wildly. She went through the back door so her grandparents wouldn't notice she was leaving the house, and in no time, she was out on the street.

She met people going about doing routine affairs, with everyone minding their business. They were smiling, but suddenly she noticed the same smiling faces now wailing, asking for help. On looking around, she noticed she was the only one seeing those people.

"What is happening to me?" Lucinda thought aloud. "Why do I see all these?" she felt within her.

She couldn't contain it anymore as she turned and went back home. Her grandparents were surprised when they heard a knock and went to check who it was, just to discover it was Lucinda.

"How come? How did you leave the house without anyone knowing?" Maya asked.

"I went through the back door. I needed some fresh air and to see the city for myself," Lucinda replied.

"Lucinda, why is your face this way? Hope everything is okay?" Greg asked.

"I told you coming to this place would be a bad idea. I just can't take it anymore," Lucinda replied, leaning on the wall.

"What happened?" Maya and Greg asked almost at the same time, surprised.

"Asking what happened isn't the issue. The issue here is that you both will never believe me. So, let's just go back home," Lucinda replied.

"This place is home too," Greg replied, a little impatient.

"Maybe for you, but not for me. I just wish you could see and hear them. Maybe only then will you understand," Lucinda said and walked out before turning back.

"Please, none of you should come to my room. I just don't want to talk about anything," Lucinda said as she left, sobbing.

"But what's wrong? Why are you crying?" Maya asked.

"Just this once, Granny, just this once, please. I want to be alone for now, please, please," Lucinda said and walked out on them.

"What's wrong with her?" Maya asked.

"We both saw what happened. I'm equally confused as well. I just don't know what to say," Greg replied.

"Maybe we should talk to her," Maya suggested.

"She made it clear she wants to be alone for now. Maya, listen, I know you still see Lucinda as that little girl who ran from the village to the mountaintop to tell us about her parents' demise, but I want to remind you that Lucinda is growing. She is seventeen. Her parents might have died when Lucinda was ten, but to date, Lucinda hasn't accepted that they are gone for good. She is hurting, and as long as she remains on that mountaintop, she will never accept the reality."

"So, we are not going back to the mountaintop. I know it's going to take time for her to get used to this place, but at the same time, I need her to heal from that pain. The only place she is going to heal is here, not there, where all those memories are still fresh in her mind," Greg replied.

"I didn't realize she was going to be like this, even after many years," Maya replied.

"What do you expect when her parents were the only friends that she ever had?" Greg replied.

When Lucinda got to her room, she locked the door from inside. She felt she needed to understand what was happening around her, just her first day in the city.

"Why do I see all these? Why do I have to be the only one seeing them? Why has life been a terror, even after taking my parents away from me?" Lucinda said, crying.

"Life isn't torturing you, Lucinda. We raised a strong girl who didn't give up all these years after our departure. So, what makes you think you can give up now?" the voice of her mom asked.

"Then why do I see those horrible things?" Lucinda asked. "What did you see?" the voice asked.

"So, you can't see them too?" Lucinda asked, surprised.

"No, we can't. But maybe if you tell us, we might help," the voice replied.

"When I went out today, I got to meet people going about their normal business, smiling. Suddenly, it felt like I saw them crying, asking me to leave, and that I had brought perpetual suffering to them. They were bleeding while calling out for help and looking around me. I became sure I was the only one seeing things," Lucinda replied.

"Lucinda, my child, those are just signs of what will happen when you don't leave on the required date. When that time comes, we will ask you to go back to the mountaintop, for what is coming is greater than you, and I doubt if you can take it," the voice replied.

"What is coming, Mom? Tell me," Lucinda demanded.

"We don't know for sure, but it won't be good," the voice replied. After considering their words, Lucinda took out her box, took out the magic seashell, and rubbed her hands on it.

"Can you at least show me what's going to happen? Tell me what the future holds for me. I'm getting scared already. At least I should know," Lucinda said, crying.

"Even the seashell won't tell you what's going to happen in the future. Do you know why the future lies in your hand, Lucinda?" the voice replied.

"I don't know. I need someone to tell me what's going to happen," Lucinda replied, crying as she dropped the seashell on the bed.

Lucinda lay on her bed curled up, disturbed.

She needed help and knew she couldn't ask her grandparents for help because they would think she had gone insane. She knew she was in this alone.

Lucinda found herself on the streets only to meet drops of blood everywhere. She couldn't fathom what was happening.

Finally, she yelled out, but everything was as silent as a graveyard.

She ran back home and called out to her grandparents, but she was greeted back with silence. The whole place was deserted.

"What's happening?" Lucinda asked, bemused.

"So, you don't know what's happening?" a voice asked as Lucinda turned to see a little girl standing at the door. It wasn't just any little girl; it was her replica from when she was just ten. Lucinda recoiled, thoughts racing through her mind.

"Where did you come from? Where did everyone go? Who are you?" Lucinda asked.

"I don't know. The entire city is deserted. My name is Lucinda," the little girl replied.

"That's my name, and you look exactly like me when I was ten," Lucinda observed.

"That's because I'm you. I'm from your past, Lucinda," the little girl replied.

"What do you mean?" Lucinda asked.

"You're letting fear consume the better part of you, and it isn't good. We're strong; we're queens who have been destined to rule immortals in the world beyond, but the question is, why are you giving up when we haven't even started the race? You're already backing down. Mom and Dad asked you to leave; will you leave?" the little girl asked.

"I have to. They said something bigger was coming and that I can't take it. I'm worried about my grandparents; I don't want any evil to befall them," Lucinda replied.

"If you left, generations of unborn would suffer for it, but that's not all. Grandpa and Grandma will get wet when the rain falls, and I'm sure you don't want it to happen. But, no matter how far you run, no matter how long you shield yourself from realizing the truth, it will come knocking at the door someday. You must answer, and guess what, it will be late by then."

"Mom and Dad want you to leave because they feel you can't tame what's coming in front of you, but if you can't take it, kill it, Lucinda," the little girl said as she turned to leave.

"Where are you going? Please don't go," Lucinda pleaded.

"I'm going so you can return to the present world. This place isn't for you. I only came to convey a message. Goodbye," the little girl said as she vanished from sight.

Lucinda started sobbing as she heard a knock from a distance. On opening her eyes, still crying, Lucinda realized she had been dreaming, with tears dripping down her cheeks.

"Lucinda, open the door, please," Maya shouted.

"I'll be out in a few minutes. So don't worry about me; I'll be fine," Lucinda said.

Her grandmother's knock brought her back to reality. What just happened? she thought. How could her ten-year-old self convey a message to her? How is that even possible? So, she felt as she stood up and walked toward the door to unlock it.

"You have been in there all day. Come and have dinner," Maya said as soon as Lucinda opened the door.

"Are you saying this is evening already?" Lucinda asked, totally lost.

"What's the time, Lucinda? Are you sure you're alright? You know you can always talk to me," Maya reassured.

"Don't worry, I'm fine. I'll be out soon," Lucinda replied as she watched her grandmother walk to the sitting room.

Lucinda lay on the bed as she kept recalling what happened in her dream, shivering at her recollections. Goose pimples appeared and disappeared on her body as she continued to think about those things. Myself as a ten-year-old, talking to me? How is that even possible?

Suddenly, she left the room and went to the sitting room to join her grandparents at the table for dinner. Soon after, her grandparents started throwing questions at her, but she responded with one-word answers, assuring them she was okay. She knew they wouldn't believe anything she would tell them, so she felt there was no need to say anything to them.

After they finished their dinner, Lucinda cleared the table and took the dishes to the kitchen to wash them off. Once she finished up, she quickly retired to her bedroom.

Just as she closed her eyes to sleep, she heard the voice. "Queen of the immortals."

Lucinda flipped her eyes open, but she saw no one. She closed her eyes tightly as she drifted off to sleep.

Lucinda had gotten to a pathway where a ray of light almost blinded her eyes; she could barely see what was on the other side. But when she tried crossing over, it felt like something held her, preventing her from moving from where she was.

"You invited us, yet your body is filled with so much fear; why is that so?" a voice said.

"I didn't invite anyone. Who are you? It isn't my mom's voice, neither is it my dad's, so who are you?" Lucinda yelled.

"Your subject," the voice replied.

"My subject? I don't know what is happening, and neither do I know what you're referring to. I've never felt responsible for anyone else apart from my dead parents and my grandparents. So, who are they? Or has my life suddenly become something else that I do not know? Have I unknowingly become something else, having some sort of subject?"

Two people are so important to me in my life, but they left so early. They are the ones that I would love to come back if I ever had the chance.

And if there were anything I could do to bring them back to life, I'd readily do that. I don't know you, and I don't want you to become my subject. Just stay where you are and allow me to live my life the way it pleases me. And talking about fear, you can't blame me.

You can't blame a seventeen-year-old girl because, for the past seven years of my life, I've been trying to heal from the death hurled against me by taking my parents away at a time most unexpected.

"Please don't add to my sorrows, whoever you are!" Lucinda replied, almost shouting.

"You are the queen. You invited your subject over here. You asked me to come. Your presence in this city woke me up, yet you can't summon the courage to talk to your subject," the voice persisted.

"Ha! What! I am not your queen, and I don't want to be. Take back your crown. I don't want to be a queen of any kingdom that I don't know. Just leave me alone," Lucinda yelled.

"How can I take the crown that was given to you even before my very own existence? And it's not a kingdom, but a world different from the world of humans. You will forever remain queen of the immortals. When I finally get here, please welcome us, or we might cause perpetual pain and agony to the surrounding people. Please do not allow fear to becloud your inherent boldness. I can still remember that girl who ran from the village to the mountaintop just to tell her grandparents about the demise of her parents. The same courageous girl who ran without fear, not minding the dangers on the road—that's the girl we know, not this new Lucinda who has been consumed by fear," the voice replied.

"How do you know my name? Who are you, and what do you want?" Lucinda asked, more disturbed than afraid.

"It's forbidden for a subject not to know the name of their queen. My name is Anya. I want nothing," the voice replied.

"What journey are you talking about?" Lucinda asked.

"The journey that lies in front of you, of course. The path is full of thorns. The path is slippery. It is dark. We don't know what lies ahead, but you will need my help when the time comes because that's your fate. But before then, I need to make my presence known in your world where you live. Goodbye, Lucinda," the voice said.

"What is happening to me? Why am I going through this? I never wanted to come to this city. Ever since I arrived here two nights ago, everything around me has been ominous; not for once have I had any reason to smile. What kind of stupid fate do I have? Why do I have to go through all this alone? Why wouldn't death have taken me too when it took my parents? I wouldn't have been going through so much pain. You all don't love me or even care about me because if you did, somehow my parents would have been here; you would have spared me. It hurts. I want to be alone, free from all this drama. I'm going to mourn my parents for as long as possible. They deserve every bit, and they are worth it. Do you know why? Simple: Because of them, there will be no Lucinda," Lucinda said as she sat down and wept. As she was sobbing, the light that had almost blinded her became dim, but no one was there anymore.

"Lucinda!" her mom's voice sounded.

"Mom, that's you. Where are you?" Lucinda asked, looking around, but to her dismay and disappointment, she was alone. She shivered as she opened her eyes, only to discover she had been dreaming all this while. She stood up and walked closer to the window and opened it to let in rays of the twinkling stars.

"What's bothering you, baby girl?" the mom's voice continued as she opened the window.

"Dad, Mom, I'm scared. I just wish to leave this city. I'm tired of everything that is happening around me. I just wish to be free. I'm afraid of what the future portends," Lucinda replied.

"Fear, that has always been the problem right from day one. Can you at least trust yourself?" the mom's voice replied.

"Mom, you have always encouraged me whenever I want to do things, but the fear aspect—I think I took that from you. And yes, Mom, you once mentioned that whatever I see, I doubted that I could handle it. What's that? Maybe you can explain better now," Lucinda asked.

"You ask too many questions, Lucinda. The journey ahead of you is way deeper than what we think, and it's connected to so many things. We don't know what's going to happen, but we doubt that our baby here can handle it," the voice replied.

"I'm seventeen, Mom; I'm no longer a baby," Lucinda reminded her parents.

"Even if your mom doubts you can win what lies ahead of you, I somehow know my girl," the dad's voice replied.

"Thanks, Dad, but you two do not understand. My life has turned into something else. I wish for this to end. What differs from what Grandpa and Grandma see? I've told you what happened yesterday."

I stepped out of this house when I saw people calling out to me and asking me to leave. They were in pain, and they were hurt.

Later, I saw blood everywhere and people asking me to return to wherever I came from. But, of course, I'm talking about what I saw with my own two eyes. And just now, someone I did not even see or had ever met called me, "Queen of the immortals."

Every human being born of a woman is bound to die someday, so where do these immortals live, and why can't I see them? Why am I a queen in a world where I know nothing? Why was I born into this world if they knew I was going to suffer? I'm tired! I'm tired, and I wish to go back to my old life there on the mountaintop, where no one will call me a queen, where I won't be seeing things differently from all others around me.

You both might think I'm crazy, but the truth is I'm not. Apart from yours, I keep hearing voices in dreams and real life. The last one I spoke with said her name is Anya. I don't know what Anya looks like, but the voice sounded feminine. She said if she comes and I don't welcome her, she will bring pain to the people around me, and guess what? I will be held accountable for it. Am I making sense to you both, or do you think your daughter is crazy? Questions, questions unanswered, or perhaps unanswerable," Lucinda concluded.

"No, you're not crazy, but have you told your grandpa and grandma about these experiences of yours?" her dad's voice asked.

"Not yet, Dad. Besides, they will think I'm crazy," Lucinda replied.

"Yes, they will because you're different from them. You're not who you think you are. I don't even know the power you possess because only one with strong power can hear people from the other world."

And about the people you see on the streets, that's just fear trying to get hold of you. Fear makes you think that something worse will happen if you stay here for as long as you want. Your mom wants you to leave when the time comes, but I want you to stay. I want you to fight this. I have always known you to be a strong girl, and I know the future is bright. Surely the path will be filled with thorns and thistles, but I know you will scale through. Don't let what you're seeing deprive you of finding out who you are. I have known you to be a normal child ever since you were born, but today, the child I gave birth to is a different person altogether. You can do this, Lucinda; yes, you can. Just let go of all those negative thoughts in your head," the voice replied.

"Thanks, Dad, but how come Mom isn't saying anything anymore?" Lucinda asked.

"She will talk to you tomorrow, but remember, don't let fear win," the voice replied. Soon after, Lucinda heard a knock on her door, and she walked toward the door to open it.

"Grandpa," Lucinda softly called as she went to a chair that was close to her window.

"Why did you leave the windows open, and why are you awake by this time of the night?" Greg asked.

"Oh, I had a dream, so I woke up, and I opened the windows. I needed to see the sky. How about you? Why are you also awake?" Lucinda asked.

"I wanted to get water to drink, and I thought I should check up on you when I heard you call Mom and Dad. Who were you talking to?" Greg asked.

"Oh, I was talking to my parents," Lucinda replied.

Greg contemplated Lucinda's words. To him, it was apparent that she was depressed. He just didn't know what to do for his grandchild anymore.

"Why are you looking at me that way?" Lucinda asked.

"You're still hurt over your parents' death. You're not over it yet, but I'm sure that soon you'll get over it," Greg said.

"You need the truth, Grandpa?" Lucinda asked.

"Yes, tell me the truth. I want to help. Tell me what the problem is; you can't keep living like this forever. You need to let go," Greg pleaded.

"I'm hurt, yes. I'm angry, yes. Life took my most priceless possession when I had just a decade with them. They might be dead, but they are around. We might not see them, but they live among us. I just want to mourn them for as long as I can. If I mourn them for two or three decades, they are worth it because there wouldn't be any Lucinda if there were no Anna and Phil. I miss them, and I can't let go, no matter how hard I try. That's the truth. I appreciate everything, Grandpa, but healing is a journey, and I'm not ready yet to embark on it," Lucinda replied.

"I miss that little girl that you were, and I would do anything to bring that smile back to her face again," Greg replied.

"I miss that little girl I was too. I miss her," Lucinda replied.

"Then why did you let pain change you? Why, Lucinda?" Greg asked.

"Fate; fate caused it all. Just maybe, death should have spared my parents," Lucinda replied.

"Lucinda, please, we need you, back. Heal for us. That pain is hurting us too," Greg replied.

"When I'm ready, I will heal, but before then, I wish to ask you a question," Lucinda said.

"Sure, why not?" Greg enthused.

"Was there any mystery surrounding my birth?" Lucinda asked.

"Why did you ask?" Greg replied.

"I just want to know. Is there?" Lucinda asked, looking at Greg in anticipation.

"Hmmm. My dear, you're exceptional. On the night of a full moon, your mom, Anna, made a wish. She said, 'I want my daughter to be a queen even though we're poor. Let her be a queen even in this world and in the world beyond.' That was her wish that night. So, when I walked up to her, I told her she wanted you to be a queen here on Earth and in the world of immortals. She said yes; she knows she wants to give the entire world to you. And when she gave birth to you, you had this birthmark on your back, the shape of a full moon with stars surrounding it. You can barely see it because it's on your back. When your mom saw 'that, she laughed and said even the stars granted her wish. Aside from that, there is nothing else," Greg said.

"I'm a daughter of the moon and the stars? But is there anything like the world of the immortals?" Lucinda asked.

"World of the immortals? That I don't know of, but that birthmark made your mom believe the stars and moon granted her wish, and yes, the mark means you're the daughter of the moon and the stars," Greg replied.

"And the seashell?" Lucinda asked.

"It was said to be magical, but little is known about that because I don't know what it does," Greg replied.

"Alright, thanks, Grandpa. I will just go back to sleep now," Lucinda replied.

"Alright, goodnight," Greg said as he walked out of the room.

Lucinda locked the door as she lay on the bed, immediately soliloquizing. "This explains it all. She was crowned even before she was born, and that was my mother's wish." Lucinda closed her eyes as she drifted off to sleep.

As soon as she woke up in the morning, she stripped herself naked and turned her back to the mirror. She saw the birthmark and wondered how come she never saw it before. Then she put her clothes back on.

"Lucinda, leave." Mom's voice came in as soon as she was through wearing her clothing.

"Leave to where, Mom?" Lucinda asked.

"You need to leave this city before the night of the full moon. Please, you need to go, as you may not survive what is coming," the voice persisted.

"Why are you getting me scared? Just explain to me why I must leave," Lucinda asked, a little irritated.

"There is nothing to explain; just leave before the night of the full moon; that's it," the voice ordered.

"Don't let fear win," were the words from her father, and she remembered them vividly. So, ignoring her mom's words, she zipped her jacket and walked out of the room.

Chapter Three

On the Day of the Full Moon

On the day of the full moon, Lucinda kept pacing around her room, thinking of the best possible way to alert her grandparents of a looming danger. She needed to talk to her grandparents so they could leave the city that night.

Lucinda wanted them to be safe, for she had already sensed that what was coming was ominous, and she didn't think she would be that brave to face it.

After pacing up and down for some time, Lucinda left her room and went straight to the sitting room. Luckily, her grandparents were sitting down, chit-chatting.

"We need to leave today before nightfall," Lucinda simply announced as soon as she entered and sat down on the sofa opposite her grandparents. Greg and Maya were bemused at her, staring at her with stirring emotions.

"Leave to where? We don't understand. I mean, why should we leave so suddenly?" Maya was the first to find her voice.

"We need to leave here. We need to go back to the mountaintop, please," Lucinda pleaded.

"Why? You have not answered Maya's question. Lucinda, what's wrong? Are you okay?" Greg asked, still staring at her.

Lucinda considered their questions in her mind before blurting out, "If we don't leave, we might all die. We might get consumed by what's coming. Just trust me," Lucinda pleaded more.

"Lucinda, please don't tell me you're going insane. What's happening to you?" Maya asked.

"I'm okay, everyone; we just need to leave before nightfall," Lucinda shouted.

"Why, why do we need to leave? Talk to us, child. Stop being uptight. Allow us to help you," Greg said.

"Please, we need to leave. I'm begging you both. Listen to me; I have never made this request before. Let's just leave," Lucinda urged.

"Why, Lucinda? Who asked you to talk to us about leaving? I'm sure you didn't wake up this morning to blab this silly idea of yours," Maya asked.

"A voice from beyond," Lucinda blurted out, unable to hold herself anymore.

"What do you mean?" Greg asked.

"I just answered your question. I said a voice from beyond asked me to tell you we need to leave today before nightfall. Mom asked us to leave," Lucinda replied.

"I will not sit down here and listen to you utter all these words from your mouth. After the incident with the horses, it seems you have lost your mind completely. What is happening to my grandchild? Understand that your parents are dead; they were my children too. Anna, your mother, was my child, but I have accepted their demise in good faith. It's been years, Lucinda, seven good years. You're yet to accept the fact that they're dead. Your grandmother and I brought you here hoping that you would heal and forget all about them, but it seems it's not working. Now answer me, Lucinda, when will you heal? When will you accept that Anna and Phil are gone for good?" Greg asked, a bit irritated. Lucinda didn't waste time before answering Greg.

"You spent quality time with your daughter before she got married, and I spent only a decade with her. How do you think I could recover from that pain, like you, how, Grandpa? No matter how hard I try to explain, you both will never understand. Besides, this is beyond healing and still bleeding. You keep misjudging me; you keep misreading the situation. I have already accepted the fate that this journey is mine alone to embark on. I lost my parents at the tender age of ten; that is already accepted by me, but I'm not ready to lose you both now, and that's why I'm asking you to please let's go back to the mountaintop where it's much safer," Lucinda replied, wiping the tears already gathering in her eyes.

"You might delude yourself, Lucinda, but we won't share in your delusion. I have watched you all these years, and I know you've yet to accept the demise of your parents. That's what is affecting your thought processes," Greg said.

"That's what you think, but they are not gone yet. They are immortals by my side, speaking to me, just as we are now talking, hearing my every word, and I hear their words. That's the fact you have refused to accept!" Lucinda shouted.

"Lucinda!" Maya shouted.

"You both want the truth? Maybe I will tell you, though I know it's useless. My parents aren't gone. I can hear them. I can hear them loud and clear, and it was Mom's instruction that I should take you out of here because what's coming is evil, and I might not handle it. You both might not hear Anna and Phil speak, but trust me, they mean well for us. The same way you both want me to heal, that's what they want too; that's why they talk to me every day. All these years, I have received nothing but love and care from you both. You both have been my parents. I can't compare the love you showered on me with anything, and I'm grateful, but the truth remains that I miss my parents. They left when I needed them most in this journey called life."

They left when I least expected it. I slept with my parents' corpses in the same house. My parents died most painfully. They didn't deserve to die the way they did. The only way nature compensated me was by giving me the ability to hear them, though they are in the world beyond.

So please, I'm not insane; I'm not crazy; stop thinking that way. I'm only fighting to make sure we all stay alive. Please, let's leave," Lucinda pleaded.

"The answer is no, Lucinda," Greg replied.

Lucinda stood up and threw one look at them before running back to her room and shutting the door.

"What's happening? Why is this happening? Why can't they make this easier for all of us? Why?" Lucinda asked as she sobbed silently, throwing herself on her bed.

"Is fate playing on my grandparents, making them adamant in their decision to stay back, so I could stay back too and fight? How can I fight this when I don't even know what it is? Why will generations of unborn suffer for this? Why should I be placed in the center of all this? Why must it be me? Why, why me?" Lucinda was muttering as she continued to toss herself on her bed.

"Because you're a queen destined to rule immortals in the world beyond," the voice said, which made Lucinda turn in the direction it came from, but she saw no one.

"That wasn't my parents' voice. So, who could that be?" Lucinda asked as she stood up and walked closer to the window.

"Don't let fear consume you; if you can't take it, kill it, Lucinda," the voice said.

"And that's all? Who is talking to me? Why can't you just show yourself?" Lucinda asked, casting furtive glances around.

"The dream, yes, the dream. Now I remember; she said these exact words to me, but how can I kill? How can I have my hands stained with blood? No, I can't. I don't know what is coming, but I'm not killing it," Lucinda said, sighing.

"Then tame it. You'll be glad you did because, in the future, you will need its help," the voice replied.

"I just need to take a nap. Then, maybe when I wake up, I'll be able to think of how to keep Grandpa and Grandma safe from these," Lucinda muttered as she went back to her bed before shortly drifting off to sleep.

"Maybe we should listen to her," Maya said.

"And head back to the mountaintop because of an illusion? That will not happen.

I love Lucinda so much, and I would stop at nothing to make sure she is healed from this pain. I don't care how many more years it will take to put up with this nonsense, but I'm willing to wait.

And if I die today, I would be annoyed with myself. Do you know why? Because I would feel I didn't try hard enough for my grandchild to heal from the pain caused by her own parents' death.

I will stop at nothing to bring back the old Lucinda. This new Lucinda isn't the girl that spent her holiday with me years back then, full of life and laughter.

This new Lucinda is uptight, sad, and she is in pain. I just want her to be happy again," Greg replied.

"I know, only that I simply don't like the way things are going. I want nothing to happen to Lucinda or us yet," Maya said.

"Nothing will happen to her or us," Greg assured.

Shortly after a brief sleep, Lucinda woke up and instantly bent over under her bed to pick up the seashell. She took it out and laid her hands on it.

"I'm worried; I'm worried over the life of my grandparents. You need to protect them. I wouldn't want the rain coming to wet them. Please protect them for me. I know they would never leave. I have tried talking to them. I have explained, but the ultimate answer was no. So, please protect them for me. Shield them from what is coming. I can sense it; it's huge. I would never forgive myself if anything happened to them," Lucinda said as her eyes became wet. She held herself back from crying.

That night, after Lucinda finished with her dinner in her room, she went back to her grandparents' room and saw them fast asleep. She then walked back to her room, but looking outside, she saw the moon was fading its color to red.

"Hmmm. The Blood Moon! It's almost midnight," Lucinda muttered under her breath as she went close to her window.

Shortly after, it was midnight, and Lucinda started feeling goosebumps all over her body. She just didn't know what was happening. Lucinda wanted to leave the house and walk on the street, but somehow, she could restrain the power urging her to go. Soon after, she started seeing blood on her palm.

"What is happening?" Lucinda asked when she saw she was bleeding from her hands. She had no injury on her body previously.

Nevertheless, Lucinda was frightened, and as soon as the drop of her blood touched the floor, she instinctively glanced at the moon again to see it had changed to a full blood moon, shimmering in its incandescence.

The howling sound that followed frightened Lucinda to her marrow that she quickly shut her windows and recoiled back to her bed.

"They are here. They are here for you, and they would never leave till they see you. The earth needed your blood for the full moon to turn red; that's why I asked you to leave. I think you can fight what's in front of you," her mom's voice said.

"But Mom, I can't do this; I don't want to fight anything that I don't even know," Lucinda said.

"You have to. I believe you can do this because if you don't, the wails of people from this city will deafen your ears," the voice replied.

"Mom, what do you mean?" Lucinda asked.

"Blood shall be spilled. That road filled with people will be silent like a graveyard. This city will turn into a graveyard, and you wouldn't want that to happen. You conquered your fear when you chose to stay, following your grandparents' refusal to leave. I believe you can tame what's in front. It's in your hands; it's your fate. Goodnight, child," the voice said.

"Why do I have this fate? Why am I destined to go through so much in life? Why is my life this way? The only thing I wanted was to grow up with my parents right beside me as a child. But I grew up experiencing their death and, after that, hearing only their voices. Now I'm being asked to protect a city I barely know. It's just been only four months of staying here. So why do I have to go through so much? Why? Why?" Lucinda asked as tears trickled down her cheeks.

"Don't let fear win, Lucinda. Why are you getting yourself so worked up when you know no journey has ever been that easy for you? The problems are just there to make you better and strengthen you more than you were before, Lucinda. You have always been a strong girl. Don't tell me you're giving up now because of the problem that is here. What happened to that Lucinda that I knew before I died?" It was her dad's voice.

"That Lucinda is still here, Dad. That Lucinda didn't change. I'm only scared that people might get hurt because of me," Lucinda said.

"Oh really? Is that what you think? People won't get hurt because of you. Even if they get hurt, then try to calm the situation. You have always been a good leader," the voice replied.

"Yes, Lucinda can do this," Lucinda said as she walked to her bed and lay down. She closed her eyes, and before she knew it, she was fast asleep.

When she woke up in the morning, the first thing she checked was her palm, but there was nothing to show that she bled the night before. Lucinda stood up and walked out of the room to the sitting room. She opened the door, walked out, and saw if anything happened in the night.

Strolling on the road, Lucinda could see drops of blood as people kept murmuring about it. Looking at them, it was apparent they were terrified of what happened and not knowing who the next victim would be. They spoke in hushed tones.

Lucinda turned, and she strolled back home, troubled. She met her grandparents discussing in the sitting room.

"Where did you go?" Greg asked.

"I just went out. It seems lives were lost after what happened last night. There were drops of blood on the road," Lucinda replied.

"That's bad. That is so bad," Maya replied.

"More will still happen; more lives will still be lost. We could have averted this if we had left the city yesterday, but no, you both thought I was crazy. I wonder what pain the family will go through right now," Lucinda replied, taking a seat.

"What happened last night has got nothing to do with us. So, what are you saying?" Greg asked.

"The incident of last night has everything to do with me. I told you bringing me to this city was a terrible suggestion," Lucinda replied as she stood up and walked into her room.

"Mom, if you can hear me, I want to ask you something," Lucinda called as soon as she entered her room.

"What you saw this morning was the main reason I asked you to leave. Your dad wanted you to stay and asked you not to let fear win, but I was scared. So, staying here is a terrible suggestion," she sounded solemn and worried.

"About my birthmark: what's the story behind it?" Lucinda asked.

"It seems I made a wish, and it came to pass. When I was still carrying you in my womb, I made a wish on the night of the full moon, and I asked that you should be a queen. We had little, and we were mere commoners, but I wanted to give you the world, and when I had you, I saw the birthmark, and I knew my wish came true. So, you're my queen, and I believe one day the world will bow before your feet," the voice replied.

"Oh, now I understand. You just collaborated what Grandpa told me about the mark and why they kept calling me their queen," Lucinda said.

"What do you mean?" the voice asked.

"Don't worry; I will figure all these out by myself. I believe I can," Lucinda replied.

"What are you going to do?" Lucinda asked.

"Never mind, and about the birthmark, why didn't you tell me all this while? I never saw it until Grandpa and I had a discussion, and he told me about it, and when I checked the next morning in the mirror, that was when I saw it. Why did you keep quiet about it for ten years, Mom? And even now, you still didn't say a word about it until I asked. Why do I feel there is more surrounding my birth? What else do I need to know?" Lucinda asked.

"I never told you because I didn't see it as anything, and the birthmark was on your back, making it difficult for you to see," the voice replied.

"Is there anything else I need to know about my birth? Tell me more. Did anything strange happen after you gave birth to me?" Lucinda asked with bated anticipation.

"That night, I heard howls of wolves. I guess your dad was fast asleep, so he didn't hear the howls," the voice replied.

"Hmmm," Lucinda grunted lightly before thinking silently: "I might not be normal, like every other person. But I think I'm different. I'm the daughter of the moon and stars. I possess powers I don't even know. Mom asked; I guess she received more than what she asked for."

"Why are you silent?" the voice asked.

"Never mind, Mom. I'm just trying to wrap my head around something," Lucinda replied.

"You have nothing to worry about. We are here for you. Though you can't see us, it's an enormous privilege that you can hear us. I love you so much, Lucinda, and even in death, I would still give the entire world to you. You're still my baby, my best friend, and my only child. You can never walk on any path alone. Your father and I will always be around to make this journey easier for you," the voice replied.

"Thanks, Mom," Lucinda replied.

"But you have to send them back, or else the entire city might suffer for this," the voice replied.

"How do I send them back? I don't know how to do that," Lucinda replied.

"Even I don't know how to, but I know with time, you will figure out how to do that. I trust you, Lucinda. I know you can win this," the voice replied.

"Thanks, Mom," Lucinda said, smiling.

"Lucinda!" Maya called as she knocked on the door.

Lucinda stood up and walked to the door of her grandmother. Maya walked in as she sat down on Lucinda's bed, tapped the bed, and instructed Lucinda to sit down.

"Is there anything we need to know?" Maya asked.

"No, nothing, but maybe if you tell me exactly what you mean, I could be able to answer the question," Lucinda replied.

"You spoke about your dead parents being able to communicate with you. So, what happened last night had a link with you. Can you let me in on those?" Maya asked.

"Hope I'm not interrupting," Greg said as he walked inside.

"So, can you answer the question?" Maya said after glancing at Greg.

"Well, everything I said out there is the truth and nothing but the truth. What happened last night? It's all my fault. Just maybe you both should have listened to me. We should have left peacefully and still come back later. Mom asked that I take you both out of here—your daughter, Anna, not even her husband, Phil. She saw what's in front, and she asked that I leave, though Dad asked that I stay back and conquer whatever it is. They are coming for me. It's just a matter of time, and they shall get me," Lucinda replied.

"Maybe we can still go back since we're going to return afterward," Maya replied.

"No. We're not going anywhere. Lucinda, what's wrong with you?" Greg asked.

"Everything is wrong with me. Maybe you should have stopped Mom when she made that wish. Maybe if you had cautioned her not to involve me with the world of the immortals, I would have been free from everything happening since their death, but you kept quiet. You keep thinking it's all about my parents' death, that I'm suffering a psychological breakdown because of that. How long could that be? Seven years? No, Grandpa. I'm hale and sound, very aware of my environment, of everything happening, mostly what neither you nor Grandma can see or hear. It's not a psychological breakdown. I'm not losing my mind! The trigger for this is traceable to Mom's wish seventeen years ago. As it stands, that wish has ruined everything. My life, my happiness, and it's so unfortunate I will have to live the rest of my life with that."

Lucinda yelled as she stood up from her bed and made for the door, leaving them with their mouths agape.

"Where are you going? Because I still don't understand everything you have said here. How do you expect us to believe you're talking to your parents, for crying out loud, granddaughter? They are gone. They are dead!" Greg said, exasperated.

Lucinda turned and, looking at her grandparents, said, "That's the only problem here. No matter what, you can never believe it. Please stop asking me what the problem is since you have always refused to believe me. Stop asking me. It's your problem, not mine, whether you believe me. I have never lied to any of you before, yet you find it hard to believe when you both ask me questions. Hence, my problem is my problem. I can only find the solution. I do not need your help, as you can see. If you cannot believe me, how can you find a solution for me? Impossible!" Lucinda yelled with tears in her eyes and walked out.

"She is hurt, but why is she talking about the wish Anna made years ago? I'm yet to understand how it ruined her life," Maya asked.

"Perhaps the moon wants her daughter back," Greg replied as he stood up and left the room. At the moment, things weren't making sense to him, but somehow, he was determined he would get the truth from

Lucinda. He knew she was going through something. But unfortunately, that problem was way too much for her to handle, from the look of things.

As Lucinda left her grandparents, she went straight for the stable at the back of the house. As she opened it and walked inside, she held the white horse and pulled her outside. Then, she mounted her and whispered something into the horse's ear as they galloped off. She was going back to her parents' house in the village. She felt she just needed time to think. She knew before she would return, it would already be late in the evening.

After two hours, Lucinda got to her parents' village and strolled down to the river. On getting there, she came down from the horse and sat on the riverbank. Then, after a few minutes of quietness, she started throwing pebbles into the river. Soon after, a voice sounded from behind her: "Hello." Lucinda turned to see a pretty young lady standing behind her.

"Do you mind if I join you?" the lady asked. "Sure."

"I'm Mia, and you're?" the lady asked.

"Lucinda."

"I've been observing you from a distance since you got here. It seems you're bothered about something. Do you mind sharing it with me?" Mia asked.

Lucinda sighed and took a glance at Mia. She picked a pebble and threw it into the river before opening up to Mia. "My heart is heavy, and right now, the wish my mother made years ago is coming back at me. It seems the problems are way too much, and I'm afraid that I may not handle them. I just feel I can't do it, that I can't win the battle that lies ahead," Lucinda replied.

"Is that all?"

"Sure; that's all."

"Well, as for now, there are no battles, but there will be battles in the few months to come. Besides, what you see as a problem isn't a problem at all; it's just a task that needs to be done," Mia replied.

"What do you mean?" Lucinda turned to have a good look at her as she asked.

"Yeah, you're scared about the howls of the wolves you heard at night and the drops of blood you saw this morning. They came for you, but they are not here to kill you or hurt you. They will hurt more people if you don't welcome them. She already told you that. So, if you don't welcome her, she will cause more pain and agony to people around you; and about the seashell, it can't protect your grandparents for a long time. Time is going quickly, Lucinda, and if you don't tame that which has come for you into this world, more lives will still be lost. As for your grandparents, don't convince them anymore as they will never believe you, but the truth is they love you so much more than life itself and will give the entire world to you."

"You're different; you're the daughter of the moon. You're a queen who was crowned even before you came into this life," Mia said.

Lucinda stood up as she took a step back from Mia.

"Who are you? How did you know she said she was coming, and she was going to cause pain to everyone around me? How do you know so much about me?" Lucinda asked.

"Anya, that's her name. I guess you have forgotten. When they told you they were coming, they weren't joking," Mia replied.

"They? Who are they?"

"Anya is three in one, an amalgam of the sort, both a deadly beast and a wonderful soul. So, you choose which side of her you want," Mia replied.

"Who are you, and how did you know all this?" Lucinda asked.

"You are finding it hard to solve the puzzle in front of you. Now I have helped you solve it. I guess you know the right thing to do now: tame the beast or send it back," Mia replied.

"Tame which beast? How can I tame what I don't know?" Lucinda asked.

"That's your puzzle to solve. No one has ever tamed Anya. Anya will kill more. Anya will render many useless, and she will come for your grandparents soon. The magic of the seashell can't keep her away for long, and about the wish your mother made, it has always been in the prophecy. But, Lucinda, you are the Chosen One; and Anya shouldn't be the problem now. The problem should be what you decide to do," Mia replied.

"But you said Anya is a deadly beast and…"

"A wonderful soul as well, depending on which side you want to see. But trust me, what's in front is greater and deadlier," Mia replied.

"Who are you?" Lucinda asked again, clearly more afraid than angry.

"My name is Mia."

"I know, but who are you? How did you know all this?" Lucinda asked.

Mia laughed as she stood up and walked towards the river. "Do I look beautiful?" Mia asked.

"Yes, sure, more than any human I have set my eyes on," Lucinda replied, genuinely enchanted by Mia's beauty.

"I'm the Goddess of this river, and I know more because I have existed for ages and ages. When you were drowning in this place years ago, I didn't want to kill you. I only wanted to show you a little about what your life is all about, but Phil came in time to save you. The Moon and stars have waited for a long time, and they want their daughter to fix this as ordained," Mia replied as she walked into the river, and before Lucinda could say anything, she vanished from her sight.

"Thank you," Lucinda muttered as she hurriedly mounted her horse and galloped home, back to the city.

Once in the stable, Lucinda pecked the white horse together with the brown horse and smiled before leaving. It was already 6 PM when she got back home. Her grandpa sat on the sofa inside the sitting room, waiting for her to walk in. As soon as she walked in, he asked, "Lucinda, where did you go? You took the horse and went off without even telling any of us. Where did you go to?" Greg asked.

"I went to my parents' house in the village. I just needed some time to think, and I guess I have found my answers," Lucinda replied, grinning.

"Sit down, let's talk," Greg said as Lucinda sat close to him.

"I want to help, but I can't if you don't tell me what the problem is. I want to be part of it all," Greg pleaded.

"I just need to fix one more thing. Just give me some more time, and I promise I will tell you everything. Do you trust me?" Lucinda asked.

"I trust you, dear," Greg replied.

Lucinda stood up as she hugged her grandfather and whispered into his ear, "When the time is right, it will all make sense."

Chapter Four

LUCINDA WALKED INTO HER ROOM, AGITATED

Lucinda walked into her room, agitated, as she kept pacing around. To her, it was apparent Mia knew so much about her. She considered going back to the river to see if she could meet her again, to find out how to end her dilemma. But she was in a quandary. After pacing here and there, Lucinda had her bath. When she finished, she went back to the sitting room to have dinner with her grandparents. However, Lucinda wasn't feeling comfortable. She felt tense as she needed to find a permanent solution to her problem.

"Anya is already here, and she won't leave until I welcome her, but how will I welcome someone who has been described as a deadly beast by Mia? What if Anya feasts on me immediately when she sees me?" she muttered.

"What's wrong, child?" the voice of her dad asked.

As soon as Lucinda heard the voice, she sat up and moved closer to the window. Then, she unlocked the window.

"What's the problem?" her dad asked again.

"Anya is the problem. She will never leave," Lucinda replied. "And who is Anya?"

Just then, the howls of the wolves sounded. It was midnight.

"The voice you heard is that of Anya. Dad, Anya stays and won't leave till I welcome her," Lucinda replied.

"But that's three; I can hear three voices," the dad replied.

"Anya is three in one, a deadly beast and also a goodly beast. I don't want to meet her," Lucinda replied.

"You said something about welcoming Anya. How do you intend to do that, child? I can see you're already searching for answers, which means you haven't given room to fear. I'm happy about that."

"Yes, I'm searching for answers. Unfortunately, I haven't found the exact thing I'm looking for. I need to welcome Anya, whom my presence brought into this world, and even if she must leave, I must welcome her first. I can't see myself doing that, and if Anya stays for long without seeing me, more souls will be lost. She will continue to kill many. I was told that even the magic seashell couldn't protect my grandparents for a long time, which means Anya will come knocking someday," Lucinda replied.

"Will you let that happen?" her dad asked.

"No, I can't let that happen. I can't let Anya hurt my grandparents. If anything happened to them, life would lose its meaning to me. I need them here; I can't be left alone," Lucinda replied.

"Then you have to welcome Anya. Even if you don't know how now, I know soon you will come up with an answer to that. I have always believed in you. I won't even stop soon," he said.

"Thanks, Dad. Thanks for your words of encouragement. Tell Mom that somehow, I will end all this and let her know Anya won't hurt her parents or me. I will find a means soon to send her back," Lucinda said.

"Alright, my child," he said.

Lucinda walked back to her bed as she lay down and stared at the ceiling. Before she knew it, she was already asleep.

The following morning, Lucinda woke up early at 5 AM when it was still dark. She stood up from her bed and walked out of her room, passing through the back door to the garden. She sat down on her favorite chair and started soliloquizing immediately.

"All my life, I never thought I was someone else other than a normal human being. It's now clear to me that even my parents didn't know whom they gave birth to. My grandparents also think I'm just Lucinda, but now I know I'm something more. Right now, I face the greatest task ever: to tame a monster I have never seen with my eyes. How difficult can that be? My life changed in the twinkling of an eye. After so many years, it is now that I realize that I'm someone else."

"You're up too early. Why?" Her mom's voice pierced through her mutterings, but she was relaxed. She had grown accustomed to her parents' voices.

"How can I sleep knowing full well that many souls are in danger because of me? I wouldn't know how many died last night. How do you want me to feel, Mom? I can't sleep. This very thing has robbed me of my sleep and peace of mind," Lucinda replied.

"Send them back," her mom said.

"You already know it's not about sending them back, but how. And even if I can send them back, how do I welcome them first? If I don't welcome Anya, there is no way she is ever going to leave. So how do I face a deadly beast though she is also good? How? Tell me how, Mom," Lucinda replied.

"I don't know, but I know you have to find out how, or else more and more will lose their lives," she replied. Lucinda cupped her head in her hands as she was engrossed in thoughts.

Soon after, she stood and walked inside the house as she went to her bedroom. Lucinda was restless. She bent down, brought out a magic seashell from under her bed, and walked back to the garden.

Lucinda rubbed her hands on the seashell as her tears dropped on it. Her desire was for Anya to go back to the world she came from. She was trying to see if anything could work out, as she didn't know how to go about anything concerning Anya.

"Don't bother because that wish isn't coming true; trust me," a voice said as Lucinda turned to see a beautiful lady sitting close to her.

"How did you get here?" Lucinda asked.

"I was here already before you came. I'm everywhere," the lady replied.

"What's your name?" Lucinda asked.

"Berta, that's the name," she replied.

"And why did you say that my wish will not come true? Do you even know what I want to wish for?" Lucinda asked.

"You want Anya to go back to the world where she came, sure, but then even the seashell can't grant that. What you hold in your hand is one of the most priceless possessions of the Royals, but mind you, there are certain requests it can't grant," Berta replied.

"Then how do I make them go back? I want to send them back; more people are dying by the night, and more will still die if I don't send them back. Please, I need help," Lucinda replied.

"I can't answer that. I don't even have the answer to that question. No one knows how you can send Anya back. But you're the queen, so you should know how to tackle that," Berta replied.

"Why should everyone keep calling me queen? How can you all place a crown on the head of one who isn't interested in the crown? I want to be free like every other young girl out there. I'm tired of being handed a task that I'm incompetent to handle. I'm tired, just tired. People are dying every night, yet I'm told that I should send Anya back for that to stop, and yet no one knows how to do that. What's the meaning of all of this? I'm tired, and I need help," Lucinda blurted.

"You're asked to save people's lives now, and without yet doing anything, you're already tired. Well, if you continue this way, soon you will be confronted with the option of choosing your parents or saving humanity," Berta replied.

"You are…"

"Joking? No, Lucinda. I'm not joking. Maybe if Mia didn't tell you, I think I should let you know now. You're being asked to solve a minor puzzle, and you're finding it so hard to do. Don't tell me you're letting fear get over you. I've not known the daughter of the moon and the stars to be a coward. No matter how hard you try to run away from this, this is your life. Welcome Anya and save everybody from the impending doom following. Keep calm and watch the bloodshed happen to someone closer to you, and when I say that, I mean either your grandpa or your grandma," Berta said, standing up.

"How did you know Mia? How did you know she already met with me? Where are you from, and who are you?" Lucinda asked.

"Mia is the goddess of the river. I knew when and where she met you. She met you at her river where you almost drowned years ago. I know because I'm everywhere," Berta replied.

"Who are you?" Lucinda asked.

"I'm a goddess, just like Mia, but I'm the goddess of the wind. Lucinda, the sooner you accept who you are, the better for everyone," Berta replied and turned to leave, but she stopped when Lucinda called out her name.

"You are leaving. Why isn't everyone helping me out with this puzzle? Is it so difficult to solve? I keep asking for help every day, but it seems everyone is ignorant of the solution. What is happening?" Lucinda asked as tears dripped down her eyes.

"That's because no one can solve the puzzle except you. Find answers to the puzzle, no matter how difficult it is. The day you fully accept that you're not only a human, then that day, you would also know why the birthmark is on your back and what it can do; that day too, you would know the powers you possess. I hope you find answers to what you seek, but when it comes to helping, you can only help yourself," Berta replied and kept moving further, and right before Lucinda, Berta vanished into the wind.

"I'm everywhere, but you won't see me. Then, one day, we will all meet," Berta said as she remained invisible.

Lucinda shivered a bit, went into the sitting room, and sat on the sofa while still holding onto the seashell. Soon, she was awakened with a tap on her shoulder. She opened her eyes to see her grandpa.

"Good morning, Grandpa," Lucinda greeted.

"Good morning, child. You're up so early; why are you with the seashell?" Greg asked.

"I'm only holding onto it as it somehow gives me strength whenever I feel weak," Lucinda answered.

"That's nice to hear. Hope you didn't sleep here the entire night?" Greg asked.

"Oh no, I didn't. I went out into the garden early, and I just came in and sat down here. I didn't know when I dozed off," Lucinda replied.

"How about Grandma?" Greg asked.

"Oh, she is still sleeping," Greg replied.

"It seems you're still feeling sleepy. Wouldn't you rather go back to bed?" Greg added as Lucinda stood up and headed to her room. She lay on the bed and drifted off to sleep.

"Grandpa, what are you doing here?" Lucinda asked.

She had found her grandpa sitting in a deserted place with blood oozing from his knee. On his knee was a bruise sustained because of his battle with a deadly beast.

"What happened to you, Grandpa?" Lucinda asked as she placed her hands on the wound, trying to stop the bleeding. But on seeing it wasn't helping, she raced into the bush and came out a few minutes later with some leaves in her hands, rubbing the leaves on her two palms before squeezing out the liquid on the bruised knee.

Greg screamed in pain as Lucinda held on to him, and in no time, the knee stopped bleeding.

"Thank you so much, child," Greg said.

"What happened to you?" Lucinda asked again as she sat on the floor and stared deep into her grandpa's eye. Right in there, in his eyes, she saw three fierce-looking wolves attacking her grandpa.

She saw how he tried to scare them away and how the wolves didn't want to kill him. Instead, they just wanted to inflict pain on him.

"Wolves attacked you," Lucinda remarked.

"Yes, and I heard them talk. They will keep killing more and more souls till you welcome them. What connection do you have with them?" Greg asked.

"I don't have any connection with them, and I certainly don't know what they are talking about," Lucinda replied.

"Are you sure? Today it's me, and certainly tomorrow, it might be my wife, Maya. What are you hiding, Lucinda? Right now, I'm in pain because of you. You know they are here for you, yet you are reluctant to see them. Now answer me: how many more souls do you want to die before you can answer them, the very reason you came into this world?" Greg asked.

"How are you so certain they came for me?" Lucinda asked.

"Simple. They mentioned your name. They aren't just animals; they are enchanted. They speak in unison, and the message was clear: 'Tell Lucinda to welcome us to the world she brought us into, else souls and souls will be lost,'" Greg replied.

"I didn't ask them to come. I never summoned them to this world. I don't even know them. Now they're killing and hurting people close to me already. How can I welcome them when I didn't bring them into this world? How do I even face something that I have never seen before? I'm scared, Grandpa. I can't do anything because I want to put a stop to all this killing. I don't want to meet any beast; that's the only truth I know," Lucinda replied.

Greg stood up as he looked at Lucinda and said, "I want nothing to happen to my wife or you, child. I might have borne the pain they inflicted on me today, but I doubt if your grandma is going to bear the same pain. They are not here to kill you. They want you to welcome them. You keep saying you didn't bring any of them to this world. I understand. I believe you, no matter how hard you try to shy away from it. You're the only one who can stop this killing. Yes, you are. Save humanity before you ruin it with your aloofness," Greg said as he began limping away.

"Where are you going, Grandpa? At least let me assist you," Lucinda pleaded.

"I don't need it, child. All I need is for you to end this chaos before it begins. This chaos that you're avoiding will come knocking at your door someday. If you don't do the right thing before the time, it might also consume us all. You started this. Please send it away before you lose any of us," Greg said and walked away.

Lucinda covered her face with her hands as she sobbed quietly. What she was avoiding was already at her door. How can she end all this? How can she end this chaos?" Lucinda muttered amidst sobs.

"That's not true," said an aged voice.

Lucinda looked up to see an older woman sitting close to her. "How did you get here, and who are you?" Lucinda asked.

"I don't have a name, but you can choose to give me any name you want. The man you saw isn't your grandfather; it's just a clip of what's going to happen to him if you don't welcome Anya. You cannot summon Anya and refuse to welcome her," the aged woman said.

"But I didn't summon her," Lucinda protested.

"You don't need to talk or even command for her to come to your world. Your presence here on Earth summoned her. You need to do the right thing and welcome her before she unleashes terror on all of humanity," the aged woman replied.

"But how do I welcome her? I have never seen Anya before. I heard she is a deadly beast as well. She is going to hurt me," Lucinda replied.

"You're so naïve, my child. Anya can never and will never hurt you. She can never hurt the daughter of the moon and the stars. She only needs you to do the right thing. The previous queen before you welcomed her, so why is it hard for you to do the same?" the aged woman asked.

"Okay. How do I welcome her? I want to put an end to this. And just like my grandpa, or rather his illusion, asked: 'How many more souls do I want to die before I end the chaos that I have created?'" Lucinda replied.

"Good, just before midnight, leave the house and go far away. Just keep walking. When it strikes midnight, wherever you are, Anya will find you, and you both will meet, but you must never cry in her presence, no matter how scared you are. Anya must never see your tears. It is forbidden for the subject to see the queen in tears," the aged woman replied as she stretched forth her hand and asked Lucinda to place her hands on it.

"You're a young lady who lost her parents seven years ago, and today you're still in pain. You're yet to heal. Your heart is heavy and filled with pain, sorrow, and sadness. You smile, but beneath that smile lies a heart asking questions every day, demanding to know why her parents had to die so early. The journey ahead isn't an easy one; more is still coming. A time will come when you will have to choose between your parents and saving humanity and your world as well. You're not just human. You are two, and when I mean your world, I mean the world beyond because that's where you rightfully belong. The journey before you is going to be difficult, but please choose between saving humanity."

"Goodbye, my child. You need to go. Maya and Greg will get worried if they don't see you soon," the aged woman said as she smiled and whistled gently before leaving.

Lucinda woke up as she rubbed her eyes, only to find out it was all a dream. The aged woman had sent her home with the whistle. She quietly stood up from her bed as she kept the seashell in the box.

She quickly had her bath, wore her clothes, and walked out of the room while her grandmother set the table for breakfast.

"You didn't wake me up to help you," Lucinda asked.

"You looked so beautiful in your sleep. At one point, you were even smiling, so I had to leave you. Call your grandpa," Maya requested.

Lucinda called her grandpa, who came out promptly, and they all sat down to eat breakfast. When Lucinda was finished, she went straight to the stable and bathed the horses, leaving them outside to dry. She then cleaned up and dropped hay leaves for them.

"What bothers you, child? Your heart is heavy, and you don't look fine," her dad voiced out.

"I have to welcome Anya. If I don't, more souls will be lost," Lucinda replied.

"Have you done that?" he asked.

"I have to meet with Anya, Dad. I'm terrified. I can't imagine standing and facing a deadly beast. It's so difficult, and if I don't do it, the killing continues, and someday it will come knocking at my door. I wouldn't want Grandpa ever to witness what I saw in my dream. I just can't let that happen. Mom would say meeting up with Anya will be a bad idea, but she wouldn't be happy with me if anything happens to her parents. The same way I was left under their care, that's the same way they are now left under my care. I have to protect them at all costs," Lucinda replied.

"I wouldn't want you to get hurt, but I wouldn't want this to linger on. I believe Anya would never hurt you. Maybe you were chosen for a purpose. I know this task isn't easy, but I trust my Lucinda to get it done," he replied.

"Do you think I can get to face Anya?" Lucinda said, sighing.

"Who are you talking to?" Maya asked as she walked into the stable.

"I'm talking to…"

"She won't understand, so no need to tell her. She will think you're going crazy," her dad interrupted her.

"I'm not talking to anyone, Grandma," Lucinda replied.

"Okay, I will wait for you inside," Maya replied and walked out. Lucinda checked to see whether she was out of sight before saying, "How I wish they could hear you and Mom. Things would have been a lot easier," Lucinda said.

"But sadly, they can't. You're fortunate enough, or should I say blessed, with powers to hear us," Phil said.

"I will have to succeed at all costs to end this, or I will die trying. I wouldn't want them to be hurt because of me," Lucinda replied.

"Alright, please try to smile for your mom and for me too," he mildly requested.

"I will, Dad," Lucinda said as she smiled. She took the horses inside and changed their water as she locked the stable and went back to the house. No sooner had she entered her room than Maya walked into the room.

"Granny, you're here," Lucinda said. "Oh yes, now sit," Maya instructed.

"Oh, okay. Hope you're not about to give me lectures?" Lucinda asked, smiling.

"I heard you talking to someone when you said you couldn't believe you would have to talk to Anya. Who is Anya? I heard you say your mom won't be happy if anything happens to her parents, your grandpa, and me. So, tell me, Lucinda, who were you talking to?" Maya asked.

"I was not talking to anyone. Anya is the name of the beast that comes to the city every night," Lucinda replied.

"It has a name? The name sounds feminine, but how did you know all this?" Maya asked.

"Some things are better left unsaid, Grandma. I don't want Anya to hurt any of you because Mom would never be happy with me. The beast is still going around killing as many as she can. Even this house can't protect us from the beast. So, I have to do something else, or I might live to regret it for the rest of my previous life," Lucinda replied.

"How do you mean? You're getting me confused," Maya asked.

"Do you trust me, Grandma?" Lucinda asked.

"Of course, I trust you. I trust you so much, more than anything else in this world," Maya replied.

"Then believe me when I say I will protect you both. Nothing, I mean nothing, will ever happen to any of you," Lucinda replied.

Maya sighed as she stood up and left the room. There was no need to ask any more questions because she knew Lucinda wouldn't answer. The day went so well, and later that evening, they had their dinner. Lucinda didn't retire to bed immediately; she stayed back in the sitting room with them, chatting. After some minutes, she excused herself as she went to the back door and unlocked it. Lucinda came back and sat with them, her face filled with smiles. She wanted to spend quality time with them because she was scared that she might not make it back alive after tonight.

GOODNIGHT, GRANDPA; GOODNIGHT, GRANDMA

"Goodnight, Grandpa; goodnight, Grandma," Lucinda said as she went straight to her bedroom. She knew she was going out that night.

Immediately, it was a few minutes before midnight when Lucinda was very sure her grandparents had gone to bed. She quietly tiptoed out of her room and out the back door. She had left the door unbolted so she could quickly leave the house with no one noticing.

As soon as she stepped her foot out of the house, she walked gently on the street with the moon illuminating the pathway. She just needed to keep going, awaiting midnight when she could meet Anya.

As she kept walking with nowhere in particular, as instructed by the older woman, she suddenly started hearing the howls of wolves, signaling it was midnight. On hearing the sound, she lost her footing and tripped to the ground, and upon getting up, she discovered she had bruised her big toe.

When she got up, with excruciating pain, she found she was face to face with her fears right in front of her—the beast, Anya, was right there before her.

Three wolves were right in front of her, but something was different about them. Their eyes were like those of the moon, illuminating like an incandescent globe. She watched as the wolves brought their heads down before her before speaking.

"It took forever for you to come for us when you are the same person who summoned us," the wolves spoke in unison.

"Summoned you? I never did. I never summoned you at all. I never asked you to come. You have done nothing but hurt innocent people who did nothing wrong to you. Why? Why would you do that?" Lucinda yelled, clearly angry instead of being frightened by the terror before her.

"Your presence on the night of the full moon invited us. Had you stayed away from here, we wouldn't have come," the wolves replied.

"Well, I'm sorry that I was present, but right now I need you all to go, go back to where you came from. You have done more harm than good. I just want to have my life back. I'm tired of seeing the people suffer, dying for what they are not aware of," Lucinda pleaded.

"Do you think it's that easy? You can't summon us and ask us to go back just like that," the wolves replied.

"But I want you all to go back. Just tell me how, and then I will do it so you would go back to where you came from. Anya, please, you have already caused so much pain to people I barely know, but although I do not know them, they're dying because of me. I feel for them. I'm the reason for what has befallen them," Lucinda pleaded.

"All this wouldn't have happened, but you summoned me. You summoned Anya, and you didn't welcome Anya. You need to welcome Anya, else Anya would cause perpetual pain and agony to the people around you," the wolves replied.

"How is it possible that you animals are even talking, and so strange that I can even understand you all?" Lucinda asked, though not entirely surprised.

"Maybe the sooner you realize that you're not just human, then all this will make sense to you. How did you think you could hear the voices of your parents? It's because you possess that supernatural power to hear voices from the great beyond," the wolves replied.

"What do you want, Anya? I'm ready to do it, so you can stop all this and then go back to your world," Lucinda replied.

"You can't send me back just like that, Lucinda. That's the only truth," Anya replied.

"I'm tired, Anya; I'm tired of all that is happening. I am. I just want to be like every other girl and live a happy life," Lucinda replied.

"But you are not like them; you're different. You're a queen crowned even before your birth. Your life was different, and no matter how you wish for it, your life is perfect," Anya replied.

"Goodbye, young queen. At least you have welcomed us," the wolves said in unison as Lucinda watched them vanish into a nearby bush.

Lucinda sat on the ground as her blood kept dripping into the soil.

"Do you mind if I check your leg?" the voice said as Lucinda looked up to see a woman squatting right in front of her.

"Who are you, and where did you come from?" Lucinda asked, a bit surprised to see she was talking to someone she had never seen before in the middle of the night.

"Don't worry. I'm not here to hurt you. I would never do that," the lady replied as she touched Lucinda's leg. She muttered some words, and the bleeding ceased. No one would believe that she had been bleeding from her big toe a few minutes ago.

"How did you do that, and who are you?" Lucinda asked.

"Call me Tara, the goddess of fire," the lady replied as she smiled.

"Mia, Berta, and now Tara," Lucinda thought inaudibly and then said, "Maybe you have solutions to the puzzle; you have the answers that I seek. How can I send Anya back? She has killed enough. She is a deadly beast, and staying here will endanger the lives of innocent people," Lucinda asked.

"The answers you seek, I do not have. You wish to send Anya back to the world beyond by all means, but I don't know. Like you know, Anya isn't just one; she is three in one, making her one of the most powerful beings in existence. Anya is an enchanted wolf. I'm sorry, but the answers you seek, I can't provide," Tara replied.

"When am I seeing the Earth Goddess? I'm yet to see her. Maybe she would have answers to my questions. Perhaps she could help me out of this mess," Lucinda replied.

"You're not in any mess. This is your fate. You have already been destined for this, even before your birth," Tara said as she stood up and headed for the surrounding bush.

"Don't tell me you're leaving. Why do you all keep coming when you can't give me answers to my questions? Why can't you all help me out? I'm tired, and I'm pleading for help. I only want to protect the lives of the people around me. I know how I felt when I lost my parents seven years ago. I wonder what the families of those killed are going through right now. I just want to help them. I want everyone to be safe. Anya is the threat here, and she needs to leave," Lucinda pleaded.

"Hmmm. Well, then you have to know this. My dear, the people of this city murdered the previous queen decades ago before you were born."

Fate made you and your grandparents move back to this place, and for the lives killed, they are not innocent. Their hands have been stained with the blood of the queen before you. Anya wants to wipe them out before coming for you. Anya doesn't believe in forgiveness; she believes in revenge. So, Anya plans to wipe out the entire city and then come for your grandparents. She won't kill them, but she will hurt them.

How do you expect her to feel when this same city killed our previous queen? The pain is still fresh in Anya's heart. Now that you have met with her, I believe she won't shed any more blood. Anya might be the deadliest of them all, but she has a sweet soul. Just too bad you met the other side of her first. And as for the Earth Goddess you think might have the answers to your questions, you're the fourth goddess, Lucinda, the Earth Goddess," Tara replied.

"How do you mean? I don't understand," Lucinda replied, shivering a bit.

"When the time is right, it will all make sense to you," Tara replied and walked deeper into the bush.

Lucinda looked up to see that the moon was still shining brighter than ever. She fell to the ground and started crying, sobbing. Nothing was making sense to her yet. With every episode that passed, she continued getting confused over the whole thing. How could she be the fourth goddess? she wondered in between her sobs.

"We came to you because you needed our help."

"You're one of us, though you possess powers that are greater."

"We have answered the questions we can, to the extent we know. It's now left for you to continue on this journey alone."

"We would return only when the time is right. We know you can win this." It was the combined voices of Berta, Mia, and Tara. Lucinda wished they could give her straightforward answers to the questions welling inside her mind.

Soon after the voices sounded, Lucinda looked up to see a bright light showing from far away. She stood up as she advanced toward it, and slowly she walked into the light.

On entering the light, Lucinda saw herself in a different world altogether. She saw a girl who looked like her run past her with tears in her eyes. Lucinda followed her closely as she watched the girl run into the hands of a mob.

"Please don't hurt me. I'm begging you. I did nothing. I'm innocent of all the crimes that I'm accused of. I didn't kill the king. He didn't die because of me," the little girl frantically pleaded.

She saw as the mob kept calling the little girl a liar, refusing to believe her. She saw as they started throwing various things at her. Finally, she saw them take her to a dungeon and lock her up as she cried bitterly.

"Why are you being tortured?" Lucinda asked, but she wasn't heard. Instead, she walked closer to the girl and touched her as she raised her chin.

"Why are they torturing you? What offense have you committed, and why is it that no one can see me?" Lucinda asked again.

"You're from the future; this is the past," the little girl answered.

Lucinda shivered on hearing that. She took a few steps backward and cast another glance at the girl before her.

"My name is Lucia, daughter of the moon and the stars. You're my incarnation. The people are torturing the people I would do anything for at any cost to protect, and me," Lucia replied.

"Since the daughter of the moon and the stars, why didn't you have powers, powers to set yourself free from these people?" Lucinda replied.

"I do, but I have been rendered powerless to use it. If I should use my powers against them, then my parents will be killed. So, I rather die than live and watch them kill my parents." Lucia replied.

"What happened then? Why are they doing this to you?" Lucinda asked.

"I have never withheld my powers from doing good. I have used it to help and heal so many. Everyone loved and cherished me, and they termed me a blessing to their generation.

My people warned me that humans could never be trusted. I was pleased to keep my powers hidden, but I didn't. I felt we are all one family. The king had fallen ill, and as usual, I had gone to treat him.

He was perfectly okay when I left the chambers, but before I got to the gate, I was handcuffed, with claims that I had stabbed the king and I was trying to run away. I escaped, but somehow, they got my parents.

I didn't escape because I wanted to run away from them, but only so I could buy more time to see if I could get the killer.

The killer is from the world beyond. She will come to you but with a different face and name. For now, she is in hibernation. Fate has it that the one that owns the seashell can kill her forever.

In between, the people somehow got to find my hiding place, and now they got me, and here I am in this cage. I wanted to rescue my parents and leave this city together, but my plans didn't work. After all that I have done for this city, they still think that I'm capable of murder.

I have been betrayed and stabbed by them. You're wondering why Anya is killing souls, the souls you deemed innocent? They aren't innocent after all; they came together and set me ablaze. They watched me burn to death despite my pleas and cries that I was innocent. I might have forgiven them, but Anya never forgets; Anya believes in revenge. I'm happy that you have at least welcomed Anya, which means there would be no more bloodshed and that the city will be in peace again. I have forgiven the souls in the city that killed me, but remember, they were never innocent. They killed me. They killed us. Keep your powers hidden from ordinary eyes. That is all that I want you to do," Lucia replied.

"I don't think I have any powers. My utmost concern now is how to put a stop to the bloodshed bedeviling the city people. The nightly cries and wails are becoming unbearable to me. You said by my welcoming Anya that it would stop, but I'm afraid Anya will hurt my grandparents who live in the city. Anya might hurt them if she finds no one else to kill," Lucinda replied.

"When the time comes, you will know the powers you possess, but don't forget to keep it a secret. You're wondering why the people cannot hear you. Of course, they can't, as you're not from this century. You've been able to see what happened in the past because Tara made it known to you that the people whom you were fighting for, whom you thought were innocent, weren't really. She is correct. Please don't repeat my mistake, your mistake indeed, because I am you and you are me. Let your powers be your only secret that they do not know of," Lucia replied. "But Lucia, I ha…"

"I don't have the answers to that question which you want to ask now. We're the same, you and me. You're just my incarnation, but soon, you will see the beauty of the great work you're called to do. So please go back to your world," Lucia replied.

Then, before Lucinda's eyes, the gate to the dungeon was opened as some soldiers came and whisked Lucia away. Lucinda followed them as she watched them tie Lucia to a bunch of sticks.

Then, after pouring a liquid substance on her, they set her ablaze. She couldn't withstand Lucia's wails and bemoaning as the fire raged.

Finally, she fell to the ground and covered her two ears as she sobbed at the agony Lucia was feeling to pass through a cruel fate.

Lucinda couldn't believe Lucia was killed in such a horrible manner, which explained Anya's anger, who would always avenge her own. Lucia was killed in such a horrible manner because she was mistaken to be the king's murderer. Despite her pleas of innocence, the people still killed her, and to think that this was the same city she protected with all her life, the same people she healed, not to mention her countless goodness to them.

How they thought she could stoop so low to kill a mere human, the same humans she had protected all her life, was something incredible. She was burned to death. It was years already, but Anya could still hear her cry. She could still see how Lucia struggled to live. Lucia submitted herself to die so that her parents could live, but the people did not spare her parents, too.

They had her parents killed and had their carcass fed to the birds of the air.

This was the act of wickedness that got Anya infuriated, and she came for vendetta. As the panorama of what happened played again in Anya's memory, she screamed as the bushes felt the gravity of her howls, which startled Lucinda.

"Lucia said she had forgiven them," Lucinda replied.

"But Anya never forgives. Anya believes in revenge. The city you wanted to save so badly killed you before, yet your heart is filled with mercy and compassion," Anya replied.

"Yes, besides feeling for them, I also feel for my grandparents, who could be hurt by you someday," Lucinda replied.

"That's true, but I will never kill them. I can only hurt them, as the killing has already stopped since the queen has welcomed me," Anya replied.

"How am I sure you won't hurt any more souls? They might have wronged me years back, but the old me forgave them even before my death. So, Anya, why can't you forgive? Please forgive and go back to the world from which you came," Lucinda replied.

"I can't!" Anya bellowed.

"But why? Why can't you? My grandparents are living in constant fear; the people too. Everyone is in fear, and to think that I brought this upon all of them and…"

"You didn't. They brought it upon themselves. They killed you even when you pleaded your innocence. How could they kill the soul that gave them everything? How could they betray her?" Anya screamed.

"I have forgiven them. Let peace reign. I don't want to cause chaos. Let this place be peaceful. Anya, my grandparents sleep with one eye closed and one eye open. You might not kill them, but you will hurt them someday. I'm tired of people living in fear. I'm tired of hearing the cries of the people calling on me for help. Please, Anya, I'm begging you from the innermost of my being. Let this go. Even if you can't forget, please forgive. I beg you as the daughter of the moon. Listen to me, Anya. Please," Lucinda said as she knelt and bowed her head.

"How could you?" Anya shouted.

Anya couldn't believe that Lucinda was ever going to kneel and bow before her. Now there was no way she was going to hurt anyone again.

That act of Lucinda's humility had hindered her. Anya knew that once the queen bowed to her, whatever she needed must be granted.

"How could you, Lucinda? These people murdered you years ago. Why have you stopped me from hurting them? Why? I only wanted them to have a taste of what you went through in their hands. I haven't had the chance to grace the human world after Lucia's death, and now that I have the chance, my only aim is to kill as many as I can before I go. Why do you have to kneel and bow before me? Why, Lucinda? Why did you have to do this? Well, keep your powers hidden from human eyes; otherwise, they might be forced to kill you again, labeling you a witch or a sorcerer or whatever they may fancy," Anya said as she howled so loud.

"I just want to have my peace," Lucinda replied as she got up from the ground.

"We waited for you this long, and now you are here. You have stopped me from feeding the blood of these humans to the earth, although you're the earth goddess. You're just so compassionate," Anya howled as she raced off.

Lucinda kept looking at the three wolves before they went out of her sight. She sighed as she sat on the ground, wondering whether Anya would ever forget and forgive what the city people did to her years back.

Chapter Six

As Soon as Anya Disappeared

As soon as Anya disappeared, Lucinda stood up from the ground and headed back home, with too many thoughts raging in her infantile mind. So, she was the fourth goddess, which summed up everything. They had waited patiently for her to become older before things would be revealed to her. But they should have waited until she was at least twenty before unleashing all this on her. She was still thinking as she walked home dejectedly, though happy with herself for at least being able to stop Anya.

When she got home, she went toward the backyard and stealthily entered through the back door. She locked the door behind her and went straight for her room. She knew she had just three hours to sleep. She lay on her bed, covering herself before she drifted off to sleep.

She saw herself taking a stroll somewhere unfamiliar when someone tapped her. She turned swiftly to see who it was. She was stunned to see a lady standing before her, with her skin glistening like the sun.

"Who is this?" Lucinda murmured, half audibly, impossible for the lady to hear, but she heard her.

"I'm such different things to different people. Perhaps you can choose a name for me," the lady replied.

"Your skin glistens like that of gems. Can I call you Sun?" Lucinda replied.

"I like the name," the lady replied, smiling.

"Who are you; I mean, what are you?" Lucinda asked.

"I'm Sun, just like you named me," she replied.

"No, not your name. I mean to know who you are and how I can help you," Lucinda asked.

"You can't help me; rather, I'm here to help you. You seek answers. Mia, the river goddess, couldn't answer; Berta, the wind goddess, couldn't answer, and Tara, the fire goddess, couldn't answer. You are searching for answers, and I'm here to give them to you," Sun replied.

"Yes, I am. You're right. First, how can I send Anya back to the world she came from? Souls may still be lost if she keeps staying here," Lucinda asked.

"If Anya stops destroying humans, will you let her stay?" Sun asked.

"Yes, I will, but that's not possible; she is a deadly beast," Lucinda replied.

"That's the side you saw first; besides, you have already welcomed her and even knelt and bowed to her so that she won't hurt a single soul anymore," Sun replied.

"Even at that, how do I send her back?" Lucinda asked.

"You want Anya to leave so soon when you haven't even gotten to know her? Anya will leave when you don't expect it. It will come as a surprise to you. Anya was sent for a reason, not just to avenge your death. In the future, you would be glad you got to know her more," Sun replied.

"So, I can't send her back?" Lucinda asked.

"I don't even know why you're so obsessed with sending her back. Well, Anya can never leave; you can't send her back. You can only tame her," Sun replied.

"How do I tame her if I can't send her back?" Lucinda replied.

"That you have already done. You tamed Anya the minute you welcomed, knelt, and bowed before her. Henceforth, she will only take instructions from you. You're the queen, and she is your subject. I'm glad you listened to your father's voice instead of your mom's. Don't let fear win. I'm so happy you didn't give room for fear," Sun replied.

"You know so much about me already, and you know about my parents too?" Lucinda asked.

"Everyone knows the people who gave birth to the supreme queen, the daughter of the moon and the stars," Sun replied and came closer to Lucinda.

"What do you want to do?" Lucinda asked.

"I'm sending you back to your world. Our discussion here is ended," Sun replied.

"But I'm not through with my questions," Lucinda protested.

"You have always wanted to send Anya back, but that's not possible. So, the next question you wish to ask now is how to drop the crown on your head, that you don't want to be the queen anymore. Am I right?" Sun asked.

"Yes, you're right. I'm not interested in any of these. I just want to be free and live like the normal young girl that I am," Lucinda replied.

"That's not possible! You can't be what you are not or not be what you are. You have always been the queen, even before the birth of your mom, Anna. So don't blame your mother for the wish she made. It has always been your fate," Sun replied as she touched Lucinda on her forehead.

Lucinda opened her eyes slowly, only to realize she had been dreaming. She sat up straight and looked at herself in the mirror. *It has never been Mom's fault. I had always been destined to be a queen,* Lucinda thought as she stood up slowly and made for her window to open it. It was already morning. The sunrays were already streaming in upon the earth. After opening the window, she went back to her bag and took her clothes out as she quickly rushed into the bathroom to have her bath and brush her teeth, after which she wore her clothes and walked into the sitting room.

"Good morning, Granny," Lucinda said to Maya, who was busy slicing the onions.

"Good morning, my dear. You woke up late. I came to your room to check on you only to discover you were asleep, and I didn't want to disturb you, so I allowed sleep to continue," Maya replied.

"Oh, good of you, Grandma. What are you making for breakfast?" Lucinda asked.

"It's a surprise, and guess what, no single soul was lost last night. So, guess the beasts didn't visit again, after all. I think they are gone for good," Maya replied.

"They are not gone; they are around," Lucinda replied.

"How do you mean they are still around? Explain better," Maya replied.

"That they didn't hurt anyone last night does not mean they are gone. They live with us now. That they are calm now is because of one reason. They will never leave. This is now their new home," Lucinda replied.

"Is there anything you're not telling me?" Maya asked, eyeing Lucinda.

"I just told you everything you need to know. They are not gone; they are still around, and they are never leaving until they decide to do so," Lucinda replied.

"Lucinda!" Maya called.

"Ask no more questions, Granny, I'm begging you," Lucinda replied as she stood up and walked to the kitchen to get drinking water for herself.

The day went well as Lucinda eagerly waited for nightfall. She wanted to see Anya. Eventually, it was night. So, Lucinda kept the back door unlocked, and when she was sure her grandparents were asleep, she crept out of the house, heading to where she had met with Anya the previous night, getting there just a few minutes before midnight.

"I hope you haven't been waiting for long, my queen?" It was Anya. Lucinda turned back to see Anya. There she was, with eyes glistening.

"Not too long, as I needed my grandparents to be asleep before I could come out," Lucinda replied.

"But how come you're now one? I thought you were three in one?" Lucinda asked.

"In my body, the other two come out only when the need arises. They can hear me; they can speak through me. I'm the enchanted wolf of the moon and the stars. Some see me as the deadliest beast because I'm three in one; while I show no mercy when I torment, fate has it that the only one whom I can ever obey is you. That was why on the day you were born, your people heard howls of wolves. It was me paying my respect," Anya replied.

Lucinda heaved a sigh of relief upon hearing the last words before uttering, "You won't hurt anyone ever again, please. I wouldn't want to be the reason for people's pains," Lucinda pleaded.

"As you wish, Your Majesty," Anya replied as she slowly transformed into a lady in her late twenties. Lucinda was shocked at that sight. She couldn't believe her eyes. She blinked a million times in under a second.

"How did you do that?" she finally found her voice to ask.

"I'm Anya, an enchanted wolf. I can transform into anything I wish, and that's what happens when you are blessed with powers; that's why they call me the deadliest," she replied as she smiled.

"In that case, I guess I will come here every night to see you. Hope I'll always see you?" Lucinda asked.

"Of course, you will," Anya replied as she stretched forth her hand and handed a necklace to Lucinda.

"What will I do with this?" Lucinda asked.

"It has always been yours. You need this to activate the powers which you possess. Lucinda, you are royalty, though you are yet to realize that," Anya remarked.

"I accept who I am. It won't lead anywhere if I keep blaming Mom or rejecting it. I accept, and I agree that this girl here called Lucinda is the daughter of the moon and the stars," Lucinda said, sighing at the same time.

And soon, there was the flash of lightning followed by the rumbling of thunder. Lucinda cowered and held onto Anya tightly as she was frightened, but Anya remained calm.

"Seems you're scared of the lightning? No need for that. It was just a sign that the world beyond has heard you. Now, look up," Anya said as Lucinda slowly looked up.

"The sky was filled with stars, and it looked so beautiful." Anya pointed at the stars and smiled.

"You are blessed with the greatest power of them all; the power to heal and the power to hurt anyone with just your pair of eyes," Anya replied.

"How can I hurt someone just by merely looking at them?" Lucinda asked.

"Maybe there is only one way to find out. Look at that cobra slithering over there," Anya pointed at a snake coming toward them. Lucinda stood up quickly and held onto Anya as she shouted, "Kill the snake."

Anya kept quiet as she watched Lucinda, a look that reminded her of what she had just told her a second ago. Lucinda caught the prompt and looked at the snake. Lucinda turned to balls of fire on closing and opening them, and as she looked at the snake, it just dried up instantly, dead.

"What just happened to me?" Lucinda, shocked, asked as soon as she got hold of herself.

"You just killed the snake. Be quick to call yourself back to reality, so you don't hurt someone else," Anya told her.

"Can you help me with the necklace?" Lucinda asked.

"Sure," Anya said as Lucinda positioned herself while Anya helped her with the necklace.

"You look pretty," Anya complimented.

"Thank you," Lucinda replied, smiling. "Anya, I have a question troubling my mind. I met this lady who told me a time would come when I would have to choose between my parents and saving humanity. I didn't understand what she meant, and I still don't understand, but it still troubles my mind. I want answers, please."

"Yes, what she said is true. It was the Wind Goddess who told you that. Berta was right. Indeed, the time comes when you have to choose, but no one knows what is going to happen," Anya replied.

"My parents are dead, and I can only hear their voices. How do I have to choose between them and saving humanity? How? I don't understand," Lucinda asked.

"I do not know, my queen, but a queen faces myriads of trials and tribulations, but what makes her a real queen is how she handles the situation. You already passed the first trial, and the second remains, and no one knows what that will be. So, get yourself ready. I'm glad you listened to your father's voice when he urged you not to give in to fear. Do not allow fear to win," Anya said, standing up.

"Where are you going?" Lucinda asked.

"It's already 3 a.m., and you need to go home, Lucinda," Anya replied.

"Wow! I didn't know how time flies. Aren't you leaving so soon?" Lucinda replied.

"Well, neither here nor there. I need you to sleep. I wouldn't want to keep you awake, and when I leave, I want you to hold the necklace and think of your room. Just do that," Anya replied as she squatted and slowly transformed into a wolf. She looked at Lucinda one more time before she raced into the bushes, disappearing.

Lucinda waved at her as she slowly closed her eyes, touching the necklace, and then thought of her room. On opening her eyes, she saw herself standing right inside her room. It then dawned on Lucinda that what she had on her neck was not an ordinary necklace. With this, Lucinda knew she could teleport anywhere.

It was an exciting feeling.

Lucinda walked to her mirror to admire her new necklace, with a unique sense of exhilaration. However, she was feeling sleepy already. She turned to her bed and switched her mind to all that happened that night.

She was awakened in the morning by the assuring hands of Maya on her shoulders as she still lay on the bed. Upon getting up, she saw her grandmother sitting close to her on the bed.

"Good morning, Grandma," Lucinda greeted.

"Good morning? It's afternoon, baby girl!" Maya replied.

"What? Are you serious? I didn't know," Lucinda said, sitting up as she stretched her dress.

"You were awake all the night, right?" Maya asked, eyeing her suspiciously.

"Yes, I was, but that's not an issue. I had something to deal with, and I had already sorted it out," Lucinda replied.

"Who gave you that necklace on your neck?" Maya asked, touching the pendant, which had the shape of the moon surrounded by stars.

"Oh, it's a gift," Lucinda replied.

"From who? I didn't see this on your neck throughout yesterday until when you retired to your room, and how come you slept and woke up with it? What are you not telling me, Lucinda?" Maya asked, still not satisfied with Lucinda's answer.

"There is nothing to know, Grandma. It's a gift from my parents. I refused to show it to anyone, and it has been with me ever since they died. So, I just felt like wearing it yesterday before I went to bed," Lucinda lied, an unavoidable lie.

"You're lying to me," Maya remarked.

"Why would I lie to you?" Lucinda asked, standing up.

"I didn't ask you a question. I know you lied because this is real gold with diamond stones encrusted on the pendant. How did Anna and Phil get such money to buy such an expensive necklace? This necklace sure costs a fortune," Maya replied.

"Maybe if they were alive, you would have asked them how they got the money to buy the necklace," Lucinda insisted as she brought out the clothes she was going to wear. She left her grandmother sitting on the bed as she walked into the bathroom to have her bath.

Maya wouldn't want to wait for her to come out. She stood up and left the room to meet Greg to tell him about the necklace.

When Lucinda finished bathing, she wore her clothes and instinctively looked at the pendant one more time before leaving her room.

"I don't know how Lucinda came about the necklace she is wearing. That necklace is real gold and diamond, and it must have cost a fortune," Maya said.

"How sure are you?" Greg asked. "I can't make up stories," Maya replied.

"Good afternoon, Grandpa," Lucinda greeted as she sat on the floor, and as soon as Maya walked closer to her and pulled out the pendant from Lucinda's neck.

"Are you not seeing that this is real gold and diamond?" Maya said, throwing it at Greg. But Lucinda wouldn't have any of that. So instead, she retrieved the necklace from Greg's hand and placed it inside her clothes.

"Lucinda, do you have any explanations on how you came about the necklace?" Greg asked.

"I already told Granny. It's from my parents. It has been with me all the while, only that I've been reluctant in wearing it," Lucinda replied.

"And how come we have never seen it? How come you've kept that away from us for so long? Besides, Anna and Phil are our children; there is no way they could afford something as expensive as this. So, tell me, where did you get the necklace from?" Greg asked.

Lucinda kept mute as she ran her hands through her hair, as she thought of what more to say.

"Lucinda, talk," Maya threatened, widening her eyes.

"Grandpa, didn't you always say that though my parents had nothing, they still wanted to give me the entire world?" Lucinda asked.

"Yes, I said so. It's true," Greg concurred.

"You once told me the story behind my birth. I asked you if I'm the daughter of the moon and the stars, and you told me yes," Lucinda said.

"Yes, I did," Greg replied, not sure of where Lucinda was driving to. "What's the symbol on this pendant?" Lucinda asked.

"The moon surrounded by the stars," Greg and Maya replied in unison.

"Well, Mom and Dad might have nothing, but they will give me everything. They were ever willing to give me the world if possible. That they didn't tell you about the necklace doesn't mean they didn't buy it. I already told you, and I'm repeating it: it's from them. I kept it away for years because I wanted to," Lucinda said as she stood up and walked into the kitchen, being already famished.

"I don't believe her," Maya said.

"Same here, but she already said it is from her parents, and of course, there is nothing we can do about it. Her parents aren't here, so who are we going to ask?" Greg replied.

Maya sighed as she sat down abruptly on the sofa. Lucinda walked out of the kitchen carrying a plate of food and went straight to her room. Once inside, Lucinda sat down as she gently ate her food in silence.

On coming out of her room, Lucinda informed her grandparents that she wanted to take a stroll on the street. Lucinda then left the house and started walking down the road. As she walked about, a little girl suddenly appeared from nowhere and hit her, falling. She bent down to help the girl stand on her feet again.

"What's your name?" Lucinda asked.

"My name is Amber," the little girl replied.

"Where are your parents? You shouldn't be all alone on the street," Lucinda said, looking around as she held tightly onto the girl.

"Thank you very much," Amber said, smiling.

"And why are you thanking me?" Lucinda asked.

"For taming Anya, and don't worry about sending her back as she will be of great use to you later. Trust me. You look beautiful, daughter of the moon and the stars," Amber replied as she smiled, flashing her excellent dentition as Lucinda stepped back and looked at her in awe. Shortly after, an aged woman appeared and held onto Amber.

"I'm so sorry; she is my granddaughter. I didn't know when she ran off. Hope she wasn't saying silly kinds of stuff to you?" the aged woman asked.

"No, not at all," Lucinda replied.

"I finally met the daughter of the moon and the stars. It's such an honor," Amber said excitedly as they still stood before Lucinda.

"You better keep quiet. Someone would never believe you're just six, yet you speak way past your age. I'm so sorry," the aged woman apologized before she left with Amber.

Lucinda smiled as she turned and walked back home. She knew the little girl wasn't an ordinary girl. Amber was a seer, and with time, Amber would get to realize the power she possessed. When Lucinda got home, she walked straight to her room, and lying on the bed, she slept off. She needed to sleep since she was going out to meet with Anya later in the night.

She later woke up late in the evening and went straight to the kitchen to pick up her dinner, after which she went back to her room and locked her door behind her.

"Are you going anywhere?" her mom's voice spoke.

"Yes, Mom. I'm going to meet with Anya," Lucinda replied.

"You can't go; Anya might hurt you one day," she pleaded.

"Anya can't hurt me. I'm her queen. Have you ever heard of a subject hurting the one who wears the crown? I possess powers greater than anyone else, including her. She can't hurt me. Not possible anymore," Lucinda replied.

"Who are you? You have changed," she remarked.

"I didn't change, Mother. Remember when you said I'm the daughter of the moon and the stars? You wanted me to be queen over all others. Well, I am now what you wished me to be," Lucinda replied.

"Please be safe. I might be dead, but I can't bear to watch anything happen to my only child," Anna replied.

"Alright, Mom. I'll be safe. My greetings to Dad," Lucinda replied.

Lucinda lay on her bed as she waited for some minutes before midnight. By then, her grandparents must be fully asleep. Once it was time for her to leave, she stood up and closed her eyes. Then, thinking of their meeting place and touching her necklace, she instantly teleported to the location.

She sat on the floor as she waited gently for midnight when Anya would appear. Instead, she started hearing the howl of wolves. Not long after, Lucinda felt someone tap her shoulder and turned to see it was Anya. She watched her as she changed into a beautiful young lady.

"Amber, you will have to find her because you need her in this journey," Anya said as soon as she completed her transformation while sitting down next to Lucinda.

"You know her? She is just six, as her granny said. But how did you get to know about her?" Lucinda replied.

"My name is Anya, an enchanted wolf, the three-in-one beast. I know things you don't know in your present phase as a mortal. Amber is a seer. Remember, she said it was an honor to meet you. But if I told you that the little girl you saw today is just an old woman in the body of a child? Amber knows more than you do. In her past life, she waited and prayed to see you, but she didn't; and now that she saw you for the first time in her existence, she was excited beyond words," Anya replied.

"How do I find her then? How do I go about looking for her? It's going to be very difficult, and how do I even need her on this journey? Everyone keeps talking about the journey. What journey is that?" Lucinda asked, a little furious.

"With time, you will know. But the truth is you have to find Amber. She sees things that the human eyes can't see. Amber is the key you would need in the future," Anya replied.

"I will try to find her. Hopefully, I will find her in less than a week," Lucinda replied.

"I never thought the goodbye would happen soon," Anya said, looking around.

"What do you mean?" Lucinda asked.

"Again, with time, you will understand. As for the necklace, don't worry; your grandparents won't question you about it anymore. Stay safe and strong, and never let fear win over you. Always have faith in yourself that you're always capable. The road will be filled with temptation and tribulations, but worry not, because I have always seen you as a winner. You will emerge victoriously. Try to keep your powers away from human eyes," Anya said.

"Why are you telling me all this? What's the problem? Is there anything that is going to happen that I'm not aware of? Please let me know; don't keep me in suspense. Let me know so I can brace myself for it," Lucinda said.

"I have to go now, and you have to go home too," Anya said as she swiftly turned into a wolf. Then, touching her paws to Lucinda's hand, she shifted backward, bowing down to Lucinda, after which she disappeared into the bush.

With tears in her eyes, Lucinda touched her necklace, and immediately she was home. She knew something was off, and she was determined to find out from Anya what the problem was by tomorrow.

In the morning, Lucinda woke up and went about her duties. She ate her breakfast and retired back to her bedroom without talking to anyone. She was eager for the night to come so she could meet Anya.

As usual, Lucinda appeared at the bush path where she always met Anya before midnight, but when it struck midnight, she heard no howl. She waited patiently, but Anya never came, and when it was almost daybreak, Lucinda had to return home with her heart filled with pain and anger. Where did Anya go? she wondered.

Greg and Maya noticed Lucinda's mood throughout that day and kept asking what was wrong, but she kept it to herself.

She just didn't want to talk about it because she knew they wouldn't understand. She just wanted Anya; she wanted to see her face again. She needed her so badly. Why would she come into her life and leave so soon, without warning?

As she paced about her room, tensed, an idea came to her to go back to their meeting place.

She then walked into the stable and took out the white horse. She mounted and raced off to the bush path where she usually met Anya. When she got there, she dismounted and tied the horse to a tree.

"Anya!!! Where are you?" Lucinda shouted. She called three more times, but all she received in return was a deafening silence.

She went deeper into the bush, hoping to see Anya, but nothing was found. Finally, she came out with tears in her eyes, and untying the horse, she mounted it and rode back home, dejected. When she got home, she took the horse inside and locked the stable as she went into the house.

"Lucinda, you're back; come and have lunch. You have had nothing to eat since morning," Maya said as soon as she sighted Lucinda.

"I'm not hungry, Grandma," Lucinda replied.

"Why? You left this morning having nothing to eat, and now you're saying you're not hungry? What's the problem? You have been moody since morning. Maya has been asking what the problem is, yet you kept mute," Greg chipped in.

"I'm not hungry. I will be in my room, and don't bother checking up on me. I'm fine," Lucinda said as she walked out when Maya called her back.

"You're not fine. Look at your eyes. They are red. You have been crying. What's the problem, girl?" Maya asked.

"I said I'm fine," Lucinda shouted as she ran into her room and banged the door. She made sure she locked the door from inside to stop her grandparents from coming inside. She just wanted to be alone.

After that day, on the following nights, Lucinda would make sure she went to the bush path to wait for Anya, but she never showed up, and it felt like Lucinda was slowly losing herself. She had formed this bond with Anya in such a short time that she couldn't believe she was gone.

Every day, Lucinda would lock herself in her room, thinking about Anya. She would remember everything that happened between them within the past few days that they were together.

Time was going fast, and it was already four months since Anya left Lucinda, but that didn't stop Lucinda from going out to wait for her. She had this hope of meeting her again.

As Lucinda lay down on her bed one particular evening, she felt a decisive breeze blow. A heavy downpour started within a few minutes, which made her get up and walk closer to the window to inhale the husky smell of the saturated soil.

"What is bothering you, my child? You have been like this for the past four months now, with no sign of it abating. So, what is the problem?" her mom's voice chimed through.

"Mom, Anya is gone. It's four months now, and Anya is yet to return. What's keeping her? Have they killed her? I can't even communicate through dreams anymore. It's been nothing since I saw her last. It seemed as if everything went with Anya," Lucinda replied, crying.

"But you wanted her to go. Why are you bothered about her now?" she asked.

"Mom, I wanted her to leave then but not now. After I got to find out who the real Anya is, I fell in love with her. She has a sweet soul, and there is a reason for the people she killed. I simply miss her company. These past four months have never been the same without her," Lucinda replied.

"So, what are you going to do?" the voice asked.

"Nothing. I don't know how to even communicate with Anya. I don't know what to do. The least I can do is just go out there every night to wait for her, believing that someday she is going to come back," Lucinda replied.

"Lucinda, Anya might never come back. You just have to accept it and live your life," Anna said.

"That's the problem. Why does life bring people to me, and just when I have formed a bond with them, life takes them away? Why is that so? Why is my own life designed that way? Why do I always have to lose people I love along the way? I'm tired of it. First, they took you and Dad away from me when I was just ten, and now they have taken Anya away. Who knows who is next, Grandpa or even Grandma? I'm tired of everything," Lucinda said as she wiped the tears from her eyes.

"You miss Anya. I hope she comes back, and if she doesn't, I hope this rain washes away the pain in your heart," Anna consoled.

It was just a matter of time before Anya came back. How long will Lucinda be able to cope with the absence of her parents' voices and the disappearance of Anya?

PART 3

Anya

Chapter One

LUCINDA WANTED PEOPLE SHE LOVED TO STAY

Lucinda wanted people she loved to stay and not leave when she got used to their presence. It had often made her sad, for to her, what was the need to get to know them when they would leave her after she had formed a close bond with them? Could her life have been fated this way, and if so, what could have been the reason for that? She had often wondered.

It had been a year since Lucinda last saw Anya. There were no dreams, communications, feelings, or voices. It felt like when Anya left, everything left with her.

"I knew I wanted her to leave at first because she was killing people, but after getting to spend days with her, I realized Anya had a beautiful soul as well. I miss her; I miss her presence; I miss everything about her help. It seemed she left with my soul," Lucinda muttered, audible enough only to herself and perhaps to the immortals by her side.

"Hey! Lucinda! Is it okay to come in?" said Maya, standing at the door.

"Yeah, sure, Grandma," Lucinda said as she sat up properly.

Maya opened the door and came in. She sat down and touched Lucinda's head.

"Is everything okay? You haven't been out since morning. You know you can talk to me if you want to," Maya said, stroking her hair.

"I'm okay, just that I miss someone special, and I hope she comes back soon," Lucinda replied.

"Ever since we moved in here, I haven't seen you with anyone, so who is the person so special that you miss?" Maya asked, popping her eyes.

"You don't know her, but when she comes back, you'll meet her," Lucinda replied. Maya considered her words in her mind but changed the topic, as her words made little sense. She took that as one of her mysterious words.

"I brought something for you," Maya said, handing a box over to Lucinda as she grabbed it and opened it immediately, eager to see what was inside. It was a beautiful bracelet.

"Thank you, but what's the bracelet for?" Lucinda asked, still holding the box of bracelets.

"Wishing you a very happy birthday, child; it's your eighteenth birthday. I know this isn't as expensive as the necklace you have on your neck, but this is all we have for you," Maya said.

Lucinda hugged her grandmother and whispered a thank you into her ear as Maya got up and helped Lucinda put the bracelet on. Lucinda smiled and said, "I love this!"

"I'm happy you love it. Well, that's just it. I made something special for you; come and eat. You have had nothing to eat since morning," Maya said.

"Thank you, Granny, but right now I'm not hungry, but I promise to eat soon," Lucinda assured.

"Okay, no problem. Your grandpa is tending the horses; make sure you come out soon," Maya said as she stood up and left the room.

"One year already, and Anya isn't back," Lucinda said to herself and sighed as she lay back on the bed.

"Your heart is heavy; your smile is gone; sadness rules over you. You have become too withdrawn. What is bothering you, my child?" Her mom's voice sounded near Lucinda's ears, but she was startled. Lucinda had become used to ethereal voices. Whenever she heard any supernatural voice, she was no longer afraid of surprise—hearing representatives from beyond the physical had become natural to her by now.

"What else but Anya? It's been one year now since she left. Ever since then, I have yearned for her presence, quested to hear her voice, but I have been met with forlorn hope. That's the reason for my sadness. I just want her to come back," Lucinda replied.

"Surely, she will come to you when it's time; I believe so, though I'm not aware when. You know, at first, you repulsed her, just like me; you were even afraid of her at one time, but suddenly you now cherish and love her. Why the sudden love for her?" her mom asked.

"Mom, it's not just sudden. I got to spend days with Anya before she left. She might be a deadly beast, but Anya is one of the best things that can ever happen to anyone who gets to know her. I miss you and Dad, but I also miss Anya. I don't just know why life isn't fair to me. They took you and Dad away, and just when it felt I had formed a bond with someone else, she was nowhere to be found again. Why is my life this way? Why does life keep bringing people into my life when they will still leave? Why the torture? Why does it have to be this way? What did I do wrong?" Lucinda asked, wiping away the tears that were already welling in her eyes.

"You didn't wrong anyone, my child; you didn't. I don't know why it is this way, but I know you will have a reason to smile. Just believe it so," the voice replied.

"What about Dad?" Lucinda asked.

"I'm here, my dear. Happy birthday to you," her dad's voice boomed.

"Thanks, Dad," Lucinda replied, smiling.

"Please be happy, at least for today. You still mean so much to us, and we need to see you happy," he said with tenderness in his voice.

"I will try to," Lucinda replied.

Having said so, Lucinda suddenly stood up, as if urged on by something else, feeling an urge to go out and enjoy the sun. She then walked out of her room to the sitting room, where she met her grandma.

Lucinda told her grandma she wanted to take a stroll down the road, which she obliged her, and off she went. It had been almost two months now since she ventured out of the house. Her grandma was glad that at least she wanted to go out. Lucinda had walked for about fifty meters when she heard a voice behind her.

"You look beautiful."

Lucinda turned to see who the person was, only to meet a girl about her age standing right next to her. Her hair was woolly white, and she had beautiful, starry black eyes.

"Thank you," Lucinda responded as she kept her gaze on the girl standing before her.

"I'm Star, and what's your name?"

"I'm Lucinda."

"That's nice. I live next door to that white house," Star replied.

"Oh, that sounds nice. The white house? That's where I live," Lucinda replied.

"That means we are neighbors. Great! I hope to see you more often," Star said and bade her goodbye without waiting for further conversation with her.

Lucinda smiled as she kept strolling down the road. She was looking around, hoping to see the little girl, Amber, but she had no success in that. Lucinda did not also know where to look for her. Having spent close to one hour outside, she went back home.

When she got back to their house, she walked straight to the kitchen and opened the plate close to the pot where her food was kept. She took the spoon and started eating the food while sitting down on a chair in the kitchen. Halfway through her meal, she became full. She covered the plate and left the kitchen, back to her room.

As soon as she lay on the bed, she remembered the girl next door she had just met outside about an hour before. She was surprised to know that such a girl lived next door to them, wondering why she hadn't met her ever since they came to live in the city. Finding the thought irritating, she waved it away and soon was fast asleep. However, she just had one name on her lips: Anya.

Three days later, Lucinda was out again, and it seemed as if Star was found everywhere Lucinda was, or instead, it was Star's silhouette. Lucinda was startled as she increased her pace, but Star kept coming closer. Finally, she had to give up and accept Star around herself. Star looked nice as a young girl at their first meeting yesterday, but it seemed something was off about her. Lucinda promised herself to find out what it was.

As Lucinda couldn't take it anymore, she returned home. She walked into the garden and sat down. Shortly after, she started hearing some noises, and on turning to the direction the noises were coming from, she saw Star coming into the garden.

"How did you find out I'm here?" Lucinda asked.

"Oh, I normally see you through my window. I saw your grandparents when they were leaving," Star replied.

"Yes, they went out to get a few things that we need here in the house," Lucinda replied.

"That's nice," Star replied, smiling.

"So why are you here?" Lucinda asked.

"Well, I was just bored at home, and I needed someone to talk to," Star replied.

"I have never seen your parents; where are they, or don't they leave the house at all?" Lucinda asked.

"Sadly, I lost my parents a few years ago, and I'm the only one that lives in the apartment. It's so sad, but I miss them. I have been alone ever since they died. I saw when you moved in last year, but I feared getting to know you because I felt you might be the harsh, snobby type, as you were always indoors," Star replied.

"I'm not harsh; neither am I unfriendly, but I just like being on my own. But, first, let me say you're the first human friend that I have ever had since I was born," Lucinda replied.

"What do you mean by 'first human friend'?" Star asked.

"Nothing," Lucinda replied and stared into thin air.

"Something is bothering you; you don't look happy," Star said.

"I just miss my parents. It's been a long time since I saw their faces, and I would do anything to see them again," Lucinda replied.

"Where are they?" Star asked.

"They are dead; they died when I turned ten. Memories of that day are still fresh in my mind. It has been eight whole years without them. The journey hasn't been easy," Lucinda replied as she quickly wiped off the tears trickling down her cheeks.

"I'm so sorry about your parents," Star said.

"Thank you," Lucinda replied.

"So, who are you? Tell me more about yourself," Lucinda asked.

"I need to get going. Your grandparents might be back soon, and I'm not sure they would want to meet me here," Star said as she quickly stood up and walked away.

"Strange," Lucinda muttered, got up, and wanted to go into the house before changing her mind. She had the urge to speak to her parents about Star.

"Mom, Dad, it's been three whole days, and I haven't heard from you. What's happening? If I have annoyed you both, I'm sorry. Have you left too? Even if you both were leaving, you would have told me, but could it be you left without a notice? I already miss your voices," Lucinda was saying to herself.

Ever since she first met Star three days ago, Lucinda had heard from her parents. She was dying to tell them about the girl next door who seemed strange and would always be elusive anytime she asked her questions about herself.

Lucinda was still in the garden when Maya walked in to inform her they were back from the market.

"I got this for you," Maya said, handing some apples to Lucinda.

"Thanks, Granny," Lucinda replied, smiling.

"You're welcome, my darling," Maya said as she left her and walked inside the house, smiling.

Lucinda knew she had all the love she needed, but she wanted more. Was she selfish? No. She was just questing for what every child out there would ask for: their parents' love. She ruminated over these as she chewed her apples.

"How I wish I could see my parents' faces again, even if it was to be for a second one last time. They were in pain before they died; it hurts so much," she said as she stood up and walked into the house to assist her grandmother.

As the days rolled by, Lucinda became more outgoing, meeting with Star often and feeling happier. Maya and Greg were elated that Lucinda wasn't always locked inside like before. But Lucinda kept wondering about the person of her new friend, Star. Though Star made her happy with her grandparents, there was this strange aura around her she couldn't place her fingers on, and she kept evading Lucinda's questions about who she was, but that didn't deter Lucinda from asking. She was a very demanding girl. She was determined to find out who Star was.

Star never visited whenever Greg and Maya were at home. Instead, she would visit when they were out. Occasionally, Lucinda had wanted to know from her why she had never visited anytime her grandparents were around. Still, she gave silly excuses, which gave her room for more significant doubt about who Star was.

"I must find out who you are and what you want," Lucinda said that night as she lay on her bed before she drifted off to sleep.

Chapter Two

HAVE YOU OBSERVED SOMETHING?

"Have you observed something?" Maya asked Greg, who was engrossed in the book that he was reading.

"What's that?" Greg asked, with his eyes still fixed on the book.

"Lucinda is not always at home these days, and I don't know who she goes out to meet. So, I'm getting worried," Maya said.

"Lucinda is eighteen, and she can take care of herself. I observed that too, but I just kept shut; at least she is no longer stuck in her room," Greg replied.

"It's okay for her to make friends; that has been our prayer, but we need to know who her friend is," Maya replied.

Just then, Lucinda walked in with a smile on her face as she greeted her grandparents.

"Lucinda, can you please have a seat? Your grandpa and I want to have a word with you," Maya said.

"Sure," Lucinda replied as she sat down close to her grandpa.

"We observed that you have been leaving the house every day, which explains that you now have a new friend. Don't you think it's okay for us to see her?" Greg replied.

"We're not saying it's wrong for you to have a friend; we are just watching out for you. We are more than happy that you no longer curl up in your room all alone, but at least we would love to see her—maybe invite her over for lunch," Maya replied.

"Oh, you mean Star; she is the only friend I have," Lucinda replied.

"So, where does she live?" Maya asked.

"So, you haven't seen Star? The girl with white hair and dark eyes? Her skin is white," Lucinda replied.

"No, we have not," Greg replied.

"But she always sees you guys when you both are going out. So anyway, just like I said earlier, her name is Star, and she lives next door," Lucinda replied.

"You're joking, right?" Greg asked.

"No, I'm not," Lucinda replied, laughing.

"You have got to be kidding. You're not serious," Maya added.

"Why? What's wrong? I don't understand you both," Lucinda replied.

"That's because there is no one living next door," Maya replied.

"I don't understand. What do you mean by there is no one next door?" Lucinda asked, perplexed.

"No one lives in that house; it's been over a decade now since the last occupant. The man who sold this house to me told me the occupants of that building, the man and his wife, slept and never woke up. So that house has been empty, even before we moved in," Greg replied.

"That's not true; Star always sees you both anytime you and Grandma are leaving together. I have seen her come out of the house countless times," Lucinda replied.

"Have you ever entered inside that house before?" Maya asked.

"No, I've not. We always talk outside or take a stroll together," Lucinda replied.

"That explains it all; your said friend isn't human, most probably. Star isn't human, most likely. No one lives in that house," Maya replied. "This whole thing is still not making sense. I will be in my room," Lucinda said as she abruptly left her grandparents and walked into her room.

"This is serious. She has seen a ghost," Maya said.

"I won't say it's a ghost; maybe someone different who lied that she is living next door," Greg replied.

"I just hope what you said is true," Maya replied as she stood up and walked into the kitchen.

Lucinda sat on her bed as she looked around her room. She became a bit terrified at the possibility of Maya's words.

"Who the hell are you, Star? Where did you come from?" Lucinda muttered.

Her grandma was right. She started soliloquizing. Most probably, Star isn't human, after all. No wonder she never let me into the apartment; no wonder anytime a question is thrown at her about herself, she deflects it. If Star isn't human, then who is she? Why did she come to me? What business does she have with me? Who is she? she concluded as she stood up and went to the sitting room.

"Tell me more about the occupants of the house next door that died," Lucinda said, sitting close to her grandpa.

"The man only told me that after their baby girl disappeared, the next day they died," Greg replied.

"Like how old was the little girl, and what's her name?" Lucinda asked.

"The girl was just ten years old then, and she should be twenty by now since it's been over a decade since it happened. Well, no one knew their child's name because no one saw the child. But what people knew was that day the man and his wife said they were looking for their child; that she was ten years old, and then the next day, they died in their house. Since then, the house has been vacant." Greg replied.

"Do you know the name of the man and his wife?" Lucinda asked.

"Why are you asking all these questions, Lucinda? We weren't here when the whole thing happened. Well, I don't know their names, but the man said the occupants of the house were magicians, but you won't know because they kept it hidden," Greg replied.

"Then how did your informant know since the man had kept it a secret?" Lucinda asked.

"The man was his brother; he sold the house to me because he couldn't afford to stay in this city anymore. He wouldn't enjoy staying in this case because staying here would keep reminding him of his brother. As for the child he had, he never got to see her," Greg replied.

"Something doesn't seem right," Lucinda whispered.

"What do you mean?" Greg asked.

"The girl child they claimed disappeared might be Star because Star mentioned her parents died when she was still little," Lucinda replied.

"Star, or whatever you said her name is, isn't the man's child. Listen, Lucinda, I have always known you to differ from the rest of the world, but whosoever Star is, she is trouble; avoid her," Greg replied.

"That's not a problem. Right now, you and Grandma are the only friends I have. Star's chapter has been closed," Lucinda replied.

"What are you up to?" Greg asked.

"Nothing, I'm not doing anything. Why did you ask?" Lucinda asked as she smiled.

"It's easy to see that your smile isn't genuine. The Lucinda I know will never agree to something without a fight, and you just agreed to something without quarreling over it just now," Greg replied.

"That's because I'm growing. Lucinda is getting older. I'm maturing. I'm eighteen, Grandpa. Let me remind you if you had forgotten," Lucinda replied.

"I haven't," Greg replied, smiling.

"Where is Grandma?" Lucinda asked.

"In the kitchen," Greg replied.

"Okay, let me check up on the horses," Lucinda said as she stood up and walked outside.

When Lucinda got to the stable, she walked in and went straight to the horses. She fed the horses hay cubes and replaced their drinking water, and when she was done, she closed the stable and made her way toward the balcony. As soon as Lucinda sat down, she remembered she had not found Amber. She immediately got up and walked outside, yelling, "Grandpa, I'm coming," and off she went down the street.

"I need to find her. Maybe I can get to ask her some questions," Lucinda muttered under her breath as she went to the spot where she had seen her months back, but she couldn't find her. She then stopped passersby and described Amber, but no one knew her. The day was losing its sun already when Lucinda gave up and turned to journey back home.

On her way home, Lucinda stopped by the oak tree that was close to their building, rested a little, and took fresh air under the branches of the tree, for it had been so long since she did that. She sat down on the ground and leaned against the trunk of the oak tree, closing her eyes and breathing in deeply.

"Have you been looking for me?" As Lucinda opened her eyes to see Amber standing right in front of her, a voice said.

"Amber, how did you know I was looking for you? I had searched everywhere, but I couldn't find you. I even asked people around about you, but nobody seemed to know who you are," Lucinda replied excitedly.

"Well, I didn't want you to meet me where ordinary eyes would see us. I knew you were going to rest on the oak tree, so I had to wait for you here," Amber said as she sat close to Lucinda.

"Is your name Amber?" Lucinda asked.

"If you don't like it, you can still call me something else," Amber replied.

"No, I don't mean that. You have a nice name," Lucinda replied.

"You're looking for me because Anya asked you to find me by all means because I'm going to be of help to you when the time comes. Guess you came a little late; you didn't make a move all this while. You were embittered about Anya's disappearance. I know you miss her, but if you had searched for me immediately after Anya left, maybe you would have easily found out who Star is by now," Amber said.

"You know her? What do you know about her? I need to know, please," Lucinda pleaded.

"All the answers you seek are in the Book of Prophecy; it holds every story you need to know; prophecies that were given even before your birth," Amber replied.

"What prophecies are you talking about? How does it link with me? Right now, the only thing I need to know is all about Star. I need answers on who she is and what she wants from me," Lucinda replied.

"Just like I said earlier, all the answers you seek are in the Book of Prophecies. So, when you get hold of it, you will know who Star is. I would love to tell you, but the truth is I can't, Lucinda. And yes, all the prophecies are linked to you because you're the daughter of the Moon and the Stars," Amber replied.

"I never wanted this life," Lucinda protested as she picked a pebble and threw it in the air.

"This life chooses you. Of course, there are obstacles on the way, but the time will come when you have to choose, and it will be the hardest task ever. But I trust you will make the right decision," Amber replied as she left.

"You're leaving already. I still need answers. I understand it's late, and your people might look for you; how do I find you again?" Lucinda replied.

"By this oak tree; when you get here, I will notice because you have a strong connection that leads people to you. That was why Star could find you so quickly," Amber replied.

"You're a child, but you're not a child," Lucinda replied.

"I'm the seer who has reincarnated four times now. I was here when you were like the other queen and was killed, but I never got to see her face. The same queen is you. You're back again; just that it took you long to come back to Earth. So, I kept reincarnating, hoping that I would someday be opportune to see the queen, and here I am today, standing right next to her," Amber said, smiling.

"Before you go: the Book of Prophecy; how do I get it?" Lucinda asked.

"It is on your own, for what you seek is closer to you. You need to hurry back home. Your grandparents are already worried that you're not yet back. So go home, Lucinda. We will meet some other time," Amber said as she raced off.

Lucinda got up and went back home. Immediately, she pushed the door open and walked inside. Maya threw the first question at her.

"Where are you coming from?" Maya asked.

"Just went for a stroll. I need to wrap my head around what you both told me about the apartment next door," Lucinda replied as she went straight to her room and lay on the bed.

"Star: who is she, and what does she want from me?" Lucinda asked herself.

"Mom, Dad, where are you both? I need you both now. I haven't heard from any of you for a long time now, and it's making me worried. Even if you wanted to leave, you would have said goodbye. Please, I need you both to say something to me. I just want to hear your voice," Lucinda pleaded.

After not hearing any voice, Lucinda removed her necklace and held it in her hands. Next, she brought out the seashell and placed both of them on the bed, but she returned the seashell after some hesitation.

Lucinda held the necklace as she looked at it, and tears trickled down her cheeks.

"The one who gave me the necklace isn't around anymore, and it's heartbreaking. Anya left, and she left with everything. And now I can't even hear from my parents anymore. Life has always been unfair to me; life has taken people whom I love and care about. They rarely get to stay with me. I hope that one day I will have a reason to put this necklace on confidently." Lucinda placed the necklace in the same box with the seashell as she closed it and hid it under her bed.

She lay on the bed, staring at the ceiling before sighing, "This isn't the life I had wanted, but here I am living it."

"Do you think Lucinda is telling the truth about the girl in the next building?" Maya asked.

"Of course, Lucinda wouldn't have come up with fabricated stories. Maybe she might have met the said girl a couple of times, and maybe the girl might have lied to her. She lives in the apartment next to ours," Greg said.

"But how come we haven't seen this girl before? Is she a ghost?" Maya asked.

"The girl has her reasons; she made herself known to Lucinda only, and I don't know why," Greg replied.

"What if someone lives there and we don't know?" Maya asked.

"Maya, the apartment has had no occupants for years now, and I believe whoever the girl is, she isn't coming back again," Greg replied.

Lucinda woke up the following day and went about her routine chores. When she was done, she told her grandparents she was going out. She didn't wait to get their permission as she jogged off.

Soon, she got to the oak tree and sat on the ground, just like she did yesterday, leaning on the trunk.

"Why did you take off your necklace?" Then, as Lucinda turned back to see Amber leaning on the tree by her side, the voice said.

"When did you get here? How come I didn't notice, and how did you know I was here?" Lucinda asked.

"I got here even before you told your grandparents you were going out. So I knew you were coming. But again, you are the daughter of the Moon and the Stars; it wouldn't be wise to keep you waiting," Amber replied.

"Thank you for coming," Lucinda simply said.

"You came here to ask me questions. The answers you seek are just close to you, and it will show itself," Amber replied.

"My parents; I haven't heard their voices for a very long time. I need to know why. Even if they were leaving, at least they should have said goodbye. I need to know what's wrong," Lucinda asked.

Amber stared at Lucinda and blurted out, "The time is fast approaching when you have to choose between your parents and humanity."

"What do you mean?" Lucinda asked.

"You still haven't answered my question; why did you take off your necklace?" Amber asked.

"It reminds me so much of Anya. I miss her, but sadly, it's like I can't see her ever again. She left without a goodbye, and when she left, she took everything—no dreams, no visits from people from the world beyond. Everything just went with her." She paused before continuing almost immediately, "Life has never been fair to me; first, they took my parents, and now they took Anya. Just this little grace of hearing my parents' voices—I don't know what happened to it; suddenly, they are mute. So, what's the use of wearing the necklace when the person who gave it to me is no more? I can't see her; I can't hear her voice. So, I had to remove it because it reminds me so much of Anya, as simple as that," Lucinda replied.

"I understand your pain, but all these are tests. You don't need to worry about Anya because when you need her, she will return," Amber replied.

"Really?" Lucinda became excited, which didn't last long before being replaced by melancholy again. "I need her now. I have always missed her presence ever since she left," Lucinda replied.

"You don't need her now. When you do, she will find her way back to you," Amber replied.

"What about my parents? What do you mean, time is fast approaching when I have to choose between them and humanity? My parents are already dead, and I have found consolation in their voices, so why should I choose between them and humanity?" Lucinda asked, trying hard not to break down.

"I understand you, and I feel your pain, but the prophecy was written years before you were born, and it has to be that way; no one can change it," Amber replied.

"All this isn't fair; all these things that are happening. I am the daughter of the Moon and the Stars, as everyone claimed. Why is my life so difficult? Why do I always lose people just when I have formed a bond with them? Today I'm with you, but I won't be surprised if they also take you away by tomorrow. Those manipulating my life have never valued my happiness. My life is in complete shambles; everything is ruined. I just want to live like every other girl out there in the world, but no, you all have made life so miserable for a little girl like me," Lucinda replied as she stood up.

"Being a leader comes with so many responsibilities, Lucinda. You just have to understand that," Amber said.

"A task which includes taking loved ones away? That's not possible. I'm fed up; I'm tired of this life I'm living. Maybe one day, you all won't have anyone to call the daughter of the Moon and the Stars because I will definitely find a way to end all of this, and even if I don't find a way, I will end this miserable life," Lucinda replied.

"You will not try that," Amber replied.

"Of course, I will. I'm completely fed up, and if at all you are worried about what will happen to my grandparents, that's not an issue as I'm ending my life together with theirs. That way, I will be at peace," Lucinda replied.

"You're angry and…" Amber was about to say.

"Yes, I'm angry; I'm angry about my parents' death; I'm angry that just this means of communicating with them has been stopped. I'm angry about Anya. I'm angry with the way my life is. I'm angry that I became friends with this girl next door, only to find out she isn't real. Maybe she is a ghost that I don't know of. I'm angry about everything; I am angry, and the only thing I'm thinking of now is how to end it all," Lucinda replied.

"This too shall pass; you just need to be strong. These are just mere challenges that will pass away," Amber replied.

"Challenges, you say? I'm tired. I don't want to be involved in any of this anymore," Lucinda replied as she turned to leave, but she stopped, turned back, and said, "And even if I were to choose between saving humanity and my parents, I would choose my parents ten times over."

Lucinda turned and walked back home. She needed to clear her head. When Lucinda got home, she went straight for the stable and took the white horse. As she mounted it, she whispered into the horse's ear before they galloped away. She was going back to their village, her parents' village.

When she got there, she went straight to the riverbank, and sitting down, she started throwing pebbles into the river.

"Surely, this isn't the life I wanted. This isn't how I thought my life was going to be. Everything is changing, and they expect me to move with every crazy change. No way. I became friends with this girl in the next building, and after forming a bond with her, I found she was fake to me. Look at my parents; look at Anya; look at my grandparents. No, I have never had a cheerful story to tell about my life. Things might have started nicely, but now everything will end in ruins. I don't want to be called the daughter of the Moon and the Stars anymore; I don't want to be the Earth Goddess again. Both are useless; they are just useless since I can't even know or see beyond what I'm permitted to see and know. It's simply frustrating. I never wanted this life. I just want to be like every other young girl out there, but my case is the opposite. I'm tired; I'm tired of being unhappy; tired of losing loved ones, and right now, the only thing I can think of is how to end this miserable life. I have always been termed strong by my grandparents, but the truth is, this Lucinda here is getting weaker and weaker every day. I just want to experience lifelong happiness like others. I don't want my life to be filled with challenges, and I don't want people I love leaving me." She paused and threw some pebbles into the water before continuing.

"Goddess of this water, I don't know if you can hear me; I need your help; I need someone to help me and end all this, else I might wake up one morning and end it all myself. So maybe you can't hear me, but you all were quick to come during Anya's time with me, and now you're all quiet," Lucinda said as tears dripped down her cheeks. "Free me, let me go! Release me! I'm tired! I don't want to be the daughter of the Moon anymore!" Lucinda shouted, holding her head as she shrieked even more.

"This isn't the life I wanted. Maybe it's the life my mom wanted, but you all should have waited for me to grow older and ask for my permission first. My mom made a simple request; she was just a poor, naïve woman who wanted to give everything to her child. She was merely dreaming, never knowing that her request could be granted. I'm one hundred percent sure that she wouldn't want me to be in this mess today. It was just a harmless wish. Now, I'm sure you were the ones that took my parents away. You were the ones that made it possible for me to hear them. I am consoled with just hearing their voices, yet suddenly you also made that cease. Just tell me, why won't I tire of this life? Anya came, and suddenly she was nowhere to be seen. Why is that so? And now the first friend I ever had, I woke up only to discover that she wasn't real, or should I say, she was just a figment of my imagination. Tell me, why won't I be angry? Why won't I be tired of the recent happenings in my life? I'm fed up, and I want to live like any other girl out there, but you all make things difficult for me. I do not wish to be one of you if I had ever been. Take the title you gave to me. This young girl here is tired, and she wants to go. You all have to end it; else, I will end it myself. How does it make sense that I will have to choose between my parents and humanity? What sort of hard choice is that? I will choose my parents ten times over. Please, please, please; I wasn't aware when this whole thing started. Please, just take it back. Free me; I'm tired!" Lucinda shouted as she covered her face with her two palms and started saying in between sobs.

"Lucinda does not want to be involved with this anymore. She isn't that strong anymore. This Lucinda is tiring of all the drama that has been happening in her life, and right now, the only thing she needs is her peace." She bent down and hid her head in between her legs.

But after a long while, she stood up and went straight to where she tethered her horse, untied it, and mounted it while saying, "I remember when my mom was in this body; and now I can't hear from her anymore. This life is so cruel, and I have done nothing to deserve it." And having said this, she galloped away.

Chapter Three

WHILE INSIDE HER ROOM

While inside her room, Lucinda was busy arranging her clothes. She had been indoors for three straight days without venturing out. She had been melancholic again, sitting all day, mourning her parents and her loss of Anya.

"Did you miss me?" a voice said as Lucinda turned to see Star right inside her room.

"The last time I checked, my room was locked. So how did you get in?" Lucinda asked. She was still busy with her clothes but casting a furtive glance at Star.

"Because I'm Star; I can do anything I want," said Star.

"Really? I thought you were the girl from the next apartment. Do girls from the next building appear and disappear at will? How did you get into my room? Who are you, and what do you want because it's obvious you have lied to me all these times?" Lucinda replied as she finally sat on her bed, clutching some clothes in her hands.

"Star, that's the name," Star replied, smiling.

"Please spare me. I already know your name—Star, the girl who lied to me so that she could come close to me. I have no time. What do you want?" Lucinda asked, clearly infuriated.

"You have been here crying like a baby because you haven't heard your parents' voices for months now. Well, I caged their spirit; at least that's the only power I have left, and I used it wisely. So if you want your parents to talk to you again, I just need you to uncage my body. I need to be free; I want to return to Earth," Star replied.

"Is that all?" Lucinda asked.

"Yes, I knew you would comply; it's very easy, the only…"

"Just keep shut, Star," Lucinda bellowed.

"You appeared in my room from God knows where, and you are here to tell me what to do and what not to do. You dare to cage my parents, and for months I haven't heard their voices, and now you're here to blackmail me. Dream on. Do you think you can walk in here and tell me what to do? Do you think you can make me do things against my wishes? You must be joking. Though you have caged my parents, I just need to make you understand it won't make me free your body or whatever you're talking about. Rather, I'll find a way to end your life forever and make you cease to exist in this world for daring to deceive and blackmail me," Lucinda thundered.

"You will never hear from your parents again," Star calmly said.

"I'm Lucinda. That's the name my mom gave to me. I am the daughter of the Moon and the Stars even before I was born into this Earth. I do things my way, and if you think you can threaten me by using my parents, then it's a failed mission. My parents will come back when I need them! You're such a pathetic loser," Lucinda replied.

"I know how close you are to your parents. You think about them every day; you would run back to me to do my bidding. It's just a matter of time," Star replied.

"I guess you have to wait forever because your wish will never be granted," Lucinda replied.

"Then we shall see," Star replied and disappeared.

Lucinda sighed as she continued arranging her clothes. When she was done, she placed them carefully in her wardrobe as she went back to her bed and lay down. She stared at the ceiling as memories of the time she spent with her parents started playing in her mind. Star was right; her parents were everything to her, though they were dead. But that which Star wanted would never happen. So, she would look for other means to bring her parents back.

"Star went too far by caging my parents. She knew what was going to hurt me. That's why she did what she did. But I will not set her free.

Rather, I will find a way to set my parents free. I didn't enjoy enough time with my parents when they were alive, and now that they are no more, they won't still allow me to enjoy their voices. Fate is trying so hard to break me down, knowing very well that my parents are my source of hope and strength.

They have done nothing to deserve what has come to them. And as for Star, she has hit me with a stone today, and I'm already so hurt and bleeding. During my time here, I will end her life. If my parents can die when they have done nothing wrong, then people like Star don't deserve to live, both spirit and body," Lucinda said as she stood up and walked out of the room.

"Where are you going to?" Greg asked as he noticed Lucinda was leaving the house.

"I just want to take a stroll," Lucinda replied.

"Are you telling me the truth, or are you just trying to deflate my question? Where exactly are you going to?" Greg asked.

"I just need to meet up with someone, but for the record, the person isn't Star. I'm going out to meet a kid I met in the market, whom I enjoy being with," Lucinda replied.

"What's her name?" Greg asked.

"Amber, that's her name," Lucinda replied.

"Reminds me of the great seer; her name was Amber too. I had wanted to meet her when she was alive, but I guess I was late; she died. That was years back," Greg replied.

Lucinda turned and sat close to her grandpa, suddenly animated. "Tell me more about this seer," Lucinda asked, her eyes flashing excitedly. "I thought you were going out?" Greg asked.

"That can wait, but at least tell me who the seer was," Lucinda said.

"Amber was her name. She was so beautiful. That's what many who saw her said. She never got old; she was always young, though she had lived for many years. She sees everything the ordinary eyes can't see. She can predict what will happen in the future; she is powerful. People who visited her said she was always sad because she hadn't met the daughter of the Moon and the Stars. No one knew who the daughter of the Moon and the Stars was. But one thing was certain; if you meet Amber the seer, she would always proffer a solution to your problems. And one day, she died in her sleep. I was hurt because I made plans to see her after you were born. I wanted to ask questions about the birthmark you had," Greg replied.

"My birthmark? Why did you say so?" Lucinda asked.

"Because I saw the birthmark change its position in the midnight with a full moon. I was with you there! I was dumbfounded; I wanted to tell your mother, but I knew she would not believe me, and that was when I said I was going to meet Amber, the great seer, hoping she would have answers to my questions. Still, unfortunately, on my arrival at her place, I was told she died the night before," Greg replied.

"Strange," Lucinda said, folding her hands.

"That was when I knew something was off. You were a special child, but I needed more explanations. Sadly, I didn't get that. So, I lived with that all my life. I didn't tell anyone because no one would ever believe me. But I'm happy you have grown to be the sweetest soul on Earth. Though your parents might have left early, I knew you were strong; and that someday life is going to return all that they took from you," Greg replied.

"I hope so; I hope life returns everything. I will be patiently waiting for that day. The darkness has stayed way too long, and it took so many things away. Right now, I only wish for the light to come because I know it's bringing all the things I lost," Lucinda replied.

"Do you care for a hug?" Greg asked.

"Sure, Grandpa," Lucinda said as she wrapped her hands around her grandpa's body.

"See you later. I promise to be home soon," Lucinda replied as she stood up and left the house.

When Lucinda got to the oak tree, she sat down and waited patiently for Amber. Thirty minutes had already gone, but there was no sight of Amber. Lucinda stood up, feeling dejected as she walked away, when a voice called her back. She turned to see Amber running toward the oak tree.

"Grandma wouldn't let me, so I had to sneak out. Sorry that I kept you waiting," Amber said as soon as she got to where Lucinda was standing. She was panting.

"She came; she is the real reason I haven't heard from my parents for a long time," Lucinda replied.

"Yes, she is! Star wants you to free her body. Only then will she free your parents. Her spirit is just wandering here on Earth, and the only power she had was what she used to cage your parents. So, tell me, will you set her free?" Amber asked.

"I won't set her free, never! She should have known by now that no one tells Lucinda what to do. I do things my way, and she made the worst mistake when she picked my parents and caged their voices. She made the worst mistake ever. So, I will not set her free. Rather, I'm going to destroy her. And about my parents, I will find a way to set them free. Star might have her powers, but I'm one hundred percent sure that she isn't stronger than me. She messed with the wrong person," Lucinda replied.

"I don't know where this courage came from, but I like the new Lucinda," Amber replied.

"She knows how much I loved my parents. She knows my parents were everything to me. She knows I draw strength from the voice of my parents, and she caged their voices, and she came back to give me conditions. One thing is certain: Star isn't human. Sure. Who is she then?" Lucinda asked.

"You are close to solving the puzzle. You have realized that Star isn't human. I'm glad you realized that quickly," Amber said.

"My grandpa mentioned the name…"

"Amber the seer," Amber said, cutting Lucinda short. "How did you know?" Lucinda asked.

"How wouldn't I know? I am she. Yes, when he wanted to meet me, I was already dead by the time he came, but I'm back now. You won't understand, Lucinda, so it's of no use explaining to you.

When I was born again a few years back, the woman who bore me died at childbirth, and people who came to see me said I look like Amber, the seer that died many years ago; and that's why I was named Amber. But I am that Amber who died many years ago. I'm back to life. I came back just to see you, and I'm glad I have been opportune to see you. Now back to why we are here: you're here because you want to know who Star is and to ask questions about the birthmark based on what your grandpa told you. Yes, the Stars and the Moon changed their position on your body, but what your grandpa failed to notice was that one Star was missing, and that was the day the people from the other world acknowledged your birth. Four Stars are still on your back, which shows you can still come back to this Earth four times. Each time you come back, one Star will miss until all disappear, and when that time comes, another will be chosen to be the daughter of the Moon and the Stars." She stopped talking and was observing Lucinda with teary eyes.

"Your heart is heavy, and you're in pain. Star has touched you where she shouldn't, and you want nothing but revenge. The last time we met, I told you a time would come when you would have to choose between your parents and saving humanity. Life has taken so many things from you; darkness is hovering around, but once Star is dealt with and cleared from the picture, the light will come back, and it's going to bring all that has been taken from you. Believe me," Amber said.

"That was the exact words my grandpa used just some minutes ago before I left the house, but do you think all that was taken from me? Do you think they will ever be returned?" Lucinda asked.

"By that, you mean your parents? Just remember, life will return whatever was taken from you. You don't have to know how," Amber said.

"How do I stop Star? I need help," Lucinda asked.

"Hmmm. Well, I can't help you with that. It's left for you to figure that out on your own. You can only fight the battle. And even if you need help, Anya is the only one who can help you out, not me," Amber replied.

"Hmmm. It's already a year since Anya left, and I don't know when she will return. How can she be the only one to help me out of this situation when I haven't seen her or even dreamed of her? Though you said Anya would come again, that is left to be believed. I'm not sure she will come back," Lucinda replied.

"Don't be so sure," Amber replied.

"I'm sure," Lucinda replied.

"Have you forgotten she told you she would come when you need her? Anya always keeps to her word. The only truth here is that you don't need Anya now. When you do, she will come; and she will run back to you," Amber said.

"What does Star want from me? I need to know," Lucinda replied.

"I might be a seer, but there are things I do not know; things that are meant for the eyes and ears of the daughter of the Moon and the Stars. But one thing I'm sure of is that the answers you seek are just closer to you. The answers you seek are in the Book of Prophecy, the only book that has been locked for centuries, and you're the only one who has the key to it. Find it, and there you will know who Star is and what she wants from you and how you can destroy her, because if you set Star free, doom and chaos shall reign upon Earth; and you won't be spared, either," Amber said and ran off. She didn't wait to listen to Lucinda speak.

"Gone! She didn't even wait to answer me or to direct me. The Book of Prophecy? Where do I even look for it? I do not know how to get the book, and talk about the key. I don't have the key to anything. This is going to be a bigger hard nut to crack," Lucinda said as she sighed and started on her way back home.

"So, did you meet her?" Greg asked as soon as he saw Lucinda step into the house.

"Yes, I did, and I'm home. Where is Grandma?" Lucinda asked.

"She is taking a nap," Greg replied.

"Can I ask you something? Don't freak out, please," Lucinda pleaded.

"Sure, what's the question?" Greg asked, dropping his glass of coffee.

"What do you know, or is there anything like the Book of Prophecy?" Lucinda asked.

"Who told you about that?" Greg asked.

"No, I just overheard some people talking about it on the street, and I felt I should ask you, hoping you can tell me more about it," Lucinda replied.

"Why do I feel you're lying?" Greg said.

"I'm not lying, Grandpa. I'm telling you the truth," Lucinda replied.

"The Book of Prophecy is said to contain prophecies and findings on things we don't think exist in this world. It is one of the most powerful and dangerous books ever. My father told me that the one who was once in possession of the book used it for evil. According to him, the book had always been kept in an ancient temple, and the only one who could read and understand the writings in the book was the priest of the temple, who changed from being good and started using it for evil. And one day, while amid prayers, the book closed by itself, and every effort was made to open it, but it proved abortive. It was left there and forgotten. Shortly after that, the priest died, and a few weeks after he was buried, the Book of Prophecy went missing. No one cared to look for it because it was locked, and no one could understand the writings, and since then, history has forgotten about it. So, can you see why I'm surprised that you are even asking me about it?" Greg said.

"But Grandpa, how can one find the book? Surely, it must be somewhere," Lucinda asked.

"You can never find the Book of Prophecy. It's not possible. It went missing from the mortals' eyes years back. My father used to say that the one who holds the key to unlock that book hasn't been born, and when she is born, the book will find its way to her," Greg replied.

"It means the one who holds the key is a woman, and that's she?" Lucinda contemplated that for a while before continuing, "How did your father know it will be a girl?"

"That I didn't ask him. Maybe if he appears here now, you can ask him," Greg said, laughing as Lucinda joined in the laughter.

"Alright, Grandpa, I will be in my room," Lucinda said as she stood up and walked into her room.

She lay on the bed as she stared at the ceiling, contemplating too many things that surrounded her life. Suddenly, she started soliloquizing.

"Book of Prophecy! Where will I find this book? Amber said the answers I seek are closer to me and that the answers are in the Book of Prophecy, and now Grandpa is saying that the book can't be found. What will I do now? I'm so confused. I just want my mom and dad free and for Star to vanish from the surface of this Earth and even in the world beyond. I want her case to be a closed chapter forever. Where do I find answers? Where do I find that book? I need to place my hand on that book; else I might never hear from my parents again. Anya, where are you? Please come back if you can hear me; I need you right now. I don't think I can do this on my own. I don't think I can win this. I'm confused. The road is getting darker, and I need a little ray of light. I don't want to give up, but I don't know if I can continue. My strength is failing me. My parents' souls are engaged right now, and I need to set them free. Why is life so unfair to me? If I'm the one to unlock this book, I need it to come to me right now," Lucinda said as tears trickled down her cheeks.

"Wake up, dear," Maya said, tapping Lucinda. She had slept off while thinking about the current travail of her parents caused by Star.

"What's the time, Granny?" Lucinda asked.

"It's 5 p.m. You need to wake up so you can also sleep at night," Maya said and left the room.

Lucinda did as she said and stood up, stretched her clothes before leaving the room. She went through the back door to get to the garden. She ran her hands through her hair as she thought about her mom and dad while she sat there.

"I miss you, Mom and Dad. I know you both can hear me even though you can't talk to me. Grandpa and Amber's exact words were life to me: that everything I've lost shall be returned. I believe that. I know somehow you two are going to come back to me," Lucinda said. After muttering these words, she glanced at the building where Star said she lived and had an inexplicable urge to search it out.

Lucinda got up and started towards the building. She got to the back door and pushed it open, and it opened.

"There is no harm checking to see what's in this building that has been locked for years now," Lucinda said as she walked into the apartment.

Everywhere was dark, and Lucinda could barely see a thing. Finally, she saw a bookshelf standing at the corner of the parlor, and she checked it out. As she walked closer to it, Lucinda turned immediately when she heard a noise, only to see it came from rats. She stiffened a bit.

"The books here are many," Lucinda said as she ran her hands over the books.

Suddenly, she heard her name from a distance and knew it was her grandmother calling. She quickly hurried out of the apartment as she closed the door behind her, sneaking back into the garden and sitting down as she shouted, "Grandma, I'm here."

"Where have you been? I have been looking for you. Dinner is ready," Maya said as she entered the garden to find Lucinda sitting on the stone chair.

"Alright, Grandma," Lucinda said as she stood up and followed her grandmother inside. Her food was already on the table as she took the plate of food and sat close to her grandpa.

"Lucinda was asking me about the Book of Prophecy," Greg began, breaking the silence.

"Where did you hear that from?" Maya asked.

"Someone was talking about it, so I asked Grandpa about it, but by the way, do you know where the book can be found?" Lucinda asked.

"You can never find that book; that's the truth. People have long forgotten it," Maya replied.

"So, there is no way I can get hold of it?" Lucinda asked.

"Even if you get hold of it, there is no way you can understand the language; the language is from the world beyond, and I don't think the girl who is said to have the key to open the book is even here on Earth yet. But perhaps she is here, and perhaps she isn't here either," Maya replied.

"That's saddening," Lucinda replied.

"Or is there anything you're not telling us?" Maya chipped in, eyeing Lucinda from the corner of her eye.

"That's true. Lucinda!" Greg said, also eyeing Lucinda at the same time.

"It's nothing. It's just that I wanted to know more about the book, and maybe I can even read it, but since you said I couldn't read it, then let it be. I only overheard some people talking about it; that's all," Lucinda replied.

"It's okay. No problem," Greg replied as they all ate their food silently.

Lucinda took the plates into the kitchen immediately after they were done and washed them up. Her grandparents were sitting down and discussing when she bade them goodnight and walked into her room.

Once inside her room, she walked straight to her window and popped her head out, staring up at the sky above. But unfortunately, there was no single star in sight, and the Moon was half full.

"Don't you want to release me so I can set your parents free? I know you miss them. I can tell you how to free my body." It was Star speaking behind Lucinda, standing there gesticulating with her hands.

"You made the worst mistake of your life when you picked my parents as bait to get to me. I'm sorry, but you just picked a fight that is bigger than you; and just for the record, I will never set you free. You can meet someone else to do that. Oh, now I remember, no one can set you free except me; you need me. I'm asking you nicely, free my parents, else when the time comes, I won't hesitate to erase your entire existence from the surface of this Earth and even in the world beyond. Please don't push me too far, Star. I have limits to which I can endure things. You wouldn't like me when I'm angry," Lucinda said as Star vanished immediately, an action that made Lucinda even more bent on finding the absolute truth about Star and why she had to be the one to set her free.

She felt deep inside her that the answers she was looking for were right there in that house. She was determined to go back and search around, hoping to lay her hands on something that could explain who Star was, and with that, she knew she would try to find out how to erase her chapter forever from existence. After staying for some more minutes, she went to her bed, lay down, and covered herself after Star had vanished.

"Getting to know how to get rid of you might take months; it might take years, but one thing is certain: once I find out, I'm getting rid of you, and I'm bringing my parents back. You know what will hurt me so much, and that's why you went for my parents. But, Star, you're going to lose this battle," Lucinda muttered as she closed her eyes and drifted off to bed.

Chapter Four

LUCINDA HAD WOKEN UP

Lucinda had woken up around 5 a.m. as she slowly tiptoed out of her room with the lantern in her hand. At night, she couldn't sleep. She was disturbed that the Book of Prophecy could be in that house. She had this eerie, though inexplicable, feeling that she was right about this.

As she picked up her lantern, she went towards the back door and gently opened it. Walking outside, she was determined to see what was inside the house.

She walked towards the back door, pushed it open, and walked inside. She lifted the lantern high so she could see. The whole building was covered in dust and cobwebs, just as it was the first time she came. She didn't waste time but went straight to the bookshelf to see if she could find anything related to Star. She instantly picked up a book that looked strange. On the book's cover was inscribed "The Prophecy." Lucinda gasped at having picked the book.

Her heart palpitated and raced swiftly. Could this be the book? she wondered. She knew her grandpa said the book had been missing for years; so obviously, there was no way this book could be here.

So, she thought as she took the book out from the shelf. Apart from the words "The Prophecy," the cover also had the symbol of the Moon and Stars on it. When Lucinda tried opening the book, it wouldn't open.

Then she realized the book was the original Book of Prophecy that had been missing, according to her grandpa.

Lucinda held the book in one hand as she sneaked out of the apartment and went straight to her home. She crept inside and went to her room. Luckily, her grandparents weren't up yet.

Lucinda placed the book on her bed as she brought out a piece of cloth and wiped the dusty cover clean.

"How do I unlock this book because I need to know what's inside?" Lucinda muttered, after which she bent down and took out the box she had hidden under her bed that contained the necklace. She opened it and took out her necklace. Then, raising it, she stared at the symbol on the Book of Prophecy.

"This is the same symbol and size. This book is indeed the book that has been missing for years," Lucinda assured herself. She thought of placing the necklace close to the symbols on the book cover.

Lucinda hesitated for a few seconds before going ahead with her intuition. She noticed a strange sound before the book suddenly unlocked as she did that. Lucinda smiled and nodded her head gently with glee.

"So, my necklace is the key to unlocking this book? Woo. Wonderful! Now is the time to read," Lucinda said as she stood up and quickly locked her room. She placed the necklace back inside the box as she hid it and sat up properly before opening the Book of Prophecy.

Flipping through the pages of the book, she saw a drawing of a monstrous beast, the "Deadliest Star."

The lettering was strange, but it baffled Lucinda that she could still read and understand it. After observing the image for a split second, she turned to the next page, knowing that the beast's description would be there.

"Deadliest Star might appear as a pretty young girl to deceive and kill as many as she wants. But unfortunately, she is just the deadly monster whose image is on the first page, the demon that can't be killed so easily. Star has lived for centuries but was sent into hibernation by the first daughter of the Moon and the Stars. Her spirit wanders about, but her body has been trapped and hibernated. The only one who can set Star free is Lucinda, the third daughter of the Moon and the Stars. Star's spirit will come for Lucinda when she is of age to deceive her into freeing her body. Lucinda has five lives, but Star would come during her second life. For Star to bring doom and chaos to the world, she must feast on the blood of the one who owns the magic seashell, Lucinda, daughter of Ann and Phil. If Lucinda ever releases Star, Lucinda must die, and sadly she won't come back to life the third time because Star will make sure it doesn't happen." Lucinda paused momentarily.

Her entire life had been written in a book, including the names of her parents, even before they were born. Beads of sweat appeared on her brow.

"I'm Lucinda, and this is my second life. So, I have three more lives. Hmmm, now I remember. The girl who looked like me told me not to make my powers visible to human eyes. That was during my first life, and that is why Amber said on the night of the full Moon, Grandpa didn't notice that one Star was missing, and now it's just three, which means three more lives are left," Lucinda thought silently, nodding continuously for some seconds before continuing.

"So, Star is a demon. It's not just about releasing my grandparents. She would come for me because, for her to achieve her aim, she had to feast on my blood. I am the one in possession of the seashell. Wow! Things are making sense now," Lucinda said as she closed the book.

"This is the book that has been missing for years, and I'm the girl child that Prophecy said will be the one to unlock it. That girl child is me. My mom gave birth to Lucinda, but she doesn't know she gave birth to another human being. She brought a queen to this Earth. If I don't release Star, I will never hear from my parents, and if I release her, I will have to die. This is tricky. What do I do now? Something has to be done," Lucinda said as she stood up and opened her windows as a glimmer of the sunray came right in.

Lucinda hid the book where her grandparents wouldn't find it as she left the house. She was going to the oak tree. Lucinda couldn't wait. Some questions needed to be answered. Maybe Amber might have the answers to those questions.

Lucinda was surprised to see Amber resting her head on the oak tree. She was waiting for her.

"When did you get here?" Lucinda asked immediately as she got closer to Amber.

"I knew you were going to find the book, and I knew you would come to meet me this morning to ask questions," Amber replied.

"Star is a demon," Lucinda burst out.

"I know," Amber said.

"You knew all about this, and you never told me?" Lucinda asked.

"I told you what I knew. Even if I had told you, there are still things I wouldn't have said because I don't know them. I told you all the answers you seek are in that book, including everything about yourself," Amber replied.

"I can't free Star. She would come for my blood because I have the seashell, but I need to know how to free my parents, and I need to know how to end and erase Star forever from existence," Lucinda said.

"You only read the first page about Star, and you're already here to ask me questions? Patience! Patience! Why don't you read more and try to find out things yourself?" Amber replied, but Lucinda thought otherwise.

"It is called the 'Book of Prophecy,' so it contains prophecies of what will happen in years. But it doesn't contain solutions on how to go about the problem. So, I need your help, Amber. I need to know what to do to stop all this," Lucinda pleaded.

"I'm only a seer, and I can only offer solutions when I know the solutions to the problem, but in this case, it is only the book and her that can help you," Amber replied.

"Who is her? Who are you referring to? What's her name, and where can I find her?" Lucinda asked.

"You're just funny. You can't find her. She will come when you need her, but now I don't think you need her. That's why she isn't here yet," Amber replied.

"But you know I need her now. I need to talk to her, whoever she is, so long as she has the answers to my questions. I need answers to this predicament. I need to know how to free my parents first," Lucinda replied.

"When you have read the important prophecies about yourself, then she will come. But for now, you need to go back home and read everything. And put your necklace away, but your bracelet is still on your wrist." So, Amber observed as she looked quizzically at Lucinda.

"The bracelet is from my grandmother; I can't remove it. She is just like my mother, and as for the necklace, it's a gift from Anya. Unfortunately, she is not here, so what's the need to put it on when the person who gave it to me has been away for about a year now? The necklace reminds me so much of Anya. So, I had to put it away, and yes, it was the necklace that unlocked the book," Lucinda replied, sighing.

"Put the necklace back for your safety. You need it now. I might be a seer, but I can't understand the writings in that book. You're the only one who can understand the writing. You're the girl child the world has been waiting for. You need to go back home. Your grandparents will be awake any moment now. The journey has just started," Amber said as she stood up and walked away.

"And she didn't tell me about the one that needs to help me. Amber is so strange. I wonder if her grandmother knows the girl she is living with isn't a child, but a grown-up stuck in the body of a child," Lucinda said as she sighed and walked away.

Lucinda got home and sneaked back into her room. Her eyes were already getting weak. She knew she had to sleep, as she didn't sleep throughout the night. By the time she woke up, it was already noon. She quickly stood up as she hurriedly had her bath, after which she dressed up and went to the sitting room to see her grandparents.

"You didn't wake me up?" Lucinda asked, looking at her grandmother.

"Yeah, because I didn't want to disturb you, as I felt you slept late yesterday," Maya replied.

"Well, she came into the room to check if you were still breathing," Greg offered.

"Your food is in the kitchen," Maya said as Lucinda smiled and walked to the kitchen to pick up her food. She then walked back to her room and locked the door behind her. Lucinda placed the food on her bed. Next, she took out the Book of Prophecy.

She flipped through the pages as she came across the words: **"ERASED FROM THE WORLD BEYOND."** And she started reading as her heart raced.

"For years, questions were being asked on how to erase Star from the world beyond, but the only one who has such powers is yet to be born. Her name is Lucinda, and she knows the trick on how to erase Star from this world. For the daughter of the Moon and the Stars to erase Star from this world, she will need the beast's help, three in one.

Star is a demon who must be erased by all means because if Star eventually wakes from hibernation, it means doom for the whole world."

"I still don't get it. Three-in-one beast? Why is this getting more complicated?" Lucinda asked, turning the pages of the book.

"Bring back the beast, and then you will find the key to how to destroy Star. Her presence is needed in the ritual."

After reading this, Lucinda kept flipping through the book's pages, but it was all blank. "No, no, no," Lucinda cried, almost at the brink of tears. She became frustrated.

"This can't be happening. Why are the remaining pages blank? I still need answers. How do I free my parents? That's the most important thing to me right now," Lucinda cried as she ran her hands through her hair and sighed. Since she knew she couldn't do anything else about it, Lucinda hid the book back as she gobbled her food.

When she was through, she took the plate and went straight to the kitchen, washed it, and placed it correctly on the rack before walking to the exit door.

"Where are you going?" Greg, who was seated on the couch, asked.

"I need to see someone; I'll explain when I get back," Lucinda said as she fled the house.

She went straight to the oak tree and was surprised to see Amber waiting for her. She sat on the ground with her back against the tree trunk.

"The book didn't tell me how to free my parents, and the remaining pages of the book are blank. I need answers, please. Setting my parents free is the most important thing to me right now. Nothing else matters to me at this moment," Lucinda said as soon as she sat down.

"The book has already covered the message you need to know for now. It is a book that opens to you as you need to know. It is left to you to bring back the three-in-one beast. Perhaps once her presence is sensed, the rituals on how to erase Star will be revealed in the book," Amber replied.

"And that's another thing I don't understand. Who is this three-in-one beast? Who is he or who is she? This isn't fair, from one thing to the other. As much as I want to erase Star from this world, I also need to set my parents free. They have done nothing to deserve to be caged by Star. I need to hear their voice even if I can't see them again," Lucinda said.

"You're so quick to forget; you can't tell me you do not know the three-in-one beast. You have met her, and you still have to bring her back to reveal the rituals to you. I believe after the ritual is done, your parents will be free, and you will hear from them again. But for now, bring back the beast," Amber said.

"I have met no three-in-one beast, and I don't know how to bring anyone. This task is tiring. I'm getting tired and fed up. Why does everything around me revolve around complex tasks? Why do I live my life in perpetual pain and agony? Why do I have to go through so much stress in doing something that would benefit the whole world?" Lucinda said.

"Do you want to free Star? If Star ever wakes up from hibernation, the whole world is in ruin. Perhaps it's time for you to ask your grandparents questions about the demon that once terrorized this world, the demon that had the mark of a Star on her. You can ask them. The beast's presence must be felt for the rituals to be revealed to you. So, bring her back, Lucinda, and stop whining. You're not a baby anymore. If you're the daughter of the Moon and the Stars, then act like one and stop whining like a child," Amber said as she turned and walked out on Lucinda.

"It is obvious she is angry," Lucinda muttered and trudged back home.

"Your time is ticking; when will you set me free?" It was Star's voice, with a bit of tease in her tone. Lucinda knew it was Star, so she didn't bother looking back.

"And what makes you think I will free you?" Lucinda replied.

"I have your parents under chains. I can hurt them if I have to. I'm already running out of patience; free me!" Star bellowed.

"I doubt if you can even hurt a fly. I'm pretty sure that the only power left in your system was what you used to stop my parents' voices from reaching me. You have no powers left. Your body is still in hibernation, so you can virtually do nothing. Only when you're free from hibernation can you talk about hurting people, but for now, you're powerless. You need me to free you and my blood so you can continue existing. So, listen, you don't have to threaten me with hurting my parents because I know you can't!" Lucinda shrilled.

For a second, Star was taken aback on hearing these words, but she suddenly exclaimed, "Whatever you're planning, you will fail. I'm promising you that. You can't erase me from this world," Star said, indignant.

"I hope you know the power to erase you from this world lies in my very hands. So, don't try my patience, Star. Don't push me to the wall because I promise I'll make life unbearable for you before I annihilate you, and let me warn you, don't you ever appear in my path to tell me anything about releasing you. Your case is a closed chapter. You have terrorized the world enough. The first Lucinda could put you into hibernation; the second Lucinda, which is me, will erase you from this world and the world beyond," Lucinda replied as she watched Star disappear right in front of her, with a hissing sound.

"Imagine the guts," Lucinda said as she sighed and continued walking home. She stepped inside, and her grandpa was sitting on the rocking chair, relaxing.

"You're back," Greg remarked as soon as Lucinda sat down close to him.

"Tell me about the demon that terrorized the world years ago, the demon with the mark of a Star on her body," Lucinda fired at Greg as soon as she sat down.

"Who told you that, Lucinda, because I'm sure you didn't hear it from the mouth of the passersby?" Greg asked, with eyes popping out in surprise.

"I was lucky to meet Amber, the seer. She told me about it. She said she would meet you when the time was right. Amber is back again, and it takes only the special ones to know she is the seer who lived years back then. Amber died and reincarnated back to life. She is on a mission close to finding that which had made her keep coming back to Earth," Lucinda replied.

Greg dropped his hand when he heard what Lucinda said before asking her, "What did you just say?"

"Lucinda…" Greg shrieked and was about to say more before Lucinda gently cut him off.

"Grandpa, please just tell me about the demon. I need to know. Don't start thinking that I'm going crazy again, please," Lucinda said. Greg considered her words, looked at her one more time before deciding to let her know what he knew.

"I was little then, but I knew what was happening around us. The demon was called Star because she had the mark of a Star on her body. She killed many. Property was lost. People lived in fear. Everyone was scared. I never got to see her because my parents ensured I was inside.

She was close to destroying this world when she engaged in a fierce battle with a young lady. The young lady looked like a normal mortal but possessed strong magical powers. Her name was Lucinda. She could defeat the demon, which she later placed into hibernation, which is more like a sleeping spell, after which Star's body disappeared. According to Lucinda, it's actually in a place where humans can't set their eyes on her. When Lucinda questioned why she didn't kill Star the demon, she replied that the one who holds the power to kill Star was yet to be born. That's the little I know, and until today no one has seen the body of Star, and history is slowly forgetting about her," Greg replied.

"Interesting," Lucinda replied.

"Don't say interesting because if you were alive during that time, you wouldn't have survived it. Now tell me where you saw Amber, the seer," Greg asked, still wide-eyed.

"She came to me because I'm special. She said I'm the daughter of the Moon and the Stars. She also said the exact words you used, that light is coming to bring back everything it took from me," Lucinda replied.

"Then why can't I see her?" Greg said.

"When the time is right, you will. I know you believe me," Lucinda said.

"Of course; I believe in you. No one knows the story behind your birth, so if she called you the daughter of the Moon and the Stars, then she is aware of the wish your mom made before giving birth to you," Greg said.

"Thanks, Grandpa. I will be in my room now," Lucinda said as she stood up and walked into her room.

"So, this is true. It happened in this world. Star is indeed a demon who has been in hibernation for years, and the day she is free, she will feast on the blood of the one who owns the Seashell, which was why she wanted to make me her friend. She wanted to manipulate me into setting her free. And when that wasn't possible, she picked my parents. It's been a whole six months, yet I haven't heard from my parents. I swear, Star, you will pay dearly for this," Lucinda said as she lay on the bed.

"How do I go about finding the three-in-one beast? Amber said I had seen her before, but I'm certain I haven't seen her. Can't she be wrong then? Why is this happening? Why does everything have to be in riddles and puzzles? Why can't they tell me things in a simplified form?" Lucinda muttered and sighed as she lay on her bed. Next, she took out the box containing the necklace, opened it, and placed it on the bed. She hid the box back under her bed after bringing out the necklace.

She held the necklace as Anya's memories flooded her mind. "Why can't you just come back and save me from all this pain and trouble? I need you. You said you were going to come back when I needed you. Isn't it obvious that I need you now? Can't you sense it, Anya? This young girl here needs you. Even if I have done nothing wrong to make you leave for this long, I'm sorry. I miss you, and I miss my parents, too. You're the only one who I can talk to now. Please come back. I can't keep wearing this necklace when the soul that gave me the necklace is nowhere to be found. Anya, come back, please. The day is getting darker already, and I need you. I want you back. I am the daughter of the Moon and the Stars, pleading and begging that you, come back home," Lucinda said as her tears dropped on the necklace. She then wore the necklace back on her neck. She closed her eyes and drifted off to sleep.

"Wake up, Lucinda; it's already late. Come and eat dinner," Maya said, tapping Lucinda, who slowly opened her eyes.

"Is it night already?" Lucinda asked, wiping her eyes.

"Yes, and you need to come and eat," Maya said and left the room immediately. Lucinda sat up and followed suit. She ate her dinner in silence as she thought of what to do that night.

But one thing was sure to her: either Anya came back to her that night, or she would never care anymore about all this. She had waited for a very long time.

"Lucinda, what's the problem? It seems your mind is somewhere else," Greg asked.

"Don't worry about it, Grandpa. I'm fine," Lucinda replied.

"Are you sure, or do you not want to share with us? You have been picking at your food, which shows something is wrong," Maya said.

"I'm fine. Never mind," Lucinda said as she hurriedly finished her food to avoid her grandparents throwing more questions at her. She took her plates to the kitchen and washed them all when she was done. "Goodnight. I'm off to bed," Lucinda said as she walked past her grandparents.

"The necklace; you put it back on," Greg asked as Lucinda stopped and answered, "I needed closure, so I wore the necklace."

Lucinda hurriedly walked into her room. She brought out the Book of Prophecy and placed it on her bed. She was tired of doing it all alone. To her, Anya had to come back. After all, she promised she would come back when she needed her.

For a year and a few months now, Lucinda had waited for her, but today she would call her out wherever she was. She made a promise to her, and so she had to keep her promise. Lucinda swore to make sure Anya would hold to that promise by coming back to her that night.

Chapter Five

When Lucinda Was Sure That Everyone Was Asleep

When Lucinda was sure that everyone was asleep, she locked her doors and clung to the Book of Prophecy while touching her necklace and closing her eyes. Then, after meditating for some minutes, she opened her eyes to see herself at the bush path where she usually meets with Anya. She sat on the ground and placed the book on her lap as she ran her fingers through her hair.

"When I was trying to heal from Anya's sudden departure, Star came in, only to cage my parents' spirits shortly after. It's been months now since I heard from my parents. It feels like the whole world is against me. I don't just know what to do anymore. Life has been terrible. As much as I want to hear the voice of my parents again, my life is also on the line. Millions of souls will be lost if Star comes back as she wishes. So again, I don't just know what to do. How do I continue living every day without hearing from my parents? I'm used to hearing their voices from the beyond; I'm used to hearing their voices every day, though I can't see them. They have become my addiction, and I want to set them free, but if I yield to Star's request, then millions of lives and my own life will be at stake as well." Lucinda muttered so long that she started weeping, and then quakes of sobs set in eventually as she continued soliloquizing.

"Anya, I need you to come home. It was here that you promised me you would come back whenever I needed you. I need you now, Anya. The whole world is crumbling at my feet. I need to do something before everyone gets hurt. I've hurt already. Star has caged my parents' souls. And somehow, I got this Book of Prophecy, and I've been told before I can do anything that the three-in-one beast has to be around before the next step on how to destroy Star begins. Anya, I'm suffering; life has been way too harsh for me. I have tried and tried, but new problems come up every morning. This isn't what I'm expected to go through as the daughter of the Moon and the Stars. I can't do this on my own anymore. Anya, I need you back. Just come home. This is your home, too. My home is your home; my birthplace is your home. I'm pleading with you, Anya. I need you now; else, I might go insane." Lucinda shouted as her voice echoed, and tears trickled down her cheeks, dripping onto the Book of Prophecy in her hands.

Lucinda was tired. As much as she wanted to erase Star forever from existence, she still needed her parents back. She was in a dilemma. She was unsure what the three-in-one beast was and where to find it. She was unaware of how she could handle the situation, where to start, and how.

To make it worse, she was on her own, with no one to help at the moment. She knew she was getting fed up with everything. She was immured, and it suddenly ceased after she started hearing her parents' voices.

All she craved was a stress-free life where she could get to listen to her parents' voices every day, interact with them, laugh with them, but sadly those were mere wishes, a mirage.

She sat there on the ground, so sad that she didn't know when it was midnight. Then, just as it was midnight, the howls of the wolves could be heard in the forest from a distance. Lucinda paid little attention as she lay on the floral ground, crying. She was on the verge of giving up.

Lucinda hurriedly stood up and heard some movements behind her, a bit frightened. Then, clutching tightly to the Book of Prophecy in her hands, she turned to look as she beheld what she had been hoping to see these past months.

"Anya!" Lucinda shouted as she ran and hugged Anya tightly.

"I'm back, and I'm never leaving again. This is my home now. You have made your place of abode my home, and I can't disobey your orders," Anya whispered into Lucinda's ear as they hugged each other.

"Is it a promise that you're not going back again?"

"Yeah, it is. Sure," Anya assured.

"I have missed you, Anya," Lucinda said as Anya slowly wiped off the tears welling in Lucinda's eyes.

"Stop crying, my dear queen. I stay; I'm not leaving you ever again. This is my home now," Anya reassured, smiling.

"Anya, I'm confused. Life has never been the same since you left. You left, and everything went with you. I got to meet this girl Star, and later on, I realized she was just a demon who wanted me to free her in exchange for my parents' souls. She caged my parents' voices so they wouldn't communicate with me. She asked me to free her if I ever wanted to hear from my parents again. But I can't. Star is a demon, and if she is eventually freed, she is coming for me because she needs the blood of the one who has the magic Seashell before she can bring total ruin and destruction to this world. This Book of Prophecy hasn't given me a clue on how to deal with Star and free my parents at the same time. Amber said the spirit of the three-in-one beast has to be felt before being told what next to do. I'm confused, Anya. I don't know who the three-in-one beast is or where or how to find it. I need to set my parents free. Life took them away from me at a very tender age, and the only thing I console myself with is the fact that I can hear their voices, but suddenly Star appeared on the scene and put a stop to that. I can't hear them anymore. Star is still asking that I free her, but this book here won't say anything about destroying her. I'm losing it, and right now, I need help before making any mistakes. Anya, I need to hear my parents' voices, or else I might hurt myself. I might inflict an everlasting injury on myself. The thought of not hearing their voices is driving me insane. Please help me, Anya. I need my parents back. I need to hear their voices again, please." Lucinda pleaded as she burst out crying again.

"Calm down; just calm down. The three-in-one beast is me. I'm the beast whose presence needs to be felt before the next clue can be given to you. How did you forget so soon?" Anya asked.

Lucinda trembled on hearing that. Everything just flooded back to her memory. How could she have forgotten so soon? She wondered. She scratched her head before saying, "Maybe I have gotten used to your beautiful human face. I forgot that the first day you approached me here, you were three-in-one."

"Well, I'm here now," Anya replied.

"What took you so long, Anya? You didn't want to come back."

"That's because you never needed me. You just wanted closeness with me and a friend with whom you can relate. The day you needed me was today when you called and asked me to make your home my home, too. That was when you needed me back," Anya replied.

"So, all this while you heard me, but you only came back because I asked you to make this place your home, too? Hmmm. Interesting," Lucinda muttered.

"A visitor will always go home. But when she moves into the house, you will have every opportunity to see her," Anya replied.

"Okay. I got it. So now that you are here, tell me how I can free my parents; I need to free them. Star has kept them hostage for so long. They don't deserve this," Lucinda said.

"They deserve it. Why can't you just free me? Do you have to invite Anya over to this place? I thought she was gone for good?" It was Star's authoritative voice that sounded nearby.

Without warning, Lucinda saw Anya turn into a three-in-one beast. Lucinda watched in awe. She hadn't seen Anya transform into a werewolf before. The words about her were right, indeed. Anya was a deadly beast. When Lucinda saw Anya was about to charge towards Star, she called out her name.

"Anya, she isn't worth it. She is just a spirit, remember? She is so powerless. She still needs me to free her body before she can do anything to this," Lucinda shouted as Anya cast a deadly look at her.

"I know you're angry, but trust me, she is not worth it. She is just here to make you angry. Please calm down, Anya, I beg of you. It's just a matter of days before I extirpate her totally from this world and in the world beyond. Her chapter is about to be closed forever. So don't worry about her," Lucinda pleaded.

"Why don't you want to hurt her? Why?" Anya growled.

"She is going to set me free. She has to set me free, or she will never hear from her parents again. But, Lucinda, you're running out of time.

Free me now!" Star shouted as Lucinda cast a glance at her. On saying this, Star bent down as she winced in pain before disappearing from view.

"What did I do?" Lucinda asked as she looked at her hands and watched Anya transform into the woman she was before.

"A three-in-one beast, a werewolf, and a shape-shifter. What else do I need to know about you?" Lucinda asked, looking askance at Anya.

"You already know everything," Anya replied.

"What happened a few minutes ago? It felt like I wasn't myself. The last thing I remember is Star wincing in pain as she disappeared," Lucinda wondered at Anya, expecting some explanations from her.

"You allowed your powers to take over you. You couldn't control yourself; that's what happened," Anya replied.

"But I thought…"

"Humans, spirits, and even vegetation; all can feel a taste of your powers; none is immune to it. You can bring unending pain to anyone. Star isn't excluded, even though she is a demon. You were angry when Star uttered those words. She commanded you without knowing you hate anyone commanding you. The person I saw a few minutes ago wasn't Lucinda. You allowed anger to control you; you need to learn to control yourself," Anya replied.

"I'm sorry," Lucinda replied after reflecting on Anya's words.

"You don't need to be sorry. You live in a world of humans. Control your anger, or else you might hurt someone," Anya replied.

"Okay. I got it. About my parents: please, Anya, do something," Lucinda pleaded.

"The Book of Prophecy wanted my presence to be felt before the clue on how to deal with Star is explained to you. So, recheck the book," Anya replied.

"It's empty. There is nothing anymore to read. The pages are blank," Lucinda replied without bothering to check.

"The Book of Prophecy can't stop halfway; check again, Lucinda. And about your parents, extirpate Star first, and then your parents will come back. And listen, you barely have enough time to do so. Star might be in hibernation, but her spirits are getting stronger. I could sense it when she came here. She might be powerless now, but she shouldn't be alive during the next full moon," Anya replied as she quickly changed to a wolf. Anya was ready to leave.

"Promise me you're going to come back anytime, any day. I need you," Lucinda said.

"This is my home. I'm not leaving without letting you know," Anya said as she raced into the woods.

Lucinda picked up the Book of Prophecy lying on the ground as she touched her necklace and closed her eyes. Upon opening her eyes, she saw herself in her room. She placed the book on her bed as she lay down beside it, staring at the ceiling before delving into her normal soliloquy.

"I hope I win this battle. I hope fate gives me the chance to hear your voice again. I miss you, Mom and Dad. I do, and I will do everything possible to hear your voice one last time," Lucinda said as she wiped the tears from her eyes almost immediately before dozing off.

"Why did you have to bring Anya? Send her back to where she belongs. I'm warning you, Lucinda," Star shouted, but Lucinda wouldn't take any of that.

"She is my friend, and she has every right to stay here, unlike you, who have killed so many people. And what makes you think I will ever set you free? I dare not, Star, and I won't. Your next target has always been me. I already know you need to feast on my blood as the one in possession of the seashell before you can bring total ruin and damnation to the world. I keep telling you, Star, soon your case will be a closed chapter; and of course, your memory shall be no more, though a sad memory it has always been. I doubt history will ever remember you," Lucinda replied.

"You're making me angry. I will hurt your parents, and you won't do anything about it. The sooner you free me from this hibernation, the better for you. Don't think I'm powerless; I'm getting stronger, you know," Star said and grinned.

"Ha-ha-ha! Alright, I have heard you, but I dare you to hurt my parents; then I'll make your exit from this world the most painful. I dare you, Star, and now listen to me; I don't know how you did it, and I don't care to know. All I want you to know is that I'm giving you forty-eight hours. If you're not destroyed within these forty-eight hours, know that I'm not the daughter of the Moon and the Stars. I accommodated you and listened to you because I thought you wanted a friend, and in the end, you were only trying to trick me into setting a deceitful soul like you free. Forty-eight hours, Star, just forty-eight; that's what you've got, and then I will wave my last goodbye to you," Lucinda replied and walked away.

Lucinda woke up only to discover she had been dreaming. She stood up and walked towards her window and opened it.

"Awe! It's morning already," Lucinda exclaimed as she sat down on her bed.

"So, she came to my dream to warn me? I can't believe this. You might get stronger, but definitely, you won't be able to hurt me because I'm sure I'll be sending you to the abyss or wherever you came from. That's a promise. It would have been okay if you didn't have to drag my parents into this mess, but you did. You knew how much my parents mattered to me, yet you played this game using them as bait. That was the worst mistake you made, and now you're threatening to hurt them. Before I destroy you, I will make you have a taste of your own medicine," Lucinda muttered as she sat at the window, looking out into the compound, with her left hand on her chin. Shortly after, she went back to her bed to look at the Book of Prophecy. She flipped through the pages and was surprised to see written on the pages she presumed blank: "Destroying Star the Demon."

"Summon her spirit, and the three-in-one beast will guide you on what next to do." Lucinda closed the book and became pensive.

"This makes little sense. How do I find where Star's body is being kept? This is going to be the toughest thing ever," Lucinda said as she stood up and left the room.

Lucinda walked into her grandparents' room to see they were still sleeping. She held her necklace as she cast a glance at her grandparents. Her eyes turned white before she released her grip on the necklace.

"I'm sorry I had to do this, Grandpa and Grandma. I'm sorry I had to cast this spell on you. I promise to wake you both up once I return. But for now, I just have to save humanity. The night of the full moon is in seven days, and I barely have enough time left. I don't even know how many days it's going to take me to find her body. It's all for our good," Lucinda said with tears in her eyes as she looked at her grandparents one more time before she left them and walked into her room.

Lucinda took the bag and stuffed a few of her clothes. She hung the bag on her back as she walked to the door. She opened the door to meet Amber and Anya standing right there.

"How did you both get to know where I'm living?" Lucinda asked.

"Isn't that a stupid question, queen? You have made the right decision. Let's get going. We are making use of your horse," Amber said as she turned and went towards the backyard.

"I can find you anywhere you are, so step outside. I need to cast a protection spell on your house because your grandparents are inside," Anya said as Lucinda locked the door and shifted from her path. Anya closed her eyes. As she rose up, she emitted a thick white net, which appeared and disappeared again.

"It's done," Anya said as she walked towards the backyard.

Lucinda followed suit. She climbed onto the white horse while Anya and Amber used the brown horse.

"How long will it take before we get there?" Lucinda asked.

"The question is whether we can find the body before the date of the full moon," Amber replied.

"I just want to end all this and free my parents. She threatened me in my dream that she would hurt my parents. I told her forty-eight hours ago. But before then, I will make her feel double the pain I'm going through right now. No one dares me and goes scot-free. I have been pushed to the wall by Star. My soul is aching; my heart is in pain. Because of Star, I have cast a sleeping spell on my grandparents. And now I'm going through the stress of finding her body. Lucinda is angry," Lucinda shouted as lightning struck, followed by a thunder strike.

Both Anya and Amber experienced some chills on their bodies before Anya waved her hand as a portal opened before them. They hit the horses as they advanced into the portal, and it closed immediately as they went inside.

They came out in a different world. Lucinda was becoming impatient. She turned to Anya and Amber and exclaimed, "I need to find her body before the next forty-eight hours!"

"Yes, my queen," Anya and Amber said in unison, slightly bowing their heads.

———•—✦—•———

Chapter Six

WERE RUNNINHG OUT OF TIME

"We're running out of time. I hope we find the body soon. Amber, you're a seer; please, you should be able to tell us where exactly we can find Star's body," Lucinda pleaded.

"You're right. That's why I'm here, and I'm taking you to where Star's body is laid. The distance to cover is much, but don't worry, in the next five hours, we will be there," Amber assured.

"What? Five hours? Is that not too much?" Lucinda exclaimed, mouth agape.

"Do you want to go back?" Anya asked, eyeing Lucinda.

"No, we have come a long way for us to turn back; and aside from my parents, Star needs to be destroyed because her continuous existence is inimical to the world," Lucinda said.

"Good," Anya replied as they continued galloping, following Amber.

They got to the foot of a mountain when Amber came to a halt, and Anya and Lucinda, following behind, also stopped.

"Why are we stopping here?" Lucinda implored a bit.

"The rest of the journey will be done by foot; we have to keep the horses here," Amber said, without looking behind.

"Hmmm. Anna and Phil might get hurt; wild beasts might attack them, and if anything happens to them, my grandparents will be devastated," Lucinda said.

"Anna and Phil?" Anya asked, surprised.

"I'm referring to the horses," Lucinda offered. Lucinda gave the horses their names when her parents' spirits lived inside the horses, which is the reason the horses held a special place in her heart.

"Don't worry, Lucinda. They won't get hurt. Anya is going to cast a protection spell around them. With that, they won't be able to run away; neither shall any harm come close to them," Amber replied.

"Alright, Anya, do it so we can get going," Lucinda replied, a bit impatiently.

Amber drew a circle around the horses as Anya cast a spell on the line that Amber drew, with a mist enveloping the horses.

"We can now go," Anya said. So, they continued their journey into the thick of the forest that stretched before them. Before long, they were to enter a hole-like cave right inside the bowels of the mountain.

"This place is dark; how do we see what's on the inside and know where we are going?" Lucinda asked, a little impatiently.

"I think that is left for you to sort out. You have the power to do that," Anya replied.

Lucinda walked into the hole as Amber and Anya followed behind. Lucinda closed her eyes as a ball of fire appeared in her hand, but she screamed, and the fire went out.

"What happened?" Amber asked.

"The fire; it was hurting me," Lucinda shrieked.

"Be in charge of your powers. They are not meant to hurt you; they are meant to obey you. Try again," Anya said.

Lucinda closed her eyes and repeated the same process as a ball of fire appeared in her hand, this time without a single heat. Finally, she raised her consciousness above that of the fire and became in control of it.

"Lead the way," Anya said to Amber as they walked deeper into the hole while the fire burning in Lucinda's hand lit their path.

"My hands are hurting," Lucinda complained after some distance inside the cave.

"That's because you're not concentrating; your powers are meant to obey you. So always stay on top of your powers; always!" Anya enthused.

As they kept walking, Lucinda hit something with her leg. She bent down to see what it was. She saw a human skull, and on looking around still, she saw human skeletons scattered on the floor. She became apprehensive.

"What are all these?" she asked.

"It is a place where Star feasts on her victims. These are their skeletons. Her body is placed inside here because this is the only place suitable for her," Amber replied.

"What's wrong, Lucinda?" Anya asked as she noticed the tears in Lucinda's eyes.

"I can hear their screams. I can hear them calling out for vengeance. I can hear them crying out to be saved. They might be dead, but their spirits still litter around here, waiting to be freed. I want to go home. They want to be free. They don't belong here. They are crying; they want to go," Lucinda said as Anya walked closer to her and placed her hand on her shoulder.

"You will free them soon, but first things first," Anya said, patting her on the shoulder.

"Let me go. Release me. I want to go home." The spirits kept wailing as Lucinda remained bent.

"They are in pain. They have been here for years. They want to go home. They are screaming; they are pleading," Lucinda said in tears. "They are my captives. You do not have any right to set them free. Go back to your world, Lucinda! You're not welcome here. Go back home. This is where they belong, and just for the record, no one can set Star's captives free. Leave my territory, Lucinda. Leave before I hurt you," Star shouted as everyone looked around, but they didn't see her.

"Lucinda, let's go," Amber said as Anya helped Lucinda up. So they continued on their journey, ignoring Star's threat. Soon they came to a fountain when Amber informed them that they were closer to the body.

"How come there is light here?" Lucinda asked.

"Her body was kept in a place where the water never runs dry. As for the light, the mystery behind it is yet to be unveiled," Amber replied.

"So, where is her body?" Lucinda asked.

"In the water," Amber said as she slowly removed her sandals, after which she walked into the water as Anya and Lucinda followed suit. They formed a circle as Lucinda looked around and asked again, "Where is her body?"

"Patience, Lucinda, patience," Anya replied as she stretched forth her hands for Amber and Lucinda to hold. They clung to her as Anya chanted strange words when the rocks inside the water started rumbling.

Lucinda was surprised when she saw what was happening, and at that instant, the rocks opened to expose Star's body lying peacefully on the cluster of pebbles and stones. She looked nothing like what Lucinda had seen. Yet, the Star she was seeing right before her was a beauty to behold, perhaps more beautiful than the lilies of the valley.

"It's unbelievable for me seeing a beautiful evil," Lucinda said as she ran her hands over Star's face.

"The stars are always beautiful. They glitter like diamonds, and everyone always looks forward to seeing them in the skies. Star might be so beautiful, but the truth remains that she is one of the deadliest beings that has ever lived, and she has to go," Anya replied.

"Her beauty is so deceptive; hope you aren't having a change of mind?" Amber asked.

"No, I'm not going back on my words."

"Now, you have to summon her spirit," Anya replied.

"How will I do that, and why do we even have to summon her spirit here?" Lucinda asked.

"We don't have time for questions, Lucinda. Try to see how you can summon her spirit because if you don't, there is no way else you can destroy Star. Just focus and concentrate. I know you can do this. You were chosen to be the daughter of the Moon and the Stars for a reason. Lucinda, this is one time to show it. Just concentrate," Anya replied.

Lucinda walked closer to the body and placed her hands on it, closing her eyes in the process. Then suddenly, she started mumbling gibberish. Before long, a ball of fire struck her hand, prompting her to withdraw her hand from the body.

"Try again. Just concentrate and call her. She will answer you. Once her spirit is here, she can't leave anymore, and she will be vulnerable," Amber replied.

Lucinda repeated the quick process, but nothing happened. She tried and tried, but it felt like Star wasn't ready to appear. But Lucinda wouldn't give up. She became agitated as she once again placed her hands on the body, closed her eyes, and summoned Star's spirit. This time around, her tears started welling in her eyes. Shortly after, they began dropping on Star's forehead, and just immediately, lightning struck, followed by a thunderstorm as Star appeared.

"Why have you chosen to do this?" Star abruptly asked as soon as she appeared.

"Perhaps I wouldn't have come for you if you had left my parents out of this, but by doing so, you misfired. You could have played your game and not involved them, and I wouldn't have been here today. Instead, you took my source of joy from me, and you lied about who you were. My parents have done nothing wrong. I'm asking you to set them free now," Lucinda bellowed her command.

"And why will I do that? You will still wipe me off from this world and the world beyond, nevertheless. So, what's the essence of setting them free? I will not lose at both ends; never!" Star bemoaned.

"I'm still asking nicely; set them free, Star," Lucinda whispered.

"And I said no! Never!" Star shouted.

Lucinda didn't waste more time with words as she bent down and brought out a dagger she had hidden in her shoes. She raised it and sliced it into the lifeless body, and just immediately, Star started bleeding at the exact place where the dagger pierced.

"It's your hand. Next is your heart. Finally, will you set my parents free, or do you still want me to torture you the more?" Lucinda asked as she raged.

"Even if she goes, your parents will still be set free somehow. It's of no use giving her enough time to talk. End her miserable life here and now. She has wasted thousands of souls. She has taken many into captivity. And even with the souls she has feasted on, she wouldn't allow their spirits to rest. She still keeps them hostage. What other punishment does she deserve, if not both physical and soulish death? Star deserves to die. Stab her in the heart. Let's end it all," Amber bellowed.

"Just do it, Lucinda. Do it and set her victims free; your parents will find their way back to you somehow; just do it," Anya added.

"Are you going to listen to them? I thought we had been friends all this while? I only wanted to be free."

"Free, so you can feast on my blood because I'm the one in possession of the seashell? Free so you can continue from where you stopped? Free so you can bring damnation and ruin to this world? Free so you can wipe out my entire existence? Why will I free you when you end up killing me just to achieve your aim of ruining humanity?" Lucinda shrieked.

"You put me into this; more reason I will have to kill you first. You placed me in hibernation for years; you ruined all my plans. That's why I'm coming for you," Star replied.

Lucinda raised her dagger and pierced it into the heart of Star's body, but as she tried pulling it back, the blade remained stuck right there.

"You have done your worst, Lucinda. You might have ended my very own existence, but I promise I will come back to Earth or the world beyond; I will, Lucinda. It might take years, but I will come back," Star screamed as she winced in pain.

They all stood there watching as Star's body slowly faded into thin air, with no trace of existence. After some minutes of silence from the three spectators, Anya walked closer to Lucinda and said as she patted her on the shoulder, "You don't look happy; you have already done it. Never mind; she isn't coming back. They are just mere words meant to scare you."

"I'm not scared or worried about her threats. I'm just sad that after everything, I couldn't set my parents free, after all. I feel I have let them down. I'm not worthy of being called their daughter. Now that Star is no more, where are my parents?" Lucinda replied.

"That's not true; you're a true queen. You have saved millions, and the world will remain entirely grateful to you. And about your parents, they will find a way to come back to you; have it at the back of your mind," Amber said and made to leave.

"Where are you going?" Lucinda asked, surprised.

"Her journey is done here on Earth. She is going back home," Anya said.

"I don't understand. I know we are on Earth but in a different place, somewhere far away from home, but what do you mean her journey is done here on Earth? You don't think about your grandmother? Wouldn't she look for you? Amber, return home with us, please." Lucinda was agitated to the point of distraught.

"Did you not read in the Book of Prophecy that after Star is destroyed, Amber will go back home to where she belongs? I have waited all these years to meet you, and I'm glad I did. I know you will miss me. I know you would visit the oak tree after I'm gone, hoping to see me, but it's of no use. I might be gone, but I'm still closer to you than you may think. Just call my name, and I will answer. Call me in times of distress, in times of happiness, and I will answer. Talking about my grandma, she wouldn't know that I was gone. All the memories we both had have been wiped from her head, same with the people who had an encounter with me. So, it's just like I never existed to them. Just call my name whenever you need me, and I will answer you. Goodbye, Lucinda; goodbye, Anya," Amber said as she waved and slowly vanished before their eyes.

"This isn't fair; this isn't the life I want. I don't wish to repeat my past again. Why do people I love leave me when I've gotten used to them? Why is that so? It's just a matter of time before you leave too, Anya. So why do you all keep leaving me? Why, why has life punished me this way? Why?" Lucinda shouted as she burst out crying.

"Lucinda, Amber isn't gone forever. She stayed this long to meet you and offer the help she is fated to offer you. And that she has done. So, she just has to return home. Amber had lived for many centuries," Anya said.

"I want to go home; take me home," Lucinda shrieked as she started walking out.

When they got to the spot where the bones were littered on the floor, Lucinda cast one glance at them before leaving, still feeling sad for them. Shortly after they got to the horses, they mounted and galloped away. Lucinda was in no mood to talk. She was just sad.

Soon after, they went to the portal that led to the visible world. "We're here. I'll open the portal, which will take us directly to your house," Anya said.

Lucinda kept mute as she wiped the tears that were threatening to fall from her eyes. She watched as Anya opened the portal, and there she was right in their backyard. She came down from the horses, same with Anya, as she held them and led them inside the stable before locking them up.

"What's wrong, Lucinda? I can see you're not happy," Anya asked.

"Why should I be? I know, of course, it's just a matter of time before you tell me you're leaving too. I think it's time I came to terms with it that everyone who comes into my life will leave when I least expect it. Thank you for helping me get rid of Star. Thank you, Anya. Perhaps I should just start getting used to how life is treating me. Somehow, someday, I will find a way to free my parents and all those souls trapped in that cave calling out for help. Thank you, Anya. I need to wake my grandparents up," Lucinda said as she walked away, but Anya called her back.

"Lucinda, I know you're sad, but I'm not leaving. I know you're angry, but there are certain prices you have to pay for being the daughter of the Moon and the Stars. Not everyone will be with you forever. You just have to get used to it and get ready because anyone might leave you. And today is Wednesday. We might have spent hours out there, but over here, we have spent days," Anya said.

"Thank you," Lucinda said as she walked into the house. She made straight for her room as she lay down and cried herself to stupor.

"What kind of miserable life am I living? Why would I ask someone to come back, and then I will still have to lose another? Amber, why didn't you tell me you would leave me soon? You just kept mute and acted like everything was fine. And now you're gone. You came, and you stole my heart, and you left like the wind? Why is it so? Why is my life like this? Why does life keep bringing people to me when they know they won't stay? Why? What is wrong with me? I hate this. I simply do!"

Lucinda started crying as she lay on her bed. Finally, after some minutes of crying her heart out, she stood up and walked into her bathroom to take her bath. Lucinda came out, changed her clothes, and walked into her grandparents' room when she was done. She then tapped them, and they became awake.

"What are you doing here? Aren't you meant to be sleeping?" Maya said, stretching herself.

"It's already evening. Get up so you can prepare something for us to eat," Lucinda said.

Maya stood up as Lucinda hugged her and did the same to Greg.

"Okay, okay. Why are you hugging us tight like this? What's the problem?" Greg asked.

"I'm surprised," Maya replied.

"I just missed you both, and I don't want any of you to leave me. I won't be able to survive if any of you should leave me," Lucinda said.

"We're not leaving you; we're going to stay here with you, okay?" Greg said.

"Thanks, Grandpa," Lucinda said as she walked out of the room.

"Strange. Something is amiss," Maya said as she left the room to prepare something for dinner. What they didn't know was that they had been asleep for days now.

Lucinda left the house as she trekked down to the oak tree. She sat on the branches as she looked around, and tears fell from her eyes.

"I will never see you again, right?" Lucinda said, picking a dead leaf from the ground.

"You were with me all these while, and you said nothing about leaving, but it was after everything that you told me you were leaving. That's not fair, Amber. I have wanted my grandpa to meet you, but now he can't. I wish you had stayed longer, Amber. I wish you could hear me and please come back home," Lucinda said as she wiped the tears from her eyes.

"You know things aren't always what they seem. We don't always get what we want. The more reason you should treasure every second you get to spend with someone." A voice sounded next to Lucinda as she looked up to see Amber.

"Amber, you're back!" Lucinda exclaimed, standing up.

"You're funny. I didn't leave you for once. I never left you, and I wouldn't leave you. I'm always with you. Just call my name, and I will be there. You will always be the daughter of the Moon and the Stars, and there is no way I can leave you," Amber replied.

Lucinda touched Amber but was shocked when she faded away.

"I wish this was real. You are gone, yet you said you're not gone. How come I can't even feel you? I need to touch you and hug you one last time," Lucinda replied.

"Call me whenever you need me, and I'll always be with you, even if you can't see me," the voice replied.

Lucinda wiped her tears as she journeyed back home. Lucinda was a few steps from her house when she heard some voices inside the portal crying out to her, pleading that she free them so they could rest.

But she kept walking, and soon after, she got home, had her dinner, and retired to her room. She locked her room as she took out the Book of Prophecy, hoping to find a clue on how to free those spirits and her parents.

She flipped through the pages, but nothing was there to grab. She then dropped the book and took out her seashell, rubbed her hands on it, and talked.

"I can't remember the last time I made a wish, but right now, I'm in pain, and I need your help. I might have destroyed Star, but the spirits of those she killed are waiting to be free so that they can find eternal rest. They are crying; they are pleading with me. They just want to be freed. I don't know how to go about it. I don't know how to set them free, but I need them to be free. They are wailing. Their tears are disturbing me. I can hear them; they just want to rest. They have been in bondage for years. They just want to rest. Please free them; free all that Star has caged so that they may find rest and reunite with members of their families who died before them. Free them; I may live without hearing the wails of these innocents. Free them because they need to be freed. They are not supposed to be prisoners. Please stop their sadness and misery and free them." As soon as Lucinda stopped talking, she heard lightning, followed by the bellow of thunder.

"I believe you have granted my wishes," Lucinda said as she wiped her tears and put the seashell back in the box with the Book of Prophecy. She then lay on the bed, and soon she started hearing the voices of laughter. She smiled, convinced that those souls had been freed, just as she desired. Finally, she closed her eyes and drifted off to sleep.

"I want to see you; it's been months, Lucinda," Anna said.

"Mom, how come you're here? What of Dad?" Lucinda asked.

"I'm here," Phil said.

"How come you're here? I thought Star caged you both. Why do I see you both instead of just hearing your voices?" Lucinda asked, pleasantly surprised.

"We want to see you," Anna and Phil said in unison as they both walked away while Lucinda kept calling them to come back. Shortly after, Lucinda woke up sweating, and it was then she knew it had been a dream. "What kind of dream is this?" she muttered.

"They both kept saying they wanted to see me, yet they were walking away from me. What does that mean? Well, I must find out somehow," she said, and she lay back on her bed and slept off.

Three months were already gone, yet Lucinda didn't meet with Anya. She had this icy feeling that she was gone, just like Amber. But she knew she wouldn't be able to hold on to the temptation of not meeting with Anya. Her soul was already knitted with Anya's.

On a specific night, when she was sure her grandparents were asleep, she locked her door and clung to her necklace. Opening her eyes, she saw herself in the exact spot where she met with Anya. She cast a furtive glance around, hoping to see Anya, but she was nowhere to be found.

"Anya, where are you? I know I haven't come to see you for months now. I only felt dejected since everyone I had ever loved left me. I felt maybe you would not stay too, like the rest of them. I was tired of bonding with people and having to lose them the next day. I was so tired. I knew you were going to go too, but today I felt unable to hold on to not seeing you anymore. I know you can hear me wherever you are now. I just thought I should say hello again, and I miss you. I miss Amber as well," Lucinda shouted into the space before her.

"When you said you wanted this place to be my home, I obeyed. This is my home, and I'm never leaving," Anya said, coming out from the bush.

When Lucinda saw the other three figures coming with her, she shifted slightly. Then, she snapped her hand, and the ball of fire appeared in her hand as she looked at the faces of the people coming with Anya and was surprised to see her parents.

She ran and hugged them, crying profusely in the process, totally short of words. She didn't know what to say. She was simply given to crying, as their appearance was unexpected to her. And finally, after a long time, Lucinda muttered, audible enough for her parents, "I missed you both." But she couldn't stop sobbing.

"We missed you too," Anna and Phil said.

"How did this happen? I thought Star caged you both. How come I can see you both in the flesh? How is that possible?" Lucinda asked while trying to wipe away her tears.

"Everything is possible because you're the daughter of the Moon and the Stars, though you are not aware of your powers. I didn't know who my child was until now," Anna said.

"We didn't know you had been conferred with so much power and the ability to do things humans can't do," Phil said.

"We waited every night for you, but you weren't coming. Then, finally, Anya assured us you would come someday. After that, we never stopped hoping," Anna said.

"I had a dream about this. Now I understand it was a message," Lucinda said.

"Yes, it was, but you did not understand it. After you made the wish with the seashell, it granted more than you asked for. It freed not only your parents; it granted them the opportunity to spend time with you from 12 a.m. till 3 a.m. They have waited for 90 days without seeing you, but I kept telling them that someday you would come out.

"Hey, wait a minute; I saw three people with you, Anya. Where is the third person?" Lucinda asked, looking around.

"I'm here," Amber said, revealing herself as Lucinda rushed and hugged her.

"Ha-ha-ha! Oh, Amber! I missed you so much," Lucinda said. "Awe, same here. I haven't seen you in the oak tree for months.

I would wait for you there in the morning, and I would be here at night. You took a long while to realize that we're never going to leave you; you're special," Amber said.

"Thank you, Anya, Amber, Mom, and Dad, for never giving up on me. I promise to come to you every day," Lucinda replied, offering a huge smile.

They hugged each other as they all sat down on the floor and talked about everything that had happened. And while they were still talking, Lucinda watched as her parents and Amber faded into thin air. She was startled.

"They are coming back, right?" Lucinda asked Anya.

"Yes, sure, they are; it's already 3 a.m. You need to go back home now," Anya said, standing up.

"Anya, thank you so much. I hope one day I can make you live among humans, not in the forest," Lucinda said.

"Till then, Lucinda," Anya said as she turned into a wolf and disappeared into the forest.

Lucinda smiled as she closed her eyes, touching her necklace, and in no time, she appeared in her room. Shortly after, she lay back on her bed to sleep.

"Thank you for bringing my parents back to me. I have my Dad, Amber, and Anya. What more do I need? I just want to live in peace forever. The daughter of the Moon and the Stars is saying thank you to the Supreme Being," Lucinda said as she smiled, and before she knew it, she was off to sleep.

THE END

PART 4

Annalise's Wish

by the best selling author
Dennis WQWong
Mansi
as Annalise
Neela
Dress Designer
Annalise's
Sequel of Arya
Wish
Published by
Sankalp Art

Introduction

A time will come when we will want nothing but answers to questions that burden us, which we cannot decipher. At such times, we leave ourselves at the mercy of fate and providence, without even having the faintest idea of how things would eventually turn out.

Our total mortality, ingrained in our weakness, is exposed in such an instance. In the case of Lucinda's situation, many issues around her had been resolved, dousing her frayed nerves, but she still had unanswered questions yet to be addressed.

Annalise's Wish gives an in-depth explanation of Lucinda's and Annalise's birth circumstances. It tells the story of how women could go the extra mile to hold their bundle of joy and for someone to call them "mother". Children bring color to a dull family. They light up the whole room with joy and happiness with their arrival into this world. The plot takes a different twist, introducing Jake, who is the son of the sun and will be Lucinda's mate, hoping that their marriage will resolve the conflict between the two worlds.

"Annalise's Wish" is the final sequel to **"*Anya*"** and it is part four of **"*Over the Distant Mountain Ranges*"**, followed by **"*Beyond the Ranges.*"**

I have provided some excerpts from the previous editions: She was named Lucinda, the daughter of a poor farmer. She was her parent's favorite and their only child. They didn't have all the good and pleasant things of life.

"Well, my parents lived on the mountain because of the calmness in that area, and nope, they don't have neighbors. I know the next question would be how do they eat? They travel to the village close to them to get foodstuffs every Friday. That's all," Annalise replied.

There was an epidemic of flu spreading across the region, and so far, Lucinda was the only one out of the three members of this household that had not yet contracted it. Her parents were already down with the virus.

"Listen, Lucinda, this illness is spreading everywhere, and it' so contagious. I want you to go back to my parent's place," They were sick, and they didn't let anyone know. Now her parents are gone.

*"Lucinda, it's me. My soul lives in this horse, "*The white horse said.

"She isn't just the only one. Your father is here too" The brown horse said.

"Since your soul lives in this white horse, I will call you Annalise, and since Dad lives in this brown horse, I will call him Phil," Lucinda said.

One won't even guess there was something under the bed or hidden in that old box. Maya unlocked it and opened it up as she brought out the seashell.

Lucinda felt something substantial as soon as she touched the seashell.

"Our grandchild is special. She is a young child filled with wisdom who doesn't act her age. Yes, she understands the language of the horses. Lucinda, your grandchild, spends quality time with the horses because her parents' spirit lives in the horses, and she is the only one who can hear them. Just let her be as she is bonding with her parents, and she barely has enough time because eventually, they will be gone forever," The old woman said.

"Lucinda, we were only given five years grace to stay with you here on earth, and the timelapses on your 15th birthday," Phil explained.

"I understand how you feel, Lucinda. We were given the privilege to communicate with you. But unfortunately, you can never see us again. So, let's be content with our voices. I have been here a couple of times. After your fifteenth birthday, I had no choice but to decide to relocate to the city with you so you could forget what happened. I was able to buy this with the little savings we have, and here we are now." Greg replied.

"You are the queen. You invited your subject over here. You asked me to come. Your presence in this city woke me up, yet you can't summon the courage to talk to your subject." The voice persisted.

"Anya is three in one, an amalgam of the sort, both a deadly beast and a wonderful soul. So, you choose which side of her you want." Mia replied.

"I am the goddess of this river, and I know more because I have existed for ages and ages. When you were drowning in this place years ago, I didn't want to kill you; I only wanted to show you a little about your life, but Phil came in time to save you. The moon and stars have waited for a long time, and they want their daughter to fix this as ordained."; Mia replied as she walked into the river, and before Lucinda could say anything, she vanished before her sight.

"But you are not like them; you're different. You're a queen crowned even before your birth. Your life was meant to be different, and no matter how you wish for it, your life is perfect." Anya replied.

"My name is Lucia, daughter of the moon and the stars. You're my incarnation. The people are torturing the people I would do anything for at any cost to protect and me." Lucia replied.

Anya couldn't believe that Lucinda was ever going to kneel and bow before her. Now there was no way she was going to hurt anyone again. Anya knew that whatever she needed must be granted once the queen bowed to her. That act of Lucinda's humility has hindered her.

"All the answers you seek are in the Book of Prophecy; it holds every story you need to know; prophecies that were given before your birth," Amber replied.

"I'm the seer who has reincarnated four times now. I was here when you were as the other queen and was killed, but I never got to see her face. The same queen is you. You're back again; just that it took you long to come back to earth. So, I kept reincarnating, hoping that I would someday be opportune to see the queen, and here I am today, standing right next to her." Amber said, smiling.

"The bracelet is from my grandmother; I can't remove it. She is just like my mother, and as for the necklace, it's a gift from Anya. It was the necklace that unlocked the book." Lucinda replied, sighing.

Chapter One

She Knew Her Mom Made a Wish

She knew her mom made a wish, but what prompted her to make the wish remained a mystery to her. Indeed, something must have happened, and she needed to know. Indeed, these questions could only be answered by her mom, Annalise.

As Lucinda lay on her bed, different shades of thoughts were racing through her mind. She was restless, tossing and turning on her bed.

Looking through the window, she saw the stars in the sky shining so bright. In the darkness are the chirping of the crickets, the hooting of the owls, and the neighing of the horses in the stable.

She waited and remained awake into the deep hours of the night, and when she was sure that her grandparents were asleep, she disappeared from the house, reappearing at their meeting place, but they weren't there yet, so she just sat down and waited for them. She waited for midnight, the very time of their meeting.

It didn't take long before it was midnight, and just like always, Annalise and Phil came out together from the nearby bush, having Amber and Anya in their tow.

After exchanges of greetings and fraternal hugging, they started playing a game of Jumanji. Still, throughout it, everyone noticed Lucinda was absent-minded, and that something was bothering her.

"You seem off. What could be the problem?" Amber asked.

"You know the least you can do is only to ask whenever you think you need answers to anything," Anya added.

"Lucinda, what's the problem? You know you can always talk to us. Something is bothering you, and it is even written all over your face. We need you to be happy so we can be happy too. Please talk to us. You need to." Phil pleaded.

"Something has been bothering me. You are right. I need to get answers based on what Grandpa told me about Mom's wish before birth. But I think there is more to it." Lucinda said.

"What do you mean, my child?" Annalise asked.

"It's all about the circumstances surrounding my birth. I need to know more about my birth. I need to know how I came back as the daughter of the moon and the stars and what prompted you to make the wish you made in promising to dedicate me to the moon and the stars.

I know I might be asking for too much, but you will lift the burden off my shoulders if you tell me everything I need to know." Lucinda said, clearly worried.

"Alright, I will tell you, but that shouldn't get you so worried. You only needed to ask." Annalise said.

"Alright, I'm all ears," Lucinda said, shifting slightly on the ground.

FLASHBACK

Annalise could be seen throwing pebbles into the river as tears dripped down her cheeks. Something was wrong somewhere. She couldn't even express herself. She was short of words about what to say. The only thing left in her were her tears, which she freely allowed to do the talking.

"Why has the world decided to be unfair to me? What offense have I committed against the universe that she feels is the right way to punish me? Am I not fit to be called a mother? Why can't I birth a child? The most annoying part is not that the pregnancies aren't coming. They are, but it will be gone once I take in less than three months." Annalise whined within herself, sobbing gently.

Phil, who had been looking for Annalise, had to check at the riverside to see if she would be there, and luckily, he found her there.

On seeing Annalise, Phil was sad, noting the dire state, but she couldn't do anything.

He had tried talking to her several times, reminding her he would love her wholeheartedly with or without a child, but Annalise wouldn't hear of that.

They had been married for two years now, and none of the pregnancies had lasted for over three months. Annalise wanted to carry her child. She wanted to be called a mother.

"Annalise, please let's go home." Phil pleaded.

"Home? That place isn't home. There is nothing special about there to be called my home. How can that place be called home when there is no child to cuddle or call me mom?

Maybe it's time for the universe to explain why they are unfair to me. She has to tell me what's wrong with me. She should tell me so I can apologize and be given a chance to be a mother. I'm tired of this pain and humiliation. I want to be a mother, even if it is just one child. Phil, we have been married for two years and six months, and until today, the cry of a baby hasn't been heard in this family. I feel so empty. The universe has a lot of answers for me, I think. I need to know my offense today." Annalise said with a teary voice.

"My dear, it's okay. I understand your condition. I fully understand the situation. A child will come when the time is right. Perhaps not now, but later in the future." Phil said.

"Future? The future is now. I want that child now, or better still, they should open up to me and tell me what I did wrong; so I can have a baby, my baby." Annalise shrieked.

"Things don't work like that, Annalise. Listen. I will love you with or without a child until the end of time. It would be best if you stopped killing yourself over this issue. I have seen couples who had children after a decade of marriage.

You just need to exercise more patience. A child will come when the time is right, and even if a child doesn't come, I will still love you, and I won't marry anyone else. I swear on my life, Annalise. This isn't the Annalise I married." Phil said bitterly.

"You're right. This Annalise you married has changed so much. Deprivation of life, pain, and anger have changed me so much, yet I disagree that it's my fault. All I ever wanted was just a child, not even riches or material things. I just want to experience the joy of motherhood. I'm not selfish to ask of that, but I don't understand why the universe has refused to give me a child despite my countless pleas. I know the universe can hear me, but I don't know why they are silent. For how long will I keep languishing in this pain and misery? For how long, Phil? Haven't I waited long enough? I'm not others. I don't have to wait for a decade before I can be blessed with a child," Annalise said with a teary voice.

Phil sat beside her, stroked her hair a bit, and rested her head on his shoulders. They were like that for a long time, and when Phil made sure Annalise had calmed down, he drew her up while standing up before they strolled down to the house. Phil helped to prepare something to eat as Annalise took her bath. Before Phil could finish up and walk into the room with the food, Annalise was already fast asleep.

Phil wouldn't wake her up. He just had to cover her up adequately because of the cold weather as he sat staring at his wife. The quest for a child was driving Annalise insane. She was now completely different, and she didn't even care about herself anymore. Annalise kept screaming out that she wanted a child. Despite Phil's love and reassuring words, Annalise still won't give up as the only thing that could ever restore her joy would be when she gives birth to her child. Yet, Phil loved Annalise so much more than anything else in this world, with or without the child.

It was already 5 pm when Annalise woke up from sleep. Phil had to warm the food up and serve Annalise. She ate half portion and told Phil she was full. There was simply no appetite for her. "But you haven't eaten anything since morning," Phil said. "Don't worry; I'm fine," Annalise said.

Phil stood up as he took the plates and dropped them in the sink, after which he came back later and sat close to Annalise.

"Phil, can I talk to you about something?" Annalise asked. "Sure, what's that?" Phil asked.

"Do you see me as someone who has lost her sanity?" Annalise asked.

"No, but why will you even say that?" Phil asked.

"It's because of my daily rants of not having a baby of mine," Annalise replied.

"It's normal; any woman in your shoes will act the same way, and I won't blame you for anything. I just want you to know that despite everything that is happening, I still love you, and I will love you till the end of time, but I just want you to promise me one thing." Phil said.

"What's that?" Annalise asked.

"I just want my old Annalise back. I would do anything to see that smile again. I don't like this new Annalise, the new Annalise that has tied her happiness to childbirth. I can't even remember the last time I saw you smile. But, please, I want you to smile and be happy always.

I know things will change soon. I just want you to be patient. Things will work out soon, okay?" Phil pleaded.

"Even though it's tough, I will try to smile even amidst these tribulations.

I wish things could change, and I would be blessed with a child. I promise to love and protect this child until the day my eyelids close in death. Even in death, I will watch over her and be with her always." Annalise said.

"Her! Do you also want a girl child?" Phil asked.

"Amazing! You also wish to have a girl child!" Annalise said as Phil smiled. Phil wanted his wife to be happy and to experience motherhood.

"Don't worry. Your wish will be granted to you soon enough. Just have faith." Phil said.

They both discussed it at length that evening. Annalise was the first to show that she was feeling sleepy. Phil covered her up as he watched her doze off. It didn't take time before Phil dozed off as well.

It was five years now as the couple kept hoping for a child, though Annalise tried to act strong. Phil knew his wife was upset.

Phil had gone to the town to sell off some items they weren't using at home. It was already 6 pm, and Phil wasn't back yet.

So, Annalise sat on the balcony as she patiently waited for her husband. As she looked up to the sky, she saw the incandescence of the moon, and the sky was filled with stars.

"They look so beautiful," Annalise said, smiling as her eyes were fixated on the starry sky.

"I wish I had a child who will sit with me and admire the beautiful scenery of the sky, a child who shines brighter than the stars in the sky, a child that even the moon would obey. I wish the moon and the stars will hear this woman's voice who wants nothing but a child. I wish my heart's desires will be granted to me." Annalise said as she smiled.

Annalise's eyes were still fixed on the sky when someone tapped her, and that was when she noticed Phil was back.

"I can see that you are admiring nature. The sky looks breathtaking today," Phil said.

"Yeah, it looks wonderful. I feel these stars came out today just because of me. I think they heard my voice, my cry, and my pain, and they are here to fix everything." Annalise said with a smile on her face.

"I hope so. Let's go inside." Phil said as he led his wife inside the house. They ate dinner, after which Phil took his bath before he retired to the bedroom.

After the incident of her last wish, it became apparent to Annalise that she was pregnant, four months counting, but she didn't want to tell her husband. She felt this wasn't going to last. She thought it was going to leave the same way others left.

Annalise was sleeping on the bed that afternoon when Phil tapped her, and she slowly opened her eyes.

"Annalise, can you sit up? I want to ask you a question." Phil said as Annalise sat up slowly.

"When do you plan on telling me, or do you think you will keep it hidden forever? I don't understand." Phil said.

"What do you mean?" Annalise said, feigning ignorance. "The pregnancy. It's four months, Annalise," Phil said.

"Well, you already know the answer. This will still go the same way others went. I will have a miscarriage soon. I'm already used to it. No pregnancy of mine stayed. So, what makes you think that this will be different?" Annalise said with a teary voice.

"Remember the wish you made," Phil said.

"What wish? I have made countless wishes, so what has it to do with this?" Annalise asked.

"The wish you made to the moon and the stars. Who knows if the universe heard you that day, and they have granted your wish." Phil said.

"But this; I'm not too sure," Annalise said.

"Wait and see, and please be positive," Phil said.

"Thank you for never giving up on me and always standing by me. It's been five years now, but you are still with me here. So many men out there would have left, but you didn't. Instead, you stood by with me. I hope I will get to pay you back someday." Annalise said.

"You're my wife; that's enough of a price already," Phil said, smiling.

Despite Phil's assuring words, Annalise had her doubts that the pregnancy would not stay for long, but she was surprised when she got to her last trimester.

She sent words to her parents, which prompted their instant visit to see her for themselves. For five years, they had waited.

When they saw Annalise and Phil brimming with joy and happiness, they joined in their joyous mood. But they didn't stay long as they couldn't exchange any home for their home beyond the mountain ranges. They came in the morning, and they were already on their way home by evening.

When they left, Annalise went to the balcony to sit down and savor the glittering sky filled with twinkling stars.

"I made a mere wish because of the agony in my heart, and somehow you heard it, and you granted that wish to me. I don't know what else to say but thank you. I'm grateful. Today for the first time in five years, I have been able to carry pregnancy till the seventh month, showing that this baby has come to stay.

I will name her Lucinda.

That's the only name I can think of, and I think that's the proper name that suits the daughter of the moon and the stars.

Nations will bow under her. She will rule nations of men and women with the special gifts.

I never got to enjoy all the things as a child, and even now, she will have them in ten folds as an adult.

I'm not making a wish this time. I'm only stating how my daughter's life will be because she has wiped my tears away and proven to all that I'm a woman." Annalise said as she kept caressing her stomach while smiling.

"**Lucinda**, *that's the name I have given to you today. You will be born to us, poor fellows, but trust me, nations will bow down before your feet. I don't know how that will happen, but I can feel it will happen.*" Annalise said, smiling as she stood up and went inside.

On the day that Annalise gave birth, they heard the howling of the wolves, but instead of being worried about that, Phil and Annalise joked about it.

"Their queen is here, so they need to pay some respect," Phil said, laughing.

"*Even though we haven't heard the howls of the wolves before, today we heard it loud and clear, which shows that the universe has acknowledged the birth of my child*," Annalise said, smiling.

"Can you see how beautiful the sky is? The stars are even shining brighter. So indeed, their daughter is home." Phil said as they both looked at their tiny baby and smiled.

"So, you see, this is the story of your conception, and that was why I was very overprotective, and I wouldn't want you to get close to the river because I waited for five years before I could have you. I wouldn't want any harm to befall you." Annalise said.

"It was a tough time for us, but I'm glad somehow the wish your mom made was granted unto her. Somehow, I felt like the universe was waiting for her to make that wish. It sounds weird, but it's like that was what happened." Phil said.

"Are Grandma and Grandpa aware of this?" Lucinda asked, keeping quiet for some time.

"They were not aware of everything I went through because I tried to keep a happy face each time they visited, and they didn't suspect that anything was wrong. But my dad was around the day I made the wish to the moon and the stars, though he didn't understand the main reason why I did that." Annalise said.

"That explains why Grandpa knows little about my birth. I wanted a full story. That's why I had to ask you. I already knew about the wish, but I didn't know why you made that wish. I'm okay with the answers now." Lucinda said.

"Deep down, you still have more questions though you're yet to put the questions together. I hope you find all the answers that you seek." Amber said as Lucinda looked at her and smiled, slightly nodding her head in acknowledgment.

Amber was right. Lucinda still had so many questions, but she didn't know how to put them all together. One thing was sure, her parents did not have answers to the remaining questions.

"It's time," Phil said as Lucinda watched her parents slowly fade away with Amber.

"I wish they could stay longer. I wish they don't have to go every 3 am. But why can't they stay without leaving? Why is it not possible?" Lucinda said.

"I don't know, Lucinda. I don't have the answer to that question, but trust me, it will come to you when you need the answers." Anya said, then, looking at Lucinda straight in the eyes added: "You have changed so much. You're growing older and wiser. I'm happy for you."

"Thank you so much. I hope someday I'll see what the other world looks like." Lucinda said.

"Soon," Anya said as she slowly turned into a wolf, and before Lucinda could say anything, she was already inside the woods.

"Too many mysteries to be unveiled and too many questions to be answered. I hope I find all the answers to these riddles that needed to be solved. I'm going to find out everything, and I will fix everything that needs to be fixed. I hope I get enough time to do all that." Lucinda said within herself.

Chapter Two

LUCINDA STARTED RECALLING

Lucinda started recalling and trying to rationalize the circumstances surrounding her birth as was told to her by her mom. She recalled that her mom said she was tired of losing her pregnancies through miscarriages and that after five years, when all hope was lost, she made a wish to the moon and the stars, which was granted.

The moon and the stars chose to send her back to earth through Annalise. But then, what could have happened if Annalise hadn't made any wish? If not for her, wouldn't her mom have given birth to anyone? Were the moon and the stars responsible for her mom's repeated miscarriages?

Lucinda concluded there was more to the story than her mom told her. And clearly, Annalise didn't know more than she narrated. She was a simple rural woman whose only wish was to have a baby girl.

Looking out into the night through her windows, Lucinda was determined to find answers to these. Soon after chewing these thoughts in her mind, she drifted off to sleep after covering herself with thick clothes.

Hardly had Lucinda woken up the following day when she heard a faint knock on her door, and on getting up, she gently opened the door to see her grandmother standing at the door with hands akimbo. Not that she was angry with Lucinda, but that was her manner of standing most of the time.

"Lucinda, it's already 10 am, and you're still asleep. Is everything okay because I know you went to bed early?" Maya asked.

"Yeah, Grandma, I'm okay. I will be out in a few minutes; just let me take my bath." Lucinda said.

"Alright, we will be waiting for you," Maya said as she walked out.

Lucinda closed her door quietly and sat back on the bed. She started thinking about her life. Rummaging through her entire life, especially her communication with her dead parents, she became tired of hiding things from her grandparents.

Lucinda tried to find out the whole truth about herself. She wanted to know everything her birth and her motive to be in this life. Lucinda knew that she had to act if she would ever get to the bottom of the riddle. Next, she stood up, walked into her bathroom, and quickly showered before wearing her clothes.

"Where is Grandpa?" Lucinda asked.

"Oh, he went out, but he will soon be back. He went to the next town to see a friend." Maya replied.

"A friend? I've never heard Grandpa mention anything about having a friend, so how come this sudden he was going to see a friend today?" Lucinda asked, eyeing Maya.

"Lucinda, you must not know everything. Your food is in the kitchen, go and eat." Maya said as Lucinda glanced at her for a split second before going to the kitchen to eat her food.

She carried the food back to the sitting room and sat on the chair close to her grandma.

Maya noticed how Lucinda was picking at her food, and it was apparent that something was wrong with her. She knew how Lucinda preferred keeping things to herself. No matter how hard one tried, she would never talk to anyone concerning her problems, but she decided just to ask, as she couldn't go on pretending that all was well with her granddaughter sitting next to her.

"Lucinda," Maya called.

"Yes, Grandma," Lucinda replied.

"Is everything okay? Don't tell me yes; because you have been picking your food, and I'm certain something is wrong somewhere. Listen, you know that Greg and I love you so much, and in as much as we want to be part of your happiness, we also want to be part of your sadness. Whatever troubles you also trouble us.

So, please tell me, what's bothering you? You have been moody even when I walked into your room. Something is eating you up. What is it?" Maya asked in a most solemn voice.

"Well, Grandma, I feel there are questions I deserve to know the answers to and I don't know if I will ever get the answers," Lucinda replied.

"And what could those questions be? If I had answers to your questions, I know I would answer you. I want you to be happy because you are all we have here." Maya said.

"My mom. I mean your daughter, Annalise," Lucinda said. "What happened to her?" Maya asked.

"I know she is your daughter, and I know she is dead, but I don't want to bring up bad memories. I'm just seeking answers. That's all." Lucinda said.

"Okay, tell me, what is the problem?" Maya asked.

"Did you have any challenges before you gave birth to my mom? Were there any unusual or unnatural circumstances surrounding her birth and even conception? I just need to know what happened before and after she was conceived and given birth." Lucinda asked.

"Why do you need to know?" Maya asked after some momentary silence from her.

"I know it will be hard on you to tell me everything, but I need to know. It will help me solve certain riddles, but don't bother asking what they are because I won't tell you. It is when I must have fixed everything I can. I will explain but for now, tell me everything I need to know." Lucinda pleaded.

"Annalise is my only child. She was my first fruit that lived, but she wasn't the first seed that opened my womb. Others came before her, but just that they didn't stay up to three months.

They died during the second month of all the pregnancies. I became tired. I was even afraid of getting pregnant since I knew they wouldn't come to fruition. What was the need to get pregnant in the first place? It was like hell to me. Depression set in.

I became melancholic. I became desperate, so desperate that I made a wish on a certain night, a wish I believe solved whatever problem it was that was stopping me from getting pregnant because after that, I became pregnant, and it stayed. When I was delivered of a baby girl, I named her Annalise." Maya said.

"Wait, wait. You too made a wish, and why, please?" Lucinda asked, shifting a bit on her seat.

"Yes, I made a wish. I pleaded with the universe, the stars, the moon to give me even if it's just one child, and my wish was granted. I was delighted, but unfortunately, my happiness didn't last for long. It was ruined the day you ran to the mountain top to tell us they were no more. I had begged for that child, Annalise.

I had waited for years to conceive her. She was the only fruit I had here on earth, the only one who made me experience the joy of motherhood. She was the only child who made me a full woman.

I was angry with the universe that she took just one child she blessed me with, knowing full well the circumstances surrounding her birth, knowing the pain and hurdles I went through before I gave birth to her. But then, I had to console myself that I had you, and I swore to be there for you always.

Anytime I look at you, I see Annalise. I know I might never fill that vacuum created in your heart by her demise, but I promise to make you happy in any way I can. That was the same promise I made to Annalise even before I gave birth to her, that I would love and care for all her children. Sadly, she isn't here today, but I'm happy that I'm trying in my little way to make you happy, Lucinda." Maya said, casting her head down in gloom.

"Well, you're right about not being able to fill the vacuum that has been created in my heart, but the truth remains that you and Grandpa are the second-best things that have happened to me here on earth and I'm happy that despite all the weird attitudes I have shown in the past, you both are still standing strong with me," Lucinda said.

"Anything for you, Lucinda, anything," Maya said.

"Now, Grandma, can you tell me everything I need to know about my mom's birth? Why did nature make you wait that long because, I mean, people are easily getting pregnant and being delivered babies daily? So, why would your own be different?" Lucinda said, dropping her food.

FLASHBACK

Maya was sitting down on the balcony discussing with her friend Martha who was breastfeeding her child.

"Your baby looks beautiful," Maya observed, smiling.

"You're a beautiful woman. I know your children will be beautiful as well." Martha replied.

"Maybe, but I don't know why life has decided to be unfair to me. I have been trying to give birth to my babies for the past five years, but it all ended in stillbirths. It's been five years of a childless marriage with Greg, my husband. It hurts.

I wish I could get to carry my children and breastfeed them. But even if it is just one seed, I will be grateful. I want to experience the joy of motherhood." Maya said with a teary voice.

"I already told you, don't worry. Children will come at the right time. You don't have to kill yourself for anything. My baby girl here, Lynn, is also your child. Please don't worry so much. Things will work out soon. I'm certain that you will carry your child someday. I'm not telling you this to comfort you, but I'm telling you this because it will happen soon." Martha said.

"How soon, Martha? Just how soon? It's been five years now!" Maya almost exclaimed.

"Don't worry, soon. You will be surprised when it happens. Trust me." Martha said.

"I hope so. I hope the child comes sooner," Maya said, revealing a wry smile, though laden with sadness.

It was already evening when Martha signified that she was ready to leave. Maya saw her off and returned home. Her husband Greg wasn't back yet, so she went into the garden to pluck some vegetables.

"Hey Maya! the way you to tend to this garden and eat the fruit it brings forth. Why don't you tend to yourself that way and bring forth fruit? Oh, now I remember, you can't. You are just a barren old hag who will never bear any fruit into this life." It was the voice of Cecilia, her neighbor shouting from her window nearby. Maya has been going through this for the past three years since she fell out with her neighbor. Since then, she had seized every opportunity to taunt her and remind her of her childlessness.

"Why are you mute? You can't say anything because that's the truth. You're a witch. Only witches don't give birth and eat their children while still in the womb, just like you. I wish Martha would stop visiting you before you kill her child." Her neighbor shouted again while laughing hysterically.

Maya picked up the vegetables as she silently walked out of the garden, but on second thought, she turned back and said, "You have made a mockery of me because of my condition. You have taunted me a whole lot and have called me barren and a witch. I hope nature steals that smile from your face someday. I hope nature places you in the same condition that I am in now. Only then can you realize the pain and agony of a childless woman."

In ennui did Maya make those proclamations, after which she went inside and straight to the kitchen to prepare dinner. She wasn't going to let what Cecilia said to get to her. One thing was sure to her that she would reap all that she had ever uttered to her in mockery someday.

When Greg got home, he noticed that Maya seemed a little off, and after eating and having her night bath, he called her and asked her why she was looking gloomy.

"What else could it be? Cecilia wouldn't have the guts to mock me if I had a child. She just mocked me again today, asking me to bear fruits, not eat the fruits from my garden. I was just on my own, and when she saw me from her window, she started talking rubbish to me. I'm not even asking for children.

Just one is enough to prove to everyone that I'm a woman, just one child so I can experience the joy of motherhood. Is that asking for too much? I need to know. I'm tired. I'm tired of waiting. I have waited for five years and nothing to show for it. Not only that the pregnancy isn't coming, it only comes to mock me. Haven't I suffered enough? Haven't I gotten enough punishment from the universe?

When will she hear my cries and give me a child? When will she shut the mouth of those who have mocked me and called me barren? Greg, tells me what I am living for because this life isn't making sense. Nothing matters anymore. If I can't have a child to call my own. I don't think I am meant to stay in the world. Maybe I need to go on a long sleep, end the pain, and be free from this endless pain, and mockery." Maya said, tearing up as she stood up to leave, but Greg held her hands as she sat back down.

"Are you giving up on everything? Are you giving up on me? For the first time since the challenge of giving birth to a child, you have talked and thought about death. That's suicidal. Do you want to go and leave everything that we both shared here on earth?

Do you want to leave without fulfilling those promises you made to me? Remember that you said you would be with me till the end of time?

Why then do you want to leave? Why do you let people's talk get to you, even influence you into making a rash decision?

Doing so will only allow them to see you as a weakling, yet I know you're not weak, but a strong woman. Maya, I need to remind you of this. Perhaps you have forgotten. You will have a child. It's certain, maybe not now but very soon. So, you don't need to keep worrying yourself over what people say.

The miracle that will shut their mouth is going to happen very soon.

Just have faith, and don't lose hope. Don't let them see this weak side of you. Remain the strong woman you are, Maya," Greg said as he hugged her tightly.

They both retired to bed that night, but immediately it struck midnight. Maya woke up and went straight to the window. She stayed silent for a long time before she started declaring some words at the height of her bitterness, desperation, and pent-up emotions.

"I'm not barren, neither am I a witch. My day will come, and I know it. I don't know long I have to wait for this special gift.

The universe, I hope you can hear me. The stars and the moon in the sky, I hope you can hear me. I just wish to have my child, even if it is just one child. I want a child who will call me mother and call my husband father. I'm not asking for too much. I do not wish for something impossible.

I wish for things that happen every day in the lives of other women. I can't sleep. My heart is heavy. My soul is bitter and my heart is aching. I have realized that the only thing that can stop all of these is only when I hear the cry of my child. I hope the universe, the moon, the stars, and all the elements of this earth tend to this heart before it loses its thirst for life." Maya said as she sighed and went back to bed.

Days turned into weeks, weeks into months, months into years, and it was already ten years now, but Maya didn't stop. Every night she would make a wish to the universe and to the moon and the stars to give her a child.

And in a month, Maya suspected that she was pregnant again. When she knew she was pregnant, she made it a point of duty every night to wish for the child's safety. She kept making wishes every night till the day she gave birth to a baby girl. Greg and Maya were the happiest humans on earth that night because their bundle of joy arrived safely.

Martha was happy for her friend Maya. She helped the new parents out in the little way she could because she knew this was Maya's first baby, and she would need all the help she could get.

At last, Maya no longer cried every night. She was happy that at least her wish was granted. Finally, she had her child, someone who could call her mother.

Maya loved Annalise so much as she was the answer to the prayers that she had made for the past ten years. She was so happy that the universe had finally remembered her. And yes, she was the most beautiful baby. People would come to see her, then tell others of the baby's beauty. Her eyes twinkled like stars.

Maya and Greg made sure that Annalise always had a smile on her face as they wouldn't want to see her cry or sad. This was the child they waited ten years for, and now that she was here, they would treasure her for the rest of their lives.

"On the night that Annalise was born, something tragic happened. Cecilia lost her three children that same day. They all slept and never woke up. She lost her home and her husband. She lost everything."

How? Lucinda asked.

I don't know what happened, but I knew nature has a way of punishing wicked people. The truth is that I was not the only one she mocked. She mocked many people, and in return, all she got were curses from them. Cecilia left, and no one ever saw her again.

She didn't die or commit suicide, though; she still lived close to the mountains. No one sympathized with her because she had done nothing but cause pain to different people. I feel karma paid her back by taking all her children. Now she has no home, no husband, or even someone to call a child. She ruined herself." Maya said, looking calm and at peace with herself.

"So that's it. Even Annalise waited for so long. I thought she had the same issue with me, but she would always assure me that she and Phil would give birth when they were ready.

After I gave birth to Annalise, it felt like my womb was closed again, but I was so grateful that I already had her. She proved to be more than just a girl child. She did work meant for boys and she would do everything to make us happy.

We would do anything to make her happy. I was so attached to her that I didn't let her out of my sight for a second. I took her to visit her grandparents, ensuring we returned the same day.

That is the same way she always wanted you close to her. The bond was beyond the natural, perhaps, all thanks to your grandfather, who made me realize that Annalise wasn't truly gone, and you're the reflection of Annalise. Anything I do for you today would have done the same to Annalise if she was still here. I would kill myself if anything happens to you, Lucinda," Maya said, almost on the verge of tears.

Lucinda stood up as she walked closer to where Maya was sitting and hugged her tightly as she whispered comforting words to her, "Nothing will happen to me. I have come to stay, and I hope someday I will reunite you with your daughter, Annalise."

"What did you just say?" Maya said, looking at Lucinda bewildered.

"You heard me, Grandma, and don't think it is impossible. She is my mother too. Nothing is impossible in my world where I rule." Lucinda said, smiling as she picked up her plate of food and walked into her room. She wanted to eat alone.

Lucinda walked into her room, sat down, and ate her food slowly. She kept the remaining food by her bedside as she recollected everything her grandmother told her, every bit of it.

"This is interesting. My grandmother had my mother through a wish, the same way my mother had. Then why did my mother die? Why wasn't she the daughter of the moon and the stars like me? Why did the mantle rest on me?" Lucinda wondered as she tried to figure out what might have gone wrong.

"Only one person has an answer to this question, and I need to know why she wasn't the one to be made queen," Lucinda said as she stood up to lock her door, after which she closed her eyes to summon Amber.

"You called." As Lucinda opened her eyes to see Amber sitting on her bed, the voice said.

"I have some questions to ask and you should have the answers," Lucinda said.

"I agree that I'm a deer who has lived for thousands of years but be assured that I do not have all the answers to things that concern the other world," Amber replied.

"You should have an answer to this. This is about my mom," Lucinda said.

"And what about your mom?" Amber asked.

"My grandmother had my mom through a wish, experiencing the same thing that my mom experienced. Though mom didn't mention that she also went through the same thing. Grandma pleaded to the moon and stars for a child, and her wish was granted, but something was off. **Why wasn't my mom fit to hold the crown?** She is also the daughter of the moon and the stars.

Why did they let her die?" Lucinda asked.

"Our destinies are tied to different things. You didn't know who you were until you came into the city." Amber said.

"That's true; it all started from Anya, and now I have realized my true being," Lucinda said.

"Let me make you understand something. It was in this very town that your grandma made that wish. I guess she didn't tell you that. Your mom Annalise was given birth to here, and after a few months, your grandparents moved out, and they went to the village mountain top to live. Maybe if they had stayed and waited for the full blood moon, the initiation would have been completed, the crown would have rested on your mom's head, and somehow her death would have been averted." Amber replied.

"This is confusing. But my mom made a wish while she was still in the village, and that's where she gave birth to me. So how come I didn't realize who I am until I got here?" Lucinda asked.

"The wish that brought your mom to earth was made right here in this city, and somehow fate drew you back here for you to complete the initiation. Your mom is also the daughter of the moon and the stars.

Even though she made her wish right there in the village, fate brought you back to your mother's roots.

Your grandma made the wish, but the initiation wasn't complete. Everything was fixed. Aside from the fact that you're a daughter of the moon and stars, the main reason why your mom and dad can still talk to you is that they are not full mortals and before you ask about your dad, the day he got married to your mom was the day he officially became the son of the moon and the stars." Amber said as she looked around.

"What's the problem?" Lucinda asked.

"I think it's time to go. The water is drying up. I have answered the questions which you want. I need to return home." Amber said.

"You can't go now. I need to know why my parents had to die if both of them were tied to the moon and stars. Why weren't they protected? Why did they let them die?" Lucinda asked, almost on the verge of tears.

"You can't blame anyone. Just like I said, the initiation wasn't complete before she was taken out of the city, which means she was vulnerable to attacks. Your grandma isn't to be blamed because she wasn't aware of the gravity of the wish she made. She knew that nature was kind enough to hear her pleas and helped her with one child.

And since your mom was tied to the village, her wombs were closed. That's why she experienced several miscarriages.

Since she wasn't in the town to complete her initiation, someone from her loins had to take over the crown that was left hanging there. They wanted her to call on the moon and the stars like her mother did.

If she had given birth freely, the moon and the stars wouldn't acknowledge the baby as theirs because it's not from them. That's why their wish had to be made, and somehow, she made that wish.

That's why you have the birthmarks of the shapes of moon and stars on your body, showing where you came from. They didn't lock her womb because of the mistake your grandmother made; rather, they did that because her lineage was found worthy and pure to bear the queen that rules the other word, and that's you, Lucinda," Amber said.

"It all makes sense now. The wish. It's all about the wish. So that's why everything started happening after I came to this town. They did not know the significance of the wish they both made." Lucinda said, nodding in understanding.

"My time is up. I need to go home now." Amber said as she slowly faded into thin air, leaving some golden dust on the bed and floor.

Lucinda took her plate with the unfinished food and unlocked her door. She went to the kitchen to wash the plate, after which she kept it in the dish rack with the other dishes. She then came out to see her grandpa conversing with her grandmother.

"You're back," Lucinda remarked.

"Yes, I am," Greg replied.

"You don't look happy. What's the problem?" Maya asked.

"Something is bothering you. You can tell us the problem and we will solve it." Greg assured.

"I think you missed something, Grandma," Lucinda said. "What's that?" Maya asked.

"Lucinda, did you promise Maya that you would reunite her with Annalise? Annalise has been dead for eight years now. Don't make promises that can't be fulfilled." Greg chided.

"Was my mom born in this town," Lucinda asked as Maya and Greg looked at each other.

"Yes, but I didn't tell you that. How did you know?" Maya asked.

*"That shouldn't be a problem. It all makes sense now. Why did you bring me here when you left this place and relocated to the village **beyond the mountain ranges**?" Lucinda asked.*

"Because, we had issues and things were tight for us, we had to go back to the village a few months after your mom was born," Greg replied.

"Maybe you should have waited longer for the full blood moon. Maybe her death would have been averted," Lucinda said.

"What are you talking about?" Maya asked.

"I am trying to say that, I don't make promises that I can't fulfill. Nothing is impossible in my world because I rule in it. So, yes Grandpa, I promised Grandma that I would reunite her with her daughter. Just watch and see. It will all make sense someday. It's my promise to both of you," Lucinda said as she walked out and went into her room.

"What did you tell her?" Greg asked.

"I just told her the circumstances surrounding the birth of her mom, Annalise. She wanted to know, and I told her. But I never mentioned this town to her. I don't understand how she got to find out." Maya said.

"And she said something about the full blood moon and that nothing is impossible in her world," Greg asked, looking worried.

"Don't be word catch police Greg, we have just this world. Which another world can she be talking about?" Maya asked.

"I hope it makes sense someday. Just like she said, because I want to know why she said all these things," Greg said.

"Let me get your food," Maya said as she stood up and left the sitting room.

As the months rolled by, Greg and Maya tried to convince Lucinda to go outside and make friends, but their pleas fell on deaf ears. That wasn't what she was after. She was determined to set everything right and she was going to keep her promise.

"I think it's time. They deserve to know." Lucinda said as she looked out to see that the sky was covered with stars and a full moon.

"They agreed with me. They are solidly behind me," Lucinda said as she smiled and covered herself up as she drifted off to sleep.

Chapter Three

LUCINDA KNEW IT WAS TIME

*L*ucinda knew it was time to meet her fellow goddesses, seek answers to her questions, and provide clues to her quest for a solution. She needed to find a way to do this and end her guilt. Her grandparents deserved the truth. After all, she surmised that Annalise and Phil were their children too.

Waking up in the morning, and after taking her bath and dressing up, Lucinda went straight to her grandparent's room. Greg, her grandpa, answered the knock on the door.

"Lucinda, you're up already and even dressed up too. Where are you going?" Greg asked.

"I will explain when I'm back. I just wanted to inform you that I'm going out," Lucinda said as she walked out of the house to the stable.

She untied the white horse's leash and mounted her. She was going back to the village where she was born. She wanted to ask questions and she was going to get it. It didn't take up to three hours before Lucinda arrived at her parents' house. She tied the horse to one of the house's pillars before walking inside.

As expected, everywhere was dusty, as it had been almost close to a decade that no one had lived there. Lucinda walked into her room and beheld the tiny bed that used to be her crib. She betrayed a wry smile, wavering her head in the process and muttering a little bit audibly, "Indeed, how time flies."

Standing at the doorway, she felt a sensation like she never experienced before. She quickly swallowed the saliva gathered in her mouth: reminiscing her childhood flooded her mind. She remembered the day she lost her parents. She remembered it as if it was yesterday.

Even though she could still get to see her parents, she wished they were alive, and if they were alive, she wouldn't have any reason to leave the village. She felt that unseen hands programmed the entire thing. Turning back, she walked out of the house and headed towards the river. She didn't want to enter her parents' bedroom.

When she got to the riverbank, she sat down there and threw pebbles into the river. She was there to find answers to her troubled mind.

"Mia, I know you can hear me, very loud and clear. I'm just here to ask questions, and I feel very strongly that you have the answers to my questions. My heart is heavy, and I have this burden on my shoulders that I need to lift. You've got to help me, Mia, please.

You, of all goddesses, need to help me. I need to bridge this gap between my dead parents and my grandparents. I know it can be done. I know that nothing is impossible." Lucinda said.

"You already have your parents back. What else do you want?" A voice sounded as Lucinda turned to see Mia at her back, about a few steps away.

Mia walked towards Lucinda with measured steps, in her full bloom, as her hair fluttered with the wind. On getting to where Lucinda sat on the river bed, she sat down but had her legs dipped into the river.

"I'm tired of living with the guilt of my grandparents not knowing what is happening around them concerning their children, Annalise and Phil. I'm tired of hiding this.

I feel that my grandparents deserve to know the truth. After all, Annalise and Phil were their children, too. I have kept the secret for a long time because they don't understand what is happening. But I don't want it to be so anymore. I want them to see and hear their children again.

They deserve to know that their children still live though they are dead. I want them to have that same feeling of excitement in them, but I don't know how to make it happen. And please don't tell me you have no idea how to go about it because I know you do. I believe you can help me out." Lucinda said.

"That's the problem. I can't help you. You see these riddles you're trying to solve. You are the only one with the answers." Mia said.

"Why do you like giving me these blank answers each time I approach you? If I know the answer to the riddle I seek, do you think I will be here?" Lucinda asked, obviously frustrated.

"I don't even know how I'm not like you. Though you do not know it, I'm different. You're wiser and stronger than the two of us, making you the earth goddess. The answers you seek and the solutions lie within you." Mia said as she slowly turned into water and was gone.

Lucinda remained there speechless, angry, and sad at the same time.

"She didn't even give me a single clue to sorting out what borders my mind. Why do they keep telling me that I have the answers to all the questions I seek? Can't they see that I am human? If I have the answers, will I even ask anyone?" Lucinda said.

"It's not frustrating. It shouldn't be. That's the truth. The truth is that for some questions, you are the only one with the answers." A voice sounded nearby.

"Tara, is that you?" Lucinda asked, still having her gaze upon the water.

"Yes, it's me. I'm glad you're able to recognize my voice. Your tears drew me down to this place." Tara said, and that was when Lucinda realized she had been crying.

"I just want my grandparents to be able to see their children. That's all that I want. I want them to hear their voices again. I have been living with them ever since I lost my parents, and they have been the best grandparents ever. They haven't given me any reason to cry. My happiness is their utmost priority.

So, I think they deserve to know that their children still live even though they are dead. They also deserve to know who I am. They know that Lucinda is just their grandchild, but I think they deserve to know that I'm not fully mortal like them, that I'm something else, and that I'm the daughter of the moon and stars." Lucinda said.

"How I wish I have the answers to the questions you seek. How I wish I could make all that happen, but the truth is, I can't, but Bertha might know how you can go about it as she is the goddess of the wind. She is everywhere. She might have answers to that which you seek." Tara said.

"But Mia said I'm the only one who has the answers to the riddle." Lucinda offered.

"Yes, Bertha can only tell you the answers, but Bertha can't make them happen. You're the only one who can make it happen, and mind you, Bertha will give you a riddle to solve. It can know how to make your grandparents hear and see your parents again when solved." Tara replied. On hearing this, Lucinda was happy that at least there was hope.

"Even though I didn't find answers to my questions but then thanks to you and Mia, at least you both gave me a listening ear and offered me a line of hope," Lucinda said as she stood up and walked away. She turned to look and saw that Tara wasn't there anymore. She had disappeared just as she appeared.

When Lucinda got back, she took the horse into the stable and went inside the house.

"You're back, Lucinda. Watch the house. We want to get something at the market and be back in the next hour." Maya said from the window as soon as Lucinda entered through the back door.

"And when we are back, you have to explain where you went and why you have a frown on your face," Greg shouted.

Lucinda ignored them and turned back towards the garden. She was there all alone in silence. Soon after, she heard the door banging to know her grandparents were on their way out.

Lucinda sat there feeling dejected. She was worried that the promise she made to her grandparents might not be fulfilled after all, and she needed to keep to her promise. Her grandparents deserved to know the truth about her. Lucinda was racking her brain.

Suddenly Lucinda sensed a strong aura lurking around her. She knew someone was around.

"You are sad. You seek answers to your questions," a voice intoned. The voice was that of a whirlwind.

"Of course, I'm sad. I lived with my grandparents for eight good years and recently learned about my grandmother's pain and stigma before she had my mother. She was telling me the story herself. All I saw was a broken woman whose death cheated, a woman who fate mistreated, taking away her bundle of joy, a woman who never spent enough time with her child as my mom died when she was just 28 years old. Even though Granny is just trying to act strong and always smile, deep down her, I know the death of her child still hurts her today.

As she was telling her story, the story of her battle with childlessness, she tried so hard not to cry in my presence. *I promised her I would reunite her with her lost daughter, and she thinks I'm insane, but I still want to keep to that promise.*

I have had the opportunity to speak with my parents and even see them, and my grandparents know nothing about it. I think the little way of saying thank you for all these years is to give them the opportunity of seeing their children, Annalise and Phil.

But the problem remains how no one has the answers to my questions, not even Mia or Tara. I still believe that nothing is impossible in my world, but I can't yet understand why it looks as if it is impossible.

You all had lived in this world for thousands of years before I came into existence, so somehow any of you should have a hint on how to make my wish come to fruition. My grandparents deserve to know the truth and see their children again.

My grandmother needs her child, Annalise. When I look at my grandmother, I only see a woman who will give up the entire world for her child, someone who will trade her own life for her child. Please help me, help me put a smile on my grandparent's faces. Help me so I can say a proper thank you. Help me so I can reunite them with their children. That's all I ask for." Lucinda concluded as tears gushed freely from her eyes.

"The seashell holds the answer to the question which you seek. Mia said only you could solve the puzzle," Bertha replied after silently observing Lucinda for some minutes.

"The seashell? What do you mean? I know the seashell grants wishes, but I doubt it can make all these come through. How can the seashell help me out?

"The seashell will give you a link to make all of these come through. You have so many powers that you do not know of. But you need to know that no road on this earth is easy. Your road isn't easy, but they knew you were fit to solve all these mysteries when the crown was placed on your head." Bertha said.

"**The seashell**?" Lucinda muttered.

"I believe you can solve this puzzle. Have faith in yourself and see things work out right before your very eyes, the way you will never going to believe." Bertha said.

"But…" Lucinda turned to say something to Bertha, but she was nowhere to be seen. Having delivered her message, she has gone back to where she came from.

"Thank you, Bertha. I know you can hear me. I hope I will be able to sort this out." Lucinda said as she looked up at the sky where she sat in the garden.

Next, she stood up immediately and went inside her room. When she got there, she locked her doors, took out the seashell from where she hid it and placed her hand on it. She said, "I know you can hear me. They said you have the link to fix this puzzle, and once I fix it, I will be the happiest person on earth.

I should have done this since, but I feel this is the time to settle everything. Indeed, there is time for everything. Please help me, seashell. I need to reunite my grandparents with Annalise and Phil's children. You have got to help me.

Though she is acting all strong and fine, that woman has been bleeding over the death of her child. Fate has been unfair to her. Nature cheated her. Death won over her several times through several miscarriages. I just need answers on making my grandparents see and hear their children.

When I said nothing is impossible in my world, I meant it. Though I don't know, I know somehow answers will get to me. Could you help me fix this and reunite them? Tell me how I need to sort this out." Lucinda finished saying as she started crying. As she was crying, she was hoping for answers from the seashell. Lucinda waited patiently, but nothing happened. She was crying softly as her tears started dropping on the seashell.

"Bertha didn't lie to me. No one has the right to lie to the daughter of the moon and the stars. She wasn't lying when she asked me to come and meet you to answer my questions.

Why then are you keeping quiet? Why isn't anything happening? You all can't shut me out like this. I want to fix this problem, to bridge this gap. I can't do this on my own. I knew you all were sent to me because I believe you will have a part to play for my journey to be easier. So, why are you all silent?

Why won't you help? Why can't you tell me how to fix this? I need to reunite them, and I will, even if that's the last thing I will do on earth." Lucinda said as she dropped the seashell and lay on her bed, crying profusely.

"The wish; she has to make a wish on the night of the full blood moon." A voice whispered slowly and quietly.

"What wish? Who needs to make the wish?" Lucinda asked, but no one replied.

"The wish; she has to make a wish on the night of the full blood moon." The voice whispered slowly and quietly, again.

It was now left for Lucinda to figure out the rest. Time was of the essence as the blood moon would happen in less than a week.

Lucinda muttered, "Now I need to fix this, Clearing her eyes. What wish could this be, and who needs to make the wish?"

When she heard the front door opening, Lucinda lay on her bed thinking hard, trying to connect things to make sense. She knew her grandparents were back, and she knew that one of them would walk into her room in a few minutes.

And shortly after, Lucinda heard a knock on her door. It was a faint knock, but a knock always filled with tenderness and much love.

"Come in," Lucinda said.

Greg opened the door as he walked inside and sat on the edge of the bed.

"It seems something is troubling you. What's it?" Greg asked. "I'm okay, Grandpa," Lucinda replied.

"But your face has given you away. It's written all over you. So what mystery are you trying to unravel this time around?" Greg asked as Lucinda sat up properly as a particular thought crept into her mind that perhaps her grandfather could be of help.

"Grandpa, can I ask you a question?" Lucinda said.

"Sure, I'm all ears. You can go ahead and ask me anything." Greg replied.

"When everything that concerns one revolves around a wish, including her birth, and to solve a problem, I mean bridge a gap, a wish has to be made, right? Who do you think should make the wish?" Lucinda asked.

"Lucinda, is this question about you? If yes, it's not going to work. Do you get it?" Greg replied.

"It's not about me, and if it's about me, why did you say it's not going to work? Maybe you should explain better." Lucinda.

"There is no need to explain since it isn't you," Greg said, standing up as Lucinda stood up too immediately and held her grandfather's hand.

"Please, Grandpa, I promise this will make sense someday. Just help me answer the puzzle, please. You don't know the weight of the burden you'll lift from my shoulders if you answer this question." Lucinda said, almost on the verge of tears.

"I said it won't work because the one who has to make the wish is gone. She has been gone for the past eight years, dead and buried, and

I think you should forget about it. So, with that, I mean your mom, Annalise, but if it's someone else, her mother has to make the wish. So, the mother has to be the one whose wish can fix the gap." Greg said as he left the room.

Lucinda sat on the bed and placed her hand on her face, buried in deep thoughts.

"So, Mom has to make the wish? How can I even ask her to make a wish? She will know that I'm up to something. Can't I do this without involving her? Why does she have to be the one to make the wish?" Lucinda asked herself, pacing up about her room as the plot seemed dead on arrival. She just didn't know what to do. She knew there was no way her mom could make that wish without suspecting that she was up to something.

Lucinda ate her dinner that night and retired early to bed. When she woke up, it was already 1 am. Lucinda stood up and locked her door. Next, she held onto her necklace, closing her eyes; and on opening it, she found herself on the bush path where she usually met with her parents, Amber and Anya. They were already sitting there in circles, waiting for her.

"I'm sorry I'm late. I was thinking about a few things, and I slept off, and when I woke up, it was already 1 am." Lucinda said as she sat down in their midst.

"Once again, something is bothering you. Do you mind sharing it?" Amber said.

"Nothing; I'm fine," Lucinda replied.

"You know we can always help when the need arises. Just tell us what the problem is, and we are ready to help." Phil chimed in.

"Lucinda, you're trying so hard to act fine, but it's written all over your face that something is wrong somewhere. I know you. I know the girl I gave birth to. I know when something is wrong with her." Annalise said.

"I feel she can sort it out. If she needs our help, she will speak up." Anya said.

"Anya is right. I can sort it out. There is nothing to worry about." Lucinda said.

"But I have a question to ask. Did Grandma tell you anything surrounding your birth?" Lucinda asked.

"No, because I didn't ask her as I felt it wasn't necessary, but what I know is that my mother was overprotective," Annalise said, smiling.

"Do you miss her? Have you ever wished that you could get to hold her and have a conversation with her?" Lucinda asked. "Why do you ask?" Phil asked.

"Nothing really; just want to know," Lucinda said, smiling.

"Your grandmother is one of the best mothers-in-law. I see her as my mother. I was an orphan when I met your mom, and Maya proved to be the mother I didn't have all these years. So, yes, we miss her, but the truth remains that she can never see us or hear from us again. We are dead, and they are alive. There is a bridge between the dead and the living. You were able to break that barrier because of the powers bestowed on you," Phil said.

"I miss her. I do. She was my everything here on earth. I loved her the same way she loved me. Even though I asked her to give me siblings, she told me she was okay with just me. Of course, I miss her. There is no way I can deny that. I still want to have that conversation with her, hug her, and I will tell her how her smile is the most beautiful thing on earth. Those are mere imaginations that can't happen. As your dad said, there is a gap between the living and dead that is impossible to bridge." Annalise replied.

"What if nature decides to turn things around, and somehow you get to do all these things with your mother again. Will you reject it, or will you accept it wholeheartedly?" Lucinda asked.

Chapter Four

Lucinda Wanted More

ucinda wanted more. She wouldn't accept having to wait only for midnights to see her parents, and even at that, once it was 3 am, they would have to part till another midnight?

She wouldn't accept the fact anymore of her grandparents not knowing about what was happening, of not being able to see their children and commune with them. Why wouldn't her grandparents be permitted to see, touch, and hear them?

It was becoming frustrating and even tasking, considering her having to come out most nights, enduring sleepless nights or half sleepless nights. Was she being selfish in demanding more? Wouldn't she have been contented with the rare opportunity already granted her to see and hear her dead parents? She pondered these thoughts as she sat on her bed, getting ready to go out for the night as usual. As she was rummaging over these thoughts, she wavered her head in disagreement, insisting that she was not being selfish but only demanding what was the right thing to do under the circumstances. She wanted to start seeing her parents daily, in everyday interaction. Any other person out there would also have asked for the same thing. Which human being would be content with this unnatural arrangement?

These were her parents she lost when she was only a child, parents she never lived with for a long time, to savor the filial love and protection good parents give to their children.

Her joy in a child-parent relationship was short-lived and was cut short by their death. And now she knew she wanted them back at any price. She was determined to get them back to herself and her grandparents. She knew she could if she tried.

As the earth goddess and daughter of the moon and the stars, if she could not get whatever she wanted, who then should? Though her grandparents had tried their utmost to make her happy, the truth remained that the joy and bond of her parents were irreplaceable to her.

They were priceless. Still bearing these thoughts in her mind, Lucinda got up from the bed and stepped out of her room into the garden. When she got there, she down on the garden seat as she waited patiently for her grandparents to go out, and they just immediately notified her that they were leaving. She was excited. Once they were out of the house, Lucinda summoned Anya. She wanted to ask questions, and she hoped Anya would give her answers to her agitated mind.

"Surely something is bothering you that you couldn't wait till midnight?" Anya said as she appeared from nowhere.

"No, I can't wait, but you just scared me by your noiseless appearance." Lucinda half complained.

"You shouldn't be scared by that. Was it to be mere humans? I would understand, but not you. Anyway, sorry about that." Anya said as she sat down close to Lucinda. Lucinda couldn't help but admire the beautiful damsel sitting just close to her, yet she knew she was sitting close to a terrifying beast in her subconscious mind.

No one would believe that this pretty young girl sitting close to her was a deadly beast, not even Lucinda herself, as a mere mortal, would assume so. It surprised the thin line between Lucinda's natural world and humans. What appeared so fundamental to humans would not be what it was. But nothing could convince humans otherwise. They only could perceive through the five senses. Anything beyond that would be impossible to them.

"It's okay to admire my beauty, but I'm sure that's not why you summoned me. So, tell me, what's the problem?" Anya asked.

"My parents," Lucinda replied.

"What about your parents?" Anya asked.

"I'm tired of this midnight ritual of meeting them at a particular place, waiting for midnights every day before I can see them, and once it's 3 am, they are gone. I want to see them every day and restart a normal, natural relationship with them, just as we had before their death. I want to start interacting with them as naturally as I can be. Perhaps you might term me selfish, but I don't care. Besides, anyone out there would also ask for the same thing.

I know you can help me out, Anya. I want them to live with us here in this house, with you too. Please, I know you can make this happen." Lucinda pleaded.

"But have you thought about your grandparents and what their reaction could be? Would they ever be able to come to terms with that?" Anya asked.

"Don't worry about them; I will fix it," Lucinda said.

"Well, I can't make it happen. The only one who can do that is you. Only you can make that happen." Anya replied.

"But you are."

"I'm Anya, the three-in-one being. I have been granted powers to do many things, but I can't promise you anything. I know that deep down, if you want this to work, you have to do it yourself. You have the powers to make it work. It's in you." Anya said.

"But how? I don't know. If I knew how I won't be asking you." Lucinda said.

"Maybe you don't know how but you have the powers to do it. You just have to go deep inside of you for the answers you seek." Anya said.

"Would Amber have an idea on how I'm going to go about it?" Digging inside wouldn't help me much, as I have done that severally without any answers. I need directions as I'm not wholly supernatural like you." Lucinda said.

"Amber won't answer the question. Listen, Lucinda, you are the daughter of the moon and the stars, and you have been bestowed with powers beyond what the mortal eyes can see, even beyond what you already know or can fathom.

You possess special powers that even you don't know. You ask questions that only you have answers to. The answer to the riddle that you seek lies in your palm. You can make it happen. You have to concentrate and figure it out, but whatever you do, make sure it won't ruin it for you in the future.

You have to be super careful because what you seek is quite extraordinary." Anya said as she stood up to leave.

"Where are you going? Lucinda protested. I'm not even finished with my questions."

"You're done with your questions, though you still have one question you can't ask me, and I don't even know what the question is. And secondly, your grandparents are on their way back so I should leave now. Check inside of your heart. Therein you will find answers to that which you seek." Anya replied as she went deeper into the garden, and just as Lucinda looked again, she was gone.

"Check inside of your heart. You will find answers to what you seek," Lucinda repeated the same thing Anya said.

"Why can't I just find the answers? Where else will I search? Why isn't my heart providing the answers that I seek? Why does everyone keep saying that I have answers to all I seek? Why?" Lucinda said, rubbing her forehead and racking her brain. She was beginning to feel frustrated.

Maya walked into the garden and sat close to Lucinda, but Lucinda didn't even notice that someone was sitting close to her until Maya tapped her, and she jerked.

"Hmmm. This is getting serious. You didn't even notice when I walked in?" Maya asked.

"Sorry, Grandma. I was lost in thoughts. You're back already. What about Grandpa?" Lucinda asked.

"Oh, he is inside, and we got something for you. Are you okay?" Maya asked.

"Yeah, can I ask a question?" Lucinda asked. "Sure, why not."

"If you keep asking for answers to your questions and people keep telling you that you should look down inside your heart, that there you will find your answers, what does that mean?"

Lucinda asked.

"It means that the answers you seek are right there in your heart. You just need to sit and think, and it will reveal itself to you. ***Sometimes we search for solutions in the wrong places while the solution is right there.*** You will figure out all that you need to solve whatever it is." Maya said.

"Thank you, Grandma," Lucinda said with a smile.

"You're welcome," Maya said as she stood up and went inside.

"I need to bridge this gap that has been created by death, and also, I need to make my grandparents stay a little longer. Now, I'm faced with two tasks that I don't know which to do first, and I don't even know how to achieve them, not at all. I'm not selfish. I'm just being normal, natural. I'm not selfish to want my parents to stay for a long time without leaving once it's 3 am.

Any other person in my shoes will request for same. They were taken away from me when I was just ten years. Death separated us, and now that I can see and hear them again, it came with conditions.

Why are things way difficult when they should be made easy for me? Why do I have to go through so much to achieve so little? Life isn't fair.

I would be wicked if I said I needed to die to be with my parents completely. Doing so will be the same as killing my grandparents; their lives will be shattered and ruined. They will never forgive me. What do I do?

How do I fix this? How do I achieve all that I have mapped out? It's now looking impossible. I need help." Lucinda said in hushed tones with a teary voice.

She was tired. She was beginning to lose faith even in herself. Her level of frustration was increasing, and if not checked soon, she could reach the level of desperation and sadness. She had started feeling she couldn't endure it anymore, yet these immortals by her side expected her to be strong, but she wasn't sure of herself anymore. Even then, she didn't know how long she would take to achieve these things if they were ever to be completed.

As soon as Maya left, Lucinda also stood up as she went inside the house where she met her grandpa, who was resting with his eyes closed, obviously in thoughts.

Lucinda was almost at the door when she heard her grandfather's voice calling her. Getting closer to him, she answered.

"Sit down," Greg said as Lucinda sat down quietly.

"I know I haven't done anything wrong, or have I done something wrong?" Lucinda asked.

"No, you haven't done anything wrong, but I have been watching you for a few days now, and it's so obvious that something is eating you up. I know you will never answer me if I ask what the problem is, but that won't stop me from asking. So, what is the problem?

It hurts that you're fine this week, and the next week you carry a long face, and no one can be able to say what the problem is. We might not be able to bring back your dead parents, Lucinda. If we had the power to, we would have brought them back because we miss them too. Surely, you can't keep shutting us out like this. It's been eight years, Lucinda, yet you still haven't gotten over their death. One minute you're happy and looking all good, and the next minute my child is down with this sadness on her face. Where did we go wrong, Lucinda? Why is it difficult to accept the reality of death? Why can you not take us as your parents?" Greg asked, looking sad.

"I'm sorry, Grandpa if I have treated you and Grandma bad. I promise I didn't mean to. I never wanted it to be that way. I'm just trying to fix up things. I'm trying to patch up things so everyone will be happy.

I know I have been crisscrossing between two extremes of emotions, but I just can't help but know that soon, everything will be just where I want it to be. You and Grandma have tried to help me, and I appreciate it. I just want some more time to fix everything, and you all will understand what I have been going through for these past few years." Lucinda said while trying to manage a wry smile.

"How can we help if you don't tell us the problem? Why are you handling the problem alone when you know we might be of help to you?" Greg said.

"Grandpa, this is not as easy as you think. You and Grandma have already helped a lot, and this I must fix alone. No one can help me. I'm the only one who can help myself. I promise this will make sense to you and Grandma soon. Have faith in me." Lucinda pleaded.

"I hope I will be alive to witness that soon. I just hope, Lucinda. My health is waning bad, and I don't have much time. I don't know when my time will be up. We are all visitors here on earth, and when the time comes, we will leave." Greg said.

On hearing that, Lucinda rushed to where her grandpa was, and she hugged him tightly, whispering into his ears, "Nothing will happen to you. It's a promise. You will live for a long time, and when you get tired of living, you can go, but you aren't leaving us for now. About your health, you've healed already," Lucinda said with every seriousness.

"You're not a physician, Lucinda," Greg said.

"I'm not, but the powers and knowledge can't be compared to what I have," Lucinda said.

"And don't ask. I will explain all these when the time comes, but believe me when I said you're healed," Lucinda added as she smiled and went inside her room, leaving Greg confused about what she just said.

Lucinda got to her room, lay down on her bed, and soon immersed in her thoughts, soliloquizing. "How did I get so caught up with things that I didn't even notice my grandpa is slipping away?

How come I didn't notice how lean he has become? All I was after my happiness and to do things that would make me happy that I didn't even notice he had been sick all this while. What if he hadn't told me today? What would have happened?

At least I'm glad it's all over now. I made good use of my powers to heal my father, and all I can say is I'm proud of myself. I will do better this time. These two have sacrificed so much for me. I need to start paying attention to them and stop hiding in my room all day. I'm going to fix everything that soon they will meet Annalise and Phil.

Mom, I don't know how it will be, but you will make that wish." Lucinda said as she closed her eyes slowly and drifted off to sleep. All she knew was that things were going to be okay soon. She was so sure of that.

Lucinda counted the days and knew that the day of the blood moon was fast approaching. Though she saw her parents every night, that didn't erase her sadness.

Even when Lucinda tried to act all happy in the presence of her grandparents because she still had this sad smile on her face, she tried hard to conceal it. She didn't want anyone to know what she was going through. Nevertheless, Lucinda was optimistic that she would fix these and make everything possible.

As the days of the blood moon drew nearer, she started spending more time in the garden talking to herself. Whenever Maya and Greg tried to strike up a conversation with her, they would notice it wasn't flowing. They knew something was eating Lucinda up, but they didn't see the issue. All she thought about was how she could get her mom into making that wish because of the conversation she had with her these few days. It didn't seem like she was going to make any wishes again.

Lucinda was out to achieve two things. Though Anya knew the second one, she kept the first one a secret.

First, she contrived to trick her mother into making the wish—the wish needed to be made. Lucinda knew the desire was pivotal to the solution, the solution that would guarantee the happiness of everyone involved.

She just couldn't imagine the smiles on the faces of her grandparents when they would get to hear the voice of their children again.

The D-day came, and she had not yet achieved her aim of making her mom make the wish. So, she prayed instead that things change so the full blood moon won't come out that night, but she was disappointed to look up at the sky through her window to see the blood moon. She sighed and sat down on her bed.

Lucinda knew it was today or never if she had to succeed, facing her fate alone and with nothing to do about the situation. Otherwise, she would have to wait till the next year before she could do what she wanted, but she wasn't prepared to wait for that long. She needed to take action that night, hoping things would turn out well for her. As Lucinda sat on her bed brooding over the problem, she didn't know when it was just a few minutes before midnight. On noticing that, she stood up and locked her door while clutching her necklace. Next, she opened her eyes to see herself standing on the path she usually met with her parents. She sat there and waited patiently for them.

"This will be either a tough night or a smooth one. I don't know which one will be, but I want everything to be perfect. To the moon and the stars of the sky, I hope you can listen to your daughter.

I need your help this night. I want everything I planned to turn out well. *Help me to make my mom make the wish.* I need her to be able to speak with her mom again. Though my grandma acts all right, she is still in pain over her daughter's death.

You know it's the same daughter she begged for, the same daughter she waited for ten years so she could have, the same child she cried to you. Now is the time to show that you can help me as I need your help to carry out this task. I know you can make this work. My mom must make the wish tonight. Please, listen to me and grant me this one wish. I beg of you." Lucinda said amidst tears.

And just when it struck midnight, Lucinda started hearing the howling of the wolves, an indication that Anya was about to appear. And soon after, Anya seemed to look completely emotionless, not happy, not sad, just plain. She came before Amber and Lucinda's parents got there later. They all sat down, and they started discussing in hushed tones, talking about the foibles of humans. Time was going so fast, and Lucinda didn't know how to bring up the discussion about her grandparents.

"The moon and the stars, help your daughter, I'm pleading. Don't forsake me now. I don't even know how to kick start my plans. I don't know." Lucinda muttered within herself, almost on the verge of tears.

"I miss my mom's stories. I don't go to bed any night without her telling me these beautiful stories. Even when I got married and visited, she would always tell me stories. I miss her." Annalise suddenly changed the topic of discussion.

Lucinda looked up as her face beamed with smiles, as this was something she was patiently waiting for.

"Does she tell you any stories?" Annalise asked, looking at Lucinda.

"Not really. Ever since you guys left, my relationship with my grandparents went from a hundred to zero. I always lock myself up in the room, though she listens and tells me if I ask her for stories. How I wish she could hear you, Mom, and also Dad. Maybe they won't have to see me as one who is going crazy anymore," Lucinda said.

"I have this feeling that someday they will be able to hear us," Phil said.

"That's true. I just want to hear her stories again. I wish my mom and dad could hear me, and my husband. I wish they could hear us." Annalise's said as she slowly faded away.

Lucinda smiled, knowing her mom made the wish at the right time. Her face was filled with so much happiness. Anya looked at her and smiled before she changed and raced into the woods.

"I don't even know how I'm going to thank you. I don't even know where to start or what to say. Just when I thought all hope was lost, that I would have to wait till next year, you changed everything. I made my wish, and you made it happen. So, thank you! Thank you so much! I'm the happiest human on earth right now! The only thing I want has been accomplished." Lucinda said, smiling as she gathered herself up to leave too.

"I heard my daughter's wish, and I acted just like she wanted. You have been sad for years. If this is the only thing that can make you happy, I will do it for you. She took good care of my daughter, so they need to reunite with each other." An old-young voice said calmly to the hearing of Lucinda. It was the first time Lucinda heard this voice. It sounded like a mixture of light and darkness, thunder and lightning, the voice of a child and that of the aged.

"Thanks to the queen mother. I hope that one day I shall see you." Lucinda found herself saying.

"Not soon, but I will always be with you. ***Your job here on earth isn't finished. You can only see me when your work here is finished.***" The voice said.

Lucinda smiled as she held her necklace, and immediately she was in her room. She quietly lay on the bed as she kept smiling.

She was so happy that she heard her voice for the first time, the voice of the one who owned her. It was the voice of the woman in whose loins she was formed and was given to her earthly mother to bear. She was so happy as she kept grinning from ear to ear.

"Lucinda, I'm happy that you're smiling right now. I don't know what you did, but whatever it was, I know it's for good since you're smiling; I love you, child." Again, it was Phil's voice.

"Goodnight, Dad," Lucinda said as she closed her eyes and drifted off to bed. She just couldn't wait for her grandparents to wake up.

Chapter Five

LUCINDA WALKED INTO

Lucinda walked into the sitting room and quietly sat down, looking as if she wasn't in the mood to talk. After sitting down and not saying anything, her grandparents became uncomfortable with her moody stare. She sat down opposite them, with eyes filled with words and a silent mouth that remained sealed.

"Is everything okay?" Maya asked as she couldn't hold it anymore and was alarmed. Lucinda pretended as if she didn't hear her, but after another long stare at her and then at Greg, she calmly started talking: "There are two people so dear to you who wish to talk. You already know them, so there won't be any need for introduction." Lucinda said as a matter of fact.

"Talk to us? Who? From where? What are you talking about?" Greg asked, confused.

"You just walked out of your room alone. Who are those that want to talk to us? Besides, no one else is here except the three of us. So, what are you referring to, or are they standing outside?" Maya asked, looking confused.

"Mom, Dad!" The voice sounded. "Can you hear us?" Phil's voice added.

"What's happening? Am I dreaming?" Maya asked, feeling so confused.

"It's Annalise and Phil's voice; Lucinda, what did you do?" Greg asked, feeling a swell of excitement in his bosom.

"She didn't do anything ill. All she wanted was for her grandparents to hear the voice of her children again." Phil's voice said.

"It's eight years now, and you can still remember our voice. I feel so happy that today you both can hear us." Annalise's voice added.

"Annalise, Phil, is that you?" Maya asked, almost on the verge of crying her eyes out.

"Yes, I'm the one, Mom." Annalise intoned.

"Someone, wake me up from this dream. This can't be real," Greg said.

"It's real. It's us. I hope somehow you will be able to see and feel us someday." Phil's said.

"Okay, this was what I have been working on. Remember I once said it's all going to make sense someday. This is what I was talking about. I have been in touch with my parents for the past eight years, but the whole issue was that you both couldn't hear them. There wasn't any need to explain to you both because when I tried to, you and Grandma thought I was going insane. I have always wanted to fix this gap, and I'm glad I can do that, even if it's still partial."

"How is it possible? How did you manage to do all this?" Greg asked.

"The wish you made, Grandma," Lucinda replied. "What wish are you talking about?" Maya said.

"Remember when you wished that the moon and the stars should bless you with a child, and they did. It turned out mother also made that same wish, but the truth is, you two considered it as mere wishes. ***This eighteen-year-old girl standing right in front of you is half-human and half-mortal.***

I am the daughter of the moon and stars, who have been bestowed with so many powers to do everything.

You and Mom's wish years ago made me who I am today. Though I didn't find it funny when I realized who I am, I had to accept it in good faith, and all I can say is that I'm happy my grandparents can hear their children's voice again after eight whole years." Lucinda said.

"I don't even know what to say," Maya said, sitting stuck on the chair as if glued to it.

"I will explain more tonight. Just wait," Lucinda said.

"This explains the howling of the wolves that I heard the night Annalise was born, right?" Greg said.

"*Exactly! The howling of wolves welcomes every daughter of the moon and the stars.* It is the same way they howled during my birth.

Your daughter, Annalise, is also a daughter of the moon and the stars, but the initiation wasn't complete because you took her out of this town and after she had me, fate brought us back here for me to pick up the crown that my mom wasn't able to wear. The universe was listening all these while weaving its ways around humans." Lucinda said.

"No wonder Annalise fell very ill after she left the town, and we thought she wasn't going to make it, but somehow she survived."

"That was when they called you to bring back their child because the place you made the wish has to be the same place where the initiation was completed. When my mom didn't return, I was brought here. I was born to replace my mom." Lucinda replied.

"Annalise! Phil!" Maya shouted in awe of what she was hearing.

"They won't hear you. they are gone, but you will hear from them soon," Lucinda assured as she went inside, but Greg was lost in thoughts.

"I see. All this while Lucinda was battling into accepting who she was. She couldn't tell us because we wouldn't understand.

So, Lucinda went on this journey alone for the past eight years. She was trying to fix the gap between us, desiring us to hear from them. Recently when I told her I was sick, she assured me I was healed, and up till today, there had been no sign of illness again.

She has been trying to fit into the life of mortals, trying to balance living with mortals with plenty of immortals by her side. It all makes sense now. I see." Greg reminisced, nodding.

"Lucinda, I'm very sorry," Maya said.

"Sorry about what, Grandma? Why are you apologizing? You don't have to, as you haven't done me any wrong." Lucinda sounded apologetic.

"I need to apologize. We didn't know you had been going through all these for eight years, trying to make us happy. Countless times you have given us hints of what you're going through, but what do we do? We continue feeling that it was the death of your parents that was affecting you, and because of that, we never paid attention to details that could have given a clue to what you were trying to do or who you are. We are sorry, Lucinda," Maya insisted.

"Yes, Lucinda, I feel the same way too. We are sorry and should have tried harder. We should have asked more questions." Greg said.

"No, you did. You did what good grandparents should have done in the circumstance. You were always concerned about me, but I kept it away from you all because I felt you were not going to believe me, and the truth was that there was no way you both would believe me if you couldn't have firsthand experience of whatever claim I would make.

Still, I knew someday things would change around. I only waited for the way you would hear them so I could explain everything that has been going on all these years.

Life has been fun and more fulfilling with you both, though sometimes I wish my parents never died. But then I would console myself with the fact that I got to hear their voices every night before eventually being able to start seeing them face to face.

I realized something the day I listened to your tale of how you had my mother. It was the same way you were hurt about her demise because of the constant pain, humiliation, and rejection you went through before you could give birth to her.

I knew I had to do something to reunite you all. I knew it was time to fill in the gap between you and them for eight years now. I started searching for ways. I asked the water goddess and fire goddess, but I got no concrete answers. When I asked the wind goddess, she gave me a clue. *And yes, the seashell you handed over to me so many years ago isn't just an ordinary seashell.*

It's a magical one, a priceless possession that can only work in the hands of the chosen one. I was able to find out that Mom had to make a wish for you to be able to hear for the gap to be closed. And somehow, she did because none of them knew what I was up to. I'm happy. I'm the most excited human on earth.

I got to reunite my grandparents with their dead children, as that has always been the task, and I'm glad I was able to put through it." Lucinda said, smiling as Greg and Maya walked closer to her and hugged her tightly.

"We are proud of you! Thank you so much for bringing them back. We can't see them, but at least hearing their voices again gladdens our heart." Greg said.

"We love you, Lucinda. Thank you for this." Maya said as tears dripped down her cheeks as Lucinda wiped them off with her hands.

"You shouldn't be crying, Grandma. Things are okay now. Don't worry. Everything will be complete soon." Lucinda said.

"But everything is completed already. We can hear them. What more can you do?" Greg asked.

Lucinda stepped back as she lifted her hands, and just with a snap of the finger, a ball of fire was sitting on her palm.

"Lucinda!" Maya shouted, shocked.

"You're going to get hurt!" Greg joined as Lucinda disappeared and appeared at his back.

Greg and Maya were shocked beyond words. "Who are you?" Lucinda.

"I'm still Lucinda, your granddaughter you have raised for eight years.

You know me as Lucinda but not as the daughter of the moon and the stars. I'm different, Grandpa; I'm entirely different. I possess supernatural powers, some of which I don't know. I'm not completely human. I'm Lucinda, but I'm immortal. That's who this girl is. Just wait, and you will see what will happen sooner." Lucinda smiled and walked inside her room, leaving her grandparents speechless.

"I guess we are in for a lot of surprises. She was either in her room or the garden. She must have been feeling lonely and sad all this while. It must have taken a whole time for her to accept who she is.

I know Lucinda to be a stubborn but sweet girl as well. I'm proud of her. I'm happy that she could pull through and how she has accepted who she is. I'm happy this new self-discovery didn't mar her. She acted wisely the same way Annalise would have acted. I couldn't have asked God for a better gift. I'm happy we have Lucinda here." Greg said, smiling contentedly.

"I'm happy she reunited me with my dead daughter and son-in-law. I don't know what to give her to thank you or appreciate her for what she did. Just when I got tired of questioning the universe on why they took Annalise from me.

Then Lucinda made it possible for us to communicate with them. Lucinda, in generations to come, your kids, strangers, and people from far and wide will bow at your feet and make you happy. You won't have any reason to cry in life. I hope all you wish for is granted unto you." Maya said, smiling as she hugged her husband.

Lucinda on bed staring at the ceiling. She was happy with herself. She was proud of herself, and best of all, she felt at peace with herself. She had just one thing left to do. She needed to behold the face of the woman whose loins she came out from.

She would see the queen of the moon and the stars. She had to meet her and thank her for blessing her with her earthly parents. Her parents and grandparents were the real deal, and she was grateful. She couldn't have asked for more.

"I guess that's why you pushed me into making the wish. I'm glad I listened to you. I could see the excitement and happiness in their faces when they heard our voices." It was Phil.

"I couldn't tell you and Dad what I'm up to. I wanted it to be a surprise. And after I listened to Grandma's tale of what she went through before she gave birth to you, I knew the only way I could make her happy was by reuniting the both of you."

She knew they were gone when she didn't hear their voice anymore. She then closed her eyes and drifted off to sleep.

Chapter Six

IN THE EVENING

In the evening, Lucinda decided to take a stroll into the town and no sooner had she opened the door then Maya wanted to know where she was going.

"To look at the environment. I'll be back before 6 pm." Lucinda promised as she left the house, leaving Maya staring at her from behind.

When she got into the heart of the town, she went to a park with concrete seats scattered all over the place. She sat down, looking around her, and she couldn't help but admire the serene environment before her. It had been a long time since she visited the town. Most of these times of her troubles, she had always been inside or in the garden. Mingling with people inside the city reminded her of her humanity, though she didn't have any human friends.

As she sat down inside the park, she couldn't help but admire a little girl who held tightly onto her mom. Lucinda smiled and muttered, "She is beautiful." The little girl and her mom were taking a walk on the street. Lucinda decided to also take a walk all by herself.

As she went into the street, she suddenly felt a hard nudge on her body, and on turning around, she saw a young boy, slightly older than her, having his baskets and their contents on the ground, littering everywhere. She had pushed the boy without noticing it, as all her attention was on the people around her.

"I'm sorry. I didn't mean to. I just wasn't looking." Lucinda apologized as she helped and picked up the vegetables littered on the ground.

"It's okay," the boy said as he clutched tightly to his basket.

On looking at him, Lucinda felt something strange and unique, perhaps. His skin was white and his hair golden, like his eyeballs. His aura was so strong. Lucinda felt it.

"I'm Lucinda; who are you?" Lucinda said, trying to strike a conversation.

"I'm Jake. Next time, you have to be more careful," Jake said as he hurriedly walked off.

"Something was so strange about him," Lucinda muttered as she looked at him until he faded out of sight. "Who is he?" Why did I feel slight pain when my hand brushed his hands?" Lucinda muttered again but, finding no answers to her questions, had to turn and stroll back home, with the thought of Jake occupying her mind. She went through the back door into the sitting room when she got home, where she saw her grandparents. She just sat down beside her grandmother but looked moody.

"What's the problem? I can see that something is bothering you." Greg said.

"I saw someone today who looked different. His skin shone bright like the sun, and his hair and eyes were pure gold. He said his name was Jake. I want to find out more about him. Something is off somewhere about him. That's it. Nothing much." Lucinda said.

"Are you suggesting he is a bad person?" Maya asked.

"No; far from that, rather, he is good, but I want to know who and why he is here. He doesn't belong here. Something is so different, but I can't place my hand on it, and I need to find out why." Lucinda said.

"Do you like him?" Greg asked, looking at his granddaughter closely.

"What! No, not that." Lucinda stammered, blushing in the process.

"It's just that he looked different, and his aura is so strong, and I want to know more about him," Lucinda replied.

"Lucinda," Greg said, smiling.

"What's the problem, Grandpa?" Lucinda asked.

"Ever since we moved into this place, you haven't had someone to call a friend. You have been alone. Either you're inside your room or inside the garden and…"

"I have friends, Grandpa," Lucinda said, cutting her grandfather short.

"I don't mean your friends who aren't humans. I mean friends who are humans like us. Having one human friend won't hurt. If you like Jake, I hope fate brings you to see each other again. At least, that way, I can say my granddaughter has a friend whom she can talk to any time, any day." Greg said.

"Your grandfather is right, Lucinda. A time comes when we will not be here for you. We won't be with you forever, and you will be spending more years here on earth when we are gone. So, you have to get used to that fact. You need someone with whom you can talk, laugh, build memories, and do many other things." Maya said.

"Well, if I'm bored, I can always talk to you both. You both make me happy. Why then, do I need a friend?" Lucinda asked.

"You need a friend, a human friend. You have to start accepting that we won't be with you forever. We are aging beautifully, and soon, we will kiss goodbye to this earth." Greg said.

Lucinda thought of what she heard and decided to go inside her room. Once inside, she concluded that her grandparents were right.

"But how is that even possible when I barely know anyone? The worst thing is that I don't even know how to make friends. I have lived in this town for some years now, yet I do not know anyone or anywhere I can visit to make friends." She was muttering as she lay on her hand, looking up to the ceiling. She was gradually becoming restless.

Next, she stood up and walked out of the garden toward her room. She kept thinking about the boy amid a potpourri of other issues bothering her. But she couldn't seem to get her mind off the boy. She knew that something was special about him, but she couldn't get to know what at the moment.

On realizing her state of mind, she wanted answers and needed to talk to someone. She closed her eyes and mumbled some words. As she opened her eyes, Anya was sitting close to her.

"You summoned me. Hope there is no problem?" Anya asked as she sat near Lucinda.

"I need your help, Anya." Lucinda pleaded.

"Okay, you can tell me what the problem is," Anya said.

"I don't have friends. I don't mean to say you're not my friend. You're my friend, but I mean like human friends. Does that make me awkward? I mean, I'm eighteen, and in a few months, I will be nineteen, and I can't even boast of having any single friend. It has always been you and Amber, my parents, and my grandparents. I need to have, even if it's one human friend." Lucinda said.

"Let me guess; something happened today. Tell me about it." Anya said, smiling.

"Who are you talking to, Lucinda?" Maya said as she walked towards the garden.

"She can't see me, so it's no use explaining to her. Just come up with any good excuse." Anya said.

"Grandma, I'm just thinking out loud. You know, thinking about life," Lucinda said, faking a smile.

"Okay, no problem. Dinner will soon be ready. So, make sure you come in very soon." Maya said as she looked at her granddaughter one more time before leaving.

"How come she can't see you?" Lucinda asked.

"Because she isn't meant to see me. So, back to the main reason why you called me here. What happened?" Anya asked.

"I saw this boy today while strolling on the streets, and something seems odd about him. His eyes are pure gold, and his aura is so strong. He said his name is Jake," Lucinda said.

"His eyes are like pure gold, and yours is like that of the sky," Anya said, laughing.

"Anya, I'm serious," Lucinda said.

"Okay, you already know his name, so why did you call me here? I'm still trying to understand why you called me and what you need my help with." Anya said.

"I need to find Jake. I want to know where he lives, his parents, and where he is from. I want to know everything about him." Lucinda said.

"Why are you interested in someone you met today, and why do you want to know more about him? Have you fallen in love with him?" Anya asked.

"No! I just want to know. I have questions, and don't ask me what I intend to ask him." Lucinda said, smiling.

"Okay, I can't help you then," Anya said. "Why?" Lucinda asked.

"Because no human fits into that description. So, most likely must have seen a spirit who came to the market to get some things. My dear Lucinda, the sooner you erase the thought of Jake or whatever his name is, the better for you. The person you saw isn't human." Anya said.

"No, he is human. Our bodies brushed against each other. You have to believe me, Anya." Lucinda pleaded.

"I believe you, but the truth is that he isn't human. His eyes are like pure gold. That sentence alone proves he isn't human like you. So, give up. You can't find him, and I can't find him too. And you made mention of friends. How did friends and this Jake relate to each other?" Anya asked.

"Ooh, you didn't get the connection? I'm looking to make him my human friend. I don't know, but my spirit accepted him. That's why I called you so you can find out everything about him." Lucinda said sadly.

"Aside from being the daughter of the moon and the stars, there are still things that you don't know. Don't worry. Soon, you will get to understand everything. It's just a matter of time." Anya said.

"I'm sure he is human. He is human." Lucinda insisted as she stood up and walked out of the garden.

"Jake met a goddess here today. What is he doing here? Why does it have to be Lucinda? I have to meet him." Anya said as she slowly faded away.

On leaving the garden, Lucinda sat on the sofa on the balcony. She just couldn't understand what Anya said to her that Jake wasn't human that made her so sad? As she was crying, she noticed someone standing next to her, wiping away her tears, and looked up to see that it was Jake. Lucinda looked at the figure to ensure the person was standing there. Lucinda was surprised.

"What are you doing here?" Lucinda asked Jake.

"I was on my way home when I saw you sitting here crying. Is there any problem?" Jake asked.

"No, there is no problem," Lucinda replied. Just then, Maya walked out to see Lucinda and Jake standing together.

"Lucinda, who is he?" Maya said, smiling.

"I'm Jake," he replied with a broad smile, without waiting for Lucinda to answer.

"I'm Maya, her grandmother. I guess you were the one who she met a few hours ago. She was right when she said your eyes are like pure gold." Maya said, smiling.

"Thank you," Jake replied, smiling.

"Is it okay to visit some other time? It's been some years since we moved in here, and this is the first time someone is coming to visit Lucinda. She will make a great friend." Maya offered.

"Granny!" Lucinda shrieked in awe of Maya's attitude.

"I'm her friend already. I will visit some other time." Jake replied.

"Nice. Lucinda's dinner is ready. Come inside and have something to eat." Maya said as she smiled and walked inside. Jake looked at Lucinda and smiled as he turned to leave, but Lucinda called him back.

"Your eyes, they are like that of pure gold. Who are you? Are you human?" Lucinda asked.

"And your eyes are like that of the sky. I'm Jake, and I'm just like you." Jake said as he walked away.

Lucinda stood there with her jaw dropped as she resolved to unravel the mystery called Jake fading away before her.

"What is happening to me?" Lucinda asked as she stood up and walked inside.

Jake was feeding the horse when he heard a noise at his back, but he continued with what he was doing as if he heard nothing.

"Why did you come to earth? Why did you choose Lucinda?" the voice asked.

"Our destinies were already fixed with each other even before she was born. Guess you told her that I'm not human. Anya, I'm a god, born to human parents. I'm still human." Jake replied as he turned to face Anya.

"Hurt her, and you will cease to exist, both human and god," Anya warned.

"I have no intention of hurting her as she is part of me. In a few months, she will be nineteen, and hope you're preparing her to meet the woman from whose loins she came out?" Jake asked.

"That isn't any of your business, Jake," Anya said. "The sooner my father and the queen of the moon and the stars end their quarrel, the better for you all. None of you can prevent this from happening. By the time she turns twenty, it will all make sense to her, and everything will be explicit." Jake said as he picked up the bucket on the ground by his side, ready to leave.

"Do they even know who you are?" Anya asked.

"Yes, they do. They found out the very day I was born on this earth. Anya, I know you're trying to protect Lucinda, and I appreciate all you have done, but you should understand that I have no intention of hurting Lucinda. I had to meet her today because she deserves to know who I am." Jake said and left, but halfway had to stop at the door as he turned to Anya and said: "Lucinda is wonderful."

He smiled as he walked out of the stable. Anya gnashed her teeth in anger.

"I hate his guts." She said as she disappeared from the stable.

Chapter Seven

LUCINDA ATE QUIETLY

*L*ucinda ate quietly with her family that evening as her grandparents talked about many things, a potpourri of issues, reminiscing primarily on their past. As Lucinda listened to them, she was prompted to come in between their conversation.

"I want to say something," Lucinda said, looking at them. "Okay, go ahead," Greg said.

"Is it possible to stay awake till midnight today, just for me? I want to take you both somewhere." Lucinda said.

"2 am? That's deep into the night. Where will you be taking us in the middle of the night? Lucinda, what are you planning?" Maya asked.

"No, you both aren't going to get hurt. I promise," Lucinda replied.

"Alright, we will stay awake just for you," Greg assured.

"Oh, my. Thank you so much," Lucinda said, smiling. She had earlier thought it would be difficult convincing her grandparents to stay awake. She knew they would be excited once they saw what she had in store.

Soon they finished up their dinner as Lucinda cleared the plates and walked straight to the kitchen to wash them. She walked back into the sitting room and joined her grandparents when she finished up.

She knew she had to engage them in a conversation to keep them awake, or they could fall asleep right there on the chair.

"So, tell me, Grandpa, do you think you will ever see Mom and Dad again?" Lucinda began.

"Sure, I will see them again. You know, no one lives forever. We all will die someday to start the journey to the world beyond. I will meet them; sure, I will," Greg said, smiling.

"What if they appear right now? What if it happens while you're still alive?" Lucinda asked.

"That can't be possible, can it?" Greg asked, looking perplexed.

"Well, with the universe, all things are possible. If the universe makes it possible, I will be the happiest human. To see my daughter's face again while I'm alive would be the greatest feeling for sure. I'm getting old, and the only thing that keeps me going is your face, Lucinda's because you look just like Annalise. Though it isn't possible to see the dead again, I know miracles happen." Maya said, smiling.

"Yea, miracles happen. Impossibilities are made possible. You just have to believe and watch how things will unfold." Lucinda assured.

"Thanks, my lovely angel," Maya said, grinning.

Greg smiled too. He knew his wife was ready to lay down her life just for Annalise to come back to life. She practically begged for a child, and when Annalise came, she became her whole world. It was so saddening to hear that fate took her away so soon.

They kept discussing, and when it struck midnight, Lucinda looked at her grandparents and asked, "Are you already?"

"Ready for what exactly," Greg asked, a bit irritated.

"Just give me a few minutes," Lucinda said as she walked into her room and returned a few minutes later. She instructed her grandparents to hold each other while placing one of her hands on her grandparent's entangled hands. She then touched her necklace, and in no time, they were standing at the pathway filled with bushes, her usual place of meeting with her parents and others.

"Wait. What are we doing here? How did it happen?" Maya asked.

"Where are we? Lucinda, what did you do? This is not even time for questions. We just have to leave here immediately. This place is dangerous. It's not safe for us to be out here inside the bush at this time. Let's go home, Lucinda," Greg said.

"Watch," Lucinda said as she pointed at the people sitting down close to a fire.

"Who are they?" Maya asked, casting a cursory glance at them.

"Before I answer that, let me tell you this. Ever since I asked you all to leave the town a few days after moving in, I spent my nights here after the monster saga. By midnight I come here and spend time with these beautiful people and by 3 am, I'm back home. They are the sole reason your granddaughter is still sane," Lucinda said.

"You haven't been sleeping at home all this time?" Maya asked, mouth agape.

"Yes, because I spend my night here. Let's move closer and see who they are." Lucinda said.

Lucinda shouted, "Annalise and Phil, look over here as they inched closer to people." They both looked up to see Lucinda standing with their parents after hearing Lucinda's voice.

"Annalise and Phil, is that you?" Greg asked as he came even closer.

"Yes, but how is this possible? How can you see us?" Phil said as he stood up with Annalise.

"Mom, can you see me?" Annalise asked Maya, looking at her with bated hope.

"You both can hug each other if you want," Lucinda said as Maya ran straight into her daughter's outstretched arms and hugged her tightly.

"It's been eight whole years, Annalise. I never thought I would see your face again," Maya said, crying.

Lucinda watched as Greg hugged Phil tightly. She left them and sat close to Anya and Amber, who watched as the four of them hugged each other without trying to let go.

"This was what you always wanted, right?" Anya asked, grinning.

"Yes, and I'm happy, but just one thing remaining, and I'm good to go," Lucinda said, smiling.

"Don't worry, the last one won't be difficult to achieve," Amber assured, smiling as Lucinda threw her hands on Anya and Amber, hugging them tightly.

When Lucinda saw that her parents and grandparents were sitting, chitchatting, she looked at them and said, "So this is where I wanted to take you both. That's why I was asking those questions. This is Anya, the three in one beast, Amber." She introduced, widely grinning.

"Three in one beast? How do you mean?" Greg asked.

"When the city was being terrorized, and drops of blood were everywhere, she was the one doing that. I will go into details later and explain her reason for doing so, but she was sent for me to realize who I was. Aside from being human, she is a wolf and a shape-shifter. I mean, not just one. They are three when I say wolf. That's why she is called a three-in-one beast." Lucinda offered.

"She is so beautiful. She doesn't look like a beast or someone who can hurt someone." Maya enthused.

Anya smiled as she said, "Don't look at the face. I'm everything she said that I am."

"Amber, the seer," Lucinda said, turning to Amber.

"You have always wanted to see me ask questions, but you have not been able to. You wanted answers to many questions. She has already had her purpose, having traced her root, knowing who she is." Amber said.

"I never believed that I would be able to see you," Greg said.

"If Annalise and Phil are dead, Amber and Anya are dead too, right?" Maya asked, still trying to collect what was unfolding before them.

"Not really; Anya isn't fully human like us. Anya is from the other world, and Amber, I won't say she is dead." Lucinda replied.

"Oh, now I understand," Greg said as they sat around the fire. "How did you do this?" Phil found himself asking finally.

"Let's say that nothing is impossible," Lucinda replied, smiling at her father.

Lucinda sat down near Anya and watched as they got along, chitchatting excitedly. Seeing the smiles on their faces, she was elated. This was what Lucinda had been dying to see, to see them meet together like this. She excused herself as she walked out of their presence, walking a bit far from them as she sat on the floor and looked up.

The moon was complete as the stars filled up the sky. She smiled and said, "I know you can hear me. I hope you're well. I know somehow I will be able to meet you someday and say thank you for everything you have done so far."

"You are my daughter. Your happiness is my happiness. I just want you to be happy," the mature voice answered.

"I want to request one more thing from you. I'm tired of coming here every night. Why do I have to wait every midnight before seeing my parents? It doesn't make sense to me. I deny myself sleep every day, and now that my grandparents are aware that they can't stay up every day because they are old.

I wish something would be done. I know I have made a lot of requests. I have asked for too many things, but I'm sorry. You know, death took my parents when I was just ten. They left too early. I didn't get to spend enough time with them. I wish their ghost would be living in our house, and we will see them every minute, living a normal human life," Lucinda said.

"But only on one condition," the voice said.

"From midnight, you will get to touch them and hug them, but once the clock strike 7 am, you can only see and hear from them, but you won't be able to touch them," the voice said.

"It's magnificent with me," Lucinda said, smiling, accompanied by flashes of lightning.

"I hope I will get to say a proper thank you one day," Lucinda said as she stood up and walked out of the bushes to go and meet the others.

"Where have you been, Lucinda?" Maya asked.

"It's night. You could get bitten by a snake. Are you're okay?" Greg asked.

"I'm okay. I just went to fix some things right. We need to get going so you can sleep." Lucinda said. Maya stood up, hugging Annalise and Phil tightly.

"I wish I could get to see you again and again," Maya said, almost on the verge of tears.

"You will. It's a promise," Lucinda said.

Greg hugged Annalise and Phil before Lucinda hugged them. She then waved at Anya and Amber before she held her grandparent's hands, and they disappeared out of sight. Lucinda hugged them and asked them to go to bed when they got home.

"Lucinda," Maya called as soon as Lucinda turned to walk out. "Yes," Lucinda answered as she turned, looking at Maya.

"Thank you, darling. You don't know what you have done for me. Thank you so much." Maya said.

"We hope your children and grandchildren and great-grandchildren make you happy just like you have made us happy," Greg said.

"Thank you," Lucinda said as she smiled and walked into her room. Her body touched the bed no sooner than she drifted off to sleep.

In the morning, Lucinda woke up and had her bath. She walked out to meet her grandparents, who were already up and chatting with excitement.

"Grandpa, Grandma, I have something to show you," Lucinda said.

"Hmm. Another surprise? I hope you slept well? And you're up so early today. Well, what's that?" Maya asked.

"This," Lucinda said as she shifted from the door, and Greg and Maya were surprised to see Annalise and Phil standing there. Maya stood up immediately to hug them, but she found out she had gone through them.

"What's happening?" Maya said.

"You can only touch them from midnight to 7 am, but once it strikes 7 am, they go back to being ghosts. I had to make them come here. I just want you both to wake up and see your children.

You miss them. Even though you try so much to hide the hurt and anger, it's still visible for all to see. You need your children. Remember what you said at night. You wish you could see them again. I promised you that you would see them, and here they are," Lucinda said as Maya and Greg hugged her tightly.

"I don't know what we would have done without you. Thank you so much for everything, Lucinda. Thank you for making us this happy. We don't even know how to repay you." They both chorused.

"You don't need to repay me. You have been with me ever since they ceased being humans," Lucinda said.

"Does that mean you can see me, Annalise, and Phil?" Maya asked.

"Yes, Mom, we can," Annalise said. "Everything. We can see everything," Phil said.

"I missed you both. For once, I thought I would never see you again after last night, but here you both are. Thank you," Maya said.

And as soon the words left Maya's mouth, Lucinda heard a knock on the door. She turned and opened it and was shocked to see who it was.

"Anya!!!" She shouted.

"The queen asked me to come. You need to be protected," Anya said as she walked into the house.

Lucinda closed the door as she dragged Anya to her room.

"Let me guess. This is what you went to the bush to consult the queen. I can see that your earthly parents treated you right, the reason you shower them with so much love." Anya said.

"If there were other words bigger than love, I would use that. Without them, then there is no Lucinda." Lucinda replied.

"Hey, look, Anya, that's Jake, the one I have been telling you about. Wait, let him come closer, then you look at his eyes." Lucinda said as soon as he saw Jake.

She had decided to take a stroll with Anya because she was bored at home. She wanted to interact more with humans and learn about their lives and everything that needed to be discovered.

She wanted her grandparents and her parents to spend enough time together, and at this moment, what she wanted more was just human friends. She wasn't getting younger. She was getting older, and she still needed human friends around her irrespective of being immortal, even if it was just one.

She waved at him as Jake walked closer to where she was standing with Anya.

"What are you doing here?" Jake asked.

"I felt bored at home, and I decided to come out with my friend. Her name is Anya," Lucinda replied.

"Oh, what about your parents and also your grandparents? Aren't they keeping you company?" Jake said, avoiding contact with Anya.

"About that; my parents died eight years ago, and I live with my grandparents," Lucinda said.

"Oh, I'm so sorry about that," Jake said, turning to Anya. He said, "And Anya, my name is Jake, Lucinda's friend," Jake said, stretching his hand for a handshake.

Anya looked at him and said to Lucinda without taking his hand, "I will be waiting for you at the tree close to the house; I will leave you two to talk to each other." Anya said as she left them to be alone.

"I'm sorry; she isn't comfortable with strangers." Lucinda apologized, feeling sad over the way Anya treated Jake.

"That's not an issue; I understand," Jake replied.

"What are you doing here? You came all alone?" Lucinda asked.

"Oh yes, I went to the market to get vegetables to make soup. As you can see, I'm on my way home," Jake replied.

"Oh, that's nice. Guess your mom is going to prepare that?" Lucinda asked.

"No, my parents have passed away. I will prepare this myself, and just so you know, I'm not a baby like you. I'm twenty-three years. I'm older than you." Jake said.

"Yeah, sure, but that doesn't matter. I'm sorry about your parents." Lucinda replied.

"Yeah, sure, it doesn't matter. I need to get going. Your friend must be waiting for you. It would be best if you didn't keep her waiting; and my parents, it's okay. It's been five years without them, and I'm adapting." Jake replied.

"Yeah, true," Lucinda said as she smiled dryly.

And without warning, Jake came closer and hugged her before leaving. Lucinda was shocked as she tried to figure out what had just happened.

"Did he just hug me, just like that?" Lucinda asked herself.

She smiled as she walked home, grinning. She loved the feeling. Along the way, she spotted Anya waiting for her at the tree just as she promised.

"You don't like Jake," Lucinda said as soon as she got close to Anya.

"Why did you say so? I don't hate him." Anya said.

"But you refused to take his hand when he offered a handshake. Is everything okay?" Lucinda asked.

"That doesn't mean I hate him, and yes, everything is okay. Why did you ask?" Anya asked.

"Because I saw how you looked at him with so much contempt and disgust. You barely know him, and you mistreated him. Remember you even said no human fits my description of him? You can now see that he is real." Lucinda quipped.

"Yeah, but the question is, is he human? Let's go home, Lucinda," Anya said.

Lucinda followed suit, pondering what Anya said about Jake not being human. Lucinda tried so many times to make Anya explain what she meant by that, but Anya remained mute. Lucinda then swore that she would find out the truth and that not even anyone could stop her.

When Lucinda found out her grandparents were still asleep, she left the bedroom the following day. As she tried walking out of the house, she heard her mom's voice.

"Where are you going? Isn't it early?" Annalise asked.

"I will be home soon. When Grandpa and Grandma wake up, tell them I went out to get something." Lucinda said and dashed out of the house.

Lucinda didn't wait to hear her mom's response or what her father would have to say. Living with her parent's spirits and seeing them every day gladdens her heart. She never for once thought that a day like this would ever come.

Lucinda strolled towards the other street. She felt that finding Jake's house won't be difficult for her, as she knew how to use her powers.

Soon she was able to identify the house. When she got to the house, she stood at the door and knocked severally; and just when the door opened, Jake was shocked to see her standing there.

"What are you doing here, and how did you find out where I live?" Jake asked.

"I'm not desperate. I'm only here to ask you a question," Lucinda said.

"Questions?" Jake said as he opened the door wider for Lucinda to come in.

"No, that won't be necessary. I'd rather sit here on the balcony and ask you what I want." Lucinda said.

Jake looked at her awkwardly as he came out and sat on the rocking chair on the balcony while Lucinda leaned against the rail.

"I'm all ears. So, what is this that you wanted to ask me that you couldn't wait, and how did you even get to know where I live?" Jake asked, still surprised.

"Finding out where you live isn't difficult for me," Lucinda replied.

"Maybe you can explain," Jake said.

"I will explain all that later, but not today. So, tell me, are you human?" Lucinda asked pointedly in her usual way.

Jake looked at her. His jaw dropped as if she had dropped a bomb. "Who knows what Anya must have told her. What is she trying to do? Anya is simply making things difficult for me. She is trying to ruin everything because she is Lucinda's guardian." Jake silently reasoned.

Lucinda waited for the answer to come from Jake, but it was taking more time than necessary, which made her suspicious.

"So, does that mean what she said is true?" Lucinda asked.

"Wait! Seriously, who is feeding you with all these? Why will you even ask if I'm human? Don't I have the same features as humans? And who even suggested that to you?" Jake said, acting upset.

"You don't need to be upset; you just have to answer the question," Lucinda said.

"I'm human, and well, if anyone tells you I'm not human, then it's obvious the person isn't human too, because it takes a nonhuman to know one who is a human and one who is not. Yes, I'm a human. I am. But why would she even insinuate such about me that I'm not human?" Jake asked.

"Your features do not fit into typical humans. Your eyes are nothing but pure gold," Lucinda said, eyeing him.

"That's because I'm different. I have always been different. I'm human, just like you. I know it's strange for a human to be blessed with eyes of gold but let's say nature has its way of blessing people, and I'm a blessing to my late parents." Jake reiterated.

Lucinda tried touching Jake's forehead, but Jake held her hand before it could get to his forehead.

"What are you doing?" Jake protested as he held Lucinda's hand.

"I wanted to check something. This mark on your forehead that looks golden too," Lucinda said.

Jake knew there was no way he would allow Lucinda to touch his forehead because once she did that, she would fully understand that he wasn't human. She wasn't human too, but some things were better left hidden.

"That's a birthmark. You need to go now. Your grandparents will be worried sick if they find out you're not at home." Jake said as he dropped Lucinda's hand and hugged her abruptly once again while whispering, "I'm a human, Lucinda." standing up, she walked inside.

Lucinda smiled as she stood up and strolled back home.

Jake opened the door to see Anya sitting comfortably on the chair. Jake sat on the other chair and looked at her without uttering. But after a minutes of silence, he started talking.

"Why are you doing this? Why are you making this difficult for me? If the two supreme beings have issues, don't drag me into it. I'm not like my father, and Lucinda isn't like her mother. We are all different people who have lived with humans, and we act like them.

Why will you stoop so low to tell Lucinda that I'm not human? Why are you trying to ruin things, Anya?" Jake asked.

"Ruin, you say? I'm only trying to protect Lucinda. Though fate has made its proclamation, that won't stop me from protecting her against you." Anya fired back at him with rage.

"I'm not evil. I'm Jake. I'm my father's son, but you should realize that we two are different. My father has unique attributes and features, and so do I. Don't try to rope Lucinda and me into the enmity between the queen and my father. Stay clear, and please do not say another word about me to Lucinda, or else you will feel my full wrath. Even if you're the three in one monster, I'm my father's son. I'm a god, the son of the sun. I will bring total doom and damnation to you. Leave Lucinda and me alone," Jake shouted and started to leave when Anya's voice stopped him.

"Do you waste time flexing your powers on people? I dare you, Jake Sun," Anya shouted back at him.

"I'm not like this. You're trying to turn me into what I'm not.

Just stop feeding Lucinda with information. I will break the news of who I am to her. Leave that to me and stay clear of our relationship. No matter how you and the queen and my father try, I will marry Lucinda. It's entire time for a new beginning," Jake said as he stormed off into the inner house.

"Bastard!" Anya said as she disappeared from the sitting room.

Lucinda was sitting all alone in the garden when she felt someone touch her, and on turning, she saw it was Anya.

"You're back," Lucinda remarked.

"Yeah, I needed to run some errands, and I'm done with that," Anya replied.

"A quick question: Why do you hate Jake?" Lucinda asked.

"I don't. I don't hate him. You went over to his place to ask questions, right?" Anya asked.

"Yes, I did. I had to. He is human, Anya, he is. I want to have just one human friend, one human friend, that's all I want, and nobody is helping matters. I wouldn't want to grow old surrounded by only the spirits of my beloved. With that, people living around will term me a witch. I need to have one human friend at least." Lucinda said, almost on the verge of tears.

"I'm sorry, I was just looking out for you. Let's say he is too handsome to be a human. That's why I made that statement. I'm sorry." Anya said, cleaning up the tears on Lucinda's eye with the back of her hand.

"Will you help me?" Lucinda asked.

"Sure, I will. If you're happy, then I'm happy too." Anya said as she hugged Lucinda, who held tightly to her.

Lucinda spent what seemed like forever in Anya's embrace before she stood up and went inside.

Anya stayed there for a few minutes before disappearing into thin air.

"You're here. How is Lucinda?" the voice of the queen intoned.

"Lucinda is fine, but I need to talk to you about something important. It's about Lucinda." Anya said.

Anya had gone to the moon to consult the queen of the moon and the stars. She needed to explain things to her.

"It's about Jake and Lucinda. Listen, Jake isn't a bad person. Maybe fate has reasons why it paired Lucinda and Jake to be together, and Jake already asked me to stay clear that I'm making things difficult for him." Anya said.

"And do you think you should stay clear?" The voice said as she turned her chair and faced Anya.

"Yes, I need to stay clear, not because of what he said but because Lucinda finds this peace around him. It feels like they have known each other all the time. The more I keep trying to get in between. I'm only hurting Lucinda. Fate has its reasons why it paired both of them together. Perhaps, this will close the bridge of rift that has been created over the ages," Anya replied.

"Prepare my daughter to meet me," The queen said as she stood up and walked out of the throne room.

Anya bowed before taking her to leave.

Chapter Eight

It Was Two Days

It was two days until Lucinda's nineteenth birthday, and it was a day Anya knew they had to make the journey. But Anya knew Lucinda wouldn't be an issue. She knew her grandparents would. How would they react if they found out that Lucinda was going on a trip to another world?

Though they had come to be filled in on some supernatural aspects of Lucinda, leaving earth on a journey to a different world entirely would be difficult for them.

Anya was sitting alone in the garden when she saw Greg walk into the garden and sat close to her.

"The only friend, my grandchild, has, you didn't go on a stroll with Lucinda?" Greg remarked.

"No, I'm here, trying to fix one or two things." Anya replied as Greg looked around and said, "but you're not busy."

"Oh no, not that actually, but can I ask you a question?" Anya asked.

"Sure. Go ahead," Greg commented.

"Will you be okay if Lucinda leaves the house for a five-day trip for something fundamental?" Anya asked.

"I doubt it, but Maya will never agree even if I say yes. We have grown to love Lucinda, and we have become so used to her that we can't spend a day without seeing her. We know someday she will get married and leave the house. She is old enough to decide, but we will be hurt if we don't get to see Lucinda, even if it's just for a day," Greg replied.

"What if she gets married tomorrow? She isn't going to live here forever, you know?" Anya quipped.

"Yea, you're right. When we lost Annalise and Phil, it was a challenging moment for us, but we tried to stay strong and act happy. Lucinda's presence matters a lot to us. We know that someday she will get married and move into her husband's home, but until then," Greg replied, raising his hands in the air.

Lucinda, who was on her way back, met with Jake in the company of two men. As soon as Jake saw her, she excused himself and walked up to her.

"Lucinda, how are you, and where are you going?" Jake asked, trying to hold her hand.

"I'm good; I'm heading back home," Lucinda replied.

"Okay, I wanted to ask. Can I come over tomorrow, Saturday?" Jake asked.

"Sure, why not? You're always welcome, and thanks for the gift.

I haven't been opportune to meet you to tell you to thank you," Lucinda replied.

"That's not an issue. Take good care of yourself," Jake said as he smiled and walked away to rejoin the men with him.

Lucinda smiled as she walked back home. When she got home that evening, she chit-chatted with her parents and grandparents during dinner. She could eat a little food, and when she was questioned, she claimed she was okay.

"Will you and Grandpa ever permit me to sleep out for five days?" Lucinda asked as Maya and Greg looked at each other.

"Where are you going?" Maya asked.

"I'm not going anywhere yet, just asking a question. I want to know like you and Grandpa won't see me for maybe five to six days. Will that be okay with you both?" Lucinda asked again.

"Oh no, we won't be okay with that. You barely know anyone here, or is it with Jake?" Maya asked.

"No, it's not Jake. Why will I stay in Jake's house for five whole days? That's insane. I agree that I like him, but I'm not obsessed with him." Lucinda replied.

"So, to where then?" Greg asked.

"Just a question, so will you both permit me, even if you do not know where?" Lucinda asked, a bit impertinent.

"The answer then is no," Maya said flatly.

"Grandpa, aren't you going to say something? Lucinda asked, looking at Greg.

"I'm with your grandma on this. I know we have lived here for a few years now, but Lucinda, the only person you know, is Jake. So how do you think we would permit you to leave the house? To where?" Greg replied.

"I'm turning nineteen in the next two days. I will still leave you, people, someday." Lucinda replied as she continued nibbling at her food.

Soon she was done with her food as she got up from the chair to tidy up the table, after which she walked straight to the sitting room.

Not long after, Lucinda said goodnight to her parents and grandparents as she walked into her room to sleep. She had a stressful day, and there was no way she could stay awake until midnight. She knew her grandparents were going to stay awake so they could talk and touch Annalise and Phil.

Lucinda lay on the bed as she kept thinking about Jake, being particularly disturbed about her identity, worried about how he would react to finding out she wasn't human. She knew there was no way she would be friends with Jake while still hiding the truth about her identity.

"How do I even get to tell him that I'm not full human? How do I tell him that Anya isn't a human too? How do I reveal to him my true identity? It's so difficult to say this to him. He might not believe me, or he might believe me but will never want to associate with me again," Lucinda groaned.

She was so confused about how to go about everything. For the first time in her life, she was making a human friend; and was now confronted with its associated dilemma, she thought. Or would she rather keep sealed lips about it all?

"How hard can this be!" Lucinda exclaimed and sighed at the same time.

"You looked worried," the voice said as Lucinda turned to see her mom's ghost.

"You're here," Lucinda asked, sitting up.

"I knew something was eating you up, and I had to come. I couldn't ask you in the presence of my parents. That's why I had to wait for you to come to your room so I could talk to you. So, is it okay to tell me what the problem is?" Annalise asked.

"It's Jake, Mom. I'm so confused. He has shown to be a good friend these past months, and he has told me everything I need to know about him, but the problem is I'm not being fair to him." Lucinda replied.

"How do you mean you're not being fair to him?" Annalise asked.

"Mom, can't you see? I'm not fully human. Someday, Jake will find out the truth about who I am, but the question is will he stay on finding out? I feel like telling him the truth, but on the other hand, I don't want to say a word to him. I don't want him to learn about the truth someday and decide to leave. I'm scared. He is the first human friend I have ever made," Lucinda surmised.

"Do you want to tell him who you are?" Annalise asked.

"I don't even know whether to tell him or keep a sealed lip, but I feel that he won't want to stay. He will leave," Lucinda replied.

"Don't dwell on hasty conclusions. You're not Jake. I won't ask you to tell him or keep him shut, but if you think he is a friend, maybe I think you know the right thing to do. A friend should know everything about you. Even if you decide to tell him and he leaves, don't worry. That would be enough to know the friendship wasn't meant to last anyway. But before then, make sure he is qualified to behold in the breath of that word called 'friend' before you spill anything to him," Annalise said.

"Thank you, Mom. I just wish I could hug you right away. Thank you so much. I wonder how life would have been without a mom by my side," Lucinda said.

"You're welcome, my darling. Don't worry. Go to bed. I know you're stressed up. It's written all over you. You can still get to hug me tomorrow or, if you're lucky, wake up early in the morning," Annalise said.

"Goodnight, Mom," Lucinda enthused before lying down and closing her eyes in sleep.

"When is she going to tell me the truth? Haven't I proven to be a better friend all these months? I've told her everything she needs to know, except that I'm the sun's son. Doesn't she consider me worthy of telling me everything about her, though I already know? Why is she scared of opening up to me? What could be the reason?" Jake pondered as he stared at the sky.

Jake has been up all night, thinking about Lucinda, feeling that she needed to hear the truth about her, which would prove that she trusted him.

"You're awake, thinking about her. What have you turned into, Jake?" The voice asked.

"Not again, father. I can think of anyone I want to. Besides, I'm not feeling sleepy," Jake responded.

"I see. Go to bed, Jake. She will tell you who she is by herself when she is ready," the voice ordered.

"Thank you, Father, but I will sleep later. You're not helping matters," Jake said.

"I don't like her, neither do I like her mother, so why will I help you get someone I don't like?" the voice asked.

"You and Lucinda's mother need help. This girl has done nothing to you. It isn't her fault she is the daughter of the moon and the stars, and it isn't my fault I'm your son, either. We are both different people, and I think fate made us fall in love with each other to solve the age-long schism between you and Lucinda's mother. Think about this. Good night, Father," Jake said as he stood up, locking the window to his room, and soon after he lay on the bed, he drifted off to sleep.

Jake stood at the door as he tried knocking, but he refrained from doing so on second thought. Too many ideas were running through his mind, and just when he turned to leave, the door flung open as Maya walked out.

"Jake, you're here. How are you doing?" Maya asked. "I'm good, and how about you?" Jake asked.

"I'm fine. I guess you're here to see Lucinda. Go to the stable. She is feeding the horses. You can go and see her there." Maya said.

"Thanks," Jake smiled as he walked down to the backyard. On getting there, Jake saw that the stable was locked, which meant that Lucinda was through with feeding the horses. He knew the next place Lucinda would be in the garden. He then strolled down; and met Lucinda watering the gardens.

"The flowers look so fresh and beautiful," Jake said as Lucinda turned and smiled on seeing him.

"Seems your favorite is the Lily flower," Jake asked as Lucinda nodded as she continued watering the flowers.

She took the can and placed it at the far end before sitting close to Jake on the stone chair when she finished.

"So, tell me, how are you doing?" Lucinda asked.

"I'm good. No need to ask you as I see you are doing just fine," Jake asked as Lucinda smiled.

"Has it been a long time since you got here?" Lucinda asked.

"No, I met your grandma at the door, and she told me you was feeding the horses. When I checked the stable and saw it was locked. I knew you were going to be here," Jake replied.

"Yeah, I just decided to water the flowers. Their colors add beauty to this garden," Lucinda replied.

"Yea. That's nice of you," Jake responded.

"I'm traveling. I won't be around for five or six days. I'm leaving with Anya," Lucinda stated.

"Oh, but what about your grandparents?" Jake asked.

"They are here. I'm still going to come back, not leaving forever." Lucinda replied as Jake nodded.

"Is everything okay? You don't look happy," Lucinda asked.

"I'm fine, just having this sad feeling that I won't get to see you for a couple of days," Jake replied.

"Are you sure that's all? It seems you're bothered about something else. You can tell me what it is," Lucinda asked.

"Lucinda, aside from the trip you're going, isn't there something else you need to tell me?" Jake asked.

"Anything like?" Lucinda queried.

"I don't know, but I feel you want to say something to me," Jake replied.

"No, nothing," Lucinda replied as she kept thinking about what Jake said, wondering whether he had by himself found out her true identity. Soon she became alarmed at what could be the outcome of such a revelation.

On seeing that Lucinda was lost in thought, Jake decided to bring her to the present by giving her a nudge. He had tried to get her attention by calling her name thrice, but she did not respond. Lucinda sat up straight after.

"What were you thinking? About what I said? I called you thrice, and when you didn't respond, I had to touch you, is everything okay," Jake asked.

"Yeah, I'm okay," Lucinda assured.

"No, you're not okay. It's written over you. What's the problem?" Jake asked to hope that Lucinda would use the opportunity to spill the truth, but instead, she still kept shut about it.

"Don't worry, I'm fine. Just thinking about some random things and also about my grandparents. But about what you said earlier, I already told you everything you need to know. I'm not hiding anything more. So, you don't need to worry." Lucinda said, smiling as Jake nodded.

"Alright, that's okay," Jake replied.

The duo was discussing when Anya walked in and greeted Jake, but Jake kept mute and made as if he didn't hear her greeting.

"I will be leaving now," Jake announced as he stood up and walked out immediately. It wasn't any use staying there for him since Anya was already there with her. He didn't even wait for Lucinda to say a word.

"Why is he leaving?" Anya asked, feigning surprise.

"Because of you, I guess. I wonder why you hate and despise him so much." Lucinda asked.

"He is the one who hates me," Anya said.

"No, it's not true. I know Jake, and I know you. He sees you as a threat because you don't want him to get close to me, which is true, but why, Anya? Jake is all shade of handsome and nice." Lucinda said.

"Perhaps both of us don't like each other. Your grandmother wants you inside for lunch," Anya tersely said.

"But you haven't answered my question; why do you hate him?" Lucinda asked.

"I don't hate him; I hate his guts," Anya said as she stood up and walked into the house. Lucinda sighed and followed suit, trying to understand what Anya meant.

"Oh, I thought you were with Jake. Where is he?" Maya asked. "Oh, Jake. He left." Anya replied.

"Why didn't he even come in to greet me?" Greg asked.

"Something came up suddenly, so he had to leave quickly." Lucinda lied.

"Let's eat then," Maya said as they all sat down while Maya dished out the food.

"I'm sure Anya is preventing Lucinda from spilling the truth. She swore to make life miserable for me, and she is at it. I just hate her." Jake cursed as he strolled down home.

When Jake got home, he walked straight to his bedroom and sat down on the bed.

"Why don't you give up on this girl?" the voice asked.

"I can't, father, I can't. Aside from the prophecy, I have grown to love Lucinda. I don't know why she finds it hard to open herself completely to me." Jake responded.

"Perhaps she doesn't love you enough." The voice said.

"Or maybe she doesn't trust me enough. Telling someone she feels is a human being and that she is the daughter of the moon and the stars are huge. That's the exact reason. As for loving me? I know Lucinda loves me," Jake replied.

"Well, when are you coming home?" The voice asked. "When Lucinda is ready to go home," Jake replied.

"You have allowed this girl to take a better part of you. You mean to hate her and not love her." The voice added.

"Father, can you please stop. I know you and the queen are arch enemies. And she already had accepted the prophecy. Why can't you do the same? There is nothing to hate in Lucinda. That girl is innocent, naive, and without stain. I'm glad fate brought us together," Jake responded.

"I need to go and rest, but I just want you to come home soon," the voice replied.

"I can't come home without leaving a child on this planet. You know that already," Jake responded.

"The time is ticking. You barely have up to four decades remaining. I need you home. You have a world to rule here," the voice said as Jake groaned and fell back on the bed, mentally exhausted.

"It's just for a few days. Not like I'm spending a whole year there," Lucinda said.

Lucinda found it hard to convince her grandparents about the trip she needed to make. She had to visit the world she was from.

"You might go there and decide not to come home. How do you think we would let you leave? It's your birthday today. For the past eight years, we have always celebrated your birthday together. So why will today be different?" Maya asked.

"No, why will you even think of that? This is still my home. Mom and Dad are here. You and Grandpa are here. So, why will I stay in another world? And of course, I know it's my birthday, the more reason I need to leave today. Please understand me." Lucinda begged.

"Truth is that we're scared. Things might go wrong. If you leave and don't come back, I won't survive it." Greg added.

"I swear by the moon and the stars. I will come home." Lucinda pledged.

"She has already mentioned the moon and the stars. So, I know she will come back. Just let her go." Phil said.

"Phil is right. Let Lucinda go. She will come back, and she means it," Annalise added.

"I promise to bring her back. We need to leave today. I swear by the moon and the stars," Anya said as Maya rushed and hugged Lucinda tightly as tears trickled down her cheeks.

Greg went closer to them as he hugged them too. Lucinda's absence would hit them hard, even if it were a temporal absence.

"I promise, I will be home in six days," Lucinda assured again. The words were scarcely out of her mouth when Anya touched her, and they both disappeared right before everyone present. Maya and Greg hugged each other as Maya cried in her husband's arms. Annalise and Phil had to console them.

Anya and Lucinda approached the entrance to the world of the moon and the stars. Lucinda couldn't help but stare at the magnificent gate right in front of her, which was made of pure gold, glistening from the incandescence of the moon.

"Are you ready to meet your home?" Anya asked as Lucinda nodded.

Anya pushed the gate slowly as they both walked in. Lucinda's jaw dropped as she stared at the new world unfolding before her.

"You mean I'm from here?" Lucinda asked with her eyes and mouth wide open.

"Yes, welcome home, Lucinda," Anya enthused.

"This place is beyond description. Saying it's beautiful is a mockery. It's beyond beautiful; it's amazing," Lucinda said as she stared at the beautiful flowers and creatures moving about.

"Let's go," Anya said as she held Lucinda's hand, and they both walked into the city made of gold.

Lucinda watched as the men standing at the entrance bowed to them. One of them quickly opened the door.

Lucinda was dumbfounded and weak to utter a word. She turned sideways, admiring the environment before as she stood beside a castle, grand and regale beyond her infantile mind could ever imagine.

"Let me guess, this is home, right?" Lucinda asked, pointing to the castle as Anya nodded.

Soon, Lucinda felt a hand touch her as she quietly turned to see who it was. Lucinda was shocked to see a woman standing before her. She was the fairest of them, and she noticed this striking resemblance with the woman. Her skin was as white as snow. Her hair as white as wool. She was aging beautifully.

"Welcome home, my child," The woman said as Lucinda raised her hands and touched the woman's face, who smiled in return.

"Are you the woman whose loins I came out from?" Lucinda asked as the woman nodded. "What's your name?" Lucinda asked. "Salle, Queen Salle," she replied.

"Would it be okay if I call you mother or Queen Salle," Lucinda asked as Queen Salle smiled and answered, "anyone can do?"

"Thank you, Anya, for a job well done. You took great care of her, and I'm impressed," Queen Salle commended as Anya smiled, saying in between smiles, "thank you, my Queen."

"You may leave," Queen Salle said as Anya swiftly changed into a werewolf and raced out of the palace.

"Is she coming back?" Lucinda asked.

"Of course, but not now. I have a lot to show you, daughter," Queen Salle said as Lucinda nodded.

Queen Salle walked down the pathway quietly as Lucinda followed suit. When they got to a door, Queen Salle pushed it open slowly.

Lucinda was shocked to see something like the moon hanging right there in the room while its light illuminated the entire room.

"What is this? It's beautiful, and it's huge," Lucinda asked. "Touch it and tell me what you see," Queen Salle responded.

Lucinda looked at the queen for something that seemed an eternity before stretching her hand to touch the moon. And no sooner had her hand felt it than she started seeing a series of visions.

"What will you call what you saw? Good or evil?" Queen Salle asked as soon as Lucinda recovered from her shock.

"I don't know. Instead of you, I was the one sitting on your throne. My parents didn't stay with me for long in the human world, and I saw my grandparents leaving," Lucinda asked.

"I'm aging, Lucinda. Someone has to take the throne when I'm no more. The moon chose you, your parents, and your grandparents. They are not leaving now, but someday they will because they need to come back and prepare for the coming of their new queen. This place is your home. You're not going to stay on the earth forever. And then when you age too, one of your children will be chosen to take over from you," Queen Salle replied.

Lucinda didn't utter a word as she walked closer to the moon, stared at it, and asked silently.

"Why aren't you showing me anything about Jake? Perhaps now is the time to tell me."

"When you get back to earth, you and Jake have to conclude whether you will end up together," Queen Salle said as Lucinda turned and asked, "how did you hear that?"

"You're asking me that? What did I not know? You don't know everything, child. Don't worry. Once you ascend that throne, the powers will be transferred to you, but for now, I can see that this Jake is making you happy. He is the luckiest man to have you," Queen Salle responded, as Lucinda blushed.

"I can't tell him anything about me. I want to, and on the other hand, I don't want to. I'm confused. He deserves to know the truth. He has felt that I'm hiding something from him. We met before I came here, and when he insinuated that, I was sad. I knew I was guilty, but how do I explain that I'm not who he thinks I am? He will leave me if he finds out who I am," Lucinda said with a teary voice.

"Tell him and allow him to decide for himself," Queen Salle replied.

Lucinda moved closer to Queen Salle as she hugged her tightly, saying, "I have two mothers, one here and the other on earth. I have done many things for her, and I hope someday I will do something in return for all my wishes you granted."

Queen Salle smiled as she said, "You're my daughter, and I have to make life easier for you on earth."

"Thank you, Mom," Lucinda said, smiling.

"Anya will be here any moment from now to take you home," Queen Salle said.

"But it's not even up to four hours that we got here?" Lucinda asked.

"The time here differs from earth. You have been away for your days on earth. Your grandparents are already missing you. They want you home as soon as possible," Queen Salle replied.

"I didn't know that's how it works here," Lucinda said.

Queen Salle removed her necklace as she put it on Lucinda, same with her bracelet, which had the moon and the stars' symbol.

"Subsequently, don't remove. Always wear them. Promise me you do that," Queen Salle said.

"I promise. I won't take them off," Lucinda said, smiling.

"Let's go then," Queen Salle said as she held Lucinda's hand, and they both walked out of the room together. Anya was already waiting in the throne room.

"Anya!" Lucinda called as he walked closer to Lucinda and hugged her.

"Thank you for keeping her safe on earth." Queen Salle said.

"You're welcome, my queen. It's my duty. I can't watch any harm befall on the queen's beloved." Anya replied.

"Thank you. You will take Lucinda back home. It's already time to leave. An hour over here is a day over there. Her grandparents are already missing her. They want her home badly." Queen Salle said as Anya bowed, after which the queen came closer to Anya and Lucinda, holding their hands tightly, as she murmured some strange words, which prompted them into fading into thin air. She had sent them back to earth.

Lucinda was surprised to see herself in her bedroom.

"Home is beautiful. I can't believe that's where I came from." Lucinda said as Anya smiled and said, "I know you will make a better queen someday."

Lucinda smiled as she walked out of the bedroom together with Anya. Maya was shocked to see Lucinda standing next to her. Lucinda had to hug her while still sitting as she tried standing up.

"I'm glad you're home. I thought you wouldn't come back ever again." Maya said with a teary voice.

"I'm home. This is my home," Lucinda replied. "Where is Grandpa, Greg?" Anya asked.

"Oh, he is sleeping and…"

"I'm awake now," Greg said, coming out of the door as Lucinda rushed to where he was standing and hugged him tightly.

"Thank you for coming home," Greg said.

"This is my home. I can't leave. A part of me still lives here." Lucinda replied.

"Jake was here in the morning. He asked about you and I told him you will be back soon." Maya said.

"Jake? Okay. I will see him this evening," Lucinda said, smiling.

"Let me quickly prepare something nice," Maya said as she stood up and walked into the kitchen.

"I know my mom and dad aren't here now, and they should be back soon. Tell them I will be home soon. Let me see Jake," Lucinda said as she raced out of the house. She didn't even wait to hear Anya or her grandfather's reply before leaving.

When Lucinda got to Jake's apartment, she stood at the door and knocked; and after some minutes, the door flung open as Jake walked out.

He was shocked to see Lucinda standing right in front of him; as he quickly hugged her.

"I know it's belated, but I can still wish you a happy birthday. I have missed you so much." Jake whispered into Lucinda's ear.

"Same here," Lucinda said, smiling as they walked into the sitting room, holding each other tightly.

Chapter Nine

ANYA WALKED INTO

*A*nya walked into Lucinda's room to meet her, lost in her thoughts. She just stood watching her and admiring her at the same time. But soon after, she tried calling her attention, but it seemed her mind wasn't in that room anymore.

Anya sat on the edge of the bed, and stretching her hand, she touched Lucinda, who instantly came back to the present. She did that a second time, yet Lucinda received no response.

"How long have you been here?" Lucinda asked.

"For over three minutes now, I called you twice, but you were thinking about something else. Is there any problem?" Anya asked.

"Yeah, aren't you noticing her absence? She meant to visit regularly, but it's been months now since she visited last. Do you think I wronged her? I can easily ask for forgiveness if I did so," Lucinda said while wearing a mournful look.

"You mean Amber?" Anya asked.

"Yes, I'm dying to see her. It's been such a long time, and it hurts not seeing her. We spent time here every night; she is part of us. She is family, but suddenly, she isn't here anymore. Isn't that strange?" Lucinda asked.

"Yeah, now I understand where you are heading," Anya said.

"You know, I miss Amber. It's been months since I last saw her. Why isn't she coming around anymore? I thought she promised she would often visit? Why isn't she keeping to her promise?" Lucinda asked.

"Lucia, I know…"

Wait, what did you just call me?" Lucinda asked, surprised. "I called you Lucia," Anya replied as Lucinda smiled.

"Listen, I know you want to see Amber, by all means. I also know you're dying to meet her, but you should know that Amber isn't like you and me. She has limited time to be on this earth."

"I can still…"

"You can't do anything about it, Lucinda. Some wishes can't be granted. You don't have to worry. Eventually, Amber will come around, then she will explain so you will understand. You were with her for a long time, so I'm sure you both understand yourself better." Anya replied.

"If she is going to come, she has to come soon. It's been months without her," Lucinda replied.

"Don't worry; you will be fine," Anya said as she stood up to leave, but Lucinda called her back.

"Are you leaving me all alone?" Lucinda asked.

"Maybe you should visit Jake if you need company, and I think you do. I'm not going inside. I'm going to the bushes," Anya replied as Lucinda smiled on hearing Anya's suggestion. She watched as Anya faded into thin air. But Lucinda did not go anywhere. She stayed in her room all day, tossing around her bed. In the evening, Anya walked into her room to meet her still lying on the bed. She stood in the doorway, staring at her.

"Why are you looking at me that way?" Lucinda asked.

"Amber is leaving. She is here to say her final goodbye." Anya dropped the news as Lucinda stood up immediately and rushed into the sitting room to see Amber with her grandparents.

"Amber, you know you can't stop visiting. You're like a family to us. I want to keep seeing you. You can't just come to say goodbye. It's not fair," Lucinda whined.

"I wanted the same too, but you know that's impossible. We are two different beings. I have to go and rest, but I'm going to make a promise to you when you birth your first child. I will come to you as a daughter. Remember that." Amber said.

"But that's going to be a long time. Can't you see how miserable I am? Please stay because of me," Lucinda said with a teary voice.

"She has to go, Lucinda. I know this will be hard for you to take in, but you just have to accept it. Don't worry. With time you will get used to her absence. She promised she would be coming back as a child in from your loins," Annalise said.

"It's hard letting her go. I can't imagine I won't see her face anymore," Lucinda said as tears trickled down her cheeks.

"It's going to be fine. You just have to hold on to the good memories you both shared," Annalise said.

"Your mother is right. Crying will never solve the problem. Just believe that someday she will come back," Phil consoled.

"It's easier said than done. How do I cope without her?" Lucinda asked.

"Your grandmother and I are here with you, your parents, can't you see?" Greg asked, hoping to bring in a measure of consolation for Lucinda.

"Please, Lucinda, clean your tears. They are hurting me. I hate seeing you like this. You just have to think of the good times you shared, please," Maya pleaded.

"Lucinda, please listen to them. I will be back soon," Amber said as Lucinda rushed and hugged her tightly.

"When you're ready to bring forth seed into this world, I will come as your first child," Amber assured.

"I know you mean it, but it's hard letting go," Lucinda said.

"Don't worry. I will be here sooner than you imagine," Amber said as she slowly wiped the tears off Lucinda's eyes.

As Amber walked closer to the door, she turned and waved goodbye to Lucinda and her family before disappearing into thin air. Lucinda fell into her grandmother's arms as she cried bitterly while they all tried consoling her.

"Your heart is heavy. You're questioning yourself on the right thing to do. To crown it all, you're confused. Hey, look at me." Jake said as he gently placed his hands on Lucinda's face and said, "you know you can confide in me. What's the problem?"

Life with Jake these past few months had been one of the best moments ever for Lucinda. Lucinda was still worried about how Jake would react if he learned the truth about who she was. She wanted to spill the truth, but on the other hand, she tried to protect her friendship at all costs.

"You're not saying anything? I'm still waiting for your response," Jake said, looking deep into her eyes.

"I want to talk to you about something important, but the truth is, I don't know how you're…" Lucinda paused as she groaned in frustration while Jake waited patiently for her to finish up her sentence. But when it was clear, she wasn't going to say anything else. Jake had to break the silence.

"What do you want to tell me, and why aren't you saying anything? Can't you see how miserable you are looking? You want to spill it out, yet you are afraid to talk," Jake said.

"You don't understand and…"

"I understand everything, Lucinda. But then, if you knew what friendship is all about, if I meant a lot to you, you wouldn't be hiding anything from me. Look around, I'm the only friend you have, and also, you're the only friend I have. What makes you think your secret isn't safe with me?" Jake asked.

Turning sharply, Lucinda asked, "How do you know it's a secret?"

"Don't try to divert from the main topic. Of course, it's a secret because you're finding it hard to say it. Perhaps, when you consider me a friend, I will know, but I think I'm just a neighbor leaving down the road for now. Take good care of yourself, Lucinda," Jake said as he stood up and left.

Lucinda tried calling him back, but he ignored her and hurried away. Lucinda sat back on the chair as tears found their way to her cheeks.

"What have I done? I have pushed out the only friend I have. Will I ever forgive myself?" Lucinda asked with a teary voice.

When Lucinda couldn't take it anymore, she ran into the house and went straight to her room. She locked the door and placed a spell on it. That way, not even Anya or her parent's spirit will have access to the room. She didn't want to see or talk to anyone. She just wanted to be alone.

"What have I just done? What have I done to myself? How do I tell him the truth? Now I only have two options: tell him and save my friendship or keep shut and lose him forever.

What if I told him and he left? And what if he didn't leave? These past few months, I have grown to love him. The only human who has proved to be a good friend," Lucinda groaned.

Lucinda couldn't imagine losing her only friend. She knew she had to explain herself to Jake somehow, because keeping shut would ruin everything. Lucinda was still in her riot of thoughts when she noticed

Anya was trying to gain access to the bedroom. She had to lift the spell, and just immediately, Anya appeared in the room.

"What's the problem? Why did you prevent me from gaining access to your room? What's wrong?" Anya asked, but as soon as he saw Lucinda in tears, she walked up to her and dried the tears.

"What's wrong? You were with Jake a few minutes ago, and now you're here crying your eyes out. What's the problem?" Anya asked.

"It's Jake," Lucinda said amidst sobs.

"I knew that boy was up to no good. How dare he…?"

"Anya, he didn't do anything," Lucinda said, cutting Anya short.

"If he didn't do anything, why are you in tears? Why are you covering up for him?" Anya asked.

"I'm not covering up for him. Whatever happens between Jake and me is my entire fault. Can't you see he has been kind and good and nice towards me all this while? He has proven to be a good human.

He accepted me with his hands wide open, and what did I do? I kept a vital part of my secret from him. I think he has noticed that I'm hiding something from him, and today when he couldn't take it anymore, he left. Even when I tried calling him back, he didn't stop.

He acted as if he didn't even hear the sound of my voice. I guess I have lost the only friend," Lucinda said with a teary voice.

"No, you didn't lose him. I'm sure he will come around. He is angry, but you can forget about him and move on if he doesn't. He isn't the only one here on earth, or is there any other thing you aren't telling me?" Anya asked.

Lucinda didn't say anything. Instead, she lay down on her bed, covering herself up. On seeing that, Anya smiled as she walked out of the room.

Jake got home and went straight to dish out something to eat. He was so mad at Lucinda. He was furious and sad that Lucinda didn't trust him enough to tell him everything.

"Hey!" the voice said as Jake looked back and sighed.

"Just because you have powers doesn't give you the audacity to come into my house anytime, any day. Have some respect," Jake scowled.

"I had to come; it's necessary. I just wanted to ask a few questions. Then I'm out of here," Anya replied.

"What do you want?" Jake asked.

"I want to ask why you're selfish, proud, and arrogant? The fact that you are the son of the sun doesn't place you above everyone," Anya said.

"Proud and arrogant? I know I'm not that, but what do you mean by selfish? What did I do? I know I have done absolutely nothing to get that appellation from you." Jake replied.

"Oh really? Then why can't you come clean and tell Lucinda the truth? Tell Lucinda who you are. You don't have to wait for her to tell you who she is, or is it recorded anywhere that Lucinda must be the first to spill the truth about her real identity?

And as if that wasn't enough, you made her lock herself up and cry like she lost someone dear to her. What manner of human are you? Ever since I have known Lucinda, I have never seen her this way. All I can say is I hate you for this. I don't know what you said to her, but I want you to go back and apologize," Anya said.

"Force me if you can, but I'm certain I didn't use any mean words on Lucinda. She is crying because she lost a friend in me.

When I said so, I meant it. I showed Lucinda my world. I told her everything she needed to know aside from the fact that I'm the son of the sun which I'm waiting for the day she turns twenty before I can tell her, but since you are too eager for her to know the truth about me, I will meet up with her and tell her, and after that, I'm gone. Now you can leave my house, Anya, and don't you ever come back," Jake said.

"How sure am I that you're not going to return someday?" Anya asked, a little excited about hearing Jake's words.

"You and your queen have always wanted that, and my father. So, exiting Lucinda's life will make you all the happiest. I want to go into my room, and when I'm out, I don't want to see you here," Jake said as he stood up and walked into his room.

"I hate his guts. I wish he leaves and never comes back," Anya howled.

"I thought you left? Or you came back for me?" Lucinda asked as she saw Amber sitting calmly on the edge of the bed.

"You need help. Why are you still delaying telling him the truth about who you are? Stop thinking of what will happen if you eventually tell him. Tell him and save yourself all this stress," Amber said.

"It's not that easy, Amber. I might lose him. He might leave me, or worst he might tell people who I am. I wouldn't want what happened years ago to repeat itself." Lucinda replied.

"You don't want to tell him, yet you don't want to lose your friendship. It's so obvious that you're hiding something from him, and he already noticed that. Now, tell me, what do you think of Jake?" Amber asked.

"Jake is all shade of nice, good, and humble. He possesses all the good characteristics one needs in a human being. He is a good friend, and I value our friendship," Lucinda said.

"What if you keep shut and end up losing your friendship? I doubt you value your friendship because you will tell him everything if you do. Just talk to him, so you don't lose everything," Amber said.

"I will try. I'm glad you're here." Lucinda said as she stretched her hands to hug Amber, who faded into thin air.

Lucinda looked around and called Amber's name, but there was no response. She slowly opened her eyes to see that she was dreaming. "Amber came to visit in my dreams. Yes, she was here. Ooh, Amber!" Lucinda said as she smiled.

"Lucinda, are you okay?" Maya asked as she walked into Lucinda's room.

"Yeah, I'm okay," Lucinda replied.

"But you were smiling a few seconds ago, and I'm sure you just woke up. So, why are you smiling?" Maya asked.

"Amber paid a visit to me in my dream. It was nice seeing her face again," Lucinda replied.

"That's nice; you should smile often. When you're done with whatever you're doing here, come to the sitting room, okay?" Maya said as Lucinda nodded.

———— • ◈ • ————

She enjoyed the gentle breeze and the silence when she heard the voice. Lucinda slowly opened her eyes to see Jake standing right in front of her.

"You are here," Lucinda remarked with her eyes wide open.

"I came to tell you what you need to know. You deserve to know before I leave," Jake said.

"You can at least sit. What do you want to say, and what do you mean before you leave?" Lucinda asked.

"Don't worry; I should stand up. I'm not going to waste much time here." Jake replied.

"What's the problem, Jake? Is everything alright?" Lucinda asked.

"Yeah, I just want to tell you the truth. You know Anya was right when she said I'm not a human and…"

"Wait. Wait. What are you talking about, and how did you know Anya said that?" Lucinda asked with her brows raised high.

"The truth is, I'm not a human. I'm a God. I don't even consider myself half-human because I wasn't born to be a human. Let me break it down. This couple has been childless for years, and throughout their lives, they have been worshipping the sun.

Before my mother passed, she handed me over to these human parents because she was sure my father wouldn't take care of me the way she wanted. I grew up with them thinking I was human, and just when I was ten, I realized who I was and why I was there with them. Life was perfect here. I didn't want to go back to where I came from. I stayed back.

But I always pay a visit to my father. After a few years, my earthy parents died in their sleep. I didn't want to go back home. I stayed here, and I was already used to being with humans.

Whenever I visit home, I feel like a stranger because I barely know who my people are. So, this is me. This is the real Jake. Therefore, my eyes are like pure gold. Anya called me selfish, proud, and arrogant, but I'm not any of those, and I sure know that your parent's ghost lives with you. If you consider me a friend, you should have opened up and told me who you are, but I won't force you since you're adamant and won't tell anyone. Take good care of yourself, Lucinda. Extend my greetings to your grandparents," Jake said as he turned to leave, but Lucinda called him back.

"You're saying you're the son of the sun!" Lucinda asked, with eyes wide open.

"That I already explained; take good care of yourself, Lucinda. I'm leaving," Jake said.

"Where are you going?" Lucinda asked.

"I don't know, and thank you for the little memories we created together." And with that, Jake stormed out of the place ablaze.

Lucinda was speechless. She just didn't know how to take in the news that Jake had just told her.

"So, Anya knew all this while. That's why she has been harsh to Jake."

Lucinda realized herself when she noticed that someone had touched her. Looking back, she saw it was Anya.

"You have been overthinking these days. I called you twice, but no response from you." Anya said.

"You knew he was the son of the sun, and you didn't tell me?" Lucinda asked.

"I tried giving you a hint, but you didn't get that. I guess he told you already. I was waiting for him to tell you," Anya replied.

"But you should have explained better," Lucinda said.

"It wasn't in my place to tell you. Now that he told you who he is, did you tell him who you are?" Anya asked.

"No, I didn't. Since he is the son of the sun, he should know who I am. He kept shut about his identity for months," Lucinda answered.

"Don't be too sure that he knows who you are. He already came clean. I think you should do the same," Anya said as she stood up and left the garden.

Lucinda sighed as she rested her back on the chair while different thoughts ran through his mind. She just couldn't believe what she heard right now. She could take it in that all this while she had been friends with a god.

Lucinda stood at the door as she tried knocking, but there was no response. She then looked at Anya, who looked away.

"We have been standing here for over ten minutes, and he won't open the door," Lucinda said.

"That's because he isn't at home."

"How did you know? We have been standing here together." Lucinda remarked.

"You're Lucinda, and I'm Anya. When you master your powers, then your soul can be able to leave your body for a few minutes just like I did and went into Jake's apartment to see he isn't in, and he hasn't been there for over a week now," Anya replied as Lucinda's face turned white immediately.

"You're joking, right?" Lucinda said as she shivered.

"What part exactly do you think I'm joking about?" Anya asked.

"About him not to have been in this place for over a week now," Lucinda answered.

"Jake isn't even in this town. Let's go home, Lucinda. Maybe he has gone back to where he came from," Anya added.

"That's not fair. He can't leave like that. This isn't fair. Was that why he said he needed to tell me the truth before leaving? So, he meant it when he said he was leaving? I tried to find out what he meant, but he was adamant about leaving. He wouldn't even say a word to me. He doesn't have to leave like that," Lucinda said, almost on the verge of tears.

"Lucinda, please don't; not now," Anya pleaded. "Will he ever come back?" Lucinda asked.

"I don't have the answer to that, Lucinda. Jake might or may never come back to this town. Why hope for the best? You can still expect the worst. I'm sorry," Anya said.

"You're right. Let's go home," Lucinda said.

Anya held her as they both walked down the road. No sooner had they gotten to the house than Lucinda locked herself up in her room while soaking herself in her tears, wondering how she could live with the guilt of not opening up to Jake before leaving the town.

"Now, I might never get the chance to see him and tell him everything. I lost a friend, a good one at that. He wasn't like Star. He was a perfect definition of a friend, and now he is gone," Lucinda lamented as tears trickled down her cheeks.

She felt she had made the worst mistake ever and may never forgive herself for losing Jake. Jake only wanted the truth from her, but it was tough for Lucinda to tell.

It had been a month since Jake left. Lucinda had continuously sneaked out of the house for these months to see if Jake had returned home, but the place was still empty.

Lucinda tried to act strong, Though it was clear that Jake's disappearance was taking its toll on her. Soon her grandparents became suspicious when they continuously asked about Jake, but Lucinda would lie to them that Jake had traveled and would be back shortly.

No one knew what was happening because Lucinda always tried to act happy, but she was bleeding and hurting deep down. Anya knew what was wrong, but she couldn't do anything.

At some point, she wished Jake hadn't left. Anya thought Lucinda would be fine, but Jake's absence turned Lucinda into something else. Anya tried to talk to Lucinda, but it fell on deaf ears. She tried searching for Jake, but it was a fruitless search.

On a starry night, Lucinda was staring right at the sky, standing by her window, when she sensed someone moving into her room.

"Is everything okay with you, child?" the voice asked.

"Yes, I'm fine," Lucinda replied.

"You know you can always talk to me. I will understand. I have noticed something very off about you for the last one month. Something is eating you up, but you're trying so hard to hide it from us. I'm your father. Talk to me. I want to share this pain with you." Phil said.

"Don't worry, Father, I'm okay. Eventually, I'm going to sort this out independently. I just need a few more times, and I will get back to my usual self. Trust me," Lucinda said.

"I thought you would get over it soon, but it's over a month now. You don't have to carry this burden all alone. I want to help my child. Tell me what is wrong," Phil asked.

"I'm okay. Don't worry about me. I will be fine," Lucinda replied with his eyes fixed on the sky.

Phil knew better. He knew Lucinda wasn't going to talk. He gently left the room.

Lucinda looked up in the sky and said, "I know you can hear me. Please bring Jake home. I promise I'm going to tell him everything.

Tell him I'm sorry for everything and I still value and miss our friendship if you see him. Life hasn't made any sense ever since he left. I want him back. I know you can do this for me. When you find him, tell him Lucinda said she is sorry."

Tears trickled down her cheeks, but Lucinda didn't bother to clean up as she continued staring at the sky in silence. She knew that something valuable was missing in her life, and she needed to get it back.

Jake frowned when the wind brought the message Lucinda had said that night.

"Why does she want me back? She doesn't even see me as a friend. She wants to open up because she hasn't set her eyes on me for a month now. I don't want to come back. I should say here," Jake said.

Jake had gone back to his kingdom because he needed some time off to think about himself and Lucinda.

"I'm proud of you, son. Lucinda isn't worth it," The voice said as Jake turned back and sighed.

"Can you be at least kind to her, father? Maybe she has her reason for keeping it a secret from me. She thought I was a mere human." Jake defended.

"Whatever the reason is, I don't care. If Lucinda loved and valued your friendship, she would have told you long ago, but what did she do? She kept it to herself, which is a sign of distrust." The king replied.

"Father," Jake shouted.

"Yes, that's the truth. I hope you're not going back there? You have been away for too long," The king said as Jake stood up and said, "someday, you will get to like her."

Jake walked out of the room and went straight to the Pinnacle of the building as he stared at the kingdom, which was built with gold, wondering whether to either stay or get back to earth.

Chapter Ten

LUCINDA KEPT QUIET

"*You love him? Don't you? It's written all over your face," Greg commented.*

Lucinda kept quiet as she observed her grandparents, not desiring to say anything, whether or not in the affirmative. They knew why they asked her whether she was in love with Jake.

Lucinda felt bored staying at home all alone. She wasn't going to sit all day waiting for Jake. She would tell her grandparents she would visit Jake, but she would stop by somewhere else and spend two hours before going home without eventually seeing Jake.

Greg and Maya were happy with the new development, but they didn't want Lucinda to go. They had become so attached to her they couldn't do without seeing her every moment of the day. They never knew what was happening. They thought their grandchild had a perfect relationship with Jake, without knowing that Jake had been away for a while.

"You are already twenty, so you should be free to answer the question. We already asked Jake, and he confessed he loves you so much," Maya started on a cool breezy evening.

"But that's not the problem. The problem is that I don't know how to tell Jake about me and the circumstances of me. How do I explain to him that my parents' ghosts live with us? How do I explain that I'm not who he thinks I am, though he has already told me about himself? He deserves to know the truth. Yes, he does." Lucinda said.

"Don't conclude yet. You haven't even told Jake, and if he can't accept you for who you are, the door is wide open for him to leave. But I know Jake. I know he will understand you. He is different, and I can feel it. You can't keep hiding the truth from him. Come up with ways to talk to him about it," Greg replied.

"But why isn't Jake coming to visit us anymore? Is everything okay?" Greg asked.

"Same here. I meant to ask Lucinda that. Why are you the one visiting him? Why isn't he visiting us like before?" Maya asked.

"What if we decide to visit him instead?" Greg suggested.

"No. There won't be any need for that. Don't worry. Jake will come around. He just wanted to sort out a few things, and he apologized. He said he would visit very soon," Lucinda replied, avoiding eye contact with her grandparents as she quickly changed the topic to something else. She didn't want her grandparents to know the truth, at least not now.

The past two months have been horrible for Lucinda. No matter how hard she tried, she just couldn't get the thought of Jake out of her head. She tried so hard to act strong, but it was apparent that something else was bothering her.

Lucinda excused herself as she went to the garden behind the house. She just sat there as different thoughts ran through her mind.

"I guess you are thinking about him; you miss him," Anya commented as she sat close to Lucinda.

"If there is another word to replace it, I would gladly use it. I miss Jake greatly, and I wish he would come home soon," Lucinda replied.

"Will you tell him about yourself, who you are, and your real identity?" Anya asked.

"Yes, I will. Jake already told me about himself, so why should I hide my identity again? I just wish he would come home. He has to come home," Lucinda affirmed.

"But what if he never comes home?" Anya asked.

"He is not that wicked and heartless to stay there because of the little issue. We didn't even have much of an issue. It was just a minor misunderstanding. Anya, if you knew where he is, tell me. I want to look for him. He has to come home. This is where he belongs," Lucinda pleaded.

"He isn't from this world. He is from the other side," Anya reminded her.

"I know, but this was his first home, so he can't just leave like that. This is still his first home irrespective of whether he isn't from here," Lucinda replied.

"Trust me, I don't know where he is right now, but while hoping for the best. Let's also hope for the worst. He might come back here, and maybe he might never come back. Whichever one happens, you should accept it. And when are you going to tell your grandparents the truth? You can't just keep lying to them. You can't keep leaving the house under the pretense of going out to visit Jake when he has been away for a month. How long do you think you can continue with this?" Anya asked.

"I don't know. That's the truth, Anya. I don't know how long I can continue with this, but I still can't tell them that Jake has been away for months now. I just wish he would be merciful enough to give me a chance to explain myself," Lucinda said.

"Okay, until then. Let's be hopeful," Anya replied as she stood up and left the garden.

Lucinda quickly cleaned the tears off her eyes as she wouldn't want anyone to see her crying.

"The first time I felt this way was when my parents died. Now, I'm feeling the same way again. I hope you will be kind enough to come home soon," Lucinda said to herself as she stood up and walked inside.

She got to her room as she took out the seashell, and ran her hands on it.

"I don't know if this will work again because I'm asking you to bring back someone who isn't ordinary. Please tell Jake to come home. I know somehow you can deliver my message to him. Tell him to come home that I will tell him everything he needs to know, that life hasn't been the same ever since he left. Tell Jake I'm cold and miserable," Lucinda pleaded. She then kept the seashell close to her bedside as she lay down and drifted off to sleep.

The following morning, Lucinda became restless. She barely touched her breakfast. Her Grandparents and parents tried to know what was wrong with her, but she dismissed the topic even before they brought it up.

"Where are you going to?" Greg asked as she saw Lucinda opening up the door.

"I'm going down the road to visit someone," Lucinda replied.

"The weather isn't too good. It's going to rain anytime. You should stay at home," Greg replied.

"Never mind. I'll be fine. Don't worry about me. I will be home soon," Lucinda replied.

"Is it Jake?" Greg asked.

"No," Lucinda replied as she swiftly left the house to avoid any more questions from her grandfather.

"Who was that?" Maya asked as soon as she came out.

"Oh, it's Lucinda. She said she was going out," Greg responded.

"It's going to rain anytime soon. I know Jake will bring her home safe," Maya added.

"She said she isn't going to visit Jake."

Maya interrogated. "Then who? She barely knows anyone else here. The only friend she has is just Anya and Jake. So, who is she going to visit?"

"When she comes home, you ask her that," Greg replied as he sat on the rocking chair.

It was already drizzling by the time Lucinda got to Jake's house. She sat on the balcony and directed her attention at the sky. It was a heavy downpour, but Lucinda sat still as the rain poured on her. To her, she wondered at the essence of going home. She needed the rain to heal this pain.

"You're going to get a cold," a familiar voice said as Lucinda turned to see Jake standing at the door.

Lucinda hurriedly stood up as she ran and hugged him tightly.

"Where did you go? I have been searching for you. I have come to this house every day, and I always sit here, waiting for you to see if you stroll down the street. I always looked out for you in the street, hoping to come home, but you never did. Please don't go, ever again," Lucinda said, crying.

Jake cleaned the tears off her face as he looked at her and said, "I'm never going away again. I will always be here with you."

Jake helped her inside as he brought out his towel so Lucinda could dry her body and her hair.

"You know you shouldn't have sat down there. It's raining heavily. You might get a cold," Jake asked.

"I always sit there," Lucinda said, pointing at her sitting point outside Jake's house. "That way, I can see people on the street; that way, I had hoped I would be able to see you when you're coming home. I'm glad you are home finally. Thank you for coming back," Lucinda replied.

"I'm happy to be back home. I missed everything here. Much more, I missed you." Jake said.

"Promise you will never leave again," Lucinda pleaded.

"I promise. This is still my home, so I'm not leaving soon," Jake responded. Lucinda smiled as she wrapped the towel around her body on hearing that.

"I told Anya that if you come back, I wouldn't hide my identity from you. Aside from being the girl who lost her parents a decade ago, I'm just like you, half-human, half-god. I was birthed by humans, though I won't say my mom is a full human. She is equally like me, but she didn't know till she died. She is literally from the moon and the stars. I'm Lucinda, the daughter of the moon and the stars, the heir to the throne. Anya isn't human. I guess you already know that. I didn't want to tell anyone because I didn't want what happened years back to happen again.

Everything about me has been kept in secrecy. I possess powers beyond human imagination, powers that I can't even control. I won't say I'm lucky, for being bestowed with all these comes with its challenges, happy and sad times.

This is Lucinda. This is everything about me. I know I should have told you earlier, but I wasn't sure if you would stay or not after hearing this. I was afraid that you might leave me if I should mention it to you. This was the reason I held back from telling you, not that I didn't trust you. I was just trying to protect myself," Lucinda explained.

"Thank you for telling me. I thought about coming back or staying back, but I felt we all deserved another chance. I realized what happened in your past life, how you were killed. I knew everything even before you told me. I just wanted you to tell me by yourself. I wanted you to trust me enough to confide in me about your identity," Jake responded.

"Then why did you leave? Why didn't you stay?" Lucinda asked.

"Because I wanted to fix a yawning bridge. I'm tired of seeing them at war. I want them to make peace with each other, and I left because I wanted to give you time to think about us," Jake replied.

"War? Who do you speak of?" Lucinda asked, surprised to hear this for the first time.

"Your mother and my father, the god, and goddess. They are enemies. Fate has assigned both of us to be together, but I'm still thinking if our union will make them become friends again. Sadly, I failed when I went home; they both detest each other," Jake replied.

"Fate? Are you the one fate has assigned to get married to me?" Lucinda asked. "I guess Anya or your mom didn't tell you about that. I found out, and I had to meet up with you. Perhaps, if I hadn't found out, none of them would have spoken to us about it," Jake replied.

"I see. Now it makes more sense. We will talk about this later," Lucinda said.

"Why? Are you scared of getting married?" Jake asked.

"I'm not scared of getting married. I just want you to follow me home. My grandparents have been asking about you. I need them to see you today at least. I lied to them for months. I would leave the house and tell them I'm coming to visit you. They have been asking me why I haven't been visiting, and I keep telling them soon. So, please let's go and visit them; at least I will be happy seeing that smile on their faces," Lucinda pleaded.

"Will you allow me to talk to your parents?" Jake asked. "Sure, since you can see them," Lucinda said, smiling.

"And also, let's talk to your grandparents about us being soulmates. I know they will understand the need to know now. It's no use hiding it from them," Jake suggested.

"But don't you think it's early to let them know. They still see us as friends," Lucinda replied.

"I know. I guess you haven't told them about the real Jake. It would help if you told them everything. Look, Lucinda, we barely have enough time. You are turning 21 in less than five months. Anya should have told you all these. I guess she prevented you from doing anything with me," Jake implied.

"Anya knows," Lucinda asked with a shock on her face.

"Yes, she knows everything. I think that's why she tried painting me bad when we first met. I don't blame her. She has just been loyal to her queen. So, once we get there, we tell them, Lucinda, they deserve to know everything now," Jake replied.

Wow, I have been in the dark all this while. What more do I need to know?" Lucinda asked.

I don't know. Consult your book of prophecy. Ask your mom questions. They will answer," Jake replied.

"You know about the book of prophecy," Lucinda asked.

"Let's say I know everything that concerns you. You should know everything that concerns me. Don't worry. I will teach you everything you need to know," Jake replied, smiling.

Thank you," Lucinda replied.

"I guess the necklace is taking us there," Jake asked. "You know so much about me," Lucinda said.

"Well, because I came out before you, and since you're my mate, I should know everything about who I'm spending my eternity with," Jake replied.

Lucinda smiled as they both stood up and held each other. Lucinda placed her hand on her necklace as they both disappeared from the room.

They both appeared in Lucinda's room. As they smiled at each other.

"You didn't tell me he was back," Anya said, sitting up from the bed as the duo turned to see Anya.

"Oh, you're here already," Lucinda said.

"Yes, welcome home, Prince Jake," Anya said.

Jake walked closer to the bed as he took the seashell and walked closer to Lucinda.

"I got the message. Jake delivered the message just the way you said it, more reason I came back home. I wouldn't want to steal the shine I brought to your life," Jake said as Lucinda smiled and hugged him.

"It's still raining. After meeting your grandparents and parents, will you take me home?" Jake asked.

"You can sleep here, right?" Lucinda asked.

"What happens to me? Where will I sleep?" Anya blurted out. "You see," Jake said.

"Anya, not like you sleep here all the time," Lucinda said. "I know, but I want to sleep here tonight," Anya replied.

"You can go to my house," Jake chipped in as Anya looked at him and lay back on the bed.

"Let's go," Lucinda said as she dragged Jake out of the room. Greg and Maya were shocked to see Jake with Lucinda.

"We have been sitting here for a few hours. How and when did you both gain entrance to the house?" Greg asked.

"My usual stuff," Lucinda replied as Maya stood up and hugged Jake tightly.

"We missed you," Maya said, smiling.

"Same here. I'm sorry I didn't stop by all this time," Jake apologized.

"We are good. I'm happy you're here with us," Greg responded.

Jake sat down with Lucinda as he slowly said to her," Is it okay to call your parents mom and dad?"

"Sure, you can," Lucinda replied, as Greg and Maya looked at them.

"What's going on?" Greg asked. "Can he see us?" Phil asked.

"Yes, I can see you both. I'm just like your daughter," Jake replied. "Lucinda, what did you do?" Annalise asked, puzzled.

"I didn't do anything. The truth is, Jake is like me," Lucinda replied.

"How do you mean?" Maya asked.

"I'm just like her. She is from the moon and the stars, and I'm the son of the sun. I knew who she was even before we became friends, and I saw your ghost each time I visited, but I couldn't talk about it. I'm just like your daughter, and I want to be seen as Jake," Jake replied.

"Wow! This is hard to believe." Greg said.

"I thought you were human like us," Maya added.

"I'm still human. I was born by earthly parents," Jake replied.

"Dad, mom, grandpa, and Grandma, I need to tell you something, Jake and I are mates," Lucinda said.

"I don't understand," Maya said.

"It means they are husband and wife, more like destined to end up with each other," Anya yelled out as she came out of the room.

"Lucinda, is she joking or serious?" Phil asked.

"I know Lucinda has a better explanation," Annalise added. "You aren't saying anything?" Maya said, looking at Lucinda.

"You all should calm down and let her explain. Jake is a good man, and Lucinda is in perfect hands if they bother to end up together. So, allow them to talk," Greg said.

"The truth is that even before we were born, it has been pre-destined that we will end up with each other. Our parents didn't say a word to us because of their hostility. I got to know the truth, and I had to search for Lucinda and luckily, she was in the same town as me.

Our spirits aligned immediately. We got to meet each other that day. Fate has it that our marriage will reunite the two worlds, and I know that's true. Aside from the prophecy talking about us, even if fate hadn't said anything, I would have still ended up with Lucinda. I love her. Life makes sense to her. I wouldn't want to throw away what we have," Jake explained.

"And they need to get married before Lucinda turns 21. You both are getting married soon," came in Anya.

"You knew about it all," Lucinda asked, surprised at Anya's words.

"Yeah, but it wasn't my power to talk to you about it. Now you know, let me tell you the truth you need to know. You have to get married before the next full moon," Anya replied as she walked inside the room.

"I thought she would stay with us a few more years," Maya stammered.

"Same here. It's so soon. Lucinda can't leave us now," Greg half protested.

"Even if I marry Jake, his house is just a stone's throw. This is my home. I will always visit. My family lives here, and I'm from here. I can't forget home," Lucinda assured.

"My daughter has grown. I thought you were the same Lucinda we left ten years ago." Phil added.

"I wish you would stay a few more years; I just wish," Annalise said.

"This is home. I'm still going to come around. You all are making me cry. No one is taking my room. Even if I turn Jake's wife tomorrow,

I'm still your daughter, and I'm still your grandchild," Lucinda said with a teary voice as Maya stood up and hugged her tightly.

"I know she will be safe with you," Phil said.

"I swear by my throne. Nothing shall hurt Lucinda," Jake replied.

They had a small wedding strictly at 12:30 am, after which Lucinda wanted to hug her parents, Annalise and Phil, before leaving for Jake's house. Maya and Greg were happy, but the tears couldn't let them say a word. They knew that Lucinda would go, but they didn't think it would be soon.

Maya and Annalise hugged Lucinda tightly after the marriage vows were taken.

"Please come back by morning. We want to have breakfast with you and Jake," Maya pleaded.

"Please, Lucinda, don't say no," Annalise added.

"I will be here; I promise," Lucinda said.

"Or we will get to spend the remaining days here. If we visit tomorrow morning, we won't leave till next week," Jake chipped in.

"That's a nice idea," Greg said.

"Thank you so much. I love you and Jake. I know you both will enjoy everything life denied us," Phil prayed.

Lucinda smiled as she hugged her father. She then took turns in embracing his family. On getting to Anya's turn, she said, "You know where to find me. You will always visit, right."

"You know I will. You're my assignment here on earth," Anya smiled as she hugged Lucinda tightly.

Lucinda held her husband as they both bade farewell to all of them before disappearing from the house.

They appeared in Jake's house as Jake wiped the tears off Lucinda's face. It was apparent she was already missing her family. It was already late. They had to go straight to bed.

Lucinda lay on the bed as he watched Jake flip through the book of prophecy.

"How long have you had this?" Jake asked.

"For some time, it came at the right time," Lucinda replied.

"Your grandparents are super excited that we bought this. They have grown so addicted to you. At some point, I thought they wouldn't let you get married, but I'm glad it's all over now. We are couples, and we still live close to them," Jake said.

"Yeah, I wish Amber was here too. I wish she were around to witness all these. I still can't believe that she is gone," Lucinda said.

"I have this strong feeling that she will come home soon. She isn't like you, and neither is she like Anya. Her time here on earth was limited. She came for a purpose, and that purpose was you, and she is through with it. You have to live every day with smiles on your face, knowing that she will come back someday," Jake responded.

"Thank You," Lucinda said, smiling.

Jake stood up as he dropped the book of prophecy on the shelf. He then came back and lay close to Lucinda.

"The world ordained our marriage even before we were born. We will make a perfect couple and bridge the gap between the moon and the sun," Jake said.

"I hope we break the enmity between those two," Lucinda said.

"Do you think our adventure here on earth is over?" Lucinda asked.

"I don't know, but the truth is, I don't think it's over. We are not mortals, so definitely, problems will come for us to solve them.

We were assigned to this world on purpose, but I know whatever will come won't be bigger than us," Jake replied.

"Thank you for coming back," Lucinda said, smiling.

"I can't be mad at you for long. I love and value what we have," Jake replied.

Chapter Eleven

LUCINDA, COME AND SEE THIS

"*Lucinda, come and see this,*" Jake beckoned to Lucinda, who *swiftly dropped the bag she was holding.* Jake handed the Book of Prophecy to her, showing her a page with an image glowing.

"Has this been here all the time?" Lucinda asked, surprised.

"No, the book suddenly glowed on its own, which made me pick it up, and that was when I saw a new message appear," Jake replied.

"This is huge. I don't even know if I'm ready to go through this stress again. Our marriage is just five months old. I don't want to be tasked with this," Lucinda replied mournfully.

"I understand if you don't want to go through this, but it will be fun doing this with you, saving the world together," Jake replied.

"This monster; I just can't deal … but wait, something looks familiar here," Lucinda said as she ran her hands on the book.

"The man bears the image of a star," Lucinda observed.

"Have you encountered him before?" Jake asked.

"No, but something seems odd. I'm trying to place my hand on it. Seeing the star on the body, why can't I fix this simple riddle?" Lucinda shouted.

"You have to take it easy. Sit and think. By so, you might be able to solve the riddle," Jake replied as Lucinda sighed and sat down on the chair.

"The mark on the body looks familiar. I'm trying to recollect something," Lucinda said.

"You mean the star?" Jake asked. "Yes, the star," Lucinda answered.

"Okay, I know you will remember sooner or later, but don't worry about it. You don't have to kill yourself about it. The main issue is how to take him out of the picture and send him to the beyond so he can never bother the world again," Jake replied.

"Why can't they just quit? Why do they keep coming back? And, why should we be the ones to protect the world, putting our lives on the line?" Lucinda asked.

"We are gods. We are special and sent here for a reason. Demons feel they have been living in the shadow of humans for so long. Since humans have no powers, they should not be allowed to stay and rule the earth. Hopefully, someday the world and the world beyond will be erased of all the demons," Jake replied.

"I just hope so," Lucinda replied as she stood up and walked into the room.

Jake took the book as he read through the content of the "**Book of Prophecy.**"

Lucinda walked into the bedroom to see Anya standing close to the window.

"Anya, you're here," Lucinda said as she quickly hugged her.

"Sagar is out. I guess he came to see if he could complete the things other demons couldn't do," Anya said.

"Do you mean the demon which appeared in the Book of Prophecy?" Lucinda asked.

"Yes."

"Wait. How did you find out?" Lucinda asked.

"Lucinda, I'm a spirit. I have lived for centuries, so I can sense whenever evil lurks. I'm a beast too. So, I can sense when demons are around," Anya replied.

"That's true. I almost forgot. I'm already getting used to seeing you as a human that I forgot who you are," Lucinda said as she sat on the bed.

'I'm just scared. I'm angry too," Anya said, still leaning on the wall.

"Is there any problem? You know you can always talk to me," Lucinda said.

"Of course, it's about **Asgard**.

I can't go with you on this one. I'm angry that I won't be part of some of your adventures to save humanity. I'm scared that something bad might happen to you. I'm scared that Asgard might try to hurt you," Anya said.

"***You're a beast.***

You shouldn't be scared. Things like this shouldn't weigh you down, but why can't you go with me? Is there any reason for that? Any

restrictions? You know I can talk to the queen, and she will allow you," Lucinda said.

"No, the rules were made even before your mother started reigning. Since you're now married, you and your husband will undertake any adventure. It can only be in rare cases that I will be permitted to go with you. I'm just tensed. I do not want anything to happen to you. I know you're a goddess, but Lucinda, this part of you is still human," Anya moaned.

"Yeah, you're right. This part of me is still human. I have emotions to start with. If I can change the rules, you know I will, but I need you to do something for me when I'm away with Jake," Lucinda asked.

"You know you don't need to ask. Just tell me what you want, and I will do it right away," Anya said.

"Protect my parents and my grandparents, and don't let them know about this adventure we are about to undertake. I will come to visit before we leave, but whatever happens, protect them all and my horses. Please take good care of them. They are still my family," Lucinda pleaded.

"They are my family too. I will protect them with the last drop of my blood. That's a promise," Anya replied.

"Thank you so much, Anya. I don't know what I would have done without you. Thank you for standing with me all these years, but I'm still pleading. Please don't disappear from me again. I don't want to wake up one morning looking for you," Lucinda pleaded.

"No, I won't disappear from you. I'm here to stay for as long as you want me to stay," Anya replied.

"Thank you so much," Lucinda said as she stood up and hugged Anya tightly.

"Send my greetings to Jake," Anya said as she bade Lucinda goodbye before disappearing.

Lucinda took the seashell as she sat down on the bed. Then, the door flung open as Jake walked in.

"Anya here," Jake asked as he dropped the book of prophecy on the shelf.

"How did you know?" Lucinda asked, smiling.

"I'm a god. I can sense and feel everything. Guess she was here to tell you she won't be going with you," Jake asked as he sat down close to Lucinda.

"Jake!" Lucinda asked with her eyes wide open.

"Anya is a beast. She senses when **demons are coming**.

I don't know how it feels like waking up one morning and being told you can't do things with someone you have always done things with. I wish somehow that some rules will be changed," Jake said.

"You know more than I do. I will change some rules when I get to that position," Lucinda replied.

"Your reign is coming with new things, I guess," Jake asked. "Exactly," Lucinda replied, smiling.

"We will visit my parents and grandparents, but we are not telling them about this adventure. We are just telling them that we are going on a trip. I don't want them getting worked up for anything. We have to come back for them," Lucinda said, betraying a wry smile.

"I will make sure of that. We will come back. That's a promise," Jake assured.

"I know I have the best husband in the whole world. I'm lucky to have ended up with you," Lucinda said.

"I couldn't thank the universe more for making us mates," Jake said as he slowly hugged Lucinda.

Jake and Lucinda got to the door and knocked. "They will be happy to see us," Jake said.

"And also angry with me that I haven't visited for a while now," Lucinda replied.

The door opened to see Anya standing there as she hugged Lucinda.

You didn't tell me you were coming here. I was with you a few days ago," Anya said.

"Who is at the door?" Maya asked, coming towards the entrance door to see for herself.

As soon as she saw Lucinda, she shouted and hugged her. After which, they all walked inside and sat down while Maya clung to her granddaughter.

"I missed my baby," Maya said.

"I'm an adult, Grandma," Lucinda said, smiling.

"And our baby, you will always be," Greg said, smiling as he hugged Jake.

"I'm happy you both came to visit today," Maya said.

"Yeah, we came to know how you're doing, but where are my parents?" Lucinda asked, looking around.

"Oh, they are not here at the moment, but I think they will soon be back," Greg replied

"Jake, you're doing a wonderful job taking care of our girl," Maya said.

"If I don't take care of her, I would have failed," Jake replied, smiling.

"Grandma and Grandpa, I want to talk to you about something important," Lucinda said.

"Is there any problem?" Maya asked.

"You know we will always do anything for you two," Greg added.

"We want to go on a trip for just a week, and we will come home," Lucinda replied slowly.

"It's important; you have to let them go," Anya added.

Maya and Greg looked at each other and nodded, but sadness was written all over their faces. Though they weren't living together anymore, they felt this uneasiness whenever they were to be separated from Lucinda, even for a moment.

"I promise. We will spend a week here once we are back," Jake added.

"Is that a promise?" Maya asked.

"Yes, it's a promise," Lucinda said, smiling as she hugged Maya. Jake and Greg stood up and left the sitting room for the garden.

The giant figure opened its eyes, revealing its purple eyes, smiling as he walked closer to the mirror to touch it.

"You know they might kill you. You just leave," one of the demons said.

"Yes, they might kill me, but that isn't certain. How long will they remain powerful to wipe out all the demons in this world? After me, another will come, and more will still come."

"So, you think they will quit and hand over the world to you?" The other demon asked.

"They have to, Elyon. They have to. This world is ours. It has always been ours. Humans can't come out and take over," Asgard shouted.

"Maybe you shouldn't have unveiled yourself right now. These tricks won't take you anywhere far. They will still defeat you," Elyon said.

"And when they do that, you all shouldn't stop fighting. Somehow the world will become ours. Someone in our midst has to make us proud," Asgard replied.

"Okay, your wish is our command," Elyon said as he bowed and left the place.

Asgard touched the mirror and smiled as Lucinda and Jake appeared in the mirror.

"Oh, it seems they are coming already, making it easier. I don't have to leave here. They will come to meet me," Asgard said, smiling.

"I hope you both have bid your final goodbye to people who mean a lot to you? Even if I don't take you both out today, someone else will. This world is ours. It's just a matter of time for the house owner to get back home. I must have my revenge," Asgard said, tightening his fist. Next, he screamed out loud, which made Elyon appear back, "you called?" Elyon said.

"Take them out. Hide them far away from where they can't be seen. You all have to leave now," Asgard commanded.

"And what about you?" Elyon asked. "I will be fine," Asgard replied.

"You know that's not true. You need us just as we need you. What will happen to you? You can't fight this on your own. Better still, let's leave them. We are okay where we are. No matter how hard we try, we won't win this fight. Star didn't win it, and…"

"Don't you dare talk about my mother in that manner," Asgard shouted, cutting Elyon off?

"She was hibernating, which made it easier for them to kill her," Asgard added.

"Then, how many more will we lose fighting over a lost battle? Asgard looks around. We are okay here. Lucinda and Jake are joined together, making it ten times more difficult to hurt them. They were sent to earth for a reason. They possess powers that they don't even know of, greater than ours. They are special," Elyon countered.

"They are not special. We are the ones. They are gods. It doesn't mean they can't be killed," Asgard shouted.

"We are special too, but the truth has been told. We can't kill them. They can only kill themselves," Elyon replied.

"I don't want to hear anything else. Leave now," Asgard commanded, but Elyon would have none of that.

"Asgard, we can live peacefully with them. We can stop this war and end all this. Creating war where there is none means we will lose our abode just for this. Why are you being so desperate?" Elyon asked as Asgard threw a slap at him.

"Leave. Take them away from here. If I don't come back, make a home there and groom someone else. This fight has to continue. We must redeem what is ours," Asgard shouted.

Elyon bowed as he quickly left the place. Asgard placed his hands on the metal lying on the floor as he muttered some strange words, making the metal dissolve into dust.

Asgard drew his strength from the metal. He needed metal to stay alive and strong.

"I'm not fighting a lost battle. Mother needs to get her revenge.

They have ruled for a long time, but now is the time for demons to take over. We can't keep living in the shadow of humans. It's now or never," Asgard whispered as he disappeared immediately.

Lucinda and Jake walked out of the lightning portal and looked around to see where they were.

"This place looks deserted," Jake said.

"I know, and I can feel this negativity hovering around here," Lucinda said.

"Let's go. I believe what we came for is somewhere around here," Jake said as Lucinda nodded, and they both walked away.

"I think we need to get closer to those pillars. Something is lurking around there," Lucinda said as Jake agreed.

Asgard smiled as he saw Lucinda and Jake approaching.

"You didn't wait for me to come. You came looking for me instead," Asgard said, laughing.

"So, should we wait till you bring ruin to the world before we stop you? We can't. What do you want? You know you can leave, and we won't hurt you," Jake added.

"Hurt me? I'm not weak like my mother. I waited patiently for this day. Now I will have my revenge. I'm sorry that you won't only be losing your wife, you will also be losing your unborn child," Asgard said as he stood up to his full length.

Lucinda touched her stomach as she looked at Jake. "Leave here; go," Jake whispered.

If it had occurred to Jake that Lucinda was pregnant, he wouldn't have gone on this journey with her.

"No, I can't leave you here. Yes, he might hurt us, but he definitely can't kill us. We possess way more powers than he," Lucinda replied.

"Asgard, when you speak of your mother, who is she? Was she that weak? I had to take her off this world permanently," Lucinda asked as Asgard growled?

"Don't you dare speak of my mother like that," Asgard shouted.

"She was weak. Why are you hurt? You're just a piece of cake when Lucinda can easily do away with your mother," Jake said as Asgard spat out a burning ball filled with sulfur.

Asgard was surprised to see Jake standing with no bruises on his body on impact with the burning sulfur.

"Let me remind you again who I am. I'm Jake, the son of the sun. I am fire itself. You can't fight me with fire," Jake replied.

"Then I will fight you with your enemy," Asgard said.

When he was about to evoke water by the side, a strong wind pinned him on the wall as Lucinda advanced and shouted, "I control the wind, water, and this earth. Everything bows at my feet, Asgard. I don't want to hurt you. Leave and never come back," Lucinda shouted as lightning struck, followed by the rumbling of the thunder.

"It was easy for you to defeat her because she was hibernating. Do you think I'm a weakling?" Asgard shouted.

"Oh, that makes more sense. Star is your mother. I knew something familiar about you, and you explained it. So, Star was your mother. I didn't hurt her. I only chose to end things peacefully for her. I didn't even inflict the right pain on her. She came for my parents, which was her greatest mistake." Lucinda shouted back. "I would have hurt your grandparents if I was her," Asgard replied as Jake evoked the rock there, and it came crashing down on Asgard's face.

"Speak one more word about our family, and I will ruin you," Jake threatened with his tightened fist.

Asgard lay on the floor as he muttered some strange words, and everything started visibly shaking as Lucinda and Jake held each other tightly.

"Don't even try because you can't stop this. The earth will swallow you up. I will make your death an easy one, and after that, I will have the freedom to do all I wish," Asgard said, laughing.

"Are you that desperate?" Lucinda asked.

"Yes, I'm desperate to bring doom and damnation to the world just like my mother wanted. She will be so proud of me," Asgard said, laughing.

"Lucinda concentrates. I know you can. Let's do this," Jake said.

"I can't. The ground is shaking. I'm trying to hold my balance," Lucinda replied. "Speak to the winds. They will hear you," Jake whispered.

Lucinda closed her eyes to mutter some words, but she opened them immediately as she whispered, "I'm sorry, I just can't concentrate,"

"Okay, just hold on to me," Jake said as he made a strange drawing on the floor while muttering some unfamiliar words.

"What did you do?" Lucinda asked.

"I summoned our parents. I'm not saying we are weak, but we can barely concentrate. Maybe when we are out of here, we can work on our balance," Jake said.

The shape of the moon and stars together with the sun appeared, and the light was so blinding that they didn't see what happened next.

Lucinda and Jake opened their eyes to see a staff right in their hands.

"You summoned the Queen and the King? What makes you think they possess human attributes like you to appear here? How dare you involve them in a party they weren't invited to. You both are fighting a lost battle. Your parents can't help," Asgard said, laughing. Jake and Lucinda joined their staff together as they enchanted some words together.

"Go home. Damnation can't be brought to the world now," they both uttered as the light from the staff fired straight at Asgard.

They both closed their eyes and fell to the floor from the ensuing explosion.

Lucinda and Jake opened their eyes to see everywhere around were ruined by the explosion.

Jake helped Lucinda up as they strolled to where Asgard was lying down, coughing.

"I know it's over for me. You have sent me where you sent my mother, Star. You both pulled a strong fight. You might have won, but unforeseen demons will always come around. The fight hasn't ended. We demons still exist," Asgard said, laughing as he slowly faded into thin air, leaving some flowers on the floor.

"The staff, where are they?" Lucinda asked, looking around.

"They are gone and belong to our parents. Asgard was right. We can't make them appear here. They have a place solely designed for them. Let's just say their spirits took over our bodies. They have done their bidding and returned to their palaces," Jake replied.

"How? Who am I married to?" Lucinda asked.

"You have a lot to learn, and I will teach you everything," Jake replied.

"Let's go home then," Lucinda said.

Jake bent down as he kissed Lucinda's stomach and said, "I'm so sorry I brought you out to experience this. If I knew you were in momma's womb, I wouldn't have stressed you. Daddy is so sorry. I can hardly wait to meet you."

"Funny enough, a demon told us we will be parents. I will tell my daughter how her presence was announced to us," Lucinda said, laughing.

"Daughter? You seem so sure," Jake asked.

"Yeah, Amber is coming back. She promised that she would come back as our first child, so I believe I will give birth to her," Lucinda said.

"Nice, is a seer, daughter of the moon and the stars, and also the daughter of the sun. How lucky can she be?" Jake replied, laughing back.

"Very lucky. We will stay alive for her," Lucinda added.

"Let's go home," Jake said as Lucinda touched her necklace, opening the portal before they both walked in.

Chapter Twelve

LUCINDA'S HAND GRIPPED JAKE

Lucinda's hand gripped Jake tightly as waves of pain and anticipation washed over her. The room echoed with the rhythm of her breaths, the moments stretching into eternity. With a final push, the cries of a newborn filled the air, and Lucinda's heart swelled with overwhelming love and relief.

As the town nurse placed the bundle of joy in Lucinda's arms, tears welled up in her eyes. She gazed down at her daughter, a radiant warmth flooding her being. "Amber," she whispered, her voice filled with tenderness, knowing this name held a significance that transcended the ordinary. She promised that she would name her child after Amber, the seer. Lucinda couldn't help but notice the subtle yet striking similarities between her daughter and Amber. From the curve of her smile to the sparkle in her eyes, an uncanny resemblance went beyond mere genetics. It felt like Amber returned to this world for the second time.

One evening, sitting with her husband Jake in the warmth of their home, Lucinda couldn't contain her observations any longer. "Jake," she began, her voice tinged with curiosity, "have you noticed how much our daughter resembles Amber?"

Jake nodded, a smile playing on his lips. "It's almost uncanny sometimes," he replied, his eyes reflecting his affection for his wife and daughter.

Lucinda pondered the resemblance, a mix of wonder and intrigue dancing in her thoughts. She traced the contours of Amber's face in her mind; the familiarity of Amber the seer features an unspoken connection between them. It was as if her daughter carried a reflection of Amber's essence, proof of the bond they shared.

"Remember Amber's prophecy?" Jake leaned back, a playful smile tugging at the corners of his lips.

Lucinda's eyes sparkled with curiosity. "Oh, you mean her claim about coming back as our child?" she chuckled softly. "Yes, she did promise that, and it's obvious she kept her promise. For once, I thought I was never going to see her again.

Jake nodded, a thoughtful expression crossing his face. "It's intriguing. The idea of her returning in a different form, possibly with powers or abilities we can't fathom."

Lucinda leaned in with her gaze fixed on Jake. "But what kind of powers could she possess? Will she be a free spirit, a wanderer between worlds?" I'm scared, Jake, even if I don't say it. I don't want my child to go through half of what I went through here on earth, discovering who I am and the battles I had to fight."

Jake's smile widened; his eyes filled with assurance. "Whatever powers she may possess, whatever form she takes, I'm certain of one thing: the convergence of our worlds, the ones she comes from, won't bring trouble upon our path. Trust me, she won't go through any of what you went through. Do you know why? Because you have cleared the path for her, that which she will be grateful for in years to come."

Lucinda sighed, a mix of wonder and apprehension evident in her voice. "It's just the unknown, Jake. The unpredictability of it all, I want what's best for her and everybody."

"I understand, love." Jake reached out and gently grasped Lucinda's hand. "But Amber has always been a beacon of positivity, a guide through uncertainty. She's not the kind to bring chaos but rather happiness. Her past life may not be easy, but her present life with us as her parents will be the easiest for her."

Lucinda's gaze softened, a sense of trust enveloping her. "You're right. She's always been an embodiment of wisdom and balance."

As they sat in contemplative silence, memories of their encounters with Amber flooded their minds. Her serene presence, her cryptic yet reassuring words echoed in their thoughts, a being who was blessed beyond measure.

"We might never truly comprehend the extent of her abilities," Lucinda mused. "But I hope she brings the same warmth and kindness she always exuded."

"I couldn't agree more," Jake nodded in agreement. "Her presence has always been a blessing, a beacon of hope in our lives."

As Greg and Maya entered the house, Lucinda greeted them warmly, embracing them tightly. Their eyes sparkled with excitement, eager to see their great-grandchild, Amber. Lucinda pointed towards Amber's room, understanding their intent, and they hurried off to be with her.

Alone in the room with Amber, the atmosphere was filled with a sense of innocent curiosity. Amber looked up at her great-grandparents with curious eyes and asked, "Why don't Grandma Annalise and Grandpa Phil play or hug me? Did I do anything wrong?"

Maya was momentarily taken aback by the unexpected question, unsure how to respond, while Greg leaned closer to Amber, trying to find the right words. "Sweetheart, they're not angry with you, and you didn't do anything wrong, okay? They're different; sometimes they can't play or hug like we do."

Amber's face scrunched up in confusion. "But I want to hug them. Can you ask them, please?" she pleaded, her innocence tugging at Greg's heartstrings.

Greg's eyes softened with empathy. "I know you want to, and they want to hug you too. But it might take some time. They're not mad, I promise."

Maya, touched by Amber's yearning, finally found her voice. "Amber, Grandma Annalise, and Grandpa Phil love you very much. They watch over you, even if they can't hug or play right now."

Amber's little face lit up with a hint of understanding. "Okay," she said, a small smile on her lips.

Greg scooped Amber into a warm embrace, trying to reassure her. "We'll all play together soon, alright?"

Amber nodded, her eyes brightening with anticipation. "Okay, Grandpa," she said, giggling as Maya joined in with a playful tickle.

Greg and Maya engaged Amber in games and playful activities throughout the day. The moments were filled with laughter and joy. Amber's innocent question lingered in the air, a reminder of the gentle patience required to bridge the gap between her and her ghostly grandparents, Annalise and Phil.

That evening, when Greg and Maya left for their home, it didn't last long for Jake and Amber to disappear into the quiet evening for their stroll. A subtle shift in the atmosphere settled over the house.

Later that night, the midnight stillness was interrupted by Jake's gentle touch as he woke Lucinda, concern etched on his face. "Lucinda, wake up," he whispered urgently, his voice filled with wonder.

Blinking away the remnants of sleep, Lucinda rubbed her eyes, a mix of confusion and concern on her face. "Is everything okay?" she asked, her voice laced with sleepiness.

Jake embraced her tenderly, guiding her gently towards Amber's room. "Come, you have to see this," he said softly, his eyes glinting with excitement and awe.

Confused but trusting Jake's lead, Lucinda followed him into Amber's room. As they stepped inside, a breathtaking sight unfolded before them. The two-year-old lay peacefully, surrounded by a celestial spectacle. Stars danced around her, and sunlight seemed to orbit her, creating a mesmerizing display that defied explanation.

Lucinda gasped in awe, her hand covering her mouth in disbelief. "What…ho…" Her words trailed off, unable to comprehend the ethereal sight before her.

A radiant smile graced Jake's lips as he held Lucinda closer, his eyes fixed on their remarkable child. "Our parents came to visit their grandchild," he said, his voice filled with wonder and pride.

Lucinda's heart swelled with mixed emotions—wonder, joy, and a sense of connection. Tears of awe welled in her eyes as she gazed upon the extraordinary scene, realizing the importance of their daughter's unique lineage.

She stepped closer to Amber, a sense of reverence washing over her.

"She truly is something special," Lucinda whispered, her voice filled with an inexplicable sense of pride and love.

Sitting together on the bed, they whispered about the strange occurrence. "Do you think we did it? Bridged the gap between worlds?" Lucinda asked, her voice tinged with curiosity.

The events of the evening left them feeling amazed and intrigued. Thoughts whirled in their minds as they dozed off, wondering what this newfound link between worlds might mean for their future and the future of their child, Amber. But whatever it was, they were sure they would handle it.

As Amber celebrated her third birthday, Lucinda observed something extraordinary about her daughter—subtle manifestations of supernatural abilities that seemed to emanate from within her. Objects occasionally levitated when Amber was excited. She communicated effortlessly with animals, giggles attracting butterflies and birds wherever she played.

Lucinda, having harbored her abilities, recognized the signs immediately. Rather than being alarmed, she found solace in realizing that Amber had inherited these extraordinary gifts from herself and Jake.

One sunny afternoon in the backyard, Lucinda watched Amber hold out her tiny hand, her eyes sparkling with innocent curiosity. A small sapling struggling to grow suddenly sprouted leaves, blooming with vibrant flowers as Amber's laughter filled the air.

While witnessing the scene, Jake approached Lucinda, his expression a mix of wonder and understanding. "She's like us, isn't she?" he remarked softly, his eyes fixed on their daughter.

Lucinda nodded, a gentle smile gracing her lips. "Yes, she is our little miracle, carrying the wonders of something beyond the ordinary. We're lucky to have her."

Embracing their daughter's unique abilities, Lucinda and Jake nurtured Amber's burgeoning powers, guiding her with love and care. They knew that within her lay a potential that transcended the bounds of the ordinary. A gift that, when honed and understood, could become a beacon of hope, and wonder in a world filled with mysteries yet to be explored.

Amber, her little feet padding softly on the floor, approached her parents, a furrow forming on her brow as she reached out to touch them. "Mommy, Daddy, why can't I hug Grandma Annalise and Grandpa Phil as I do with Big Grandpa Greg and Grandma Maya?"

Jake and Lucinda exchanged glances. Their hearts softened by Amber's innocence. Jake crouched down, meeting her curious gaze. "Sweetheart, it's not that they don't want to hug you. It's just that they can't."

Amber's eyes widened. "Why not? Don't they like me?"

Lucinda kneeled beside her, wrapping her arms around Amber. "Of course they do, darling. They have a special way of being here."

"How?" Amber's voice carried a hint of confusion.

"Your grandparents turn into something called ghosts during the day," Lucinda explained gently.

"Ghosts?" Amber's voice quivered slightly.

Jake nodded, trying to find the most straightforward words. "Yes, they're like spirits, sweetie. People who have left this world."

"But why are they here if they're gone?" Amber's innocence begged for understanding.

Lucinda smiled softly, tracing a finger along Amber's cheek. "You see, honey, Mommy and Daddy are different. I come from the moon and stars, and your daddy comes from the Sun. So, some things work differently for us."

Amber blinked, trying to make sense of the magical explanation. "Who am I then?"

Lucinda's eyes twinkled with affection. "You, my dear, are something special. With time, you'll discover who you truly are."

Feeling curious and fascinated, Amber took her parents' hands as they led her back to her room. They tucked her in, showering her with kisses, and left her to drift into the realm of dreams, unaware of the enchanting encounters awaiting her as the clock struck midnight.

The clock's chime pierced the silence of Amber's room as midnight arrived. Annalise and Phil, the spectral forms of her grandparents, appeared, their translucent figures casting a soft glow in the dimly lit room. With a tender longing, Annalise extended her hand towards Amber, intending to stroke her hair as she slept.

"Grandma! Grandpa!" Amber's voice filled with excitement.

Surprised, Annalise asked, "My dear, why are you awake late?"

Giggling with innocence, Amber sat up. "I was waiting for you!"

Phil couldn't help but chuckle at her sincerity. "You were waiting for us?"

"Yep!" Amber affirmed, enveloping her grandparents in a heartfelt embrace. "Someone told me that if I want to hug you, then I have to wait until midnight; she is right,"

"And who is that," Annalise asked.

"It's my secret; I promised her I wouldn't tell anyone about her. "Have you been coming every night?" Amber asked smiling.

A tender warmth enveloped Annalise and Phil at Amber's innocent inquiry. "Yes, darling, we have," Annalise replied, her voice filled with affection.

Happiness flashed across Amber's face as she nestled back onto her pillow. "Don't worry, I'll find a way so you don't have to wait till midnight to play with me again, and Mommy doesn't have to wait till midnight to hug you both."

Annalise and Phil exchanged glances, a shimmer of hope reflecting in their translucent forms. Their heart swelled with gratitude for the unwavering love of their grandchild, even though they both knew it wasn't possible. Lucinda had already done what her powers could do.

Amber closed her eyes with a comforting smile, her breathing becoming steady and calm as sleep gently reclaimed her. Annalize and Phil watched over her for a moment. Ensuring she was deeply asleep, they reappeared in the familiar surroundings of their parent's home before slowly fading away from her room.

Greg and Maya were overjoyed to see their daughter and son-in-law, the ethereal reunion filling the room with warmth and love. Conversations flowed effortlessly, recounting tales of the past and sharing glimpses of their unseen world.

Greg bid them goodnight as the night deepened, his heart full from the brief yet cherished encounter. It didn't take long before Maya bid them goodnight. Annalise and Phil sat on the balcony and watched the stars and the moon that night.

"What Amber said will hurt when she realizes she can't do anything. She is such a sweet little child," Annalise said, breaking the silence.

Phil chuckled and said, "She will grow to understand the realities of life."

"The truth is, I'm happy that Lucinda and Jake aren't fully human. Laying on the deathbed and thinking about my child was the worst thing ever. I fought death. I wanted to stay alive for my baby, but I guess I didn't fight enough. I watched my daughter go through hell, even though my parents were taking good care of her. All she wanted was her parents. I'm happy that whatever happens, Amber won't have to go through the same thing Lucinda went through. She won't bear the same scar that our death caused to her daughter," Annalise uttered as Phil shifted closer to her and hugged her tightly.

Phil smiled as he looked at the Stars. "I'm happy that things turned out well for Lucinda. It would help if you were happy, too. We got the chance that many never got."

Alone in the dimly lit room, Lucinda gazed at the night sky through the window, the stars twinkling like distant whispers. She couldn't shake off the unease about her daughter's future and the unknown path ahead.

With a heavy heart, Lucinda whispered into the silent room, Lucinda stood up as she walked into her room. Jake was fast asleep already. She lay down on the bed, staring into blank space. Thoughts of Amber and the complexities of being a mother swirled through Lucinda's mind. The soft glow of the moonlight seeped into the room, casting shadows that seemed to mirror the uncertainty she felt.

Despite the tranquility of the night, Lucinda's heart remained restless, haunted by the unspoken worries about her beloved daughter. The night went on, leaving Lucinda in a state of contemplation, hoping for clarity and reassurance amidst her apprehensions.

In the calm stillness of the night, Jake stirred from his sleep, sensing an unease that permeated the room. He turned to see Lucinda, her eyes open, staring into the darkness, a troubled expression on her face.

"Lucinda, what's wrong?" Jake's voice was soft, laden with concern.

Startled, Lucinda turned to face him, trying to mask the worry in her eyes. "I'm okay, Jake. Couldn't sleep," she replied, attempting to dismiss the gravity of her thoughts.

Jake could sense her hesitation. "Please, talk to me. I can see something's bothering you," he pleaded gently, reaching out to comfort her.

"You're worried about Amber. This has gone far too long, and it's unhealthy," Jake said.

Lucinda turned and said, "I know, but the more I try to get the thought off my head, the more it returns. I have tried Jake, but it's not working. I don't want to lose Amber, and I don't want Amber to lose me; I don't want my daughter going through the same thing I went through after my parents died."

"You're immortal, Lucinda; you can't die," Jake assured.

What if fate has destined for Amber's parents to die," Lucinda asked.

"Okay, my wife has gone crazy; fate hasn't destined anything evil to happen, hey? This isn't the woman I married; don't let fear turn you into what you're not. I'm begging you," Jake pleaded.

"I will try not to let fear win over me, I promise," Lucinda said as she turned and closed her eyes.

Jake, though worried, respected her wish for solitude. He watched as she closed her eyes, pretending to sleep. Feeling less, he silently gazed at the full moon outside their window, an unspoken plea escaping his lips, "Please, the moon and Stars, help your child; don't let fear win over her."

With a heavy heart and a silent prayer for guidance, Jake settled back into bed, hoping for peace to envelope their home and soothe the anxieties that had gripped Lucinda.

Chapter Thirteen

LITTLE AMBER

*L*ittle Amber tiptoed into her mother Lucinda's room, her wide eyes filled with wonder and innocence. "Mommy, do you think my grandparents Annalise and Phil will ever come back to life?" she asked, her voice conveying hope.

Sitting on the edge of the bed, Lucinda paused, her smile softening at Amber's question. She looked at her daughter, her heart swelling with a mix of emotions, memories flooding back. Her gaze was Amber's; momentarily, the room seemed to hold its breath.

"Sweetie," Lucinda replied gently, "life can be tricky sometimes. We don't always have answers to everything, do we?"

Amber furrowed her brow, contemplating her mother's words. "But if they do come back, how would you feel?" she persisted, her curiosity unquenched.

Lucinda's smile remained, but her eyes carried a hint of something more profound, a mixture of longing and acceptance. She placed a hand on Amber's shoulder, drawing her close. "If that were ever possible, I think I'd smile and say nothing at all," she said softly, her voice conveying mystery.

Amber pondered Lucinda's response, trying to decipher the meaning behind her words. Sensing her daughter's confusion, Lucinda tousled Amber's hair affectionately. "Sometimes, love, the most powerful feelings, are the hardest to put into words."

With a contented sigh, Amber nodded, feeling a sense of comfort in her mother's embrace. Lucinda's smile lingered, hinting at a story untold, a journey of love and loss that only time could unveil. She didn't want to think about anything that would end up dashing her hopes. How was she even going to explain to her daughter that she could still see her grandparents, all thanks to the newfound powers, and they would never be humans again? She didn't want to ruin her daughter at such a tender age.

Jake walked into the room. His face was etched with concern as he found Lucinda deep in thought. Sensing her unease, he swiftly approached her, concern evident in his eyes. Lucinda turned to him, a mixture of worry and confusion on her face.

"What's wrong, Lucinda?" Jake inquired, his voice tinged with concern, as he took her hands.

With a furrowed brow, Lucinda divulged, "Amber asked me something odd earlier—how I'd feel if my parents came back to life." Her voice held a trace of disquiet.

Perplexed, Jake's expression mirrored the confusion. "Where could she have gotten that idea from?" he pondered aloud, trying to decipher the reason behind Amber's unexpected question.

Looking slowly, Lucinda murmured, "I have no idea, Jake. It caught me completely off guard. She asked with so much happiness on her face, like it was something that would happen. How do I break it to her that people who are dead can never come back to life?" her concern was palpable.

Fearing that Lucinda might be growing anxious, Jake held her hands tighter, gazing deeply into her eyes. "Please, don't let this unsettle you; you don't need to tell Amber anything. Let her come up with her questions. As she grows older, the realities of this world will make sense to her," he urged, trying to calm her unease. "Amber and I will visit your grandparents, Maya and Greg, today. What if you come with us? Maybe being around family will help us understand what's happening."

"No, I'm okay; I still have some things to sort out here. You both should come back in time for dinner," Lucinda said.

Jake looked at his wife and said, "Promise me you will be good. Remember, nothing will happen to her. She is just like us, and whatever she is displaying now shouldn't bother us, okay," Lucinda nodded in agreement, finding solace in Jake's assurance as Jake and Amber prepared to leave for Maya and Greg's place. An eerie feeling settled within her. An unspoken tension lingered in the air, an unexplained sense of foreboding that made her heart race faster.

Deep down, Lucinda couldn't shake off the unsettling feeling that something was amiss—something lurking beneath the surface, hidden within Amber's innocent words. It left her with a chilling sensation, a silent apprehension that lingered ominously in her mind. Something might have made her daughter ask that question, but she knows Amber is not one to force answers from her.

The Sun began its descent as Jake and Amber arrived at Big Grandma and Big Grandpa's house. The air filled with the warmth of family. Amber dove into playtime with Grandma Maya; her laughter echoed through the house.

As the evening progressed, Greg gestured for Jake to step outside momentarily. Concern etched on his face, Greg asked Jake if everything was alright. Jake nodded but shared his worry about Amber's peculiar questions regarding Lucinda's parents, Annalise and Phil. Despite her efforts to conceal her distress, he explained how it seemed troubling Lucinda.

With a comforting tone, Greg reassured Jake, "Kids ask lots of questions, Jake. The last time we were there, she asked us why Annalise and Phil didn't touch or play with her. We were shocked by the question, but we managed to reply. Amber is just curious. Lucinda will figure it out. It's tough, but she'll manage." His words carried a sense of understanding and wisdom.

Jake smiled, grateful for Greg's reassurance. "Okay, then," he replied, feeling somewhat relieved by Greg's words of wisdom.

Soon, Maya emerged from the house with Amber, who reluctantly bid goodbye to her grandma. Maya gently handed Amber over to Jake, a tender smile gracing her face as she wished them well on their way home.

"I love you," Amber said innocently as Maya and Greg replied, smiling.

As Jake and Amber made their way down the quiet streets, the Sun setting in the distance, a sense of tranquility enveloped them. Jake held

Amber close, cherishing the bond between father and daughter. The streets, usually bustling with activity, now lay empty, painting a serene backdrop for their evening stroll.

In the peaceful embrace of the twilight hour, Jake and Amber walked hand in hand, the fading light casting long shadows across the pavement. Despite the day's mysteries and worries, the quiet stroll with his daughter brought a sense of solace to Jake's heart.

The serenity of the room was disrupted as Anya entered, her presence startling Lucinda. Anya observed d the troubled look on Lucinda's face, her eyes scanning her friend's worried expression.

"What's wrong, Lucinda?" Anya's voice broke the silence, tinged with concern.

Lucinda hesitated, unsure whether to divulge the complexity of Amber's recent revelation. "It's nothing g, just…thinking about Amber and her abilities."

At dinner that night, Amber, in her innocent curiosity, asked her mom and dad if they didn't want Grandma Annalise and Phil to be humans again. Lucinda stayed quiet, but Jake responded, "We'd love that, sweetheart, but it's impossible."

"When you say it's not possible, how do you mean," Amber asked curiously.

"They are dead, Amber; my parents died when I was still a child. During that time, I wanted nothing but to bring them back to life. I asked questions and did everything within my power, and nothing happened. So, when Daddy says it's not possible, believe him. We can't bring back dead people," Lucinda explained calmly.

Amber nodded. Her eyes filled with a child's understanding. "Okay, but Mommy, you and I don't have to believe in what people say is impossible," she replied, her tone accepting but still curious.

Jake looked at his daughter and asked what she meant, but Amber smiled happily and continued with her food.

Intrigued by Amber's sudden smile, Lucinda pressed, "Why are you smiling, honey?" But Amber grinned mischievously, knowing how to dodge questions like any four-year-old might. Lucinda attempted to maintain a serious tone, saying, "No more games, alright?"

After dinner, Amber dashed excitedly to her room, her parents trailing behind to tuck her in. Yet, as they leaned over to kiss her goodnight, Amber feigned sleep, stifling giggles as they left her room.

"Do you think she is up to something?" Lucinda asked as soon as she got to the room.

Jake looked at his wife and smiled. "What could a four-year-old possibly be up to at this time of the night? You worry too much about Amber,"

"She just said that we don't have to believe in everything people say is impossible," Lucinda replied.

"Your parents are ghosts that we can see and touch once it's midnight. That is what others term impossible. So hey, Amber is right, let's sleep," Jake said as he pecked his wife.

Lucinda stared at the ceiling with different thoughts racing through her mind before she drifted off to sleep.

Once alone, Amber sat up, her imagination brimming with excitement. She glanced at the window and noticed the full moon casting its silver glow. It was exactly midnight. With a gleam in her eye, she stood on her bed and whispered some peculiar words that seemed to flow effortlessly from her lips.

"Thank you," Amber whispered to the stars outside, feeling a strange sensation coursing through her tiny frame. As she uttered those mysterious words, the stars twinkled and danced in a dazzling display, brighter and more vibrant than she had ever seen before.

"Don't worry, Mom, when you wake up by morning, you will be the happiest person ever," she said, giggling, content with her secret little ritual. Amber settled back into her bed, a satisfied smile gracing her lips as she drifted off to sleep as the stars twinkled in the night sky.

This moment marked another instance where Amber's mysterious abilities hinted at something beyond comprehension, leaving both her parents and herself unaware of the vast power she wielded. A child's innocent words whispered under the moonlit sky, invoking a shift in the world.

Lucinda stirred awake to tiny footsteps shuffling excitedly across the wooden floor. Amber's giggles filled the air, pulling her from the depths of sleep. Blinking away the remnants of dreams, Lucinda sat up, her heart pounding with curiosity.

"Mommy, wake up! I have a surprise for you!" Amber's voice bubbled with enthusiasm, tugging at Lucinda's hand.

Rubbing her eyes, Lucinda followed her daughter. A mixture of drowsiness and anticipation filled her. Amber led him into the sitting room, her tiny hand gripping Lucinda firmly.

With a flourish, Amber stepped aside, revealing figures standing by the window. The morning light illuminated their silhouettes. Lucinda's breath caught in her throat, her eyes widening in disbelief. Before she stood, her parents—Annalise and Phil—were alive and vivid as if plucked from a distant memory.

Shocked, Lucinda stumbled backward, her heart racing with a whirlwind of emotions. "How... How is this possible?" Her voice trembled, eyes darting between her parents and Amber.

Amber beamed, a radiant child's smile lighting up her face. She looked at Lucinda with a knowing innocence that belied her tender age. "Surprise, mommy! I found them in the pictures and brought them here!"

Lucinda's gaze darted from Amber to her parents, her mind struggling to grasp the inexplicable scene before her. Tears flew up in her eyes as she stumbled forward, embracing her parents tightly, feeling their warmth, and hearing their comforting words.

As Lucinda held them close, a flood of emotions surged within her—a mix of joy and disbelief. She glanced at Amber, overwhelmed by the inexplicable miracle her child seemed to have woven.

With a tender gaze, Lucinda looked at Amber, her voice quivering with emotion. "My darling, how did you...?" Her words trailed off, lost in the wonder of a child's imagination, realizing that sometimes, the innocence and magic of a young heart could create moments that defied all logic.

Jake emerged from the kitchen, and Amber dashed to him, laughing and joyful. "Did you wake your mom up?" Jake asked, his voice filled with amusement.

Amber giggled mischievously and nodded, "Yes!"

Curious about the commotion, Lucinda inquired, "What did you do, Jake?"

Looking surprised at himself, Jake explained, "I was shocked too. I could find Annalise and Phil this morning. In short, they're not ghosts anymore; they're human."

Everyone turned to Amber, eyes wide with astonishment. "What did you do, Amber?" Lucinda asked gently, trying to understand.

"I brought them back to life so I could play with them. Aren't you happy?" Amber replied innocently, her eyes wide with confusion.

Lucinda and Jake smiled warmly, assuring her, "We're delighted, sweetheart. Thank you."

They gently asked Amber to go to her room, wanting to speak privately. Alone together, Jake and Lucinda's faces lit up with joy and relief.

Lucinda hugged her parents tightly, a sense of happiness washing over him. "I think, Mom and Dad, I'm going to have breakfast with you for the first time. You died when I was 8. I didn't even know this was possible."

Lucinda's eyes welled up with tears of joy. "Yes, I'm here, Lucinda. We're all here now," Annalise said, holding her close, feeling an overwhelming sense of gratitude for this miraculous moment.

With tears of joy streaming down their faces, Jake and Lucinda embraced Annalise and Phil, their hearts flowing with happiness at the reunion they thought was impossible.

Amid the emotional embrace, Lucinda's words lingered in the air, marking a moment of importance in their lives—a breakfast together after years of separation caused by death, a symbol of the miraculous second chance they had been granted.

Amid the quiet midday, Annalise and Phil stood at the doorstep of her parent's home, exchanging glances filled with anticipation. As

Annalise gently rapped on the door, a faint sense of nervousness mingled with excitement coursed through her veins.

The door creaked open, revealing Maya, her mother, her eyes widening in sheer surprise. "Annalise?" she stammered in disbelief etched across her face. It was a usual hour for her daughter to be present, especially considering their peculiar circumstances. She barely had time to process before Annalise rushed forward, enveloping her tightly.

"Mom, it's us!" Annalise's voice was filled with an undeniable joy. Maya was taken aback, still trying to comprehend the situation. "But it's noon. How...?" his voice trailed off, confusion and amazement intermingling in her words.

Before Maya could finish, Greg, her father, appeared behind her, observing the unexpected reunion. His eyes widened as he caught sight of Annalise and Phil, frozen in a moment of astonishment. "What's going on here?" His voice held a mix of concern and fascination.

Phil stepped forward, a faint smile playing on his lips. "Amber, she did something incredible. She found a way to bring us back to life," he explained, his tone tinged with disbelief as if even he was still coming to terms with their newfound humanity.

Greg's expression had shifted, a glimmer of hope mingled with disbelief in his eyes. "Amber? But how? It's impossible." His curiosity was palpable, a father's concern and fascination blending seamlessly.

Annalise chimed in, her eyes shining with unshed tears of joy. "Dad, Mom, it's true. We're humans again!" Her words hung in the air, a sense of surrealism enveloping the moment.

Greg's initial shock melted into an overwhelming wave of relief. Without hesitation, he pulled Phil into a tight hug, a silent expression of happiness for their salvation. Then, turning to Annalise, he embraced her just as tightly, his eyes glistening with tears of joy.

Finally reunited in this unexpected turn of events, the family gathered around the table for a long-overdue lunch. Laughter and conversation filled the air as they savored this precious moment together. Annalise and Phil shared stories of their ghostly adventures while Greg and Maya listened intently, their hearts filled with wonder at the unbelievable twist of fate.

As they relished each other's company, the hours seemed to slip away, lost in the joy of the present. It was a moment they had longed for, a simple yet profound reunion that mended the years of separation and uncertainty caused by their untimely death.

The sunlight streamed through the windows, casting a warm glow over the room as the afternoon waned. With hearts full and spirits soaring, they savored every minute, grateful for the unexpected miracle that brought them together once again.

As the afternoon drifted into early evening, the atmosphere remained charged with an indescribable warmth. Annalise, Phil, Greg, and Maya lingered at the table, reminiscing about moments long gone, sharing anecdotes from their ghostly and human experiences.

"Remember that time we got stuck in the body of the horses?" Phil chuckled, glancing at Annalise with a playful grin.

Annalise rolled her eyes, a smile tugging at her lips. "Oh please, it was hell, but I was grateful we could talk to Lucinda and share some time with her. Dad, you and Mom kept thinking Lucinda was insane, but she was just bonding with her parents."

Laughter filled the room, a harmonious blend of shared memories and newfound joy. Greg and Ma watched their daughter and Phil, their hearts swelling with contentment at the sight of their happiness.

"How did Amber manage to do this when Lucinda couldn't?" Maya's curiosity sparked a new wave of conversation, her gaze flickering between Annalise and Phil.

Annalise took a moment, gathering her thoughts before speaking. "It was a combination of things. Amber discovered ancient magic, though she won't say where, which she performed exactly at midnight today with the help of the moon, and here we are, Mom, as humans, not ghosts, not anymore.

Maya shifted close to her daughter and said, "Your death created a scar in our life, and your return today has somehow cleared that scar. Please don't leave us, Annalise; your mother won't bear it if anything happens to you or Phil again. Promise me that this return is for a lifetime,"

"I promise, Mother, I won't go anywhere," Annalise assured as she hugged her mother tightly. Tears flowed freely from their eyes as Phil and Greg watched with smiles on their faces.

Lucinda arranged the room, feeling a sudden breeze that whispered across her skin. "Anya, I know it's you. What is it? she questioned, sensing the familiar presence.

Anya's voice resonated softly, carrying a weight of revelation. "I hope you know what Amber did has granted immortality to your parents and grandparents," she conveyed, her words hanging in the air.

Startled, Lucinda clutched a vase, her heart pounding with realization. As Anya's words sank in, the vase slipped from her hands, shattering into pieces on the ground, mirroring the shattering realization of the enormity of Amber's actions.

Before Lucinda could respond, Anya continued, preempting her unspoken question. "Before you ask me how she did it, I don't know.

When a child is from both worlds, I guess the powers she bears are more than the eyes can see. The truth is that Amber will do things that the world terms impossible," she explained, fading away into the ether, leaving Lucinda standing in stunned silence.

Jake rushed in, concerned, asking if everything was alright. Lucinda struggled to gather her thoughts, trying to explain. "It's Amber. It's something she did. We need to go to her room," she replied, her voice tinged with urgency and a sense of disbelief.

Jake could see the worry etched on Lucinda's face as she struggled to explain. "Amber did something when she brought my parents back to life. It involves making them and my grandparents both immortal," she managed to articulate, her voice trembling slightly with unease.

Concerned by Lucinda's distress, Jake gently urged her to calm down and share what had happened. Lucinda recited Anya's revelation, and in response, Jake surprised her with a probing question, "What are you so scared of, Lucinda?"

Feeling overwhelmed, Lucinda sighed heavily and sank onto the bed. "I don't know, Jake. I don't. I lost them when I was very young; I guess that messed up with my mind," she admitted, her gaze fixed on the world outside the window, lost in uncertainty.

Jake enveloped her in a reassuring hug, comforting her. "Our daughter's fate has already been decided. Whatever you do won't change that; if you try to alter it, there will be consequences that we won't like. Just let him be," he reassured, hoping to ease Lucinda's worry.

"Okay," Lucinda murmured, accepting Jake's reassurance and feeling more at ease.

Once Jake felt Lucinda had calmed down, he suggested they go and talk to Amber. Amber was found in the sitting room, engrossed in playing with the wooden toys Jake had bought her. Lucinda approached her gently, her heart full of apprehension.

"Amber, Mommy needs to talk to you," Lucinda said softly, trying to hide her concern.

Amber's eyes sparkled with curiosity as she looked up, eager to hear what her mom wanted to say, her innocent gaze fixed on Lucinda, waiting for an explanation.

Lucinda stared at the moon, which cast a gentle glow through the window, painting the room with a soft luminescence. Her daughter's innocent gaze held an unspoken wisdom as she explained the aftermath of her act of magic.

"Mommy, I made everyone who shares my blood immortal," Amber said, her voice tinged with the innocence of a child.

"What's immortal?" Amber asked, her curiosity shining through.

Jake, standing nearby, knelt, attempting to simplify the concept. "It means they won't ever die, sweetheart."

"I did it because you're sad," Amber continued, her voice tinged with a sense of understanding beyond her years. "You keep lying to yourself that you're happy but not."

Lucinda's heart skipped a beat at Amber's words, caught off-guard by her daughter's perceptiveness. "Amber, I…"

"No, Mom," Amber interjected gently. "You would have done it long ago if you knew how. I want Grandma Annalise and Grandpa Phil to play with me, not just at midnight. And you want to hug and hold them, too. Do you think I don't know that they died when you were little?

I brought them back so you could play with them since you didn't get the chance to when you were little. I did everything for you, Mom.

Walking inside, Amber left Lucinda standing there, her thoughts swirling in a whirlwind of emotions.

Alone with Jake, Lucinda felt a wave of confusion and sorrow. "Amber is right. But it's not that simple, Jake. Bringing back the dead…I don't know if it's right."

Jake stepped closer, his voice a soothing balm to her troubled soul. "Lucinda, wouldn't you have done it if you knew how?"

Her heart heavy with the weight of past losses, Lucinda hesitated. "Their death has changed me. I thought I healed, but maybe I didn't. I know that I am the happiest person on earth right now that my parents are back to life, but deep down, I'm concerned about who I gave birth to. What kind of power have I unlocked on this planet."

"But now they're here," Jake said softly. "You and I are immortal, together with Amber; what's wrong with having your parents and grandparents turned immortal, too? We didn't know how, but Amber knows how, and she did it. It's not wrong to want that. You talk about the pain of your parent's death. I'm sure you wouldn't want to wake up one morning to hear that Maya or Greg is no more, and with the connection you have built with them over the years, their demise will wreck you."

Lucinda's eyes filled with tears as she realized the depth of her longing for her parents. Jake's words pierced through her inner turmoil, melting the icy walls she had built around her pain.

"You have been thinking about my grandparents, haven't you? Lucinda asked, and Jake nodded and said, "I also don't want them to leave, so I'm happy with what Amber did for them and our happiness."

Embracing her husband tightly, Lucinda let out a choked sob, the dam of emotions finally breaking. "I don't want to lose them again."

Jake held her close, his arms a sanctuary of comfort. "We won't. You're a family, immortal now. Let's cherish this gift Amber has unlocked for all of us."

In that embrace, amidst tears and unspoken words, Lucinda found hope. The magic Amber had unleashed had granted her parents and grandparents immortality and unlocked a path to healing the fractured pieces of their family, bridging the divide between the living and the departed.

THE END

Main Characters

Lucinda

Mía

Anya

Annalise

Phil

Grand Father

Grand Mother

Elyon

Asgard

Amber

Star

Jake

Credit

Annalise: **Mansi**

Amber: **Nicolette Bett**

Lucinda: **Chioma Rachel Chukwu**

Anya: **Natsyu "K"**

Grand Father: **Dennis WC Wong**

Grand Mother: **Jocelyn N. Wong**

Elyon: **Zarek Wong**

Asgard: **Kayin Wong**

Star: **Robin Michaels**

Annalise's Dress Designer: **Neela** form SankalpArt

All the illustrations, distribution (print and digital) is subjected to copyright @ SankalpArt LLC, an author's dream 2022.

About the Author

Dennis W.C. Wong

Mr. Wong recently retired at Kaiser Permanente in Oakland, CA as a Nurse Assistant in the Operating Room Department and became a Licensed Vocational Nurse in home health care. It was only after exploring the paint sales industry that he felt drawn to pursue a career in healthcare. Backed by an Associate of Arts in Retail Marketing from Chabot College, Mr. Wong earned a Bachelor of Science in Business Management-Personnel and Industrial Relations from California State University, Hayward. He was presented with the Albert Nelson Marquis Lifetime Achievement Award by Marquis Who's Who in 2020. Also, as a Sterile Processing Technician, Mr. Wong volunteered with Surgical Missions to Guatemala and Ecuador. He owned a 1969 Ford Falcon Futura Sport Coupe. It has won several awards at car shows and was featured in the February 2024 American Muscle Car calendar.

In January 2018, he published "**The Apricot Outlook of Katherine Koon Hung Wong**," a memoir about his mother. This book originated as a term paper for a psychology class in 2005 titled "Senior Biography of My Mom Aged 77."

His mother's Chinese middle name translates to "Outlook Apricot." Apricots symbolize female elegance and the large ovoid seed resembles the eyes of an Oriental beauty.

Mr. Wong's second book "**The Power of Passion**," is a fictional story that intertwines themes of love, passion, and empathy.

He continued the apricot theme in his children's stories, starting with "**The App I Cot Journey to Plumville**," where the main character faces adversity. Its sequel, "**The App I Cot Goes to College**," follows Appy's journey to becoming an engineer. "**Appy Overcomes Covid**" addresses family challenges during the pandemic, while "**Appy Retires**" reflects on his career. In "**Grand Appy's Family**," Appy looks forward to becoming a grandfather. Appy and June received a Lifetime Achievement Award in Engineering in the finale, "**Grand Appy's Achievement**." This six-book series has now been combined into a single volume titled "**The App I Cot 6 Series**."

In 2002, Mr. Wong's poem "**My Journey**," written during his nursing assistant class, inspired the poetry collection titled "**Ode to Thy Apricot - Reimagined**."

Dennis's granduncle, Philip, and his wife, Kyau, embarked on a 14-1/2-month journey to the Orient from April 2, 1947 to June 17, 1948. With granted permission, he published the travelogue diary from his granduncle Philip's pocket notebook in

"Chronicles of An Oriental Adventure."

www.ingramcontent.com/pod-product-compliance
Lightning Source LLC
Chambersburg PA
CBHW051134300726

48978CB00011B/267